THE RESURRECTIONIST

THE RESURRECTIONIST

A NOVEL BY

Jack O'Connell

ALGONQUIN BOOKS OF CHAPEL HILL 2008

Published by
Algonquin Books of Chapel Hill
Post Office Box 2225
Chapel Hill, North Carolina 27515-2225

a division of
Workman Publishing
225 Varick Street
New York, New York 10014

Printed in the United States of America.
Published simultaneously in Canada
by Thomas Allen & Son Limited.
Design by April Leidig-Higgins.

This is a work of fiction. While, as in all fiction,
the literary perceptions and insights are based on
experience, all names, characters, places, and incidents
either are products of the author's imagination
or are used fictitiously.

Library of Congress Cataloging-in-Publication Data
O'Connell, Jack, [date]
The resurrectionist : a novel / by Jack O'Connell. — 1st ed.
p. cm.
ISBN-13: 978-1-56512-576-6
1. Chemists — Fiction. 2. Clinics — Fiction. 3. Coma — Patients —
Fiction. 4. Fathers and sons — Fiction. 5. Comic books, strips, etc. —
Fiction. 6. Psychological fiction. I. Title.
PS3565.C526R47 2008
813'.54 — dc22   2007049423

10 9 8 7 6 5 4 3 2 1
First Edition

To James Daniel

Mea maxima culpa.

—*Menlo*

THE RESURRECTIONIST

1

Alone in the doctor's office, Sweeney's eyes lingered on the final panel and, once again, he found himself feeling something close to sympathy for the cartoon strongman, exiled and adrift, the world torn down in a random instant and supplanted with a precarious replacement.

Closing the comic book, Sweeney tried to bring himself back to the here and now. But in seconds he found himself studying the cover, this grotesque family portrait of circus freaks that an artist had elevated into icons. Then he heard the door open and, immediately, he rolled the book and slipped it into his back pocket, covering it with the tail of his sport jacket.

"Sorry for the interruption," Dr. Peck said, coming around the desk and sliding back into his seat.

"Not a problem," Sweeney said.

Dr. Peck was one of those individuals whose voice, on the phone, had conveyed his appearance: entirely bald, bordering on gaunt, well groomed but with lips that were too thin and pale. He looked as if his grandfather had owned the most efficient general store on the prairie. But Sweeney knew this wasn't the case.

"We were speaking, I believe, about the accident," Peck said as he reopened Danny's file, then sat back and waited.

Like everyone else, Dr. Peck wanted a recounting. One more smug little prick who had to have the story. He sat and waited, actually folded his hands across the hollow that passed for his belly and assumed a position of clinical concern. His vision seemed to focus on the knot of Sweeney's necktie, a Christmas present festooned with chicken boys.

Sweeney cleared his throat and tried to stay calm.

"As I was saying, it's been a difficult year. But I think this move will be a step in the right direction for us."

"The doctor in Cleveland —"

"Lawton."

"He *will* be forwarding the rest of the boy's records?"

"Daniel."

Peck squinted as if he didn't understand. As if the name weren't on the file in front of him.

"The boy's name is Daniel," Sweeney said and crossed his legs. "You should have received the records already. I'll call this afternoon to remind Dr. Lawton."

Peck nodded and opened the manila folder on his desk.

"Coma is a complex condition, Mr. Sweeney. The word itself is used incorrectly more often than not."

Sweeney nodded back. He needed the job and he'd burned all his bridges back in Ohio. But there was still a limit to the amount of patronizing shit he'd endure.

"As you might imagine, doctor," he said, "I've immersed myself in the literature since the accident."

Peck sniffed and closed Danny's file, pushed back just a bit from the desk and lifted the coffee mug that featured a line drawing of the Clinic.

"I'm not trying to be difficult, Mr. Sweeney," Peck said. "I understand what you've been through. This is a heartbreaking situation —"

"This is my life, doctor. This is not a situation, this is my life. And I don't mean to be disrespectful or ungrateful. But your associates offered me this position and I accepted it. I pulled my son out of the St. Joseph and moved us eight hundred miles from home. And now you're sitting here telling me I might not have the job."

Peck put the mug down on Danny's file.

"That's not what I'm saying, Mr. Sweeney. Not at all. I simply want to make sure things are clear here at the start. I'm certain we both have some natural concerns and —"

"I have one concern and that's the well-being of my boy. You tell me what your concerns are and I'll address them."

Peck picked the mug up and Sweeney saw that it had left a brown circle on Danny's folder. The doctor was quiet for a minute and then he sniffed again. His voice, when it came, was lower.

"I want to make sure you have a realistic picture of what we can and cannot do here. Your son, Daniel, has had minimal brain activity since the day of the accident. According to the records I've received, the doctors at the St. Joseph have administered all the standard and appropriate therapies. We're a research facility and we do good work. But the last thing I would want is to give you false hope."

"I can promise you," Sweeney said, "I'm a realist."

They looked at each other until Peck blinked.

"All right," the doctor said, putting on the weary voice. "I'll take you at your word."

"I appreciate that," Sweeney said.

Peck looked at his watch and then slid another file out from beneath Danny's. Sweeney felt some relief — the interview was coming to an end.

"Your CV looks fine," Peck said. "You studied at Ohio State?"

A nod, waiting.

"Concentration in pharmacognosy?"

Another nod.

"But you never went into research?"

"I had intended to," Sweeney said, trying not to sound defensive, "but it didn't work out that way."

Peck smiled as if he understood, then asked, "What made you decide on pharmacology in the first place?"

"My father had his own shop."

"You liked working for the big outfits?"

Sweeney shrugged. "They paid well. They moved you along. I was thinking of buying my own franchise before the accident."

Peck let the last sentence hang for a beat or two.

"And your wife was a pharmacist as well?"

A nod, thinking, *Just ask, you little hump.* When the doctor refused, Sweeney said, "We met in school."

"May I ask if you've pursued any counseling in the last year?"

It was not what Sweeney expected and he took a moment before saying, "May I ask how that's pertinent to my job here at the Clinic?"

Peck maintained a bland expression but scratched his nose.

"You've suffered extraordinary stress and grief. You've lost your wife and, for all intents and purposes, your son. And I'm about to put you in charge of the Clinic's drug room. Which is to say, I'm giving you responsibility for all of the Clinic's patients."

Sweeney wanted to stand up. He wanted to move around the desk and pick up the coffee mug and break the man's stuffy nose with it. He wanted to put the fucker on the floor and kick him in the head until Dr. Peck was a patient at his own Clinic.

He did none of those things. He folded his hands on his knee and said, "You've got my letters of reference there, doctor. You've got my employment history and you've probably got the results of your inquiry to the Ohio board. I've never been cited for anything. My performance reviews have all been excellent. This position means a pay cut for me. But it seems to be the best place for my son. Now either I have the job that was promised me or I don't. If I don't, please let me know. Because if that's the case, I have to phone my lawyer and make new arrangements for my boy."

Peck let the room go quiet before he stood up.

"I apologize," he said, "if you feel my question was inappropriate."

He extended his hand. Sweeney stood and took it across the desk.

A smile now, as the doctor moved to the exit.

"You'll call Cleveland and see about those missing records?"

"I'll call," Sweeney said.

Peck opened the door to the office.

"You'll find human resources downstairs. They'll have some paperwork for you to fill out and you'll need to have your photo taken."

Sweeney stepped into the reception area and said, "Thank you, Dr. Peck."

Dr. Peck nodded and said, "Welcome to the Clinic."

THE PERSONNEL MANAGER was an older woman named Nora Blake. She wore a white summer suit and a perfume that Sweeney hadn't smelled in twenty years. She filled out his paperwork in the basement cafeteria, where she bought him coffee from an antique vending machine.

The coffee was wretched but Nora Blake was delightful and Sweeney almost sprayed their table when she called Dr. Peck a vain little bastard.

"Do you talk like this to all the new hires?" Sweeney asked.

"I'm retiring in three months," she said. "I've been at the Peck for thirty years. I've met a lot of arrogant doctors. But Peck is just a shit."

"I wish I could disagree."

Nora actually patted his free hand. "Not to worry, Mr. Sweeney. You're working nights. You won't see much of him."

"You can just call me Sweeney," he said. "Everyone does."

"All right, Sweeney," pulling a pack of Virginia Slims from a jacket pocket and lighting up. "You want to tell me why you asked to work third shift?"

He shrugged. "I'm a night owl."

"Okay," mouth working around the cigarette. "You want to tell me why you left the senior pharmacist position at the largest CVS in Cleveland to come to this nightmare?"

Sweeney sat back in the chair. It moved and the legs screeched a little against the linoleum.

"You're really the personnel manager, right?"

"For another twelve weeks."

"Why'd you stay for thirty years if it's such a nightmare?"

"I got bored," Nora said, contorting her lips to blow her smoke away from him, "living off the trust fund."

"Ms. Blake," Sweeney said, "I've never had a job interview quite like this."

"This isn't an interview. According to this," indicating his paperwork with her cigarette, "you already got the job."

He decided to let himself banter.

"You're allowed to smoke in here?" he asked.

"This is the smoking section," she said.

"I don't see a sign, Ms. Blake."

"When I'm sitting here," Nora said, "it's the smoking section. And knock off the Ms. Blake, all right? You make me feel like a stenographer."

"Well," Sweeney said and drained the last of the coffee, "you've sold me on the place so far."

"That's what I'm here for," Nora said. "For another ninety days, anyway."

She squinted at him through her smoke, shifted in her seat, and stifled a wince. Then she pointed at him with the cigarette and said, "In the beginning, I came here for the same reason you did."

"Your son?" Sweeney asked.

She shook her head. "My husband, Ernie." She threw out a hand and leaned toward him, an instant confidant. "He was a gorgeous man, let me tell you."

"Your husband's a patient?"

She smiled at him and he saw some of her lipstick had smudged across her front teeth. He wasn't sure whether or not he should tell her.

"He was," she said. "For almost twenty years. Industrial accident. He worked the line over at the Gordon Brothers. It was a slip and fall. We got a little settlement, but what am I going to do? Sit home and feel awful?"

"Twenty years," Sweeney repeated.

Nora shrugged. "You know they can go that long. Don't tell me you haven't read all the books. That's what the families do. We read all the books. We look for the answers. We become goddamned specialists, don't we? Twenty years isn't so unusual. Ernie was young and strong."

Sweeney had nothing to say to that.

"You know, he didn't hurt anything else. No broken bones. Just his head. The first doctor says to me *It's a fluke.* If he'd hit the floor at another angle, who knows? A concussion. A week off from the mill. As if this is supposed to make me feel better. All these years later, I'm still frosted."

Sweeney had a response to that. "Their job isn't to make you feel better," he said. "You find that out immediately."

Nora saw the opening and used it. "How'd it happen to you? Your son, I mean. Do you mind me asking? I know some of the general details, but . . ."

He did mind. He hated it every time and it never got easier. But he'd found a way to tell it. He'd made it into a story. Like a joke you've memorized so that you use the same words. The same tone and the same pauses with each telling. He took a breath, got himself ready.

"I was working," he began and wished he hadn't finished the coffee. "It was about seven o'clock. I'd gotten called in. The night shift guy — Anwar — he'd phoned in sick. I couldn't get anybody. So Kerry was home alone with Danny. This was early summer and we'd just gotten the pool going. We'd had a barbecue on Memorial Day. Invited the neighbors. We were new to the neighborhood."

But this wasn't how he normally told it. Why did he mention the barbecue? He looked across the table at Nora, took another breath, and started again.

"Danny had just turned six that spring. Kerry had gotten him started with swimming lessons at the Y."

The instructor had been nineteen. He couldn't remember her name. She wore a red lifeguard's suit and had blond hair, chopped at the neck. He'd made it to the lessons only that one time. The lifeguard had freckles and a tattoo on her ankle.

"And he loved it. He was a real waterdog."

He remembered Danny in the girl's arms. Holding these colored plastic rings in each fist. Danny would scoop them off the bottom of the pool. He was so light — thirty pounds on his sixth birthday — that the lifeguard had to help him dive down to grab the rings.

"You were at work," Nora said, nudging him along.

"I was at work," he said. "I must've filled a dozen asthma inhalers that night. The air quality was terrible all week. I had all these parents hovering in front of the counter. They haven't had dinner, you know, and the kid's gone from a wheeze to a real gasp."

He sees the black woman, young, her first child, terrified. She can't find her insurance card. She dumps her purse into her lap.

"And your wife," Nora said, "was home with your boy."

He felt the coffee start to churn in his stomach.

"He was in his pajamas already. Kerry had gone out to the patio to turn on the grill. She was going to throw a kabob on for dinner. She left the sliders open. And she went back in and poured herself a glass of wine."

He stopped then and stared at the old woman in her white summer suit, with lipstick on her front tooth. He swallowed and changed his voice and said, "I'm sorry. Is there a restroom around here?"

Nora Blake motioned with her head.

"Turn left out of here and go to the end of the corridor."

THE MEN'S ROOM was empty. He walked into a stall and closed the door. He put a hand across his mouth and tried to breathe through his nose. He felt his pulse hammering in his neck. He felt his bowels going loose and that instant jet of perspiration breaking under his arms and across his groin. He pulled down his tie, unbuttoned the shirt. The room tilted and he leaned against the green metal partition. He could smell something like bleach. Some old-fashioned disinfectant. Then the pain broke across his forehead and temples. His vision blurred. He bent, went down on one knee, and vomited.

Afterward, he splashed his face with cold water, washed out his mouth, and popped a peppermint candy. He bought the candies in bulk and always kept a half dozen in his pocket. He put a hand on the sink and steadied himself, then looked in the mirror. He rebuttoned the shirt and adjusted the tie.

He stood up straight, brushed at the knee of his pants, and walked back to the cafeteria. Nora Blake was still seated at their table, writing something in his employment file. She closed the file as he sat down.

"You all right?" Nora asked.

Sweeney bit into the peppermint and nodded.

"The first year after Ernie's accident," she said, "I lost twenty-five pounds."

He was still breathing heavily, but the sweats and the pain in the head were gone.

Nora watched him as she tongued her front teeth. Then she added, "And I've never put one of them back on."

HE SPENT THE rest of the morning getting the Nora Blake Tour. It was an amazing performance, one part architectural lecture, three parts stand-up routine. And all of it seasoned with a little social commentary and a lot of staff gossip. Nora could spiel. Nora knew her shtick. Three decades showing new recruits the inside of the nightmare had honed her travelogue. She delivered it with a dry and deadpan voice that had been refined into gravel by years of cigarette smoke and stoicism.

The Clinic was a sandstone monster on fifty acres of private land near Quinsigamond's western border. It sat between a wildlife preserve and an abandoned quarry. The Peck family had owned it from the beginning. Generations of doctors begetting doctors, a priestly clan of cool Yankees elected by God to care for the sick and the dying. They made their money in cotton and wool, but they gave their hearts to disease and deformity. And over time, the family hospital became the model for American health care, the kind of place where charity and science could lie together in order to breed healing.

This history weighed heavily on the current Pecks. They knew their tradition and they let it guide their decisions. Especially the decision, made a little more than thirty years ago, to alter their mission, to specialize. Many felt it was a radical break with the past, but Dr. Peck has never looked back. And today, the Peck Clinic is breaking new ground once again, setting the standard as the finest long-term care and research facility for patients trapped inside coma and persistent vegetative state.

What others might call grand or stately, Sweeney saw as ominous. The Clinic was heavy and dark on the outside, a Romanesque mausoleum with a central manse and two dark wings that fanned out from each side. And the inside was even worse, a maze of cavernous rooms and bad lighting and narrow, vertigo-inducing corridors.

At full capacity, the Clinic could maintain a hundred patients. But fees were so high and Dr. Peck's criteria for admittance so stringent that there were rarely more than fifty sleepers at any time.

That was how Nora referred to the patients. Even though she knew the term was medically inaccurate and annoyed most of the staff doctors. "Drives them crazy," she said. "As if I was insulting someone. But for twenty years I sat next to my husband's bed. Room 103, I'll show you. And that's how I did it. I sat there and I held his hand and I told myself he'd just finished a plate of stuffed cabbage and was dozing. I told myself we were in the living room and he was watching his Red Sox and he'd just drifted off. And any minute he'd start up with the snoring and I'd have to wake him and send him up to bed."

"But isn't it harder that way?" Sweeney asked as they rode the elevator up to the third floor.

"How so?" Nora asked.

"If you tell yourself they're just sleeping, then aren't you also telling yourself that one day they're going to wake up?"

Nora got a little stiff.

She said, "Mary Rowlands."

Sweeney said, "Pardon me?"

"Of Rockhurst, Maryland. Went through the windshield of a '72 Camaro. Severe head trauma. Fourteen years in PVS. One morning she wakes up and says, 'Is my husband all right?'"

"I read about that case," Sweeney said. "She died a week later."

"So she died a week later. The point is, she woke up. She regained consciousness and she talked to her people."

"I don't know," Sweeney said. "For me it would be harder. Imagining Danny's dreaming about some cartoon or something."

"Maybe he is," Nora said.

"But they don't dream."

She gave a laugh that carried just a touch of pity.

"Who've you been talking to?"

Ordinarily he would have let it go. But two days away from Danny had him edgier than usual.

"No, I'm sorry, they *do not* dream," he said. "They just don't. There's no activity in that area of the brain. It's documented. If they're dreaming, then it's not true coma."

The elevator came to a stop with a jerk that one of them finessed and the other did not. The doors slid open and as she unlatched the mesh gate, Nora said, "Jesus, we got to you just in time."

They stepped out into a small foyer that led to the nurses' station. No one was at the desk, but a tall black man in green scrubs was just beyond it, mopping the floor of the corridor.

"Hey, Romeo," Nora called to him, and Sweeney cringed at her volume. "Where's the princess?"

The janitor had a thick accent that Sweeney couldn't place. "She gone to get the coffee," he said.

Nora rolled her eyes for Sweeney's benefit and in a mock whisper said, "We'd pay her in coffee but we couldn't afford it."

She led him down the hall and into the first wardroom. And though a year of daily visits to the St. Joseph should have steeled him to the sight, he had to fight the impulse to run as soon as he stepped into the room.

A shaft of sunlight pouring through the oversized windows made everything seem ethereal. Six beds were filled with six bodies. Men and women. Old and young. Dressed uniformly in hospital johnnies. White sheets covering them to the waist. Some skulls were heavily bandaged, the heads mummified. Some were intact but fully and freshly shaven. Others sported luxurious hair that looked newly washed and styled.

All of them were hooked to IVs. One young girl wore a crown of elec-trodes that coalesced into a fat braid that, in turn, fed into a machine at the side of her bed. Harsh respiration came from a shriveled old man, the only one turned on his side, his face bathed in sun. The noise did things to Sweeney's stomach.

The first week that Danny was at St. Joe's, the boy had shared a room with what the nurse called "a hard breather." The sound never stopped, that chronic, laborious gasping and one night Sweeney caught himself in a suffocation fantasy, imagining himself holding the pillow over the roommate's face until the lungs at last gave up and the brain, finally, shut down.

He realized Nora was watching him.

"You can see they're well taken care of," she said.

And it was true. The room and its patients were clean and well tended. There was nothing immediately horrific here. At least nothing particu-larly visceral. And he knew that this was exactly what unnerved him, this outward appearance of tidiness and normalcy. As if he'd wandered into some Victorian napping parlor and the lot of them would awake at three when the bell was rung for tea and cake.

"Third floor," Nora said, lowering her voice again, "is for the short-timers. Or, at least, those diagnosed as possible short-timers. They've in-dicated moments of consciousness since their incident."

He flinched at the word *incident*.

"These are Dr. Peck's prime candidates for arousal. Good brain activ-ity. Promising response to therapies. These are the ones who have the best chance of walking out of here and suing somebody."

Sweeney motioned to the young girl with the mane of wires.

"What happened to her?"

"Thrown from her horse," Nora said. Then she began to point to each bed in turn. "Car crash. Car crash. Stroke. Car crash." And turning to the last one, a woman about her own age, "And I think she was a fall down the stairs. The cellar stairs, I think. Her son found her."

Sweeney led the way back into the corridor and started for the elevator before Nora could show him another ward.

"For a personnel manager," he said, "you know an awful lot about the patients."

"I spent time on all these floors," she said. "Ernie started out on three. After a month, they downgraded his condition and moved him to two. He spent his last ten years on the first floor."

He stopped walking and waited for her to do the same. When she turned to him, he asked, "Do you know what floor Danny will be on?"

She said, "Would you believe me if I said I didn't?"

He shook his head.

All the wiseass gone now, she said, "He'll be in my husband's old room."

THEY DIDN'T SPAR much after that. They breezed through the second floor, the patients looking paler and more fragile than their counterparts upstairs. Nora had a penchant for narrating the proximate cause of each catastrophe before them. He heard about drug overdoses and viral attacks, embolisms and encephalitis and diabetes, hepatitis and botched suicide.

He was brought to the bedside of Mr. Lawrence Belmonte, who got lost in the woods during a hunting trip in Maine last March and suffered a near fatal case of hypothermia. He lost both his feet and all trace of consciousness. Sweeney was paraded before the bed of Mrs. Honey Lieb, who'd been shipped up from Fort Myers after she failed to wake from her gallstone procedure. He gazed upon the comely face of Ms. Tara Russell, a twenty-four-year-old media consultant from Atlanta who fell ill at a conference in Michigan, was hospitalized for what one doctor still insists was Legionnaires' Disease, slipped into a coma the night she was admitted, and ended up unaware, alone, and in the void, floating here in the Peck Clinic.

"Such a shame," Nora said, patting Ms. Russell's leg through the sheet. "You say it over and over. It becomes a little prayer."

THINGS WERE DIFFERENT on the first floor. There were only three wardrooms and only three beds to each room. And though the rooms had long ago been gutted and refitted for such purposes, they retained a residential feel. It was darker down here. The walls preserved a lot of the house's original heavy wood and the floors were covered with an old-fashioned carpeting rather than tile or rubber.

The wardrooms were located in the rear of the building and as they walked down the central hall, Sweeney could feel Nora tensing. She stopped in the door of 101 and Sweeney entered first. There were three beds, two on the back wall and one on the front. All three of the patients had gone decerebrate, the arms rigid, bent at the elbow and locked. The hands clenched into fists and pulled up to the chest. The legs raised up into a fetal crouch.

Sweeney made himself move deeper into the room. He stopped at the foot of the first bed and saw a middle-aged woman, eyes blasted open, staring at the ceiling. His eyes followed down her body. When he came to the gastrostomy tube snaking out from beneath the sheet, he turned to another bed. A young man, maybe early twenties, though it was hard to say. The gauntness obscured age, made them all into skeletal angels.

Nora had stopped volunteering stories, so Sweeney asked, "What's his deal?"

"Spring break," she said. "Daytona. About five years ago. He tried to jump into the hotel swimming pool from his balcony."

The third patient was suspended in a Stryker frame.

Nora saw him looking and said, "Bedsores."

Sweeney said, "Take me to Danny's room."

They exited 101, moved past 102 without looking inside, and entered 103.

"Do they always leave the lights on?" Sweeney asked.

"It's easier," Nora said, "on the doctor's eyes."

The first two beds were empty.

"Which one will be his?" Sweeney asked.

"I'm sure you can take your pick," Nora said. "Would you like to meet his roommate?"

Instead of answering, he approached the occupied bed. He began to run through the routine, to pull in the deep breath and crack the first two knuckles of his right hand with his thumb. But what he found at the far end of the room was not what he expected.

"She's been here three years," Nora said, at his side now. "Her name's Irene Moore."

There was no decerebrate rigidity here. No swollen or shaven head. No sunken cheeks, no mummified extremities. The eyes were closed. She was turned on her side, dressed in a white cotton nightgown.

"And what's her story?" Sweeney heard himself say.

"Unfortunately," Nora said, "no one really knows. She went to sleep one night and she never woke up. There was no head trauma. No drug or alcohol overdose. And as far as they can tell, no stroke or seizure. Dr. Peck says it's got to be viral. But he's guessing if you ask me."

"Does she have family?"

"She's got a husband. Ex-husband now. In the beginning he was here all the time. He took an apartment in the city. He's a lawyer in New York. Lots of money. He tried to commute back and forth for a while. But after a year, when she wasn't responding to any of the therapies . . ."

She trailed off, then added, "He still pays the bills, though. I'll give him that."

Sweeney asked, "No kids?"

"No. And her parents have been gone forever."

He nodded, started to turn toward the empty beds and heard Nora say, "Irene, dear?" as if she were talking to someone with a hearing impairment. She was leaning over the comatose woman, rubbing her arm and tucking some hair behind an ear. "Irene, this is Mr. Sweeney. But we just call him Sweeney. His boy Danny is going to be sharing the room. You'll be meeting Danny tomorrow."

Normally, Sweeney found such displays patronizing and showy. He'd seen a lot of it at the St. Joseph and thought it more for the benefit of the visitor than the patient. As if she sensed his disdain, Nora looked backward at him, still rubbing Irene's arm, and said, "She hears me, you know."

"Just like your husband," he said before he could catch himself.

"That's right," Nora said and turned her face back to Irene Moore. "Just like my husband."

The window for apology slipped past and, not knowing what else to do, Sweeney walked down to the first bed in the ward and said, "I think this one will be good for Danny."

Then he took the rolled comic book from his back pocket and placed it under the bed's pillow.

THEY WERE SILENT on the ride down to the basement. But when the elevator opened onto a dim junkyard, Nora said, "Oh, this is going to be just charming." They stepped into a storage area crammed with piles of furniture and equipment — gurneys, desks, IV poles — some of them shrouded with tarps and sheets.

"One of these days," Nora said, "somebody's got to clean this place out." She fished in her jacket pocket and brought out a set of keys and they made their way through the maze to the door in front of them. She had a little trouble with the lock. Sweeney took the keys from her and managed to turn the bolt.

They stepped into the apartment.

Nora said, "I'm guessing you got a bargain on the place."

Sweeney found a light switch, flipped it, and said, "This is what closed the deal."

He'd meant it to be funny. The ceiling light flickered, then caught, and the room took on a yellow tinge.

"It's not as big as I expected," he said.

"That's always been my experience," Nora said, moving to the box windows up near the ceiling, pulling back the minidrapes and sending clouds of dust into the air. She put her hands on her hips and shook her head. "You've got a real talent for punishing yourself."

Over the phone, Dr. Peck had called it a "three-room efficiency" and used the word "cozy." But the kitchen was really just a galley along the rear wall that housed an antique stove and refrigerator. In general, the apartment looked like the set of a 1950s sitcom about a bachelor janitor.

The air was close and stale. Sweeney pointed to the windows and asked, "Do those open?" Then went to check on the bedroom before Nora could answer. He found a nice four-poster with matching bureau that sported a mirror. Sitting on the bureau was what looked like a Sears catalog but turned out to be *The Big Book of Logic Problems*. There was a coat post in one corner of the room and a calendar nailed into the wall above the bed. The calendar featured Miss January 1973, a naked brunette kneeling on a white shag rug.

Nora came to the doorway and said to Sweeney's back, "Let me find you a place in the city."

Sweeney shook his head without turning around. "It's fine," he said. "I won't be in here much. And I'll be right below Danny."

"Let's see what we find in that refrigerator," Nora said, "before you make any final decisions."

LIMBO COMICS

ISSUE # 1: "Exile"

They came from the city of Maisel in the heart of Old Bohemia, land of pogroms and demonology. They became a family in the most binding way of all, through a shared and pitiless suffering. Make no mistake, the oldest truths are the most reliable: persecution ties a people together. To be different is to invite oppression. To wear your difference on your body, on your face, this is to invite eradication. Unless, of course, your difference is so grotesque that the crowds will pause to study, to celebrate, to marvel at your misfortune for a short time before they smite you. Then, and only then, will you have a chance to escape.

What does it mean to be a freak? For the Goldfaden Freaks it meant, for a time, a brief period in the beginning, that they were stars. They had been handpicked, assembled over years and miles by Tedeo Bluett, showman extraordinaire and inheritor of the Goldfaden Carnival, the premier—and, perhaps, the most notorious—of all the traveling circuses in all of Old Bohemia. The circus featured the standard fare of all the major bazaars—acrobats and aerialists, fortune-tellers and magicians, trained beasts and juggling clowns, games of chance and skill. So what was it that set the Goldfaden apart from the many other cavalcades of garish drama and comedy that patrolled the gypsy circuits? Its tents were no larger or more colorful than those of the Theatre Magika. Its rings of fire no hotter than those of Valli's Cabaret. Its gorillas were no more savage than those of the Kabalist's Revue and its human cannon was no braver than that of the Circus Herman Nevi.

No, the single feature that separated the Goldfaden from all the other touring spectacles was the infamous Freaks' Promenade. Staged just before the finale of each evening's show, this procession of unsightliness and deformity was unmatched in the history of sideshow lore. Truly, the Goldfaden Freaks were the stars of not just Tedeo Bluett's circus but the entire carny world. Legendary monstrosities, they were the only freaks whose appearance in the flesh was more unsettling than even their most hyperbolic promotional posters. And because of this, Bluett saved their act for the climax of each performance and kept it short and simple.

Every night, after all the lions had been tamed and all the swords had been swallowed, after the clown king had chased his nemesis, the thief of hearts, around and into the rolling fountain, after one of the Flying Zhilinskis had dropped Little Sonya into the arms of Count Leonid and the Weatherman had been electrocuted and revived by his curvaceous assistant, and the Halloween Killer had lost his head to the Magic Guillotine, then, and only then, did Ringmaster Bluett unleash his freaks. And they marched around the perimeter of the center ring and then up, up, into the audience, right up close and personal, where the customers could see for themselves the horrible mistakes that nature makes on rare occasions.

Physically, it was not a tough gig. And this proved to be the freaks' downfall. Because while their "act" consisted solely of a ten-minute nightly stroll of ogling and groping amid shrieks and curses, the freaks' pay and accommodations rivaled those of the acrobats and lion tamers—a fact that triggered no end of jealousy among the rest of the Goldfaden performers. And nowhere was that jealousy more inflamed than in the spleen of Shoshone McGee, the infamous "Blade of Zürau," a half-Cherokee, half-Irish, and fully psychotic knife thrower who functioned as the Goldfaden's resident diva.

McGee lived in a state of perpetual crisis, a melodrama of alcoholism, amphetamine abuse, manic depression, and bad karma. He went through assistant-wives like sour candies and his colleagues agreed that he approached anything like happiness only in the midst of performance, throwing his blades at a human target. He was a tall, muscular man of dark, movie idol looks, except for an enormous protruding brow that was never quite mitigated by the black, luxuriant hair, which he wore long and swept back. His cheekbones caused marital discord in the towns through which he toured. He lived his life barefoot and bare-chested, though he favored expensive leather trousers, the tighter the better. The bulk of his salary from Bluett went to liquor, pills, and knives. But when the throwers of Old Bohemia talked shop, most agreed that McGee had the finest collection of steel in the business. He may or may not have been the most skilled bladesman on the circuit, but he was certainly the most daring. He fired his daggers while blindfolded and drunk and from distances that no Entertainers' Guild would ever sanction.

All of this, however, is mere addendum to the central fact of the knife thrower's existence: Shoshone McGee hated freaks.

No, this is too generous. Truth be told, McGee abhorred freaks. He despised freaks. He loathed them with an antipathy that seemed to grow with each new day. Freaks lay at the center of a furious rage that boiled, year after year, in the heart of the knife thrower. And though there were many legends regarding the source of the man's fury, no one could say with any certainty which one was closest to the truth.

But as far as the Goldfaden Freaks were concerned, the reason for McGee's hatred was an academic mystery. What mattered was staying away from the madman and his cutlery. And so a system of avoidance grew up organically within the troupe. The freaks' trailers were always parked at the opposite end of the campsite from the knife thrower. They dined in separate mess tents. And Bluett slipped Glomo the clown an extra kroner and a bottle of schnapps each week just to make sure that McGee was absent from the big top when the Freaks' Promenade occurred each night.

And yet, for all of these precautions, Shoshone McGee's hatred only grew as the years went by. And, over time, that hatred slowly poisoned the rest of the Goldfaden troupe against what the knife thrower, in his inimitable way of turning bile into poetry, called the devil's putrid afterbirth.

And so it was the fate of the freaks that, even within the liberal world of a circus clan, they became outcasts, exiled from the bosom, show dogs kept forever beyond the warmth of the family fire. Of course, it was natural that they would build their own fire, their own family, constructed of their ill-fitting parts and bound together by an empathy that knew no limits. That family was comprised of:

Fatos, the mule-faced boy, guileless and playful and dreamy despite his large and perpetually infected ears and the mange that spread across his cheek each spring;

Aziz, the human torso, the stoic of the family, swinging himself forward on his thickly callused knuckles, a fat lower lip tucked up over his mouth;

Nadja, the lobster girl, whose claws could clip a cigar neatly in two, who relished a good party and hinted, in the small hours of too many drunken nights, of love affairs with princes and opium;

Durga, the fat lady, a half ton of matriarchal earth goddess, who dressed in flowing silk and would listen to any problem and provide counsel and solace and Bavarian chocolate;

Jeta, the skeleton, outfitted, always, in a navy singlet, so shy that the nightly Promenade could reduce her to tears;

Milena, the hermaphrodite, proud and testy, with a wit as sharp and fine as a German scalpel;

Antoinette, the pinhead, who adored gingham dresses and piano music, and who tended to wander if not properly supervised;

Marcel and Vasco, Siamese twins who loved and squabbled by the phases of the moon and who once passed a full year without speaking to each other—though today, neither can recall the source of their argument;

Kitty, the elegant, delicate, raven-haired dwarf, with just a touch of the femme fatale, of which she was mostly unaware;

And Chick, the chicken boy, the conscience and spirit of the freak clan, with his patchy coat of feathers and the hard cartilage that formed a beak of a mouth. Chick, the boy without a past, whose mother had given him to Tedeo Bluett to raise. The chicken boy whose spirit was so pure and whose soul was so wise that his tenure in this foul world was forever problematic. With a tendency to fugues and trances, with a notion of a long-lost father, with his tender love for the dwarf, his Kitty, and a knowledge that his destiny lay beyond the borders of Old Bohemia, in the legendary country of Gehenna.

We know little about the chicken boy's origins. And, as usually happens in the absence of fact, legend has descended to fill in the gaps. Chick himself will not dignify the legends with discussion. But late at night, walking in the woods or huddled in a trailer with his beloved Kitty, he sometimes allows himself a nip of analysis and a shooter of speculation. Tedeo Bluett has told him the same simple tale from the start.

The troupe, stranded outside of Worgl when a show had fallen through, was camped on the edge of town, on a bluff overlooking the River Kalda. It was a season of recession and grippe and people were not venturing to the theaters. Troubled by another bout of worry and insomnia, the ringmaster had taken a walk to clear his mind. He was thinking that night of getting out of the circus business altogether. Selling the Goldfaden to Herman Nevi or Kalli Kraus or one of his other competitors. Lost in thought, stumbling through the fog, a young woman's wailing suddenly startled him. He made his way toward her cries and found himself on a slimy jetty that protruded into heaving winter waters. And at the end of the rocks, he found her.

She couldn't have been more than sixteen years, he told Chick. She was hysterical and distraught and, beyond this, Bluett would say, somehow he knew that she was the saddest creature he had ever encountered. This is a bold statement for a circus man to make and it is the one part of the story that Chick has never doubted. The girl was dressed— *hidden* was the word that Bluett used most often—in the kind of flowing, hooded cape that had been fashionable many years previously. Beneath the cape, she wore a serving girl's frock, the tattered uniform of someone's maid. A washerwoman-in-training, was Tedeo's initial guess, but when he saw her face peek out from the hood, he knew he was wrong. No, even in this hysterical state, with her hair tangled and matted by the spray, this one was a beauty of rare breeding and grace.

Her crying ceased when she saw Bluett approaching on the jetty. But she was silenced for only a moment.

"Don't try to stop me," she screamed over the wind.

And Bluett knew that she meant to throw herself into the chop.

He halted and held a hand up, both to reassure the girl that he understood and to block the water blowing into his eyes.

The girl looked from the ringmaster to the river, as if suddenly unsure of her next move. And that was when Bluett saw she was holding
a package, something the size of a bread loaf, wrapped in a rapidly de-
composing newspaper—what he would later discover to be a medical
tabloid known as *The Journal of Physical Abnormality.*

"Please," he yelled over the screeching winds, "let me help you."

With this, the girl threw back her hood. And even in the darkness,
Tedeo Bluett could see that she had eyes as striking as the emperor's
emeralds.

"You want to help me?" she asked, her contempt cutting through
the gale. "Get him to Gehenna." And with that, she tossed the bread
loaf at the ringmaster and threw herself off the rocks.

Instinct born of a lifetime in the circus caused Bluett to go down on
one knee and catch, perfectly, the tossed burden that he understood, at
once, to be something other than a loaf of bread, something alive and
moving and making sounds of its own. Torn, he ran to the jetty's end
before allowing himself to inspect the creature in his arms. His eyes
swept the water but there was no sign of the jumper. He called out to
her but knew, as he called, that it was futile.

Then he peeled back the news wrap and took his first look at the
child inside.

"I have lived a life in show business," he would tell Chick over the
years that followed that night. "I have trafficked all my days in spectacle. I come from a people who have made their living mining the
most curious parts of this astounding world. But in all my time, in all
my travels, I had never seen anything like you."

IT WAS THIS very chicken boy, born into tragedy and mystery, who
drew the bulk of the "normal" performers' wrath. Too innocent and
pure-hearted for his own good, Chick had become the crowd's favorite absurdity, a creature whose deformity could not camouflage his
deep sense of compassion and truth. That Chick was a religious seeker,
given, rumor said, to prophetic dreams, made him only more suspect
and, ultimately, despised by the rest of the Goldfaden troupe.

During the final tour with the Bluett show, the freaks' popular-
ity peaked. It was in the city of Smetano that the problem came to a

head. The audience had been impatient all week and even the master showmen had trouble commanding full attention. During Magda Zhilinski's neck twist there had been catcalls, genuine boos and hisses, though Magda had performed perfectly. When Grendal Romain attempted to put his horses through the synchronized folk dance, the music could not be heard above the crowd's impatient grumbling. But the last straw was heaved on during Shoshone McGee's knife-throwing exhibition, when someone yelled, "Bring on the freaks!" and the crowd cheered at an inopportune moment—causing McGee to nick, for the first time, his latest wife's inner thigh.

At this, McGee's long-seething rage boiled over into murderous rebellion and the Goldfaden troupe revolted en masse. They issued Bluett an ultimatum: Choose the freaks or choose the rest. One or the other. To share a stage with these blunders of God was one thing. To be upstaged by them was something else entirely. Something evil and unnatural and, finally, intolerable.

That Bluett was not a stupid man goes without saying. He had the savvy of a fifth-generation showman. True, the freaks were his finale, the most popular attraction of the whole circus. But their act consisted of nothing more than a ten-minute parade. And you cannot book a tent with ten minutes of deformity. As a climax, the freaks were gold. As a beginning and an end and everything in between, they were death.

And so, on a cold autumn night, when a harvest moon blasted the forests with blue light and the fog rolled in cold and wet, Tedeo Bluett banished the freaks from the only home that most of them had ever known. To his credit, he paid them a month's wages and let them keep their costumes.

The freaks were dumbfounded. By and large, these were not wily individuals. Most had been coddled throughout their lives, tended and managed by Bluett like prized sheep. They were not idiots but they were all spoiled to a greater or lesser degree and had little sense of how to take care of themselves in the wider world.

So, when Bluett abandoned them at a campsite on the edge of Village Odradek, the freaks were confused and terrified. Fat Durga went to work at once, playing the mama to her misshapen brood. She draped her gargantuan arms over several sloping shoulders and dispensed a

rosy future. The freaks would stay together, she proclaimed, and remain a family. They would apply for a state license and get out on the
road, on their own. This was the best thing that could have happened
to them. No more suffering the pettiness of the mundane jugglers. No
more living off an allowance from the ringmaster. They would form
their own troupe and control their own destiny.

Jeta and Antoinette were comforted by Durga's prophecy. And most
of the others were at least calmed enough to sleep. But Chick and Kitty
weren't fooled by the big lady's dreams of blue skies and gravy. They
said nothing aloud, but they exchanged a lovers' knowing look across
the evening's campfire. The look said: What do we know about licensing? What do we know about bookings and ticket sales? About promotion and advertising? About tent riggings? About union rules? About
the twisting back roads of Old Bohemia?

The look said: What do we know about putting together an act?

Chick appreciated, even loved, Durga's optimism and her way with
a cheerful story. But what the family needed most in this instance was
a new patron. Someone strong and smart who could guide them, keep
the clan together and manage the business aspect of their collective
life. While Durga sketched out the details of their gleaming future,
Chick wracked his brain trying to think of a new and worthy patriarch. It was not an easy task—most of the circus owners in Old Bohemia made Tedeo Bluett look like a saint—and Chick fell asleep before
he could conjure a candidate. And woke an hour before dawn with a
hand clamped over his beak and a knife tip poking into his neck.

His eyes, wide with shock and betrayal, opened and looked out on
Bruno Seboldt, the Goldfaden strongman, an authentic Hercules who
had joined the troupe a year before, hiring on during a matinee in
Krappl. Bruno, who could burst iron chains and heave a dozen clowns
the length of the tent and lift a small horse straight over his head, was
said, from the start, to be a wanted man. He had never warmed to the
freaks. And now it looked like he was ready to murder at least one of
them.

But after a horrible moment of mutual staring, Bruno sheathed
his knife into his boot, brought a sausage of a finger to his mustache-
hidden lips and made a shushing sound. Then he released Chick's beak

and motioned to the trees beyond the campfire. Chick rose silently, stepped over a sleeping Kitty and followed the strongman into the woods.

"You almost scared me to death," Chick said to Bruno's back.

Bruno found a stump and sat on it, which brought his head even with the still-standing Chick's. Despite the nighttime cool, the big man wore a training shirt that exposed his enormous arms and the identical tattoos on each — pictures of Atlas hoisting the earth. Bruno kept his eyes on the ground, as if, even in the shadows, he could not bring himself to look at the chicken boy.

"If I had wanted you dead," Bruno said, "I would be roasting you on a spit right now."

It was always an unsettling image, no matter how often he heard it, and Chick allowed himself a shudder.

"What's all this about?" he asked. "You're rid of us. Isn't that what you wanted?"

Bruno shook his head.

"It's McGee," he said, scratching the back of his skull. "He says you're all abominations. That if we just let you go free, you'll only find another circus that will take you in."

It was as if someone had read Chick's mind, though he knew that Flora Kino, the troupe's resident gypsy, was more grifter than psychic.

"And what business is that of yours?" Chick asked. "You don't have to look at us anymore. You don't have to share the tent or the trailers with us. You got what you wanted."

Moonlight reflected off Bruno's forehead.

"McGee says it's too dangerous. The competition is fierce these days. We can't afford to lose our audience to the monsters."

Chick nodded, unable to hide from the logic. At a loss, he simply said, "And what do you think, Bruno?"

The strongman scratched at his cheek, pulled on his mustache. Finally he rose from the stump, came forward, and towered over Chick.

"I don't like the lot of you," he said. "But McGee is on his way. He plans on butchering every last one of you. And I couldn't let that happen."

"What will you do," Chick asked, trying to look into the dark woods behind Bruno, "when he gets here?"

Bruno's hands went to his hips and his head tilted just a bit toward a shoulder.

"I was thinking," he said, "that there might be a solution to this problem."

It was at this moment that Chick felt the first symptoms of the seizure. It came as an instantaneous wallop of déjà vu, accompanied by a cold rush of current up his spine and into his brain. He staggered, regrouped, and asked, "What do you mean?"

Maybe it was the darkness or perhaps his self-absorption in the moment, but Bruno didn't notice the change in the chicken boy.

"I mean," Bruno said, "what if you left?"

"Left?" repeated Chick as his stomach began to churn and his eyes to lose focus.

"Yes," said Bruno, warming to his idea as it took on weight with his words. "What if you left the country? Got out of Bohemia? Especially you. You're always reading those newspapers and pamphlets about Gehenna. You could go there. You could take all of them with you."

"Go to Gehenna?" in a breathy whisper, as if voicing a dangerous heresy.

"I know a man," said Bruno, anxious to keep talking, to continue rolling out his plan. "He used to come by the gym in Maisel. We would play cards together sometimes. He has a boat. A ship. He owes me a favor. I could get you passage. To Gehenna."

"Why would you do this for us?" Chick asked.

And Bruno muttered, "I won't have murder on my hands again."

No man ever spoke with more sincerity or better intention. But the vow proved impossible. Before they could wake the rest of the freaks and decamp the area, they were ambushed by Shoshone McGee, nastily drunk and thirsty for freak blood. He came out of the tree line with a knife in each hand, raving, screaming like a demon, promising rape and dismemberment and lingering death to the filthy abominations. And then he saw Bruno Seboldt.

"Betrayer," he screamed and charged with both knives outstretched.

For a huge man, Bruno was nimble and fast. And, of course, it helped that McGee was wretched with alcohol. Bruno sidestepped the attack, knocked the madman to the ground with a blow to the neck, came down on the knife thrower's back as if genuflecting, and in a single, fluid motion, took McGee's head in his bulging arms, like a soccer ball, and twisted it until the neck snapped. It happened in an instant, a child quieting a baby goose.

The sleeping freaks woke with McGee's war cry just in time to witness the killing. Everyone remained on the ground, silent and in shock, except for Antoinette, who crawled into Durga's arms and began to whimper.

Bruno got to his feet and heaved a sigh and said to Chick, "We don't have much time. Help me bury him."

But the chicken boy was in the midst of a full-blown seizure, his arms and legs twitching, his eyes rolled up past his lids, a soupy bile running from his beak. He was in the Limbo now, the place of visions, of warning and prophecy. Where the voice of the father spoke its cryptic messages of possible salvation.

On this night of expulsion and killing Chick had his first vision of Gehenna. And of his nemesis, the mad doctor called Fliess. And of the doctor's laboratory, a clifftop castle called the Black Iron Clinic.

Chick hallucinated in the Limbo throughout that night, while Bruno Seboldt carried him like a corpse across the dark countryside and a parade of freaks followed behind them both, their last Promenade in Old Bohemia.

BY DAYLIGHT THEY made it to the docks of Studl. And by the next nightfall, they were steaming out of Fleischmann's Harbor, bound for distant Gehenna, a land known only through legend and folktale. It was a momentous turning point for the freaks. And even the pinhead knew it.

But if there was great fear—and, certainly, there was—the escape also brought a sense of hope and possibility, a sense of new beginning. Because while the freaks had escaped their first death sentence, they had also found a new, if unlikely, patriarch.

Bruno Seboldt stood at the bow of the *The Touya* throughout that first night at sea, staring into the ocean as waves broke to either side of the ship. He took no food and he spoke to no one. And when Chick approached him in the morning with some of Durga's cinnamon coffee, handed the strongman the mug and whispered, "You're one of us now," Bruno never responded. As if he had not heard the words.

3

Every freak and his mother were out on the streets of Bangkok Park, running or hobbling as best they could to their sundry negotiations. In the daylight, the Park was an even greater spectacle of degradation, the freest of all markets, where bloody money and rough sex could purchase any commodity. In this tenderloin, more often than not, a flamboyant violence was the service fee paid on the edgiest transactions. And into this bazaar, strolling from the west, his hair greasier than usual, his bad knee acting up with the weather, and the crotch of his jeans tacky with drying blood, came the Spider.

If who we are is best defined by our bad choices, then Spider was the kind of raging fuck-up destined to ruin most of the lives into which he wandered. This morning, he was wandering down Watson Street, trying to remain inconspicuous in this sea of human detritus. And though he was not wearing his colors, the eternally pissed-off squint and the tattoo on his neck would have given him away to both rival and cop as a stone biker, if not necessarily an Abomination. So he hurried, bouncing the antique satchel off his bad leg, limping to his grisly appointment on Watson, like one more rancid pilgrim trying to slake a chronic thirst or score some dirty capital.

Made of gleaming black leather, handcrafted in Spain long before Spider fell into this world, the satchel looked like a doctor's bag on steroids. But its bottom was growing damp as the biker made his way through the maze of alleyways and ruined factories and cryptlike saloons of the Park, toward a cross-dressers' bar called the Grand Illusion.

Spider had intended to be late for his meeting, if not quite this late. But he'd been up half the night, running a hundred bullshit errands for Buzz

Cote. And then, at dawn, there was one final errand of his own, which had taken a lot longer than he'd anticipated.

The thing was, most of Buzz's chores felt like idiot work that even the Fluke could've done. Every now and then, Buzz got that way — usually before he decided to break camp and head for another farm. That's what Buzz called the clinics — the farms. Where you pick the turnips for the soup. Buzz had a way of going all stressed and pissy before a move. And of making sure that Spider knew his place. "Remember," Buzz would say through that fake laugh, "you're the deputy, not the fucking sheriff."

The truth was, it stung, and it was one of the reasons why Spider was willing to risk going solo into the Park to make a move on his own. He was tired of being second in command. Tired of following orders and running errands for Buzz Cote. And tired as all fuck of the arguments between Buzz and Nadia over where the family should go next. It was building toward something ugly no matter how they tried to hide it. Buzz mumbling all the time about how Nadia'd gone round the bend with all her "last clinic" bullshit. Nadia laughing at Buzz last week, saying his imagination was even smaller than his pecker. It was like being a kid again, back in one of the foster homes.

One of these days, Spider would split off from the Abominations, and then Buzz would know the cost of disrespect and thoughtlessness. But starting your own crew took money. Which was why Spider found himself jogging toward an eye-opener with a soggy-bottomed satchel, headed for a sit-down with the mad scientist.

The bar was a narrow hole that straddled the oscillating border between Little Asia and Latino Town. Jammed like a middle child between an abandoned appliance showroom and an abandoned rod and wire mill, the Illusion bathed the street, all year long, with its strange bouquet of lavender, sweat, skunk beer, and rain. No more than a dozen feet wide but running deep into the block, the G.I. was known to give even long-time customers the occasional sense that they were inside a dark train, swaying and hitching along the roughest of track. It was a good place to bring someone if, like Spider, you wanted to fuck with him a little before you took his money. And while there were other drag clubs in the Park that stayed open night and day, the Illusion was said to host the meanest transvestites in the city.

Spider entered through the rear door and stood in the shadows, letting his eyes adjust to the darkness. A long black marble bar ran the length of the place, opposite a row of tiny, two-man booths mounted against the far wall. The ceiling was made of acoustic tiles gone yellow and brown and interrupted by a large circular vent, a broken paddle fan and a working disco ball. Two cement support columns split the narrow aisle between bar and booths, both columns wrapped in deep shag carpet, one pumpkin orange and the other a faded aqua.

There was no natural light in the bar. The windows up front were blacked out by velvet curtains upon which were painted nude portraits of the great belters of American cabaret — Ethel, Carol, and Judy. The juke, an old Wurlitzer, was tucked safely behind the bar and featured songs by that trinity and other, less well-known goddesses. The booths were wooden and scarred with a century of burn-and-cut graffiti. The tables were red Formica trimmed in silver and sporting disturbing patterns of gouges, and the seats were red Naugahyde and often sticky. The floor featured several layers of linoleum worn into a gully along the heavily trafficked path to the restroom, revealing what seemed to be lower geological levels.

And there, in the midst of this submarine gloom, was Dr. Peck, fidgeting in one of the booths that lined the side wall. The doc was dressed like an embezzler, in a pricey gray suit that needed a pressing. He had a charcoal raincoat folded next to him and a hat resting on top of it. And Spider wanted to kick his ass just for bringing the hat.

Peck hadn't sounded happy with the choice of meeting ground but he was a smart guy and knew when he had no leverage. He'd been waiting for close to half an hour, nursing a sour coffee in a dirty mug while Jared, the former linebacker and current barkeep, done up this morning in a Balenciaga gown, played the juke — some Kurt Weill song by way of Anne Shelton.

Jared pulled a bag of trash from beneath the bar and moved for the rear exit, spotting Spider at the last minute and letting out a squeal before finding his balls and warning, "I'm strapped," in a voice that insisted it was true.

"I'm not looking for trouble," Spider said, amused and maybe even a little flattered. "I got a business meeting, that's all."

Jared looked the Abomination over and thought about this. "You even raise your voice," he said, "I'll start shooting."

Another time, Spider'd have told him he'd be shooting out his ass, 'cause that was the only place he'd find his gun. But this morning was business, so he let the threat go and walked past the barkeep, sliding into the booth opposite Dr. Peck and noting that, aside from Jared, they had the place to themselves.

"You're late," Peck said.

"And you're an asshole," Spider said. "It's not a perfect world."

Peck leaned forward and asked, "Why here?" in a low voice.

"Change of pace," Spider said, starting to enjoy himself. "I worry about you, Doc. Stuck up on that hill all day with the turnips."

"The turnips?" Peck said.

"The sleepers," Spider explained. "The coma people."

"My patients are not vegetables," Peck said, as if talking to a dim journalist. "And, technically, they're not asleep."

"Yeah," said Spider, "but they're not exactly square dancing either, are they?"

Peck knew going in that the biker was insecure and moody, probably dangerous, possibly psychotic. But until this moment, he hadn't realized that he was dealing with a moron.

"I was in the middle of a meeting when you phoned," Peck said. "I thought we agreed that you wouldn't call me at the Clinic."

"I doubt there's very much you and I agree on, Doc," Spider said. "But just so you know? I'll fucking call you whenever and wherever I need to fucking call you."

"Look," Peck said, "I don't want to argue with you —"

"That," said Spider, "is the first smart thing you've said this morning, Doc." Then, before Peck could respond, Spider lifted the satchel and placed it on the table.

Peck looked from the bag to the biker and back again.

"What's this?" he asked.

"That," Spider said, "is the merchandise."

"The merchandise?" Peck said, confused, and then, in an instant, not at all confused. "Good God, you're telling me . . ."

He trailed off and suddenly reached for the bag, but Spider was faster and swatted Peck's hands away from the latch.

"You don't touch it," Spider said, "until I have my money." He paused and let the gravity of the moment settle in. Then he sat back in the booth and added, "And you don't look inside until you're back at the farm."

"This is outrageous," Peck said.

Spider put on a surprised face and, in one casual motion, picked up Peck's cup and tossed the remains of the coffee on the doc's suit. Peck reared back but didn't make a sound. He looked down on his shirt front and then up at the biker.

"You don't know outrageous," Spider said. "Now stop fucking around before you piss me off."

Peck sat in silence for a few seconds, trying to think. Then he eased up off his ass, pulled a handkerchief from a back pocket, and started to dab at his collar and lapels as he stared at Spider, who hung his head forward, smiling and waiting.

"This," Peck said, gesturing to the satchel with the handkerchief, "is not what we agreed on."

"You saying you don't want it?" Spider asked.

No one spoke to Dr. Peck this way and the experience was upsetting the rhythms of his thought and his speech.

"What we had agreed . . ." he began, then stopped suddenly and re-grouped. "*I* was to perform the procedure."

"That's right," Spider said, "and I saved you the trouble. You're not careful, I might start thinking that's worth a bonus."

"You don't understand," Peck said, his anger not yet in the voice but visible in the face and in the way he was holding his hands. "There's a protocol. There's a way that things need to be done for a successful harvest."

"Successful harvest," Spider repeated. "Jesus, listen to you. Successful harvest. That's a fucking riot, Doc."

"There are questions that I needed to ask," Peck said. "Blood tests and tissue samples."

"You're a detail man, Doc," Spider said. "I can see that. You take your work seriously."

"There are time constraints," Peck said. "I don't even know when —"

"About five this morning," Spider said. "And you know what? I just decided you owe me a new pair of jeans."

Jared the bartender appeared at the table.

Spider startled a little, looked up, and said, "You're like a fucking cat."

"All those years of dance," Jared said. "You want to hear the breakfast specials?"

"Get out of here," Spider said, amused and delighted. "You serve *food* in this place?"

Jared just stared down at the biker, hands on hips, tired but smart and, always, professional. Dr. Peck stared at the black bag.

Spider asked, "What do you got? You got any eggs and hash? I'm in the mood for some eggs and hash."

"We don't have any hash," Jared said. "Do you want to see a menu?"

"Fuck it," Spider said. "Just bring us a couple of hairy knuckles and some doughnuts."

Jared nodded and walked away.

Peck waited a second, then folded his hands on the table in front of the satchel and said, "I don't think you understand my situation."

"I think I do, Doc," Spider said. "I don't think it's that hard to understand. I think even a shit-for-brains retard like me can understand your fucking situation." And then, below the table, he gave the doctor's shin a quick but solid kick. Peck grunted and lurched forward, but he kept his hands on the table.

"I didn't mean to insult you," Peck said.

Spider kicked the other shin and said, "Then you fucked up, didn't you?"

Peck was careful to nod. "I suppose I did," he said.

"I suppose so, too," Spider said.

They sat in silence until Jared returned and transferred two highball glasses and a plate of chocolate-glazed doughnuts from his tray to the table.

"Will there be anything else?" the barkeep asked.

"Anything else for you?" Spider asked, leaning toward Peck.

The doctor shook his head without shifting his eyes from the satchel.

"Then pay the man," Spider said.

Peck looked flustered for a moment, then shifted his body, rummaged in his pocket, and came out with an antique clip filled with neatly folded bills. Spider reached across the table and grabbed the money from him, handed the wad to Jared uncounted, and said, "You keep the change."

Jared remained placid, accepted the bills, and moved back to the bar. Spider slid one glass in front of Peck, lifted the other, and said, "How 'bout a toast? How's that sound to you, Doc?"

"You're generous with my money," Peck mumbled.

Spider laughed, spilling some of the drink. He put his glass down in front of the doctor and picked up its twin.

"I'm about to get real generous with an ass-kicking, too," he said. "What the fuck do you care, anyway? You got more money than you'll ever spend up there in the clinic."

"The majority of my money," Peck said, "is poured into my research."

"Yeah," Spider said, "me too. That's why I'm in need of a grant. You aren't the only one with big plans, Doc. So gimme my money and I'll let you have a doughnut and we can both call the morning a success."

"Why would I pay you," Peck asked, "when you didn't do what you promised to do?"

And in this way, the time arrived for Spider to get serious.

The biker sat back and wiped a hand across his mouth. He let his head fall back on his neck until it bumped against the back of the booth.

"You take that tone with me," he said slowly, "and I hear it as disrespect. And you need to believe me here, Doctor, you do not want to disrespect the Spider. Sooner or later, that is always a fucking mistake. And in your case, it'll be sooner."

Peck was stubborn enough to fight his own good judgment. He made Spider wait while he stared at the satchel and pretended to think things over. Finally, he gave a single nod of the head and slipped a bulging envelope out of his coat pocket. He placed the envelope on the table and slid it toward the Abomination.

"I'll pay you," Peck said, "because it's in my interest to pay you. And because it's possible that I can use something of this harvest. But our business is finished. If you'd performed the way we agreed, we might have had an ongoing relationship. But apparently you're not a man who thinks about the future."

"That's where you'd be all kinds of wrong," Spider said, leaning his chest into the table, reaching down into his boot to pull and open his Buck knife, and jabbing it into Peck's thigh, just enough to puncture trouser and skin and draw a run of blood.

This time, Peck yelled out, a shocked little scream that, for a moment, drowned out the jukebox rendition of "Night Has a Thousand Eyes." The doctor pressed a hand against the thigh, took it away bloody, grabbed his soiled handkerchief, and applied pressure to the wound.

"You stabbed me," he said, as if Spider didn't know.

"I stabbed you," Spider said, "you'd be holding your guts in that snot rag. I poked you's what I did. Just to show you I'm thinking about the future right this minute. I'm thinking about how I'm going to come up to your turnip farm one of these nights and cut your dick off. And I'm thinking about how I'm going to use it to choke the life out of that bitch daughter of yours. And I'm thinking how after that, I'm going to burn your fucking clinic to the ground along with all your fucking sleepers. How's that for the future, shithead?"

On the last word, he picked up the envelope with his free hand and slapped Peck across the face with it. Then he got out of the booth, stood in the aisle, tucked the envelope into the front of his jeans, tucked his knife back into his boot, grabbed two doughnuts, and limped out the bar's back door.

Peck sat still for a minute, then looked across the aisle to Jared, who was wiping down the bar and humming along to the juke, unconcerned, lost in a familiar daydream. The wound was starting to burn, but Dr. Peck couldn't help himself. He pulled the satchel down onto his seat and unfastened the hasp carefully, as if disarming a bomb. Pushing both flaps back on their hinges, he took a breath and peered inside at the fetus. It had taken on a blue and purple hue and he guessed it was roughly four months gestated and had been terminated about five hours ago.

Whoever had performed the procedure had done an adequate job. The fetus appeared normal and very likely harvestable. Peck closed up the satchel, relieved, and exited the bar, bleeding his way out the front door, suddenly excited despite the hole in his leg.

Behind him, Jared began to sing something bold and brassy.

4.

Sweeney had the hotel send over his luggage. He'd traveled light, a canvas duffel and a garment bag. He had arranged with the real estate agent back in Cleveland to sell whatever furnishings she could to the buyer and dispose of the rest in an estate sale. Corrigan at the pharmacy said this was a sure way to get screwed but Sweeney liked the idea of getting rid of everything and starting fresh.

He hung his whites in a closet full of cobwebs and breathed in the smell of oil from out in the cellar proper. He unrolled his ties and hung them on the pegs of the coat post, put his few casual clothes in the bureau drawers. From the bottom of the duffel, he took out two bath towels and laid them on the bed. He unfolded one to reveal a framed photo. It was a snapshot of Kerry and Danny that he'd had blown up. A vacation shot from two years ago up at Put-in-Bay, posed on the deck of the cottage they'd rented. It was dusk and Kerry had lifted the boy up to show him something out on the lake. Sweeney had grabbed the camera off the picnic table and snapped them without warning. The sun was just about spent for the day and the horizon was a slash of bright red below the clouds.

He propped the photo on the bureau and picked up the puzzle book. The apartment's last occupant had been the Clinic's longtime custodian. Nora said he'd been a drinker, but not so bad that anyone had to act on it. Sweeney had no problem imagining the man after a few pops, admiring the charms of Miss January and wishing he were a decade younger. But as he lay down on the bed and sank into its middle and opened *The Big Book of Logic Problems,* he couldn't quite imagine the custodian wrestling with two trains hurtling toward Chicago at different rates of speed.

He dozed off while trying to puzzle out the cost of the largest pumpkin at the farmers' market. And was woken some time later by Romeo, the janitor from the third floor. Sweeney answered the door a little sleep drunk, having napped just long enough to feel disoriented.

"They told me to come get you," Romeo said. "Your son's on the way."

"Danny's here?"

The janitor shook his head. "I said he's on his way. They called from the airport."

"Thanks," Sweeney said. "Let me throw some water on my face and I'll be right up."

Romeo didn't answer and he didn't step away from the door. After a second, Sweeney moved to the bathroom. He stood before the toilet and took a long and pain-relieving leak. Then he moved to the pedestal sink, rolled up his sleeves, and splashed himself into the present.

He patted his face dry and looked in the mirror. He ran a hand through his hair and reminded himself to buy some mouthwash. Then he left the apartment and followed Romeo upstairs. When they reached the front porch, he knew something was wrong.

Too many people were milling around — two orderlies with a gurney and three women huddled together, all of them looking as if they were on their way to a wake. Two of the women were crones, gnarled and as wide as they were tall. They were dressed in old-style nurses' uniforms, complete with hats, and each one carried a large red plastic toolbox from which protruded tangles of tubing and swabs and packages of sterile wraps. They were listening intently to the third woman, who was a fraction of their age and wore a lab jacket and had a stethoscope slung around her neck.

One of the crones indicated Sweeney as he came down the stairs, and the young woman turned to greet him.

She said, "Are you the boy's father?"

"Is everything all right?" he asked.

She put her hand out and said, "I'm Alice Peck, the chief of rehabilitation."

"Is Danny all right?" he asked.

"We're not sure," blunt and emotionless. "They called as soon as they landed. The nurse practitioner that's traveling with your son said there was a problem with his shunt. I've notified Dr. Siegel at City."

"Jesus Christ, are you going to operate?"

The woman shook her head. "Probably not. We're closer than City

General. I've instructed the EMTs to bring the boy here. I'll take a look at him. If it's something we're not prepared to handle, I'll send them on to Dr. Siegel."

"How did this happen?" Sweeney asked, trying and failing to keep his volume normal. "What's wrong with the shunt?"

"I don't know. I haven't seen the patient yet."

"His name's Daniel," though he never called him that.

"I haven't seen Daniel yet. The NP said there could be a backup. His vitals had dropped a little but were holding steady — "

Sweeney tried to think. "Did this happen on the plane? I knew I should've traveled with him."

"Mr. Sweeney," the woman said, "right now I don't know much more than you. Now when the ambulance gets here, I'm going to ask you to stand back and let me have a look at Daniel. And you're not going to want to do that. But you're going to have to."

He had already quit listening. And then they all heard the sirens and, moments later, saw the red and white van turn onto the circular drive and start up the hill to the Clinic.

It came to a stop in front of the porch. The driver and his partner jumped out of the van simultaneously and Alice Peck yelled for the driver to get back behind the wheel. He did as he was told. The partner was already opening the back doors. They swung past their hinges and locked in place.

At first, Sweeney couldn't see Danny. A third paramedic jumped out of the ambulance and began to talk to Alice. Sweeney couldn't hear a word. The nurse practitioner he'd hired from the St. Joseph was on her knees next to the stretcher. Alice climbed inside the van and knelt on the opposite side. Her two crones moved to the lip and stood at the ready with supplies.

Sweeney came up behind them and leaned over their shoulders. Now he caught a glimpse of his son, the body in its familiar hunch, covered with a sheet to the waist. One of the nurses felt his presence, turned, and said, "You'll have to stand back, sir."

He said, "That's my boy," but he did as he was told.

Dr. Peck had her hands on Danny's head and she was speaking in a low voice to the nurse practitioner, whose name was Mrs. Heller. Mrs. Heller had a blood pressure cuff on Danny and she was staring at her watch while nodding her head to everything Dr. Peck said.

On Danny's second day in the St. Joseph, there had been a problem with the shunt. It had blocked off or backed up. Something went wrong. Two doctors and two nurses had gone to work on the boy and Sweeney had overreacted, yelling obscenities at the LPN who had tried to lead him into the solarium. The doctors had fixed the problem and Sweeney had spent weeks apologizing to the young woman.

That panic came back to him now and he tried to work on his breathing. It didn't help and he shouted out, "Get him to the hospital."

One of the EMTs gave him a look. Everyone else ignored him. Dr. Peck came up off her knees into a squat, pivoted, and started grabbing some things from the nurse's toolbox. Sweeney saw latex gloves on her hands — when had she put those on? Mrs. Heller said something about blood pressure that Sweeney couldn't make out. He moved to touch the shoulder of the paramedic to ask what had been said. He stopped himself, tried to breathe again.

Now the doctor had a handful of gauze panels, thick and soaked. She handed them to one nurse and took a fresh supply from the other. In her free hand, Sweeney saw what looked like a pair of pliers.

That was when he turned around, sat down on the porch steps, and supported his head with his hands.

That second night at St. Joe's — when the shunt had blocked off or backed up, when the doctors had walked quickly into Danny's room and asked Sweeney to wait outside. When he'd called that patient young nurse a fucking bitch — that night had ended with Kerry saying to him *It would've been better if he'd died.* And with him slapping her across the cheek.

He had never hit a woman in his life. He had rarely raised his voice to his wife. He did not hit her hard. There was no bruise. She had run away from him. And he had made his way to the men's room and sat down in an empty stall and wept and gagged and punched the partitioning wall until he couldn't feel his fist.

Now he felt a hand on his arm and looked up to see Alice Peck in front of him. He stood and almost bumped into her and she steadied him.

"He's okay," she said.

"Thank you," he said, too loud. And then, "You're sure?"

"You can go to him," she said.

Mrs. Heller was climbing out of the van, looking more angry than relieved, with the *Limbo* backpack slung awkwardly over her shoulder. Sweeney started to climb in where she'd been and a paramedic said, "Why don't you let us get him out? You can see him better."

Sweeney nodded and stepped back. The driver and his partner were in the rear of the ambulance now, throwing latches and sliding free the gurney. They held it above the driveway and one of them kicked loose and lowered the retractable wheels.

Danny was in his standard position, on his side, arms bent up to his chest, hands balled and tucked just below the chin. He was dressed in a johnny, and Sweeney made a note to ask what had happened to his pajamas. He had specifically laid out the *Limbo* pajamas. He leaned down over the boy, his chest shrouding most of Danny's body. He kissed the boy's cheek, brought his lips to the boy's ear. He said, "Dad's here," and felt himself start to slip.

Coming upright, a little too quickly, he said to no one in particular, "Can we get him into his room now?"

There was a moment of group hesitation before Alice said, "We'll be right along." Then they wheeled the boy around the stairs and up the handicapped ramp and the crones followed behind with Mrs. Heller bringing up the rear, lugging a small travel bag.

As the group negotiated the front doors, Dr. Peck said, "Are you all right?"

He nodded and swallowed and said, "You're sure he doesn't have to go to the hospital?"

"I'm sure," she said. "It wasn't as serious as it looked. But if you'd like us to arrange for a consult with Dr. Siegel, we can do that."

"If you say he's okay," he said, "I believe you."

"And how about you?" she asked as she stripped off the latex gloves. "Are you going to be okay?"

"I'm just a little off balance. A lot of changes."

She put her hands in the pockets of her lab coat. "Must be a big move."

"We've been in Cleveland for almost ten years," he said.

"I know," she said. "The St. Joseph is a good facility. I know Dr. Roth pretty well."

"I've heard the name, but I never met her." After a second or two of silence Sweeney said, "So you're Dr. Peck's daughter?"

She smiled and her eyes widened a bit and she said, "My father's the head of the Clinic, yes."

He saw no resemblance.

"So it's a family business?" he said and flinched at how lame it sounded.

"Not quite," she said. "The Clinic's a privately held corporation but we both sit on the board."

Sweeney laughed before he could stop himself. "I was just making a little joke there."

Alice leaned her head forward a bit and said, "I know."

Sweeney couldn't think of anything to say but "Oh."

Alice Peck motioned to the front door with her head and said, "Listen, I'm going to collect all your son's paperwork and get his new files going. We'll give him a day to rest up from his trip before we start his assessments." She put out her hand and said, "It's a pleasure to meet you, Mr. Sweeney."

He took the hand and said, "Thanks for taking care of Danny, Dr. Peck."

She started to walk away, turned back, and said, "I look forward to working with you."

HE SAT DOWN on the steps so that he wouldn't be following on Dr. Peck's heels. He tried the breathing again. He put his hand on his knee and realized he was still shaking. He inhaled, held the breath, exhaled. He rolled his head around his neck. He took in and let out another breath. He smelled apples and Alice Peck's perfume.

Over the last year, he'd read a couple of books on stress reduction. Both texts agreed that breathing correctly was key. Breathing was the answer. You learn the techniques. You practice them and make them reflexive. You become conscious of your breathing and you learn to alter it. You do all these things and you'll manage to relax both your body and your mind.

So far it was bullshit.

The attacks were happening more frequently, not less. They manifested in two ways. Either he panicked, as he had this morning in the cafeteria, or he became enraged. As he had last month, when he got into an argument with a retiree over the cost of a prescription. He ended up screaming at the old man, opening the customer's vial, and throwing the pills at his back as he ran down the stationery aisle.

He'd tried grief counseling. His doctor had recommended a woman who practiced out of her home in Shaker Heights. She'd been pleasant enough. Sympathetic and well meaning. She'd asked him to find a mantra, something short that could catch his mind and focus it. He'd picked a prayer from childhood — *Mercy and justice belong to the Lord*. He could tell the therapist disapproved, but once he'd chosen the phrase it wouldn't go away. There are still nights when it repeats in his head through a run of unsleeping hours.

He stared at his hand until he brought it under enough control to be inconspicuous, then moved up the stairs and into the Clinic. The EMTs passed him without a word on their way out. He walked to room 103 where he found Danny already installed in his bed. Mrs. Heller was at his side, adjusting the sheet.

Sweeney stood in the doorway. They'd cut the boy's hair before he left St. Joe's. It was a razor job, military close. It made him look older and made the bald patch around the shunt seem less severe. In the beginning, there had been a few arguments about the hair. The clinic's policy, when there was any skull care involved, was to shave the entire head every other day. It made Danny look cold and vulnerable and sick and Sweeney put up a stink. He'd been a real pain in the ass to Dr. Lawton until they relented and allowed a small cover of fuzz to grow. The first crop that came in was downy, silky, and Sweeney had spent countless nights compulsively stroking his son's head and shivering. He couldn't believe more parents didn't question the hair ruling. He'd have to ask Alice Peck about her policy.

Mrs. Heller sensed him, turned, and frowned.

There was nothing subtle about Mrs. Heller.

"It's a gloomy place, Mr. Sweeney," she said.

"They're all gloomy places, Mrs. Heller," he said.

"But it's so old."

He came into the room, sat on the edge of the bed, and picked up his son's hand. "Dr. Lawton says they do amazing work with long-term patients."

"They've had two arousals. And one of them reverted," she said, taking some lip balm from a pocket, rubbing it on her fingers, and then running the fingers over Danny's lips.

"Did you wash your hands, Mrs. Heller?"

It was the kind of thing that angered her the most and he knew it. He'd found a dozen ways in as many months to question the woman's professionalism. She ignored him, recapped the balm, and snatched some Kleenex from the bedside table. Then she surprised him by saying, "I'll miss Danny."

"I know you will, Mrs. Heller," he said. "But this is the best place for him right now. It was time for us to get out of Cleveland."

She nodded and jumped back into the clinical.

"You can let the front desk know when you're ready for the admitting team to run the checklist. They wanted to give you some time with him before they started. I've checked and they've got his list of meds. But apparently some of his records haven't arrived yet."

"I'm going to phone Dr. Lawton today."

"I'll check with him when I get back."

He wasn't sure he was going to ask until the words came out. "Mrs. Heller," he said, "I was wondering what happened to Danny's pajamas."

She immediately looked down at the boy and then back to the father.

"I thought you packed them," she said.

Sweeney shook his head. "He's got two pair of those cartoon pajamas. I packed one and I wanted him to travel in the other."

"I thought you took all of his things."

"If you could check his room at St. Joe's —"

"I checked the closet before we left," Mrs. Heller said. "It was empty. I was certain you'd taken everything."

"There's no need to get defensive," he began.

"I'm not getting defensive." Her voice rose a bit. "I'm simply telling you that the closet was empty."

"It's no big deal," he said. "I just thought I'd ask."

She pulled back a little, put on her rare puzzled look. "I'll check again, but I'm certain that closet was empty. I'll call you if I find anything."

"Don't worry about it," he said. "I'm sure I can buy another pair in town."

He wanted her out of the room and gone. He reached into his pocket and pulled out a wad of bills, then hesitated. Did you tip someone for this kind of thing? Mrs. Heller looked at the money in his hand, then looked away. Apparently you did not. He put the cash back in his pocket.

"I want to thank you for the care you've shown Danny," he said.

She put her hand on the boy's forehead as if checking for a fever. She let it linger for a second and then pulled it back across the soft bristles of hair. Without looking up, she said, "He's a wonderful little boy. And I'm sorry for all your troubles, Mr. Sweeney."

He nodded but she didn't look up, and then it was too late to say anything. Mrs. Heller picked up her travel bag in one hand and her nurse's kit in the other and said, "I'll let you know if I find the pajamas." Then she left him alone with his son.

He stood staring at the boy for a while, as if fixing the child again into his memory. He moved to the closet, removed the *Limbo* backpack that Mrs. Heller had stowed there. He placed the pack on the bed and studied the grotesque illustrations screened on its flap. The chicken boy. The skeleton. The Siamese twins. All in vibrant primary colors.

Sweeney unzipped the pack, reached inside, and withdrew a fat stack of comic books, which he placed inside the drawer of the nightstand. He selected the top issue, closed the drawer, climbed onto the bed next to his son, brought his mouth to the boy's ear, and, softly, began to read.

LIMBO COMICS

ISSUE # 2: "A Treacherous Passage"

The crossing to Gehenna was, at times, perilous, and at other times, monotonous. The seas were often stormy and nauseating, and the ship was always cold. The freaks dressed in layers of costumes and passed the time imagining the riches and the fame that they would claim in the new world. Durga braided Antoinette's sparse strands of hair. Marcel and Vasco played poker for matchsticks. Milena and Nadja occasionally tried to cadge drinks from the surly crew in the boiler room. And Chick scribbled in his diary, last year's Christmas gift from Kitty.

Mostly he recorded and analyzed his visions, the messages he received during his seizures. He had them, on average, every third day throughout the voyage. All of them involved the doctor, Fliess, and his enormous laboratory castle, the Black Iron Clinic. All of them relayed in the voice of the Limbo, which had come to mean, in Chick's mind and heart, the voice of his long-lost father. Calling out to him. Guiding him in fits and starts. Leading the son to communion and healing.

Kitty sat watch during the seizures, holding her love, cradling him as best she could, stroking the feathers of his cheek, kissing the feathers on his forehead with her seasick lips.

The Touya was a tramp steamer that managed fourteen knots on a good day and boasted a skeleton crew of fifty men, all of whom had more than a passing acquaintance with the darker side of human nature, and none of whom lost any love on the freaks. The Captain of *The Touya*, a hatchet-face bear of a man named Karl Gunter, communicated with the freaks through Bruno, the strongman, who conveyed the skipper's insistence that the freaks confine themselves to the ship's hold for the duration of the passage. Here they lodged among the freight — thousands of sealed drums filled with expensive fertilizer made exclusively from the excrement of Royal Bergauer Stallions. Twice a day, Bruno brought down a crate of food, mostly overripe oranges and tins of salted pork. The conditions were stark and filthy, but these were circus folk, after all, well used to improvisation and the uncertainties of nomadic life.

It took weeks to reach Gehenna and toward the tail end of the trip they caught the last slap of a nor'easter that snapped the freaks like marbles across the floor of the hold all night long. Jeta became hysterical and Aziz was forced to backhand her with one of his enormous paws.

Landfall came just after dawn one morning. Captain Gunter dropped anchor and summoned Bruno to his quarters for a card game and a conference over a breakfast of hardtack and Becherovka.

"My debt," the Captain said, "is paid."

Bruno nodded, raised his glass to the man.

"You kept your word," Bruno agreed.

Gunter smiled, pulled out a small canvas pouch filled with snuff, and offered the strongman a pinch. The Captain's ego was larger than his legendary belly. An autodidact, he had a well-known passion for the Bible and the Bard, and Bruno hoped that he wouldn't have to endure a reading from the Song of Solomon.

"And what now?" Gunter asked. "What will you do?"

Seboldt waved off the snuff and tried to shrug his muscle-bound shoulders.

"We'll look for work," he said. "People are the same all over. Everyone wants to see the freaks."

"So you're staying with them, then?" said Gunter, a man not normally given to surprise.

"For a time anyway," Bruno said.

"I could take you back home," the Captain said. "You got them out of harm's way. Most men would say that was enough."

"I can't go home," Bruno said. "Shoshone McGee had a lot of friends."

At this, Gunter spit out the latest sip of his drink.

"The hell he did," the Captain said. "I knew McGee. Even his parents hated that bastard. He was a boil on the ass every day of his life."

"The ladies liked him enough," Bruno said, getting up from the table and moving to look out the Captain's porthole. The small room smelled of oil and sweat and the odor combined with the low ceiling to produce in the strongman a touch of claustrophobia.

Gunter refilled Seboldt's glass and carried it to him.

"The ladies," he said to Bruno's back, "feared him and loathed him. He was a bully on his best day and a rapist when he drank. And he drank whenever he was awake."

Bruno turned around but didn't argue.

The Captain handed him his drink and moved back to the bottle.

"The fact is, Bruno," he said, "no one would give a goddamn that you killed the knife thrower. You did a favor for all of Bohemia. And I think you know that."

"Murder is still murder," Bruno said, but it came out weak. "There will be a warrant out on me."

"There won't be a one," Gunter said evenly. "Teddy Bluett will find a new bladesman and life will go on."

"Tell it your way," Bruno said, wishing they could move on to a new subject.

"It's my ship," the Captain said. "I'll always tell it my way. But this time it's also the truth."

"There's nothing for me back in Bohemia," Bruno said.

"Maybe not," Gunter said. "Probably not. But I think you're off to Gehenna because you want to stay," his voice suddenly rising here, "with those pathetic vermin in the hold."

Bruno was caught off guard.

"You're touched," he said to the Captain, but there was no force behind the insult.

"Careful son," Gunter said. "You're strong as Krok's mule, but this morning you're in the Captain's quarters."

"What are you getting at?" Bruno asked.

"I think you're hard for those filthy monsters down below."

Bruno spoke slowly and deliberately.

"I hate those miserable abominations. As much as you. As much as McGee."

Gunter nodded and smiled in response.

"Son," he said, "you might be a murderer. But you're still a pathetic liar. And I say you're sweet on the freaks."

Then there was a moment of possibility in which one or the other might have thrown a punch. But both were smart men with a wealth of experience in the area of dismal consequence.

"Why don't you just bring us into the harbor," Bruno said, "and we'll be out of your hair?"

Captain Gunter stared at the strongman, expressionless, then he moved back to his mess table and sat down again. He lifted his glass of spirits, brought it to his lips, and said over the rim, "Who said anything about the harbor?"

As a boy, Bruno Seboldt had survived daylong strappings from his maniac father. As a teen, he had seen trench combat in the Budwein province. As a young man, he had lived through the cholera epidemic and the Krumloff Circus fire. To say that Bruno Seboldt was a man of courage and tenacity was a more than reasonable statement. But that morning, as he heard Captain Gunter deliver those six casual words, he shuddered and was overcome with the kind of doubt that can render a man impotent for the balance of his life. And though Bruno could not have known it, down in the hold, at that exact moment, the chicken boy was starting to sweat and ache.

"I don't understand," Bruno finally managed to say.

"You don't?" said Gunter, enjoying the taunting.

"You have to put in," said Bruno. "Your hold is full of cargo."

"So it is," said Gunter. "Fertilizer and abominations. The shit goes down to the Port of Chaldea. That's still a good hundred kilometers away. But I'm afraid you and the monsters are getting off here."

Bruno squinted at him and Gunter barked out a laugh.

"I liked you, Seboldt," the Captain said. "Truly, I considered you a friend. You could hold your liquor like a Russian and you played a fine hand of cribbage. But you're sweet on those freaks. I've seen it. Don't try to deny it. You've turned. You've gone over. And I can't help you. I've got a business to run and I've got a reputation. If even one of my importers knew I brought those deviants to Gehenna, he'd tear up my compact. And if they knew their goods had been bunking with freaks, they'd dump all that expensive dung in the deep."

"What are you going to do?" Bruno asked.

"You sound like a eunuch already," Gunter said. "Good Christ, it's an awful thing." He shook his head and motioned to the porthole.

"We're less than a kilometer from shore. That's Bezalel out there. A terrible city. A place without God. Makes Maisel look like Eden. But it's a fine spot for freaks. And their handmaids."

"Then bring us in and we'll be gone," Bruno said.

"I've no business in Bazalel," Gunter said. "You want to go there? Then jump in the sea and swim."

It took Bruno a second to realize that the Captain meant his last words literally.

"You know they can't make it," Bruno said.

Gunter smiled as if on an indulged child.

"You had the strongest back in Bohemia," he said. "Put it to work."

"There are eleven of them," Bruno said.

"Is that all?" Gunter said. "It seemed like a multitude."

Then he called for his first mate, who was waiting outside the Captain's door. Landau entered already smiling, as if in on the joke for a year.

"Mr. Landau," Gunter said, "escort Mr. Seboldt topside. And have the rats brought up from the hold."

WHEN THE SWABBIES came for them, the freaks went passively. Getting the fat lady and the Siamese twins up the iron ladders to the top deck was no easy task. But everything progressed peacefully until curiosity overtook one of the sailors, who tried to cop a feel on Milena, the hermaphrodite.

Milena had one method for dealing with gropers—knocking the molester to the ground and stomping repeatedly on his crotch as if trying to kill a cockroach. The man's mates came running and a melee broke out until Landau appeared and restored order. By then, Antoinette and Jeta were hysterical and Chick was sliding rapidly into an ill-timed seizure.

As the crew began to rig an iron conveyance beam off the starboard side of the ship, Captain Gunter arrived on the scene. The presence of Gunter brought a gravity to the situation that silenced even the pinhead.

The Captain was a dramatic man, given to ritual and the big gesture. So he couldn't resist turning a childish, if murderous, stunt into high theatrics. While the crew finished securing the beam, he had Landau arrange the freaks into a semicircle on the main deck, with Bruno, the reluctant patriarch, centered among them all. The crew stood in small groups, ripe with anticipation. Several men carried wrenches or hammers. Gunter glared them into silence, then began his speech.

"I've spent my life at sea," he said, "like most of the Gunter men before me. So I know how wondrous the sailor's life can be."

Now he began to pace, as if inspecting new recruits. He did not hide his disgust as he studied Nadja's claws and the bones of Jeta's face.

"But for all the beauty and the marvels, a mariner knows that the ocean can be a place of monsters. A refuge for abominations, which God, in his wisdom, banished to the cold fathoms, far from the decent company of man."

Gunter stopped before Kitty, looked down, and shook his head as if overcome with a disappointment that rivaled his revulsion.

"The world is an imperfect place," he continued. "And on occasion, some monsters free themselves from their briny crypt and find their way to the surface. And when this happens, it is man's turn to do God's work and to send the beasts back to the blackest depths."

He turned to his men now, lifted his face to the sun and closed his eyes.

"That, gentlemen, is what we're going to do this morning."

The sailors began to cheer, but after a moment, Gunter raised a hand to quiet them.

"Being men of God is not an easy thing. We want to do His work and we want to do it well. So we will leave the final judgments to the One above."

He opened the eyes, turned back to address the freaks.

"If you can swim to shore, then God be with you, and welcome to the land of Gehenna."

A dramatic pause here, as understanding spread among most of the freaks and they began to look to one another for direction.

"And if you can't swim," Gunter added, as if an afterthought, "then a hell of another sort awaits you today."

At these words, Bruno moved to grab his betrayer. But Karl Gunter was no drunken knife thrower and Mr. Landau had a pistol to the strongman's temple before Seboldt could lay a hand on the Captain.

Gunter seemed thrilled by the attempt on his life.

"Why don't you show your grotesque friends how this is done?" he said to Bruno.

Landau repositioned the pistol, pressing the barrel into the small of Bruno's back and shoving him forward to the crates that were stacked into steps before the ship's rail. Extending off the rail was the iron girder used to lower freight to the docks.

The freaks' semicircle broke open and Bruno moved between Kitty and Chick as he approached the railing. He tried not to look at either one, but the chicken boy suddenly reached out and touched him and it felt like ice against the strongman's skin. He glanced quickly at the feathered face and saw the beak move, and the boy, who was drooling a white bile, tried to whisper something before a crewman clubbed him to the deck. Seconds later, while falling through the skin of the water, Bruno realized that what Chick had said was, "Forgive me."

Bruno leapt off the girder without waiting for a command or a shove. The water was frigid, but he was not worried about himself. Often, he had swum miles at a time in the River Kalda when training for a new touring season. But he didn't imagine that any of the freaks could manage the kilometer to shore. And he was certain that some of them would sink like stones as soon as they hit the drink.

They picked Aziz first, grabbed him by his arms and placed the human torso up on the iron bar. He didn't make a sound, but immediately began to swing himself forward, down to the end of the beam. Then he took three rocking swings, each bringing his trunk higher into the air until, on the last, he let himself fly and arced up and out and into the sky, forming his arms into a perfect V as his trajectory reversed and he began to plunge downward. He knifed into the ocean, disappeared for a few seconds, and then emerged near Bruno, who was treading water in a controlled panic.

Aziz spoke quickly to the strongman, blinking the sea out of his eyes. "I can make it," he said. "So can Fatos, Milena, Durga, and the twins. But you have to help the rest. I'll wait for you on the beach."

With this he began an impressive breaststroke away from the ship, toward the rock-strewn shores of Gehenna.

Up on the deck, one of Gunter's men was poking a hysterical Jeta down the length of the girder with a massive gaff. Bruno squinted through the sun, trying to see what was happening. The gaffer toyed with the skeleton, feigning a poke at the head and then drumming on the girder with the steel of his hook. Jeta screamed and danced as if the beam were ablaze and the crew laughed as if in the grip of a wonderful mania until, finally tiring of the routine, the crewman swung his pole up and spanked the boniest ass in all of Eastern Europe. Jeta went sailing off the girder and fell, those ridiculous arms and legs spastic all the way down. She went under the water and bobbed up once.

Bruno swam to her, dove down, and just managed to grab a twig of a wrist. He pulled her up into the air, supported her around the waist, and yelled, "Can you swim?"

The skeleton couldn't speak. Her head was snapping back and forth on her bird's neck. She made deep sucking noises and her eyes blinked open and closed and open again.

Bruno got up into her face and tried to speak clearly and slowly.

"I'm going to bring you into shore," he said, "but you have to calm down or we won't make it."

He could see her making the effort to detach from her panic. The blinks came more slowly and her breathing became more deliberate.

"That's right," Bruno said, encouraging her. "That's good. You're going to be fine. I'm going to bring you to land."

He kicked his legs, moved around to her backside without letting go of her, then repositioned his arm around her waist. She allowed herself some whimpering and he didn't call her on it. He brought his mouth to her ear and asked, "Do you know how to float, Jeta?"

She could only shake her head *no,* and he was quick to say, "That's all right. That's not a problem."

He could see her tiny ears turning blue and understood that she had no body fat to insulate her and that this meant it was possible she could go into shock before they reached the shore.

"Now, listen to me, Jeta," Bruno said. "I'm going to put my hand on the small of your back and push you up to the surface. All right? I want you to try and lay back and let the water float you up."

He eased her supine, positioned himself, and got a new grip on her—higher up on her chest and under her armpits. He began to swim sidestroke, pulling her along. They glided, quickly gaining some distance from the boat. Bruno's arms and legs were enormous and Jeta weighed less than thirty kilograms. But when Gunter whistled at him from the deck, the strongman couldn't resist turning his head to look.

And what he saw was Durga, the fat lady, being lifted over the rail by five straining crewmen. The Captain wasn't risking the girder to this kind of girth. The crew heaved once, then twice and managed to toss the corpulent ball of flesh overboard. Durga fell like a refrigerator and hit the water in a cannonball splash that rained for long yards.

Bruno stopped swimming, pedaled his legs to tread in place and Jeta began to scream and thrash. He had to tighten his grip to keep the skeleton from going under. It was a minute before Durga surfaced, like a leviathan, spouting water and howling with the shock of the cold. But when she began swimming, she did so effortlessly, powerfully, even beautifully. She made it to the strongman in no time and they floated like happy mammals for a moment.

"You can swim," was all Bruno could think to say, and the words came out high-pitched and delighted.

"In the water," Durga said, "I'm petite."

She reached out and squeezed the skeleton's trembling shoulder.

"I'm fine, Jeta," she said. "We're all going to be fine."

Then she made serious eyes at Bruno and said, "Let me have her. You'll need to take two at a time."

They both looked back to the ship where a defiant Nadja was trying to keep herself between Antoinette and the jabbing of the gaff.

Antoinette was behind the lobster girl, still as a statue and weeping. Nadja's best show dress had been torn half off her.

Bruno placed Jeta in Durga's outstretched arms and began swimming frantically back toward *The Touya*. The lobster girl and the pinhead fell within seconds of each other. Antoinette howled the whole way down, a shriek of pure terror. Bruno got to her only seconds after she went under. He yanked her back into the air by an arm and as soon as she cleared her throat of water, the screaming began again.

He wasn't as lucky with Nadja. The lobster girl fell off the far side of the conveyance beam and went under about twenty yards away. Bruno pulled Antoinette along with him but the pinhead's thrashing slowed him. He switched his grip from arm to neck and tightened it until he choked her into silence. But in that moment of distraction he lost sight of the spot where Nadja had broken the water.

Bruno scanned the ocean and at last spotted a single claw as it bobbed up once and then slipped below the surface.

Grabbing Antoinette around the waist, the strongman swam to the claw site and dove. With his free hand, he grabbed and grabbed until he clasped a handful of the lobster girl's hair, snatched her up by the scalp, and pulled all of them up past the surface.

Nadja broke into the air choking and heaving. Her convulsions triggered a new level of hysteria in Antoinette, which threw Bruno off balance. He began to dip to one side, immediately tried to compensate, and pitched to the other. Somewhere above him, the crew of *The Touya* was yelling, whistling, taunting. And then he became aware of small objects striking the water around him—banana peels, cigar stubs, and something that hit hard, maybe a rock or a bolt.

"Get on my back," Bruno screamed at the lobster girl, trying to sling her over his shoulders and, at the same time, contain the pinhead.

He felt Nadja repositioning herself and then saw her claws jutting out below his chin. Somehow, he ignored the impulse to shake her free. He clutched Antoinette under his left arm and began to swim with his right. Keeping his head down and kicking his legs, Bruno aimed for the shore and tried not to think about what was happening up on the ship's deck.

It seemed to take forever, but finally he could hear Durga and Aziz calling to him, cheering him on. Nadja and Antoinette stayed silent through it all, until they coasted onto the beach in a pool of foam and were scooped into Durga's abundant arms, where they let loose all their fear and sorrow in terrible, wailing cries.

They'd come into a tiny cove, a horseshoe of sand cut out of a coastline that was mostly boulders and, further in, a plain of smaller, shinier, well-washed rocks. The human torso was in the surf up to his nipples.

"Do you need to rest?" he asked Bruno, who stood, then hunched, bracing his hands on bent knees. Water dripped steadily from his mustache.

He didn't answer. He didn't say a word. He turned around and dove again into the ocean.

Halfway back to the ship, he passed the twins, Vasco and Marcel. They were swimming as one body, Vasco manning the left arm and leg, Marcel, the right. Under different circumstances, it would have been something to behold. But Bruno had no time to marvel. As he glided past, Marcel said, "You must hurry," before plunging his head back into the water, and Vasco, whose head was emerging in perfect synchronism, added, "Fatos is unconscious," and then his head submerged and Marcel's reappeared, saying, "and they're about to rape Milena."

Approaching *The Touya*, Bruno could see the body of Fatos hanging limp, suspended over the end of the beam. The crew had given up any pretense of ritual and the proceedings had degenerated into an unmitigated debauch. If this was God's work, the deities of Gehenna were even more sloppy and perverse than the strongman had imagined.

Milena had been stripped naked and was bent over the railing at the waist. The angle prevented Bruno from getting the full picture, but it appeared that the hermaphrodite was being beaten with a sounding pole. The crew was into full rampage by the sound of things and the strongman began to suspect that the dwarf and the chicken boy were already at the bottom of the ocean.

He swam until he positioned himself directly beneath the hanging body of the mule. It was all he could do and it gave him time to catch his breath and rest his arms if not his legs. And though the noise of the collective sadism above was almost unbearable, the strongman's admiration for Milena grew by the second. Bruno could see that, though s/he hadn't yet passed out from the scourging, s/he wouldn't give them the satisfaction of even a scream, let alone a pleading. It inspired Bruno to start his own taunting and he yelled up to the sailors, "She's got testicles you'll never have, you *arschfickers*."

And though he couldn't have known it, Bruno's timing was crucial. Because just at that moment, Landau, the first mate who had been wielding the sounding pole, made the decision to use it as more than a cudgel. And upon hearing the taunt from below, Landau's associates, who had been holding Milena against the rail, released the hermaphrodite's arms in order to spit and gesture and scream down at the strongman. And so, a moment of opportunity presented itself as the would-be rapist shortened his grip on the pole and moved closer to his victim. And all Milena needed was that moment.

S/he whirled and kicked and caught the scourger in the very groin that Bruno had just disparaged. Landau fell to the deck on his knees and before his men could react, Milena had taken the sounding pole from the first mate, thumped him just once across the face and broken his jaw, then got behind the torturer and brought the pole up to his throat to choke him. Seeing their leader in peril, the other crewmen backed off as Milena maneuvered the hostage up onto the beam and began edging backward toward Fatos.

Looking down just once, s/he spotted Bruno treading below and made the decision. S/he got a foot beneath Fatos's chest, lifted and sent the mule plunging down to the strongman. Then s/he jumped, taking the pole and the first mate with her.

Bruno almost caught the mule. The shock of the water brought Fatos back to some semblance of consciousness and he let himself be pulled onto Seboldt's shoulder as the others exploded the sea a few yards away.

Milena and Landau bobbed up at the same moment and immediately began to wrestle, each trying to choke and drown the other. Bruno swam to Milena's aid, grabbed the first mate by the collar and submerged him, while Milena found and took possession of the sounding pole, then thrust it like a spear under the waves and into the opaque figure writhing below.

Minutes went by, Fatos lolling on Bruno's shoulder, Milena and Bruno staring at each other as Landau drowned and his men screamed from the rail above. But not a single man jumped from the ship to try and save their drowning officer. Not even Captain Gunter, who stared down at Bruno with a look of hateful surprise.

The Captain turned away first, just as Landau ended his struggle and his body began to float languidly down to what Gunter had called "the briny crypt."

When the body had vanished from sight, Bruno looked at Milena and asked, "Can you swim?"

The hermaphrodite looked toward the distant shore and said, "Some of it. Probably not all of it."

Bruno nodded.

"Give me the pole," he said.

Milena released it reluctantly. Bruno passed it across his chest until he reached the midpoint. Then he placed Fatos over the far end of the pole and let the mule's face dip into the water for a second. Fatos came awake again and Bruno said, "Just hold on and keep your head up. I'll take you in."

Turning to Milena, he said, "Get on the other side. Give me some balance."

Milena swam to Bruno's left, arms draped over the pole. Up close, Bruno could see the cherry welts rising like bulbs on the hermaphrodite's neck and shoulders. Bruno straightened himself out and began to kick his mighty legs and the trio was propelled away from the ship.

Bruno kept an eye on Fatos to make sure that the mule was staying awake, but when he spoke it was to Milena.

"You took that beating like a man."

"Is that supposed to be a compliment?" Milena said, but the words didn't have the performer's normally dry sarcasm.

They stayed quiet for a while, Bruno kicking with everything he had, until finally he had to know and he asked, "The dwarf and the chicken boy. Did they suffer in the end?"

Milena didn't answer and Bruno was forced to imagine the worst. He kicked harder, until the hermaphrodite finally said, "They're still up there. The Captain was saving them for last."

It wasn't what the strongman was expecting and he almost stopped kicking. But Fatos was passing out again, so he brought up a leg to nudge the mule awake, then focused on the last sprint to shore.

When they rolled into the beach, Antoinette and Jeta were calmer but still curled in Durga's lap. Aziz and the twins had collected driftwood and scrub and Nadja was digging a pit for a fire.

"I told you he'd make it," Durga said to her clan.

The twins ran to retrieve Milena and Fatos from the surf, dragging them up onto the beach and gently tending them. And though some of the clan had never before seen the hermaphrodite naked, none thought to gape.

Aziz approached Bruno and asked, "Can you go back?"—his way of asking if there were, in fact, any reason to swim out to the ship one more time.

Bruno was starting to tire. The lungs of even the strongest man in Bohemia have their breaking point. His legs were cramping and weak. And he was so chilled that his skin was entirely puckered.

He spoke softly to the human torso.

"They were alive when Milena jumped."

"Then I won't keep you," Aziz said, already assuming, there at the start, that Bruno was a patriarch who would sacrifice anything for his brood.

Bruno nodded, spat into the foam at his feet, turned and began to trudge back into the sea. He chose a simple stroke and maintained a consistent speed. He tried not to think of all the hours he had spent playing cribbage with Karl Gunter in the basement recreation room of the Jungborn Gymnasium in Maisel. He tried not to think of the sound that Shoshone McGee's neck had made when he twisted it and all those tiny bones had cracked like knuckles. He tried not to wonder what was compelling him to risk his life for the sake of some hideous abominations. And he tried very hard not to think about what was transpiring aboard *The Touya* at this moment.

AND WHAT WAS transpiring was a kind of sadism that, with the death of First Mate Landau, had escalated from dangerous hazing into an orgy of brutality and humiliation.

The chicken boy, fully in the grip of the Limbo now, had been trussed at the feet and hoisted to hang upside down from a cargo boom suspended off the mizzenmast. There he hovered, a feathered and twitching piñata, assaulted by both his visions and the group of crewmen who took turns batting his body with clubs and shovels and mop handles.

Inside the Limbo, the illusions had never been so vivid before. It was like watching a film at the Kierling Theater back in Maisel, but better, sharper, more colorful. More real, like a play, a tragedy in which the chicken boy was the main character. He was running from Dr. Fliess with the rest of the freak clan. He was running through a desert, the sand burning his feet. And then the desert became a swamp, a dank, fetid marsh that gave birth to enormous flies. The flies bit at his face and tried to hide in his feathers. And then the swamp became a beach, where terrible waves broke over massive boulders, this romantic nightmare taking place under the shadow of a looming black castle where the doctor and his creatures lived and worked.

Chick cried out with the terror of the hallucination, but his cries were no distraction for the crew of *The Touya,* half of whom had pinned the dwarf, Chick's Kitty, to a bulkhead, a chain wrapped around her neck like an iron snake.

Captain Gunter had only a tentative control over his men, mad as they were with lust and hate. And, of course, the Captain himself was fighting a siege of powerful and complex urges. Landau's attempted rape of the bi-genitaled creature revolted him, but the first mate's murder by the hermaphrodite enraged him. In the beginning, he had wanted nothing more than to frighten and humiliate the abominations and then be rid of them forever. But, as the Captain should have known from all his reading, such plans have a way of not only unraveling, but of coming back to ravage the planner.

Gunter had lost an efficient, if depraved, first officer. Now he wanted only to dispose of the last two monsters and get the ship to the Port of Chaldea. The men, however, had other ideas. And to oppose them, while they were in this agitated state, was to invite mutiny and, perhaps, even his own dispatch off the conveyance beam.

So he decided to allow one last ritual of exorcism, one final venting of the crew's fear and discomfort, before tossing the chicken boy and the dwarf into the blue. But when he came upon a sailor—Hoess Wirth, by name—standing over the chained dwarf with his pants around his ankles, he couldn't help but forbid the congress, saying, "Son, would you know an animal in this way?"

Possibly Wirth was ashamed of his answer because his johnson immediately went flaccid. Enraged by this, he looked at the Captain and said, "Anything wrong with *this*, sir?" and began to urinate upon the helpless Kitty.

The Captain allowed for the lesser of two evils, but when one of the crewmen who'd been waiting on the sidelines for his turn yelled, "I've got a better idea," Gunter was truly frightened.

The sailor ran to the hold, calling for his mates along the way. They disappeared for a time, made abundant noise down below, and reappeared, each carrying a full drum of the Bergauer fertilizer, which they at once began to open, prying off welded lids with fire axes and shovels, and dumping the excrement in a growing mountain all over the Captain's once-gleaming deck.

"The skipper says they're animals," said Wirth, the urinator, taking the late Landau's position as leader and spokesman. "And animals love to rout in their own shit."

Cheers went up and crewmen began to pull down the still-quaking Chick, while others hauled Kitty up off the bulkhead. They threw the freaks like sandbags into the mountain of feces and then began to cover the misshapen bodies with shovels full of night soil until there was no part of the deformities remaining to be seen.

Completely encased in the world's most costly dung, Kitty found it difficult to breathe. She tried to work her hands up to cover her face, forced herself to keep her breakfast down in her stomach where it belonged. But before she could stop herself, she found her brain rejecting any chance at hope and began thinking, *This is how it ends, smothered in a casket made of horseshit.*

And then she felt herself being lifted. Felt herself being moved roughly through the air. And then she was dropping, rapidly, that plunging sensation erupting in her stomach and her temples.

She hit the water hard and the outer layer of filth was instantly washed away. The falling feeling was replaced by a sense of drifting, an almost peaceful languidness. She began to dig with her hands, used them like claws, tearing away the pasty crap above her eyes, shaking her head to dislodge the turban of *scheisse*.

Her mouth and nose sealed, she floated downward for a while, though her sense of time had been obliterated by trauma. She came to a stop suddenly and lay a second before the panic ignited. And then she was flailing. Her body was writhing, twisting, shaking, her arms and legs trying to thrash and kick. She opened her eyes, could see almost nothing, a pale shaft of light corrupted by free-floating clods and particles swirling away from her frantic dance.

And then even the light was gone. And she felt herself grabbed anew, manhandled and lifted up again. Felt other hands, bigger hands, wiping at her head, her face. She turned and saw the strongman, cheeks puffed out with captive air. Bruno knocked away the last of the clinging dung from Kitty's face, pulled her into his arms and began to ascend.

They broke into the air, both of them gagging. Bruno seemed unsteady, his eyes overlarge and bulging a bit.

"Can you tread?" he asked and when Kitty nodded, he released her at once, took a huge breath and dove out of sight.

Kitty knew she was close to shock but she pedaled her feet and scrubbed at her face and neck with salt water and scratched with fingernails. From the deck of *The Touya*, crewmen threw shitballs, but managed only to pock the water around her. They yelled vengeful obscenities, but Kitty couldn't hear them anymore.

Bruno was gone for what seemed like hours, maybe days. Kitty was woozy. She had to remind herself to work her legs and feet. Her head lolled and bobbed and she thought she heard Ringmaster Bluett calling her to perform.

When Bruno finally popped up again, he was alone. He heaved several times, got hit in the back of the head with a ball of shit, and said, "I can't find him."

Kitty moved her arms, propelled herself into the strongman's chest, then, without a word, she put a hand on the top of Bruno's skull and used the last of her strength to press down on that massive, shit-stained cranium.

Bruno stared at her and after a moment, said, "Once more. That's all I can do."

Kitty just stared back as Bruno filled his lungs and pitched himself down once again.

This time, he seemed to be gone weeks, perhaps months. But this time, when he broke the surface, he had the chicken boy in his arms. Chick was unconscious but not quaking—the seizure had ended. His feathers, even wet, were black and tarry with horse manure.

Bruno didn't speak. He turned his back to Kitty, who took a moment to understand that she was to climb on and wrap her tiny arms around the strongman's neck. When she had positioned herself, Bruno shifted Chick to keep the boy's face in the air, then began swimming.

The last thing they heard from *The Touya* was a single curse—*Missgeburten*—in the horrible new voice of Captain Gunter.

IT WAS A LONG, painful trek into shore, and several times Bruno thought his absurd trio would go under. But the waves and the currents were with them, and when Bruno washed into Gehenna for the last time, the others were waiting. The clan was whole and again united.

Somehow, Aziz had managed to start a fire. Fatos was awake and lying next to the flames. Milena was still naked but the sarcasm had returned, fully intact.

"Smells," s/he said, "like we're home."

Durga took Kitty off of Bruno's back and proceeded at once to wash the dwarf in the surf. But it was Bruno himself, the new patriarch, who insisted on tending to Chick. Years later, the twins would say that this was the moment when the bond between the strongman and the chicken boy was first forged.

Bruno laid Chick on the beach, cradled Chick's head with his massive hands, put an ear to the boy's chest to confirm the heartbeat, and put mouth to beak to assist the struggling lungs. In seconds, the chicken boy heaved the last of the Limbo bile and a gallon of seawater into Bruno's lap. And then he awoke, looked up into Bruno's face, and said, "I knew you would save us."

Upon hearing Chick's voice, Kitty broke away from Durga and ran to her love. There were tears of both rage and joy then, from every eye in the troupe.

Sometime later, they all fell asleep and dreamed, restlessly, through the remainder of that day, huddled together near the warmth of the fire, like infant creatures in a cold and fearful new world.

6

Over the last year, Dr. Peck had become devoted to the sherry. It was a Manzanilla and had been shipped to the Clinic straight from Spain by Mr. Moore, the husband of the patient in 103. Peck had found it an odd choice for a Christmas gift and, upon sampling the first bottle, decided it was too pungent for his taste. He'd thought about giving the whole case to the housekeeper but Alice had discouraged him and, upon further consideration, Peck had come to agree with his daughter. Such a gesture would have been inappropriate. But in the end, after several more samplings, the doctor had grown accustomed to and, ultimately, quite fond of the wine.

Now he swirled it in his grandmother's antique *copita*, as he climbed up the brief curve of stairwell that led to the tiny cupola above his study. This was where he learned to appreciate the Manzanilla, sitting under the low, copper-domed roof after a night of reading. The little round room was sealed but fitted floor-to-ceiling with glass, like a lighthouse, and on full moon nights, Peck loved the way the rays lit up the amber tinge of his wine. The room appeared designed for children, two, perhaps three of them at most, and Peck had spent a large percentage of his childhood here. The space limitation always produced a calming effect on the doctor. He liked to lounge on the narrow window seat and look down over the grounds of the Clinic as if gazing out on a vast sea. On a windy night, the pines that spread out across his acreage rippled like a black ocean. And when he spent enough time staring at the patterns of the waves, he sometimes reached a state of higher thinking, that realm in which the breakthroughs could come.

Tonight, as he sipped and brooded, Dr. Peck was thinking about his newest patient, Daniel Sweeney. It looked like Ohio was right. Everything indicated that the boy would be a premier candidate for arousal. Aside from the immediate area of brain trauma, he was young and strong and healthy. And the father, the pharmacist, was the perfect profile — devoted and unstable, desperate and drowning in guilt. The man was pliable and would be easily convinced. The trick was always to give them more hope than information. If you overwhelmed the families with the realities of procedure, you only confused them. Confusion led, inexorably, into fear. And though fear, on occasion, could be used as a persuasive tool, the more frightened the loved ones, the harder they were to control.

Everything requires balance, as the universe chronically reminds. The doctor needs to sense when to be authoritarian and when to be sympathetic. When to offer possibility and when to pull it away. When to be available but silent, and when to be absent but hovering as an unseen presence in the wardroom. The ghost with the only solution. The redeemer with magic scalpel and syringe.

Family tradition and a lifetime of study had taught Dr. Peck that neurologists were the priests of modern consciousness. He regularly reminded his daughter of this truth and pointed out that, like a priest, one must tend his flock with a rigorousness that others might define as inhumane. It was an irony the doctor could appreciate only after his third glass of sherry.

We are mapping the location of the human mind, he would tell his daughter and his colleagues and his students at the medical school. *And our maps are not aligning with the received wisdom.*

As a groundbreaker in a field that operated on the slippery edge of both medical science and philosophy, Dr. Peck could make such statements without apology. At the age of twenty, Peck had removed the brain of a salamander, transferred the brain into the animal's tail fin, studied the creature for six weeks, then replanted the brain in the cranium and watched the salamander reassume all its normal functions, as if the operation had never taken place.

Peck first reported the results of his experiment to his father, who responded with a wry smile and the question, "Are you telling me that you plan to specialize in salamanders?"

Since the day that question was asked, Peck had cut out, divided, rotated, transposed, and shuffled thousands of brain parts of thousands of salamanders. Also of mice, rats, turtles, gerbils, chickens, cats, and rhesus monkeys. Between all of the cutting and rearranging, he had written some of the most radical and hotly debated papers in the young history of the neuro-transplantation field.

On nights like this one, safe in the cupola, brooding and sipping his sherry and looking out on the pattern of the wind, the doctor was beginning to realize that his life had been one long and steady journey. A pilgrimage to a place of certain, verifiable truth about the human mind. About what the mind is and where it can be found. About how, once stolen, the mind might be reclaimed.

Peck's father had been too much the Yankee to speak, at least publicly, of a belief in the idea of personal destiny. But while Peck had inherited his progenitor's brilliance — and then some, he knew — he had claimed none of the man's modesty. And that was a fine and lucky thing. Modesty had no place in the high drama of revolution.

Peck's wife, in the midst of one of the later binges that had made her stunningly crude, had called her husband a *dickless genius*. He seized on the term as a perverse badge of honor and never touched the woman again. That was the night he first slept in the cupola. His daughter had found him in the morning, curled up and shivering, dreaming of patterns and waves and the shuffled brains of salamanders.

Draining the last of the sherry, he heard movement below in his study, leaned his head over the stairwell, and called down, "Alice?"

She hesitated before answering.

"I was looking for a file," she said.

"The Sweeney boy?" he asked and already knowing her answer he added, "I've got it here. Come join me. And bring the bottle from my desk."

He listened closely, heard her approach the bend of stairs and begin to ascend. And then she was before him, looking like her mother before ruin, the moonlight making her face even softer, younger. She was still wearing her lab coat, but she'd let her hair down. Peck leaned back, held out his glass with one hand, and patted the files on the window seat next to him with the other.

Alice poured and said, "It's cold up here."

"You didn't bring a glass for yourself," Peck said. "It's all right. We can share."

Alice lifted the Sweeney file and sat down next to her father.

"Have you spoken to Lawton?" she asked.

Her father squinted.

"What for?"

"To touch base," Alice suggested. "Let him know they arrived safe and sound."

"I'm not a travel agent, Allie," Peck said and sipped. "And the boy is no longer under Dr. Lawton's care."

Alice looked at him, hoping for a smile. When one failed to materialize, she opened the file in her lap and turned to read its contents in the moonlight.

"Everything seems to check out," she said. "Precipitating incident was a fall that caused cerebral trauma. Buildup of blood on top of the brain caused compression of the brain surface. MRI revealed subdural hematoma."

"No retention of consciousness since the incident," her father said, taking over from memory. "No response to pain, temperature, or touch. No pupil reaction to light. CT scan reveals herniation of the right cerebral hemisphere across the midline and into the left cranium. But no apparent damage to the brain stem or spinal column."

Alice nodded as she turned pages and read. "Weaned off the respirator and transferred from the admitting hospital to St. Joseph's one week after the incident. The assessment team, under the direction of Dr. Lawton, found the patient totally unresponsive and requiring full nursing care, tube feeding, frequent turning, suctioning—"

Peck interrupted again. "They doused the boy with methylphenidate. Ten milligrams, twice a day, with no results. His GCS score has remained at four, unchanged for the last year."

He took a sip of sherry, licked his upper lip, and added, "Lawton went through the motions. As he tends to do."

"Well," said Alice, "he's ours now."

"Another exile," said Peck.

And his daughter responded, "Ten thousand strong and growing."

This was as close to a motto as the Doctors Peck had yet to find. It referred to the fact that at any given time, some ten thousand individuals across the country were being maintained in a condition of profound unconsciousness, in some degree of coma or vegetative state.

"If it's all right with you," Alice said, "I'd like to head up the assessment."

Peck put on a surprised look.

"I thought your plate was full," he said. "I was going to ask Tannenbaum."

"I'd rather handle it, if you don't mind. I already met the boy and the father."

Peck didn't say yes or no. He rubbed across one of his overgrown eyebrows with a free index finger and said, "What about the mother?"

Alice was taken aback for a second.

"As you know," she said, getting nervous and, so, too clinical, "the mother is deceased."

"Does it say in that file," asked her father, "the cause of death?"

"In the file?" she repeated and he didn't wait for her to go on.

"The mother killed herself," Peck said, "six months after the boy's incident. Lawton said she opened her wrists in the bathtub."

"Lawton?" Alice said. "I thought you hadn't talked to Lawton?"

"I didn't say that. I said that *I* hadn't called *him*."

She was beginning to feel claustrophobic in the tiny room, as if the copper dome above her head had been inching downward while she wasn't looking.

"Did Dr. Lawton say anything else," she asked, "that was pertinent?"

"He warned me to watch out for the father. That he's ready to explode."

"And we put him in charge of our drug room?"

"It was an appropriate incentive," Peck said.

Alice shook her head, suddenly finding it difficult to keep her thoughts ordered.

"The man has lost his wife and his son," she said. "He's suffering catastrophic stress. Do you really think Tannenbaum is the right person to steer him through the process?"

Peck put the sherry on the floor between his feet, unfinished. He straightened up and reached out to put his hand on the back of his daughter's neck.

"Allie," he said, "if you want to handle this case, you know it's yours."

"Thank you, Poppa," Alice said. "It's just that the boy, Danny . . . Have you taken a good look at him?"

Peck didn't say anything but he took his hand away.

"He looks," Alice said, "a lot like Alvin did at that age."

And the hand came back up and Peck slapped his daughter across the face.

The action was as controlled and neat as the voice that followed it.

"We don't mention that name," Peck said.

Alice kept herself from touching the cheek, she nodded and tried to breathe, but the claustrophobic feeling was flooding through her now.

"Enough shop talk," Peck said, putting both hands on his daughter's shoulders and positioning her away from him on the window seat, so that he could come up against her back and wrap his arms around her. He let his chin rest on her shoulder, brought his nose into her neck, and took in her scent.

"Look at how beautiful the woods are tonight," he said. "It's like we're the only people left in the world."

1

Sweeney hooked his feet under the bureau and did sit-ups. This was his preferred method for avoiding sleep. He had been getting by on three to four hours a night for months now. What sleep he did get was fitful and, because of the dreams, sometimes more debilitating than restorative. The therapist out in Shaker Heights had promised they'd stop eventually. So far, she was wrong.

The dreams didn't always center on Danny. Occasionally, they would feature people and places from Sweeney's childhood. Sometimes the setting was the pharmacy. Sometimes an enormous shopping mall or a hot and confining bus or a stretch of off-season beach. But in every dream, whatever the locale, he was searching for something he had lost — money, keys, jewelry he'd bought for Kerry, the deed to his father's house. In his dreams he had searched for his Honda, a beagle puppy, his college diploma, his driver's license, his uncle's toolbox, and an overdue library book titled *Roots of the French Revolution*. The therapist had suggested he keep a notebook by his bed and write the items down.

She had also suggested he attend the coma families support group that met once a month at the Holiday Inn on Royalton. His first meeting was also his last. He was horrified to find that members new to the group had not only to introduce themselves but to explain their loved one's condition and the coma's proximate cause. On impulse, he'd made up a story about a swimming pool accident. But when the group broke for coffee, a woman approached and called him on the lie. She had someone at the St. Joseph. She knew all about Danny, she said. Mrs. Heller had told her about Kerry and she knew "the whole truth."

He ran from the Holiday Inn and almost hit a taxi on his way out of the parking lot.

But one good thing had come from the meeting. He learned that the dreams weren't uncommon. The wife of a man who had been shot in the head told about a recurring nightmare in which she exited a car but closed its door on her raincoat. She ended up being dragged down the block as the car began to accelerate. At that, the woman next to Sweeney had leaned into him and whispered, "In mine, I'm at the zoo and all the animals are getting loose."

Now he avoided sleep as much as possible, drinking coffee all day, keeping the lights and the radio on whenever he was at home. He'd been tempted to try some chemical solution to the problem. To either dose himself with amphetamine or narcotize his brain into his own, controlled coma. But like most of his colleagues, he'd been conditioned at school against self-medicating.

What he did in lieu of sleep was exercise. He couldn't bear the sociability at the gym but he loved the old-fashioned regime of solitary calisthenics. In the privacy of his bedroom, by the glow of the muted TV, he jumped rope, pulled on a chin-up bar he'd mounted in the doorway, and ran through sequences of push-ups and sit-ups. As a result, he was college weight again and his arms and legs and abdomen had become toned and taut. And if his brain still, sometimes, screamed for sleep, he was learning to ignore its demands. What he found more difficult to ignore was the irony his new habits had produced. His muscles had grown hard as his son's had atrophied. And Danny had achieved perpetual sleep while his father had made himself into an insomniac.

He hit three hundred, unhooked his feet and lay down on his back. The ceiling was cracked and water-stained. His room sat directly below 103 and he tried to picture where, exactly, Danny's bed was located.

The admission and assessment team had spent two hours with the boy. Sweeney liked the idea that they were starting fresh instead of relying on the St. Joseph files. Alice — she insisted he call her by her first name — had explained that the doctors would meet in the afternoon, compare notes, and work up a prognosis and a schedule of therapies and medications. She told him that at the beginning they'd be reassessing almost constantly. Then she had dismissed the team and bought him dinner in the cafeteria.

The place was even seedier at night. They ate a runny stroganoff and

Jell-O and, as he knew she would, she asked about the circumstances of Danny's accident. He didn't want a replay of the morning's episode with Nora, so he said, "It's all in his records," and Alice didn't push for anything more.

He stripped off his trunks and his T-shirt, threw them in the sink, and stepped in the shower. The water was hot and the pressure was high. He sat down at the far end of the tub and let the spray blast his body.

Kerry and he had often showered and bathed together before Danny came along. She'd reach up to wash his hair and he'd run the soap over her belly and between her legs. Afterward, he liked drying her off, wrapping her in a towel, and pulling her backward into his arms.

Now he placed a hand on his cock, then just as quickly took it away. He thought he heard a phone ring, got up on his feet, and turned off the water. The bathroom was entirely fogged. He climbed out of the tub and ran, dripping, into the living room. An old black rotary phone sat on the floor next to the sofa, but it wasn't ringing. He squatted and picked up the receiver, put it to his ear, and heard nothing. Tomorrow he'd have to call from the pharmacy and have it turned on.

THE CLINIC PHARMACY was a cave. It was located in what had been a walk-in bank vault built, by the original Peck, in the recesses of the family manse.

Ernesto Luga, the second-shift pharmacist, asked more questions than he answered. He was leaving the Clinic in a week. He had scored an opening at the new Wonder Drug out at the new Wonder Drug Plaza in Flanders. According to Ernesto, he'd be making double his current salary by the end of his first year.

"An' you actually get to work with people," he said, "instead of, you know . . ." trailing off because he knew about Danny.

"What's his story, anyway?" Ernesto asked.

Sweeney was doing Ernesto's inventory. Ten minutes into his inaugural shift, Sweeney knew there was nothing he needed to learn.

"He's in a coma," Sweeney said and began to count the bags of saline again.

"Everybody in here's in a coma," Ernesto said. "I meant, you know, how'd it happen?"

Sweeney braced the clipboard and jotted numbers, then looked up. Ernesto was sitting on a countertop, eating a tuna sandwich.

"You really need to know?" Sweeney asked.

Ernesto chewed with his mouth open and nodded.

"We were at an Indians home game. They were playing the Tigers. We'd been given box seats by a drug company rep I know."

"What company?"

"What difference does it make?"

"Forget it," Ernesto said. "Go 'head."

"Bottom of the eighth. We're down by one. Sizemore hits a shot into the stands. And I didn't manage to stop it."

Ernesto stopped chewing and they stared at each other. Then he swallowed and said, "You mean it hit your kid?"

Sweeney continued to stare at him. "It was the first game I'd ever taken him to."

He started to turn back to the inventory and Ernesto said, "Bullshit."

It sounded more friendly than angry, and when Sweeney looked up, the pharmacist was grinning and had strands of tuna and mayonnaise on his chin.

"Excuse me?" Sweeney said.

"C'mon," Ernesto said. "That's bullshit, right?"

"Why would I lie about my son's coma?"

"Beats the shit out of me," Ernesto said. "But if that's what happened, you'da sued the shit out of the franchise and you wouldn't be living down in the basement."

Sweeney pointed at the chin with his pencil. "You got some tuna there," he said and Ernesto wiped it away with his hand.

"You're not gonna tell me what happened, are you?" Ernesto said.

Sweeney smiled and said, "What else do you do all night besides eat tuna sandwiches and flirt with the nurses?"

Ernesto slid his ass off the counter and tossed his brown bag and empty Coke can into the trash.

"These nurses?" he said and threw up a hand in disgust. "Don't even bother. None of them got a sense of humor. 'Cept the ones with that bitchy sense of humor. And you don't need that. This place is gonna drive you crazy, you know."

"Why's that?"

"Lots of reasons. You were running a big store back home, right? Lots of customer service, dealing with the people. You don't deal with no one here. Specially on third shift. I did eleven to seven my first six months, I almost went batshit. No kidding. You're filling the same meds, night after night. You got the skeleton crew, right? You dying for the janitor to come down, tell his same stupid jokes. Really, I don't mean to depress you or anything, but you made a bad move here."

"Thanks for the concern, Ernesto."

"Big turnover on the third shift. That's another reason I'm getting out. I earned my way to second shift and they keep scheduling me back to third every time we're short-staffed. Look at tonight. I'm supposed to be down La Concha — hey, you play dice?"

Sweeney shook his head and Ernesto went on.

"Here I am training you instead."

The notion of Ernesto training him struck Sweeney somewhere between sad and annoying, but he said, "Speaking of training, maybe you could run down the routine for me."

"Good idea. I told Nora I'd give you an hour and if you knew your shit I'd leave you alone."

The room was more drug closet than pharmacy. A claustrophobic wouldn't have lasted. There were no windows beyond a small pass-through rectangle cut into the wall where the nurses and the occasional doctor would pick up their orders.

"You won't see much of the doctors," Ernesto explained. "They keep one resident on at night. Right now it's Tannenbaum. You meet Tannenbaum yet?"

Sweeney shook his head and Ernesto went on.

"Unless there's a problem he just sleeps all night in the lounge. Anyway, you'll find all your med orders there in your in-box when you get here. Mostly it's the same old shit unless one of the patients develops an infection or something. Sometimes Dr. Peck, the lady, she'll mix things up on you. But basically, you'll just be filling your bags and syringes and putting them up on the tray. There are six night duty nurses, two to each floor."

"For fifty patients?"

"It's not exactly intensive care, you know? They do their rounds, check the monitors, hang their bags, maybe roll somebody or give a sponge bath or change a diaper. But mostly they're drinking coffee with Romeo and reading their romance novels."

"Back up a second," Sweeney said. "The nurses don't fill their own syringes?"

Ernesto shook his head.

"So there's nobody double-checking the meds?"

"It's all on you, bro," Ernesto said. "So you got to pay attention."

"That's unbelievable," Sweeney said.

Ernesto seemed amused. He checked his watch, clapped Sweeney on the back, and said, "I got to get running now. My boys are waiting for me. If you get hungry you can have the rest of my sandwich. It's in the fridge."

He moved to the door and said, "Anything I forget?"

"I don't think so," Sweeney said. "Thanks for staying late."

"*De nada,*" Ernesto said, slipping out of his smock and hooking it over his shoulder. "You'll get the hang of it real quick. And listen, if you start thinking you made a mistake, I can put a word in for you down at Wonder Drug."

"I appreciate that," Sweeney said.

And then Ernesto was gone and he was alone in the vault. He turned the radio on and fiddled with the tuner until he found a station playing Philly soul. That was one improvement over the chain stores. Most of them pumped in a loop of Muzak day and night. The same shit over and over.

He moved to the service window, stuck his head out, and looked down the corridor, then turned up the volume on the Stylistics doing "Stone in Love with You." Kerry had loved this stuff, called it "blue lightbulb" music, and would never tell him what that meant.

He took a small stack of med orders from the in-box and thumbed through them. Lots of requests for bags of Jevity, various antibiotics, insulin, blood thinners and diuretics, Verapamil. Light work and nothing out of the ordinary. He could fill everything in less than an hour even if he dawdled. If nothing new came in he'd be sitting on his ass until dawn.

Which, he knew from experience, was unacceptable. It was never a good idea to leave his mind unoccupied for too long. To be idle was to be in danger. Because in unoccupied moments, he would remember. Images would come. Sequences from the old life. One man at that group meeting had used the phrase *memory is the enemy* and Sweeney had seized on it.

He worked as slowly as he could, rechecking each script he filled, hoping that one of the nurses would visit and he could introduce himself, try to pull someone into a conversation. But by 1:30 all his work was done and his in-box was empty. No one had come by to meet the new guy.

For the next half hour he went through the room methodically, played cop, opened every drawer and cabinet. Then he played efficiency expert and rearranged everything he found. And then he put it all back the way he'd found it.

By 2:30 he decided to find the floor nurses and introduce himself. He pulled the steel shutter down over the order window and secured it, moved into the corridor, and locked the door. It was silent in the hall. He walked past a row of closed doors, trying and failing to keep his steps from echoing.

He came to the nurses' station and found it deserted. Ernesto had said there were two nurses assigned to each floor. It seemed unlikely that they'd all break for coffee at the same time. Then again, this wasn't an ordinary hospital and he had no idea what Clinic protocol entailed.

The station consisted of a tall, grand semicircular desk made of glossy wood and set in the center, but toward the rear of the first floor's enormous foyer. It was flanked by a chalkboard that had been mounted on the rear wall. The board had been gridded and patients' names were written in boxes down the left margin. Next to the names were written various notes — vitals, meds, therapies, schedules, and, Sweeney assumed, attending nurse. It was an intricate system of notation, using shorthand and different colored chalk.

He found his son's name, printed in yellow, and read across the grid. He could make out the meds, of course, and the latest BP, pulse, and temp, but there were several boxes that he couldn't decipher. The final box in Danny's row read "Rey." He decided to look in on room 103.

The door was partially closed. Rather than push it open, he squeezed inside. A woman in white was bent over Danny's head doing something to the boy's mouth. Sweeney didn't want to startle her but she seemed unaware of his presence. Finally, he cleared his throat.

She didn't respond. Didn't turn or flinch.

He said, "Excuse me?"

In a low voice, she said, "You must be the father."

"I'm sorry to bother you — " he began and she cut him off.

"You're not bothering me," she said. "I'll be with you in just a second."

He took it, for some reason, as a request to wait outside. He stepped back into the hall and then felt stupid when he heard her say, "Where'd you go?"

He stepped back inside. She was standing now, stroking Danny's forehead. And she was stunning. Tall and lean, she gave off an immediate impression of physical strength and, just beneath that, even in the archaic nurse's whites, a kind of dark carnality. Her hair was black and long, brushed back over her head, barely tamed and at odds, somehow, with the uniform. Her eyes were a brown or a blue that was so deep they appeared black. But it was her cheeks that dominated the face — high and protruding and just short of jeopardizing her beauty. Sweeney noticed she had what may have been the longest fingers he had ever seen, and they were holding what looked like a miniature bottle of catsup in her free hand. He gestured to the bottle and said, "What have you got there?"

She held the bottle out in the air. He stepped forward, grabbed it, looked at the label, and said, "What the hell is this?"

"Just what it says. Tabasco."

Sweeney looked up at her and waited for the explanation. There was a clipboard resting on Danny's stomach and the woman picked it up and hugged it.

"What were you doing with this?" Sweeney asked.

"I was swabbing a half teaspoon onto your son's tongue."

He felt anger coming on now and, right behind it, the fear that he'd lose control.

"And who told you to do this?"

"Your new best friend," she said.

He looked down at Danny and then back at the nurse.

"Alice," she said. "The amazing Dr. Peck."

He stood there trying simultaneously to process the words and calm himself.

He said, "Who the hell are you?"

She came to him and took the Tabasco from his hand. He surrendered it and she shifted the clipboard under one arm, took Sweeney by the elbow, and walked him into the hall. The light was better and he got his first close look at her.

"I'm Danny's nurse," she said, releasing his arm and extending her hand. "Nadia Rey."

He shook and forgot to introduce himself.

"Is this a standard thing? Putting Tabasco on a patient's tongue?"

She nodded. "In some cases."

He tried to think, tried to gauge how upset he should be.

"You don't think that's intrusive?"

Nurse Rey brought her own tongue out and wet her top lip before she said, "Does Danny like spicy foods?"

It caught him off guard, her referring to his son as if he existed in the waking world. Before he could reply, she said, "There's no wrong answer, Sweeney. If he did, then we're rousing a favorable memory. And if he didn't, then the possibility for response is even stronger."

She'd called him Sweeney. Not Mr. Sweeney. As if they'd already met.

He said, "And was there any response?"

"He just arrived here today," she said. "It's too early to start looking for signs."

"I'm aware of that," he said.

She looked down the corridor beyond him but she said, "Did you get lonely down in the vault?"

He followed her gaze but the hall was empty. He turned back to find she was staring at him. "It's a little slow," he said.

"There's really no need for a pharmacist," she said. "It's just a state requirement for licensing."

He wondered if he should take offense at the comment. But he was glad to have someone to talk to and he wanted to prolong the conversation.

He changed his voice and said, "So you met Danny?"

She smiled for the first time. "Danny and I are going to be good friends," she said and there was nothing patronizing or phony about it. He was about to ask her if he could buy her a coffee, but she looked at her watch and said, "Are you looking for the game? Did Ernesto fill you in?"

He didn't know what to say.

"Look," she said, "it's not like I approve. I'm down here doing my rounds."

He nodded and said, "I can see that. I'm not accusing you of anything."

"It doesn't make any difference to me," she said, "if you want to play or you want to talk to them about it. But whatever you do, if you want some advice, handle it yourself. You don't want to bring either Peck in on this. You just got your son settled in here."

"Who said anything about Peck?"

"They're up in 306," she said.

"Thanks," Sweeney said. "I'll go talk to them."

"Do whatever you want," she said. "I've got to get back to work." Then she turned and started toward another room and he heard her mutter to herself, "Fucking Ernesto."

8

In its day, Harmony Prosthetics had provided something resembling wholeness to generations of the maimed and the amputated around the globe. At one time, it was the second largest replacement limb, bone, socket, and eyeball manufacturer in the world, shipping "artificial anatomicals," as the catalogs called them, to every industrial sector on the planet. Founded by the Hanger family in the wake of the Civil War, the company prospered for a century, bingeing on government contracts with every martial conflict, and reinvesting in R & D during the periods of peace. But markets and technologies tend to change and those that can't adapt die ugly deaths. And in the end, so it was with Harmony, which had succumbed more than a decade earlier to a combination of blows from both its Asian rivals and the miracles of microsurgery.

All that was left of this proud enterprise was the factory on Grenada, in the heart of Bangkok Park, a classic red brick mill, six stories tall and a full block wide. It had once employed two shifts of three hundred men each, and its smokestacks loomed over all of Bangkok like crosses on the road to Rome, spewing the plumed black smudge of rubber and plastic by-product seven days each week. Since then, most of the smokestacks had half fallen, leaving battered towers crumbling lazily beneath Quinsigamond's toxic rains. And the mill beneath the stacks was a mausoleum of fiberglass hands and silicon palates, housing the typical urban scavengers — rats, pigeons, cockroaches, and, of late, a pack of nomadic bikers known as the Abominations.

Run by Buzz Cote, a burly veteran of the crank wars, the Abominations were classic renegades. Unaffiliated and proud of it, they swooped into towns like a plague, announcing their presence but never their agenda. Coming to Quinsigamond out of Phoenix, they found their way to the

Harmony as if it were the ancestral home. They installed themselves in
the mill and put their bikes on display in the gravel lot next door, as if
taunting the local gangs, daring an offensive.

It had been six months since Buzz and his creatures arrived but, so
far, no one had challenged them. Which was, to Buzz, a mixed blessing.
Tranquillity begat productivity, but it tended to make the boys edgy. And
being in one place for too long made them downright pissy. That's when
they started to fight amongst themselves. With any luck they'd be pulling
out of the city in another week or two but Buzz knew, from experience,
you don't rely on luck. So tonight, he was sending the boys out on a run,
to let them gorge on a little speed, maybe find a roadhouse where they
could kick some ass and steal some poon.

"Ladies," he said, as he walked inside the circle of revving hogs, clapping his boys on the back or the head, "do me proud, but come back in
one piece."

When he got to the end of the line, he laid a hand on the shoulder of
his second in command and leaned in to the Spider's ear.

"I need you to hang back with me," Buzz said.

Spider let up on the throttle but squinted at Buzz to show his confusion.
Buzz shook his head.

"Can't be helped," he said. "But I'll make it up to you, I swear." Then
he stepped back to the next in line, the Elephant, and yelled, "Spider's
hanging back with me. We got some business. You're in charge, Tubby.
Keep the family circle."

The Elephant nodded, both thrilled and frightened by the responsibility. Then he signaled with his pudgy hand and led the pack out of the lot
and out of the Park, headed for some restorative mayhem.

Spider waited until all the boys had departed and the roar of the hogs
was fading down Grenada. Then he leaned back in his mount and said,
"The fuck, Buzz?"

Buzz chucked his deputy under the chin and said, "What's the matter,
boy? You ain't getting enough?"

"I get all I need," Spider said, shutting down his bike and climbing off
to hover under Buzz's chin.

"Ain't that the truth," Buzz said, slinging an arm across Spider's neck to
walk him back into the factory. "You barely got enough left for our girl."

"I ain't heard her complain," Spider said.

"Well, now," Buzz said, "complaining ain't exactly Nadia's style. Is it?"

Spider started to laugh and said, "I guess it ain't." And then they were both laughing, punching and poking each other, just a couple of irrepressible rebels, like in the old days back in Oakland, when they'd first gotten together. Back when the family was new and everything seemed inevitable. They'd met at a swap out in the hills of Berkeley, a kind of underground flea market for bikers and dopers and anarchists. Spider was buying a unit of crank and Buzz was picking up a case of test tubes and they almost came to blows over who would get the same issue of a favorite comic book.

Until that day, Spider had been a committed loner. On his own since the age of ten, he'd imagined himself the last individual, and he'd valued independence over any other virtue he'd ever sampled. But here he was, three years in, an Abomination. Another motherless brother, as the song put it. The thing was, Buzz had offered what no one else could — a *shared* independence. A liberty so radical it could scorch all the old freedoms and deliver an emancipation too real to refuse.

Spider wasn't sure when he'd stopped believing Buzz Cote's bullshit. Maybe it was Cincinnati. Maybe Louisville. But wherever it had happened, it was, he knew, the first time he'd experienced genuine grief. In the wake of that grief came the decision to split off from the family and form his own crew. And now, whenever the thought of fucking over Buzz and the boys started to bother him, Spider just remembered the fact of his own disbelief and the anxiety melted away instantly.

"You really think it's a good idea, though," Spider said as they entered the mill, "lettin' the boys ride without me?"

"The boys'll be fine," Buzz said. "You got to have more faith."

"But what was so important, you needed me to hang back?"

"It's a bird problem," Buzz said, his face as serious as his tone.

"A bird problem," Spider said. "What the fuck's that mean?"

"I'll show you," said Buzz, and he led the way through the first floor toward the rear of the mill.

The factory was organized by product makes and models, with each floor given over to the many shapes and sizes of a particular replacement part. The layout followed the logic of the human body itself: feet and legs were manufactured on the first floor; testicles and hips on the second; hands, arms, elbows, and shoulders on the third; all manner of oral implements — from tongues to teeth to palates — on the fourth; and eyeballs and sockets, ears and noses on the fifth. Skull plates, administrative offices, and research and development shared the top floor.

Buzz had poked around a bit up on six, rooted through R & D prototypes that had been left behind. He didn't recognize everything he inspected, but some of the products left him with a queasy feeling that lasted several nights.

The work area of each floor was a plain of open space, made into intricate mazes by aisles of mammoth heavy machinery, all of it gunmetal gray or dull green. The floors were cold concrete, stained black by oil; the ceilings, a tangled canopy of wiring and piping. There were small, boxy windows fit into the brick here and there, but the glass was a heavy, opaque variety that let in little light. In addition, the windows were fitted, inside and out, with security grates, a black wire mesh, which gave a sense that the building could be converted from factory to penitentiary in a heartbeat.

The rear of the first floor was outfitted with a huge cafeteria. When the Abominations first colonized the Harmony, Buzz had the boys cart out all but the largest of the round, aluminum lunch tables and the bikers dropped their bedrolls and turned the room into a dormitory and clubhouse. They had running water and the Fluke had managed to jerry-rig some electricity to power the lights, stove, and refrigerator.

Beyond the cafeteria, at the very back of the mill, was a freight lift whose car remained locked up on the sixth floor no matter what the Ant tried. So, instead of elevator races for entertainment, the boys had begun climbing in the shaft, hauling themselves up and down like apes on the chains and wires that dangled into the blackness of the cellar.

As he moved through the central aisle between the gargantuan lathes, Buzz suddenly let out a war cry and started to sprint toward the shaft. Spider flinched but caught on fast and began to race after his leader. And when they reached the shaft, the two men flung themselves at the same time, catching different cables and lowering their bodies, hand over hand, into the bowels of the factory.

They emerged into the basement, a cavern of piping, storage, and furnaces that stunk of chemicals and sewage. Buzz pulled out a flashlight and clicked on a beam that revealed hundreds of drums of dyes and oils, countless barrels of paints and pigments. And though neither one of them said anything, they could both feel the rats breathing among the abandoned supplies.

In the center of the darkness sat a monster of an incinerator, a huge brick kiln, like a prison house for elves, with a cast-iron door on its face big enough for a man to climb through. The top of the oven fed into a steel funnel that tied to the factory's main stack, which rose up through all the floors and, finally, through the roof.

Buzz put down the flashlight and took hold of the gear wheel on the furnace door as if he wanted to pry it loose from the incinerator. He made a face as though furious and constipated, then he used all of his upper body strength to budge the wheel. It groaned through years of rust but it turned, slowly and with a terrible sound. And when it could turn no more, Buzz took a breath, stepped back, and pulled the door open.

Spider hunched to look inside. He stared for several seconds but could see nothing. Straightening up, he looked at Buzz and shrugged.

"I need you," Buzz said, "to climb in."

It was a moment before Spider could laugh and, when he did, Buzz joined in. But when the laughing faded, awkwardly, Buzz said, "In you go."

"The fuck you say?" Spider asked.

"Look," Buzz said, "I'd go myself, but I'm just too big."

Spider hunched again, tried to see inside the incinerator and came upright, just as confused.

"I'm not going in there," he said.

Buzz sighed.

"It's like this," he said. "Somehow, a bird got in there. Made a nest, you know. Up in the stack."

"A bird?" Spider said. "Who the fuck cares?"

"That's the thing," Buzz said, upbeat, as if his deputy were about to see the light. "It's Nadia. She says she can't sleep at night. The bird's making all these noises. Keeping her awake."

"I ain't heard no bird. What the fuck kind of bird is it?"

"How do I know what kind of bird it is? What difference does that make? Nadia wants it gone."

"I'm telling you," said Spider, "I ain't heard no bird."

"And I'm telling you," Buzz said, "Nadia says it's there. And she wants it gone."

"I'm a light sleeper," Spider said. "I'd have heard a bird."

Buzz waited a second, scratched his belly, drummed on his leg with the flashlight.

"You calling Nadia a liar?"

"'Course not," Spider snapped. "That's not what I'm saying at all." He tried to think and then said, "Maybe it's a bat. Maybe that's what she's hearing."

"She said bird."

"How'd a bird get in the stack?" Spider asked.

"How the hell you think?" Buzz said. "It came down from the top."

"So you're saying I have to go in there?"

"It's a piece of cake," Buzz said. "There's a ladder mounted on the inside of the stack — "

"You're shittin' me," Spider said. "A ladder?"

"A ladder," Buzz insisted. "For maintenance. You got to clean these out, you know. They're just like chimneys. Only worse. They get buildup."

"This is fuckin' nuts," Spider said. "Couldn't Nadia just sleep someplace else in the building?"

"You want to tell her to move?"

"I could get burnt up in there."

"This thing," Buzz said, kicking the incinerator, "hasn't fired in ten years. There's no power."

"So I go in?" said Spider.

Buzz nodded.

"And I find the ladder?"

Another nod.

"And I climb up till I find a bird's nest?"

"That's it," said Buzz. "It'll be up near the top."

"Up near the top? I can't fit up there."

"You'd be surprised," Buzz said. "There's more than enough room."

"And when I find the fuckin' nest? What do I do?"

"Well, if the bird's there, you kill it."

"Kill it?"

"Yeah, grab it and kill it. Just twist the neck."

"I never killed no bird."

"That," said Buzz, "I find hard to believe."

"What if it ain't there?" asked Spider.

"Just knock down the nest. It comes back, sees you been up in there, it'll fly off."

"This is fuckin' stupid."

"You're making a big deal out of nothing," Buzz said. "Five, ten minutes, we're done. Then we'll kick back, have a few drinks, and wait for Nadia. We show her the bird is dead, you know she'll be grateful."

"You're sayin' I missed a run with the boys for this?"

"You're my deputy, Spider," Buzz said. "It's not all privilege. There's some responsibilities, too. Now get the fuck in there."

The tone said that Buzz's patience was gone, so Spider pushed his head through the incinerator door, hesitated a second, then hauled the rest of his body inside. Buzz kneeled down outside and thrust his head and the hand that held the flashlight into the furnace.

"I'll be right here," he said to the Spider. "I'll light it up so you can see."

"Christ," said Spider, "I can barely breathe in here."

"Go up, kill the bird, and come down," said Buzz. "A moron could do this."

And with that comment, Spider began climbing up the walls of the stack. In seconds, he was covered in soot and ash. Each time he passed through a flue, the stack grew a little narrower and Spider muttered to himself. Down below, Buzz ignored the curses and tried to make light.

"Stop whining," he said. "You can have Nadia first."

The words echoed and crumbs of rusted iron rained down from the rungs beneath Spider's hands and feet and settled on Buzz's head and arm.

"For this," Spider yelled down, "I should get her first *and* second."

"Fine with me, son," Buzz said, "but I don't think you'd live to tell that story."

"Maybe," said Spider. "But I'd die a happy man."

He climbed more quickly, trying to think of Nadia and the night ahead. But the stack contracted dramatically now and the rungs of the ladder began to shrink.

Finally, Spider stopped his ascent and said, "There's something blocking the stack."

"Is it the nest?" Buzz asked.

"I dunno," Spider yelled and Buzz could hear the strain in his voice. "Whatever it is, I can't reach it. And I can't go up any higher. It's too tight."

"Take another step," Buzz said, pulling his trunk farther into the mouth of the furnace. "You can do it."

"I can't," Spider said. "It's too narrow."

"Christ," Buzz said, "you're almost there. Just stretch up and grab. You can do it."

"I'm stretching," said Spider, angry now. "I'm telling you, I can't reach it."

"All you have to do," said Buzz, "is knock it down."

Spider cursed and struggled. The bricks were rubbing against his shoulders and his lungs were starting to convulse on him.

"I gotta come down," he screamed in a voice too loud and high to plausibly deny panic.

Buzz stretched out his arm and shined his light up the cylinder. "You've almost got it. Just reach up. I know you can do this."

"This is bullshit, you son of a bitch," Spider yelled, enraged.

"Push yourself up," Buzz yelled, in the voice of the father, a sound so weighted with threat that he saved it for the rarest of emergencies. "Force yourself up there."

Spider gritted his teeth and jammed his body forward with everything he had. He felt the bricks squeezing in on his shoulders and his ass but he managed to raise his knee until his foot found the next rung and he hoisted himself that much farther. He was wrapped in brick now, corseted in mortar and creosote, but the nest was just above his head.

He stopped in place, took in some sooty air, got control, and said, "I get back down, Buzz, you and I are gonna have some words."

"Just get the fucking bird," Buzz said.

Slowly Spider found a way to inch his arm up over his head. He poked at the bottom of the nest and found it so dry and brittle that it began to break up with his touch. He fingered away at this dry bowl of twigs, leaves, wire, and plastic. And when he reached inside the bowl, he found no bird, only a fat wad of paper, which he grabbed and pulled down before his face.

"Did you get it?" Buzz asked from below, his voice now soft and emotionless.

Spider didn't answer. Between the beam of Buzz's light shooting up and the slice of moonlight that drifted down into the stack, he was able to see the object in his hands — a filthy envelope full of cash.

And just as Spider made out the logo of the Peck Clinic beneath a stain of ash, Buzz snapped off the flashlight.

Spider startled and dropped the envelope and money floated down over Buzz and into the belly of the furnace.

"What the fuck," Spider yelled. "Turn on the light, asshole."

He tried to take a step down to a lower rung only to find that the bricks refused to let go of his shoulders. The Spider screamed and tried to thrash his way free but his jerking and bucking made his situation only worse.

"You stupid bitch," Buzz yelled from the belly of the furnace, his tone just short of regretful. "You think Nadia doesn't know every goddamn thing that happens at that clinic?"

"Get me out of here," Spider hollered, enraged and terrified, his body futilely trying to convulse within its minute confines. Dirt and rust and soot and some twigs from the nest fell into his eyes.

"I bring you into Limbo," Buzz yelled, not caring if Spider could hear him over the screaming. "And this is how you repay me."

Spider tried to push himself off of the ladder, but nothing happened. Pieces of the nest fell into his mouth and he began to spit and choke.

"I bring you to meet the freaks," Buzz yelled, "and you do business with the enemy? You give that fucking doctor exactly what he needs. And then you hide the fucking money from *me*?"

At the height of his frenzy, Spider was granted the single moment of clarity in a life so twisted by violence and bad luck that it could culminate only in this kind of demise. He used the moment to make a request.

"Buzz," he yelled. "Don't do it this way. Help me come down and you can cut my throat."

Buzz stayed silent for a minute, letting the Spider think he was mulling the option. Then he laughed and yelled up the stack.

"Can't do it, Spider. I want you to think about what you've done while you're drying out up there. You know, I might've even understood if you'd thrown in with Nadia and the last clinic and that fucking madness. But to choose that asshole Peck. You're a real disappointment to me, Spider. And I want you to really understand what you've thrown away. Should take you three, four days to dehydrate —"

"The boys won't let you do this," Spider screamed.

"As far as the boys are concerned," Buzz said, "you're headed south to scout things out for us."

"But they'll hear me."

"The boys won't be back till sometime tomorrow," Buzz said. "By then, without any water and with all that soot and shit in your lungs and throat, you won't sound like much more than a bird that got stuck in the stack somewhere."

The words yanked Spider back into his panic and he began to holler again, something about Limbo being bullshit, and Buzz, a fool and a liar. And then the yelling degenerated into a kind of scatological prayer, made of equal parts terror and rage, and losing meaning as it progressed.

The big man pulled himself out of the furnace, stood, and pushed the door closed. He could still hear the screaming, but now it was muffled, the words indistinct. Taking hold of the gear wheel, he began to turn it like a skipper steering his ship through a chaotic sea. When he heard the furnace door lock, he left his hands on the wheel for a moment and let his body slump, suddenly exhausted. And he thought, once again, about the obligations of the patriarch.

9

Sweeney used the stairs rather than the elevator. He took them two at a time. It was a grand staircase that wrapped itself around the elevator's well, and he ran the last third of it. He had no idea why he was running. Not a clue why he was heading for the third floor, taking the stairs because he didn't want to announce his approach with elevator noise.

He found them in 306. Four nurses, Romeo the janitor, one of the EMTs who had carted Danny from the airport, and a young guy in green surgical scrubs and a John Deere cap. Each was seated on the end of a bed, back to the bed's occupant, leaning over a tray table that was covered with playing cards and money.

They all looked up as he stepped into the room but no one spoke until Romeo said, "You got to show fifty to sit in."

Sweeney stared at him. The vague island accent was gone and in its place was an overdone street drawl, something from an early '70s movie.

"Who's he?" the guy in the scrubs asked and one of the nurses said, "He's Ernesto's replacement."

The male nurse said, "His son's down on one."

Sweeney felt like they were watching him through a one-way mirror.

"Ernesto's such a little shithead," said a girl who looked too young to be up this late.

"Well c'mon in, for Christ sake," said Romeo, "now you're up here."

Sweeney stayed where he was.

He saw Romeo look at the guy in the scrubs. Then the EMT said, "You here to play?"

"What's the game?" Sweeney asked.

"There's only one game at the Clinic," said Romeo. "You know Limbo?"

Sweeney shook his head and everyone went quiet again until the guy in the scrubs crossed the room with his hand out.

"I'm Dr. Tannenbaum," he said. "This looks awful to you, I'm sure —"

"Man didn't say that," Romeo interrupted. "Did you, Sweeney?"

Tannenbaum went on. "It's really not as bad as it looks. Honestly, the game is in keeping with the mission of the Peck."

"Listen to this guy," said the EMT, mimicking. "Mission of the Peck."

Tannenbaum ignored him. "We play *for* the patients. When the game is on, really, we *become* the patient. It's an inclusive activity. We envision them wakeful." He gestured toward a bed behind him. "Until you walked in that door, I *was* Mrs. Oliphant."

Romeo had enough and said, "Yeah, and it's Mrs. Oliphant's turn to deal. So we got to know, did you come to play?"

There was no mistaking the question for anything but a threat.

"Not tonight," Sweeney said.

The young nurse let herself ask, "Are you going to tell Dr. Peck?"

Before Sweeney could answer, Romeo said, "Now that's just a stupid question, Debbie," the sass a little too theatrical. "'Course he's not gonna tell."

"Just don't bring the game to my son's room," Sweeney said and waited a beat before leaving the ward.

He took the elevator down to his apartment and grabbed *The Big Book of Logic Problems*. He carried the book back up to the drug vault and spent the rest of the night trying to work out the puzzle of the Chinese triplets.

SOMETIME BEFORE DAWN Sweeney put his head down on the counter and dozed off. He was woken just before seven by the first-shift druggist, a pale and lanky woman named Adele. They both made bad first impressions. He was asleep his first night on the job. And she struck him as yet another person who thrived on suppressing chronic anger. He decided not to linger in the vault. But before he could get out the door, she handed him an envelope from the in-box. It was sealed and his name was written across the front.

"Someone must have dropped it off," Adele said, "while you were napping."

He stuffed the envelope in his back pocket and left without a word.

He bought a pecan muffin and a coffee in the cafeteria, took them down to his room, and watched the morning news while he ate his breakfast. There was something comforting about listening to the catalog of the previous night's horrors on a black and white television.

When he'd finished the muffin, he got up and rummaged around the apartment until he found a pencil in a kitchen drawer. The only other things in the drawer were a ball of wrapping twine and a bottle opener. He moved back into the living room and rotated the TV channel. It was an odd sensation, tuning the set manually, finding only a handful of stations, and watching how the reception varied from one show to the next. When he came to *Limbo*, he sat back down on the couch and drained the last of his coffee.

He opened the book of logic problems and began to write a to-do list on the inside back cover. He needed to stock the apartment with some groceries, open a checking account at a local bank, buy some new sheets — his old ones were for a double bed. He needed to call Dr. Lawton and remind him to forward the rest of Danny's files. He wanted to get to the mall and pick up some new *Limbo* pajamas. And he had to have the phone turned on.

He closed the book and dropped it on the floor. He brought his legs up and stretched out on the couch and tried to watch Danny's favorite cartoon through a haze of snow. He'd been making an effort for the past six months to comprehend the program, but the number of characters and the complexity of their interweaving and always-changing relationships continued to elude him. The more confused he became, the harder he studied. And this morning, studying *Limbo* was all he wanted to do. He'd use the show to block the growing possibility that moving Danny and himself to Quinsigamond was the biggest mistake of his life. He'd use the epic cartoon to keep himself from thinking about the pervasive gloom of the Clinic. Or the nurse and her Tabasco bottle. Or the floating card games that the patients endured, unaware, every night.

Instead, he stared at the grotesque little figures on the TV screen and tried to remember all their names.

To Sweeney, everything about *Limbo* was complex and unsettling. The concept was created, written, and drawn by a mysterious recluse known only as Menlo. The artwork was antithetical to the classic American style of Disney or even Hanna-Barbera. And because of this, he felt that something was a little decadent about the very look of the show. It didn't help that the main characters were all freaks and outcasts. Classic circus numbers, disfigured and unwanted. The hermaphrodite. The fat lady. The skeleton. The Siamese twins. And the protagonist, Danny's favorite, the chicken boy.

Sweeney first became aware of *Limbo* on the day Danny came home from kindergarten with a chicken boy trading card in his lunch box.

"I got it from Timmy Roache," Danny said. "He had two of them."

And that night, instead of reading another page of *Mike Mulligan* before bed, Danny had asked that Sweeney read the back of the chicken boy card.

The obsession grew out of that single dog-eared bubblegum card. And in the year that followed, Sweeney had cursed Timmy Roache more than once. It became a kind of tagline around the house. Every time Danny discovered a new *Limbo* card deck or comic book or videotape or board game, Sweeney would say to Kerry, "Thank you, Timmy Roache," in a kind of mock-exasperated whisper.

In fact, he didn't mind his son's new enthusiasm. He saw it as a positive development. That was the line he preached to Kerry anyway. *At this age,* he'd tell her, *it's good to see that kind of focus and concentration. And he's picking up a lot of new words and concepts.*

Sweeney actually felt the cartoon had brought him closer to Danny. Up until the discovery of the chicken boy and his world, Kerry had been their son's favorite. But all of those Saturday mornings, driving to the comic book store for a pack of trading cards and, if it were the first Saturday of the month, the latest issue of the *Limbo* comic, had bonded father and son.

Before the accident, Sweeney had never made much effort to understand the dimensions of the *Limbo* story line. Danny's enjoyment of the show was all that mattered. But since the onset of his son's coma, Sweeney had begun trying to figure out who was who and what was what inside the world of the concept.

That this was not an easy task shocked him at first. It was a cartoon, for Christ sake. Designed for and marketed to little boys. And yet, the scope and complexity of the concept was daunting. Its evolution over time was ridiculously detailed. And the intricacy of the minutiae built into the story was overwhelming.

The marketing sages who disseminated *Limbo* into the kid culture appeared to work in tandem with Menlo — maybe even dictated to the creator — so that the overall myth expanded with each new *Limbo*-inspired product to hit the street. The backstory and the various side stories all grew richer and denser and more detailed with the release of the latest card game, cereal box, action figure booklet, or text message. How, Sweeney wondered, with each exposure to each permutation of *Limbo*, did a six-year-old master it? And with such ease and grace?

The stories of *Limbo* took place in a realm called Gehenna, which seemed to Sweeney a series of enormous and decaying and desperately crowded cities separated by massive tracts of desert and swamp and forest. There was a core group of characters, a traveling band of circus freaks. Sweeney thought of them as repertory players, who surged to the forefront or faded to the background, depending upon the needs of any given story.

The freaks were led by Bruno, the bald strongman with the walrus mustache and the tattoos, the unofficial patriarch. But the heart of the clan — and the point of view for most of the stories — was Chick, the boy with the grotesque mouth and the body covered by a coat of feathers.

They traveled from city to city, often pursued by a cabal of scientists and soldiers in the employ of the heroes' nemesis, the mad Dr. Fliess. They had, of course, all manner of adventure, traversed perils, found and lost allies, dispensed assistance and experienced betrayal. Whatever the medium — comic book, TV cartoon, or the touring ice show that had cost Sweeney a bundle — the freaks of Gehenna remained true to the integrity of their world. History mattered in this open-ended narrative. Past events had consequences and repercussions that played out in future episodes. The characters endured loss and change. The nature of the relationships within the group shifted and matured. Occasionally, someone would suffer and die.

The overall principle that gave a framework and a purpose to the freaks' ceaseless wanderings was the quest to reunite Chick with his long-lost father. The gimmick that steered their travels was the trance into which

Chick fell at unexpected and, usually, inopportune moments. This dream state was called "the Limbo" and, once in it, the chicken boy would experience visions and receive messages. These messages were delivered by a disembodied voice, which Chick believed to be that of his missing dad. The voice was erratically guiding Chick — and, so, the rest of the troupe — on a chaotic pursuit of sanctuary and, perhaps, healing. But unlike his compatriots, what Chick desired more than refuge or normalcy was simply to encounter and embrace the papa he had never known. It was a peril-ridden process and Chick had no control over any of it. And more than once, he'd endangered the whole troupe by trancing out at a crucial instant.

The whole trance shtick was the thing that confused Sweeney the most. Just when he'd begin to think he had a handle on the dimensions of the story, the chicken boy's eyes would roll back and Bruno would look to Kitty, Chick's love interest, and shake his head as if to say *not again*. Sweeney felt the same way. Because when Chick went into the Limbo, all the rules and logic of Gehenna were thrown out and replaced by a realm that was even more surreal and difficult to follow.

Danny had tried to explain it now and then, but grew frustrated with his father's inability to remember key facts, to grasp what, to Danny, was an instinctive language of self-evident truths.

Now Sweeney had an opportunity to pay attention. To listen and look, closely and carefully. But the story made little sense to Sweeney and he was glad when the knock on the door gave him an excuse to get up and shut off the TV.

It was a disheveled young woman who looked as tired as Sweeney felt. She was dressed in a short denim skirt and a leather jacket and her hair was pulled into a ponytail.

"Are you Mr. Sweeney?" she asked.

He nodded and said, "Can I help you?"

She reached into the pocket of the jacket, pulled out a car key on a rubber fob and held it out in the air.

"I've got your Honda."

"Oh," Sweeney said, "you're from the agency."

She nodded and he took the keys, then hesitated a second, unsure of the etiquette here, if he should invite her in.

"Have you been driving all night?"

He saw her look past him into the apartment and motioned with his thumb. "I'd offer you a coffee, but I just got into town myself. Haven't made it to the store yet."

She ignored the explanation and fished, first in one skirt pocket and then in the other, until she pulled free a crumpled receipt. "You're supposed to sign that," she said.

"Right," Sweeney said. "Of course."

He left her standing in the doorway and went back to the couch, retrieved his pencil from the puzzle book, returned to the door, smoothed the receipt against the jamb and wrote his name on the bottom line.

"You're supposed to keep the yellow copy," the girl said, and Sweeney tore the backing sheet free and handed over its mate.

"This is a little awkward," Sweeney said. "I'd like to give you something, you know."

"You don't have to do that," the girl said. "I left the car in the lot out in back of this place."

"Thanks," Sweeney said, "but really, I'd like to, you know, tip you. For all that driving you did. And you got here ahead of schedule and all. But I haven't gotten to a bank and I've only got large bills. What if you give me your address and I can mail something to you?"

She put a hand over her mouth and yawned, then said, "It's not necessary. You saved me bus fare."

Finally, he stepped back and asked, "Do you want to come in for a while? You really look bushed."

"My friend's waiting outside in her car," she said. "I've got to cruise. You could call the agency though. Tell them I did a good job."

"I'll do that," Sweeney said. "Are you staying in town long?"

"We'll see," she said, turned to leave and turned back to add, "Your Accord really burns a lot of oil. You should have it looked at."

"I'll do that, too," he said. "Thanks again."

By now she had moved across the storage area, thumbed the elevator, and was yawning again. She gave a halfhearted wave and Sweeney couldn't decide if he should stand watching her until the lift arrived.

But the girl looked back at him and said, "I'm all set," through a yawn and he closed the door. He started to put the receipt in his pocket and touched the envelope that Adele had given him up in the vault.

He pulled it free, tore it open, and removed a prescription sheet. Dr. Alice Peck's name was at the top of the sheet, but the note underneath read

> I'd like to talk to you about Danny.
> I'm working third shift again tonight,
> if you'd like to come by and visit.
>   Nadia Rey

He read it twice and reminded himself not to overreact. Back at the St. Joseph, every call, every note, every meeting had been a problem. Not once in the last year had a single request to talk resulted in good news.

He carried the note into the bedroom and dropped it on the bureau, then looked at himself in the mirror. No wonder the drive-away girl had refused to come into the apartment. He stripped off his clothes and took a cold shower. Then flopped back on the couch and tried, once again, to understand the world of the freaks.

LIMBO COMICS

FROM ISSUE # 6: "The Roving Jubilee"

... The purchase of the bus hadn't left much of a bankroll. And Bruno had to deplete it even further the next day by buying a route card at their first gas stop.

The next week was one long blur of driving through farmlands and pastures and skirting the bigger cities. The freaks were hot and dirty and regularly hungry. They ate two meals a day, cooked hobo style on the roadside. Gehenna became a different land with each day that passed, and the extent of the differences from day to day suggested an enormity that began to awe them.

They stopped twice for provisions—once at a roadside produce stand and once at a blighted general store. Bruno knew they would run out of money for gas and food before they reached the interior plains, but he chose not to share that fact.

Chick had a couple of low-grade seizures during the trip, which bore a couple of names that, as usual, didn't yet mean anything to anyone. But he did hear the Limbo voice, the father voice, mention a show title that was featured prominently on the route card. *The Bedlam Brothers Present the Roving Jubilee, a Pious Entertainment for the Righteous and the Reborn* sounded both impressive and a little frightening and there was some debate as to whether or not such a show would want a freak act on their bill. But the card said the Jubilee was playing a weeklong stand at the county seat, a village called Mach'pella, which, according to the map, was only a day or two away. So that was where the freaks were headed.

They almost made it, too.

The bus broke down just ten miles outside of town. When he felt the engine start its death rattle and the noxious, black smoke being spewed became too much to ignore, the strongman veered off the road and coasted to a stop in a field that stretched to the horizon, a field barren of anything but scrub weeds.

Bruno put his head down on the wheel and said, to himself, "I'll drive it and I'll sleep on it, but I'll be damned if I'll push it."

Then he climbed out of his seat, stood in the aisle to stretch, and said to the freaks, "Looks like we're walking to work this morning."

No one complained. Like good soldiers, they filed off the bus and lined up by its side. They had no possessions to collect, no clothes to gather and pack beyond what was on their backs.

"Okay," said Bruno, taking his place before them, "we're on the hoof and you all know what that means. We stay together and close. I'll walk lead. Chick's behind me. Fatos will bring up the rear. Nadja, you hold hands—" He stumbled over the word, regrouped and rephrased. "You hold Antoinette's hand. Durga, we'll try to keep the pace moderate. But it's all flat land, so you shouldn't have too much trouble. Holler when you need a break."

And with that, they began their march. It was blazing hot and, though the twins tried to sing as they moved, the day proved too buggy for even a short medley.

BY MIDAFTERNOON, the big tops became visible in the distance. The skeleton was the first to notice, though she was in the rear of the parade. Jeta had terrific eyes and when she spotted the flashes of painted banners and flags against the pale blue sky, she let out a shriek that brought the troupe to a standstill.

"That's it," said Bruno. "And, Jesus, it looks big."

"A fest that large," said Aziz, swinging on his hands in excitement, "they're bound to have some annex shows."

They started moving again now, their voices competing with the rush of their speculations. Did the Bedlam Brothers have their own freaks under contract? And if so, what was the makeup of that troupe? Would they be frauds or second-raters? And if not, would the Brothers hire the clan? And if they did, what would be the fee?

Bruno let them theorize. The adrenaline was nudging them forward faster than a whip could have. Even Durga's abused knees seemed suddenly oblivious to the pain of ambulating.

"I'm spending my first envelope on pie," the fat lady said. "That's all I've been able to think about since we left home."

The remark struck Chick as so wonderfully absurd that he found himself laughing. His beloved Kitty was so thrilled to see her paramour tickled that she, too, let loose with a burst of tittering. The chortling spread like a virus through the clan and soon everyone was venting their shared travails in a parade of unstoppable revelry.

But when they got close enough to read the bannerline on the main tent, Bruno began to shush them and asked them all to have a seat and settle in. The freaks fell into a natural circle on the ground.

Bruno stood behind Chick and said, "I don't know how long this will take. The route card said that they open for business tomorrow, so things should be plenty hectic on the fairgrounds right now. I'll search out the head canvasman first and see if they've got a sideshow annex. One way or another, I should be back before nigthfall."

He started to leave, turned back and said to Durga, "Maybe I'll bring back some pie."

IT TOOK BRUNO longer than he expected to make it to the fairground entrance. As he drew nearer to the run of canvas walls, he was able to read the bannerlines that advertised the show's various headliners. He saw intricately drawn and wildly colorful notices for aerialists and animal trainers, fortune-tellers and firewalkers. It seemed to Bruno a standard collection of acts and one geared to a rural, less sophisticated crowd. That opinion changed, however, when his eyes landed on the biggest banners of them all, the ones posted on either side of the main entrance flaps. The panels depicted a magician dressed in what seemed to be Joseph's own robe, a turban on the man's head bound together with a ruby of heavenly brilliance. The man's eyes had a definite satanic cast to them. On the left-hand canvas, the magician was depicted kneeling in an Edenic garden of greenery and rainbow flora. Around him circled an angry mob, its members outfitted with all manner of brutal weaponry, from crude cudgels and stones to gleaming axes and swords. On the right-hand panel, the magician was depicted in the same garden setting, but this time he was emerging from an open grave, caught in shafts of radiant light that gleamed down from above. The bannerline read

The Amazing Dr. Lazarus Cole,
The Resurrectionist
See him murdered by an angry mob
Watch as he is declared legally dead by a state-certified physician
Stand stunned as he is buried in a grave six feet beneath the earth
And be astounded as he rises from the dead on the last
day of the Jubilee.

Bruno stared at the banners, trying to decipher the trick. He had known packs of stage magicians, from the obvious to the baffling. And he had even assisted some of them in a pinch. But he had never seen anything like this. He dismissed the banner's claims as this country's love of hyperbole. But he could not walk away from the illustrations. There was something about the man's eyes.

"Show doesn't open till tomorrow."

The voice came from behind him and he pulled himself out of his reverie, turning to look at a skinny old man dressed in overalls and carrying a hammer in his left hand.

"Looks like a big one," Bruno said.

"You're not from around here," the old man said. "The Jubilee is the biggest show on the tour. They don't get bigger than the Jubilee."

Bruno nodded and gestured to the banners.

"You have an impressive lineup," he said.

"Top drawer talent," the man said. "Every one of them."

Bruno smiled, took a breath and made himself say it.

"You got any freaks?"

The old man didn't answer right away. He leaned his head from side to side like a deaf mongrel, sniffed and wiped at his nose.

"Not this time," he finally said. "We tried freaks before. It didn't work out. Maybe you heard about the problems, huh? Maybe that's why you're asking?"

Bruno began shaking his head vigorously.

"I'm show folk," he said. "I'm looking for work."

The codger's shoulders slouched a little and he shook his head. Then he looked Bruno in the eye and said, "Well why the hell didn't you say so at the start?"

The old man was named Forrest DeWitt and he said he was the best canvasman west of the Desirea Range. He took Bruno to the mess top and bought him a cup of coffee and a tin of slop. He waited until the strongman had finished his meal before he asked, "So what's with you and the freaks?"

Bruno made the decision to level with DeWitt.

"The truth is," he said, "I've got a troupe of them on my hands."

"You?" said DeWitt. "I must be losing the knack. I would've pegged you for a musclehead."

Bruno followed his meaning and nodded.

"I am," he said. "Back home they called me the Behemoth."

"And where," asked DeWitt, "might home be?"

Honesty was a fine policy as long as it didn't endanger you. Bruno said, "I've drifted so long, I'm not sure anymore."

DeWitt loved the answer.

"I know that song by heart, son. Place I was born? It's not even there no more."

"So," Bruno said, "just between two old road dogs like us, can you tell me where the Bedlam Brothers come down on the freak question?"

"Thing is," DeWitt said, seeming to get a little squeamish, "this is a big stop for us. We play Mach'pella every year this time and we always leave with piles of loot. Not much in the way of entertainment in these parts and the folks are a little, you might say, repressed."

"Repressed?"

"Little bit restrained, you might say. And more'n would do a person any good, if you follow. They're a religious people out here on the plains. You have to understand that. We brought in a sideshow of freaks, what, three, four seasons back. It didn't sit too well."

"Not much draw?" asked Bruno, disappointed.

"Worse than that," DeWitt said. "The crowd got, let's say, uncomfortable, in their presence. Things were thrown, you see. Bottles. Rocks. It got a little bit ugly. The crowd drove those freaks right out of town. We never seen them again. And the kicker was, most of them weren't real freaks at all. The bearded lady pasted on her beard. The monkey man was just a pygmy in a fur suit. And the rest of it was all pickled punks and shrunken heads."

"Well, maybe *that's* what got the crowd so riled," Bruno said.

Forrest DeWitt simultaneously shrugged his shoulders and shook his head.

"Hard to say anything for sure when it comes to the marks," he said. "You know that."

"Well, where does that leave us?" Bruno asked. "You think there's any chance of us hiring on?"

DeWitt laughed.

"This is a goddamn carnival, son. There's a chance of anything happening, isn't there? I'll tell you what. You go fetch your performers and bring them back to the fairgrounds. We'll look them over and see what we see. How's that sound?"

"That sounds," said Bruno, standing up, "like the fairest words I've heard since I came to this country."

He shook hands with the canvasman and left the mess top. And on his way off the fairground he thought for sure he smelled pie.

SOME OF THE FREAKS were still seated in a circle when he returned. Chick and Kitty were huddled together not far away and Durga was holding a sleeping Antoinette in her arms. All eyes were upon the strongman as he approached the clan. He didn't want to make them overly optimistic. But at the same time, he didn't want to kill the hopefulness that had been building since Jeta first glimpsed the tents.

Milena, of course, was the first to speak.

"So what's the story?" s/he asked. "Are they hiring?"

"They might be," said Bruno and all of the freaks looked at one another.

"What kind of an answer is that?" Aziz wanted to know.

Bruno shrugged.

"I think there's a good chance we can sell ourselves," he said. "The canvasman said this wasn't historically a sideshow kind of crowd. But the owners might give us a tumble if we got the goods."

"Then what are we waiting for?" said Nadja, getting to her feet and slapping her claws together.

They began the march to the Jubilee, Bruno in the rear this time and lost in thought. He didn't notice that Chick had stepped beside him until he heard the boy's voice whisper, "So, did you meet the Resurrectionist yet?"

Before the strongman could respond, Chick moved up to the front of the parade and stepped into the lead position.

THE LEGEND WAS that the Bedlam Brothers had started out as ordinary gazonies, signing on with a lower tier show when it passed through their hometown of Mt. Seir one summer's day. And as far as anyone can tell, the legend is mostly true. Suffice it to say that the brothers worked their way up in the outdoors entertainment business. They approached the game like a problem to be solved, mastering each area of carny expertise and moving on to the next. In this way, they had done it all, been barkers and candy butchers, ticket hawkers and twenty-four-hour men. They had labored as concessionaires and cleaned up the most gruesome donnikers in the land. One brother was said to have served some time as a musclehead on the rural Athletics Show circuit. The other was known to have mastered an imposing array of skills in the magical arts. But through all these years of training and traveling, the brothers' true genius lay in that most misunderstood of all arts: showmanship.

Gladys Bedlam's boys were both masters of, and innovators within, the mystical art of the ballyhoo. They knew more about the techniques of hype and fanfare than entire generations of showfolk combined. This was their secret and their golden goose and it paid off in spades. The boys bought their first circus before they were out of their teens, a ragtag company long past its prime, staffed by reprobates and perverts and mangy, disease-ridden animals. But by the end of their first season, the boys had somehow transformed the cavalcade into a must-see event and word of its thrills passed from village and parish to town and county. Every night saw a straw house crowd and the brothers reinvested the bulk of the profits, adding more acts, upgrading the talent, and sprucing up the sets and the costumes.

Now they were the preeminent circus owners in Gehenna and, with nothing left to accomplish, they had managed to turn their legend into myth. No one saw the brothers anymore. They still traveled with the Jubilee, but in a massive rig that was their home and office, a sanctuary declared off-limits to everyone. They continued to supervise every element of their extravaganza, but they did so through their puppet, an operatic ringmaster named Renaldo St. Clare.

It was to St. Clare that the freaks were presented by Forrest DeWitt. The ringmaster walked the parade line, which was set up along the hippodrome, inspecting each member of the clan silently but carefully, scrutinizing the extent of their anomalies and hunting for signs of fraudulence. St. Clare plucked a feather from Chick's arm and held it up to the sunlight. He knocked on Antoinette's skull, had her kneel so he could check for seams. He poked at the web of flesh that bound the twins together, put his fingers between Jeta's ribs and even tried to pull off one of Nadja's claws. But when he began to lift the hem of Milena's makeshift dress, the hermaphrodite pinched the ringmaster's cheek and said, "I'll show you what you want to see. But if you try to touch anything, I'll knock your teeth down your throat."

Bruno thought that display of cheekiness would kill any chance of employment. But when the ringmaster approached him, St. Clare was in good humor. When Bruno expressed surprise, Renaldo explained, "Every real he/she I've ever known was a ball-breaker. Your crew gets my vote. Now I just have to convince the brothers."

And he disappeared into the massive black trailer that was parked at the end of the midway.

Twenty minutes later he was back, carrying Jubilee badges for the entire clan.

"Congratulations," he said to the freaks, passing out the pins that would grant them admittance to the mess top and the bathhouse. Bruno got the key to the double-wide that they would all have to share until other accommodations could be arranged.

That night, the freaks slept like full-bellied lambs and used all of the next day to familiarize themselves with the Jubilee and get ready for opening night. By and large, the carnies treated them warmly. The clan had its run of the wardrobe trunks and was given a tour of the sideshow annex where they would be on display. They were pleasantly surprised to find that the facilities rivaled those of the Goldfaden. The stages were clean and ample and the lighting was first-rate.

Ringmaster St. Clare gave them a quick breakdown of the Jubilee method of sideshow performance.

"What you make, of course, will depend on your ability to fill the top," St. Clare said, turning to Bruno and Milena, neither of whom could hide their shock. "And your ability to fill the top will depend on your talker. I've always been of the opinion that a freak is only as good as his bally. No matter how strange and terrible your performers, if you can't get the marks into the annex, you can't show them your wonders."

He clapped Bruno on the arm and said, "But you look like a seasoned barker, my friend. I'm sure you'll have no problem seducing the citizens of Mach'pella."

"Barker?" Bruno said, suddenly confused. "I'm not a barker. I'm a behemoth."

St. Clare looked at the strongman and then at the freaks.

"I'm sorry," he said. "You're not their barker? I thought you told my canvasman that they were your act."

"Well, they are," stammered Bruno. "I mean, that is, I'm traveling with them. We're traveling together. We used to perform together. In the same circus. That is . . ." and he looked to Chick for help.

"Mr. Seboldt," explained Chick, "was the strongest man in our homeland. He can pull a locomotive for over five hundred meters."

St. Clare said nothing for a few seconds. He stood smiling and nodding, as if thinking of something else. Finally, he said, "That's very impressive, young man. Quite a feat, I'm sure. But we don't have any locomotives here."

"What I'm trying to say," Chick said, "is that Bruno is a strongman, not a barker. He's never worked the bally."

It came out sounding like an accusation.

Ringmaster St. Clare nodded his understanding.

"The trouble is," he said, "we already have a strongman. And, with all due respect to our friend Bruno here, and meaning no insults at all, I assure you, we think our strongman is a fine one. He's been with us for many seasons now. Micmac Shawnee. You've heard of him, perhaps? We call him the Chief. An authentic savage, strong as a dozen bulls and meaner than a cornered snake."

St. Clare took a breath and shook his head.

"Now, what we didn't have, until yesterday, was a genuine, state-of-the-art freak troupe or a barker that could sell them."

Everyone stood looking at the ground and one another as if trying to solve a math problem that had been carved in the earth.

Finally, Bruno clapped his hands together and said, "Mr. St. Clare, you've been very generous with us and I want you to know how much we all appreciate that. If you say we need a barker, then we need a barker. And though I may not have any experience, I've been on the circuit most of my life and I'm a fast learner. And the truth is, I'd be proud to bally for my friends here."

Renaldo St. Clare looked like he'd just dodged a hail of bullets.

"Excellent, Mr. Seboldt," he said. "I look forward to working with you and your entire troupe. The show kicks off at sundown tonight with the opening ceremonies. You won't want to miss that, I promise you. We'll open the sideshow annex at seven. Should you have any questions or concerns between now and then, you can find me on the midway. Good luck to all of you."

And he gave a little bow before exiting the annex.

"You?" Milena said immediately. "A barker?"

"I didn't have much choice," Bruno said. "He was getting ready to give us the heave."

"But can you do it, Bruno?" Durga asked. "Can you run the patter?"

"I guess we'll find out," Bruno said, "come sundown."

THE INAUGURATION OF this season's Mach'pella stand seemed to the freaks no different from the kick-off performance of dozens of other circuses they'd witnessed over the years. Professionals, they stood and sat away from the crowds who had flocked in full capacity to turn the midway into a straw house, standing room only, not a remaining ticket to be had. It seemed every man, woman, and babe in the county had come to the opening of the show, their hearts swollen with the promise of premier entertainment and who-knew-what thrills and surprises.

The ceremonies began with a meeting, under the big top and in the center ring, between Renaldo St. Clare, in full spangled costume, and the mayor of Mach'pella, who read a proclamation that officially declared this "Jubilee Week" in the town. The ringmaster enthusiastically thanked the crowd and then began a run of adjective-laden puffery that even Milena had to admit was impressive. Then the band began playing a rousing chorus of the Jubilee theme, written, St. Clare reminded all, by the Bedlam Brothers themselves—*those mysterious ministers of modern magic and miracles, who just might be sitting next to you at this very minute!*

And as the audience began to look right and left in the hope of spotting one the brothers, the opening processional began, led by a dozen Indian pachyderms, each one bearing a member of the Romero family, fearless trainers who could make any beast do their bidding. The costumes were splendid, trimmed with colored lights and bells, and the family's boots gleamed with countless layers of French cream.

The acrobats and aerialists came next. Family units from around the globe, and all of them born with a magnificent talent for equilibrium and self-control. They marched with grace and vitality, ran up each other's back and leaped off shoulders, flying ridiculous distances and landing like statues carved of the coolest marble.

Next followed an amalgam of contortionists, bird trainers, fire-eaters, sword swallowers, hand walkers, stilt walkers, glass walkers, a trick pony, and an abundance of jugglers who made airborne everything from pitchforks and babies to fireballs and wagon wheels. The clowns took their turns, causing a very efficient mayhem at the tail end of the parade, driving tiny cars in circles, throwing buckets of water or confetti, honking horns and blowing balloons and running madly from mechanical mice. They proved a sharp contrast to the penultimate parader, the Jubilee's lone strongman, Chief Micmac Shawnee, billed as "The Brawniest Brave on the Ballyhoo," according to his bannerline.

"He doesn't look so tough to me," said Durga.

"Looks," reminded Bruno, "can be deceiving."

The Chief marched defiantly, decked out in tight buckskin pants, barefoot and bare chested, a crow's feather lodged behind one ear and his bulging chest decorated with war paint tattoos. No one said it aloud, but he reminded all the freaks of the Goldfaden knife thrower, except for the fact that the Chief's head was shaved clean to the skull. Shawnee glared at the crowd and a few brave souls let fly some good-natured booing. To which the Chief responded by plucking a hatchet from his pants and waving it in the air menacingly. That this brought a round of laughter and cheers did nothing, it seemed, to lighten Micmac's mood.

"Does anyone find it odd," asked Milena, getting bored with the pre-show festivities, "that we weren't asked to march in the parade?"

"I told you," said Bruno, "they had a bad experience with some bogus freaks a few seasons back. Besides, if they see you all in the parade, why would they pay money to see you again in the annex?"

This satisfied everyone but Chick, who decided to keep his unease to himself.

The parade seemed about to conclude when the ringmaster stepped back into a sudden hail of spotlights and the band abruptly played out the last of the Bedlam Brothers' anthem, "Pandemonium (We Will Astound You)."

"And now," bellowed St. Clare, projecting out past the farthest seats in the house, "to officially kick off the twenty-seventh visit of the Bedlam Brothers Roving Jubilee to our special friends in Mach'pella, the man you've all been waiting to see, a legend of colossal proportions, known and marveled at from the palaces of the Far East to the local grange halls, the wizard who has rewritten all the science books and put the undertaker on the dole, here he is, ladies and gentlemen, please welcome back to your town and your hearts, the one and only Dr. Lazarus Cole," and here he screamed out the last two words, "The Resurrectionist!"

An explosion sounded at the entrance to the midway and a cloud of purple smoke mushroomed. The band's drummer erupted with tympani and the percussion goosed every heart under the big top and focused all eyes onto the gust of vapor, out of which now emerged what seemed to be two creamy, brawny unicorns, pulling an open golden carriage festooned with luminous jewels of every hue. The man within the carriage held the reins with one hand. The other was pointed defiantly up into the air.

He drove the unicorns to the big ring and brought them to a stop. He stared up at the crowd for a long moment, a bemused look on his face, as if he had sized them up and found them all wanting. Then he roused himself, stepped out of the carriage and down onto the midway. He was tall and gaunt, dressed in formal attire, a black tuxedo with long tails, crimson shirt and cummerbund and a narrow black tie. He wore French cuffs and elaborate gold cufflinks and, on his head, an enormous white turban bound by a ruby.

He threw his head back and, into the silence of the crowd, he shouted, "I am Dr. Lazarus Cole," paused and added, "the Resurrectionist."

And then he bowed elaborately, one leg propped behind the other, knees bent slightly and the turban tipping close to the ground.

The crowd went berserk. The cheers and screams, the overflow of uncontrolled emotion, was unlike anything that Bruno and his freaks had seen through the course of their travels. The ovation went on for so long that Antoinette became agitated and Milena had to wonder, aloud, what kind of act could warrant such acclaim.

It didn't take long to find out. And, at least in its early stages, it wasn't what the hermaphrodite—or any of the others—had expected.

Aziz had pegged the guy as some kind of faith healer, who'd whip the hicks into a frenzy of righteous and woozy belief and then slay a few spirits by laying on those big, milky hands. He couldn't have been more wrong. Because when the applause finally faded, what the Resurrectionist launched into was a kind of comedy act from hell.

First, he prowled the midway, giving a general introduction—*great to be back in your wonderful town, we've got a great show for you tonight*—taking the audience's mean temperature, getting a read on the marks, singling out a few probable rubes. But then he went up into the bleachers themselves, like some common clown, and it didn't take long for things to get ugly after that.

Chick saw that Lazarus Cole *was* possessed of a first-rate talent, but that it was vicious in nature. A natural insult comic, he raised the

tease and the rib to torturous levels, a cruelty inherent in his barbs
that the chicken boy had never before witnessed in his short life. It
became apparent, quickly, that the Resurrectionist was a miner of outrage. He had a magician's skill for sizing up the stooges but rather than
focusing on the good-natured or the serene, the gullible or the naive,
he seemed to be targeting the most aggressive, the most perturbed,
and the most choleric individuals in the sizable crowd. And then, once
he'd identified these human time bombs, he went to work on them
with a daring and an expertise that would have made an abusive parent envious.

Cole baited the crankiest of the cranks. He found twelve marks, dys-
peptic malcontents in this sea of happy revelers. And he goaded those
twelve, poked at them, taunted them. He degraded and humiliated
them. He seemed to have the ability to find their weakest spot, their
particular hot button. And then he drilled into it.

And it was nothing short of agonizing and fascinating. A staged
train wreck of human emotions. The freaks found it impossible to
look away. In bursts of brilliant and, apparently, dead-on-target vi-
tuperative, invective and accusation, Cole abused his marks to levels
of rage that were poisonous to behold. He stripped bare the dynamics
of their damaged psyches and went to work on them with a verbal
jackhammer, boring into their deepest fears with a diamond bit. The
collective mood under the big top went from joyous and celebratory to
furious and hateful. This was abuse comedy transformed into obscene
sadism.

Five minutes into the routine, Kitty whispered into Chick's ear,
"What have we gotten ourselves into?" Five minutes later, Durga had
to escort both Antoinette and Jeta back to the trailer. Milena, however,
was more entranced than repulsed. And even the chicken boy felt the
need to see where it was all headed.

When the twelve rubes were on their feet, red faced, adrenaline
surging, larynxes close to rupture with the ferocity of their screams,
their hands balled into fists of ire, Dr. Lazarus Cole folded his arms
across his chest as if ennobled by their fury and asked, "Wouldn't you
love to kill me?"

And then, reaching into the interior breast pocket of his tuxedo, he produced a glass bottle, a classic seltzer dispenser. He held it up in the air for a second so that the crowd and the twelve rubes could inspect it. Then he took aim, depressed the dispenser's handle, and began shooting streams of carbonated water into the faces of his victims.

It was like pulling the pins on a dozen live grenades. There was a moment of stunned silence when space and time appeared to freeze. And then the rubes screamed en masse and broke out of their seats, charging after the evil Doctor Cole, their tormentor. They snatched wildly at the air as the Resurrectionist led them through a wild chase up and down the bleacher aisles, through the bloodlusting crowd.

While the chase was transpiring, Chick looked away, feeling light-headed, as if a seizure were on its way. In fact, he was reacting to the effects of the display he'd just witnessed. But by turning his head, he happened to notice the small gang of gazonies who had taken to the midway and began collecting from the circus rings a series of canvas tarps that he had not previously noticed. Beneath the tarps lay piles of rocks, bricks, lead pipes, and crockery. And all at once, Chick understood, too well, the intended purpose of these items and the intended outcome of this act.

He looked back to the bleachers just in time to see that Cole had run his gauntlet in such a way that his pursuers had been united, swept up into a single small mob. And with this accomplished, the doctor sprinted down from the stands and into the midway, where he was picked up by every spotlight in the house.

Now he dashed into the center ring, twirling and feinting until he manipulated his enemies into a circle around him. At which point, he held up his hands and came to a sudden stop. For a moment, the enraged dozen, and the audience, were unsure of what to do. It seemed the doctor might be about to give up and apologize, beg forgiveness for his abuse.

Instead, he put his hands on his hips, looked each man in the face, and said, "My God, you're all too revolting to live."

You could hear a single gasp somewhere out in the crowd. It sounded like a match being struck. And then the dozen rushed him at once, knocking Lazarus Cole to the ground, kicking him, punching him, stomping him. When a single gazonie ran from the sidelines into the ring, it seemed for a moment as if someone were attempting to rescue Dr. Cole. But the young man was only calling attention to the piles of pummeling material lying at hand, waiting to be used.

The attackers did not disappoint. They seized stone, block, tube, and plate and had at the prone doctor with the release of a dozen infuriated lifetimes. The crowd cheered the massacre. Kitty looked away, hiding her eyes in the feathers of her beloved. Bruno stared in disbelief. The other freaks muttered to themselves as if lost in a childhood nightmare they'd thought long past.

The batterers exhausted themselves before they exhausted their weaponry. In the end, as the cheering began to fade, one by one they lifted themselves from their work and staggered, blood drenched, out of the center ring, escorted by showgirls who would bring them to the bathhouse.

The body of Dr. Lazarus Cole lay in a messy heap, now illuminated by a single white-blue spot, a hot light that revealed a hideously disfigured corpse, something no longer identifiably human and surely, certainly, definitively dead.

The cardinal rule of all show business, and especially of the circus trade, is: keep things moving at all times. The fact that Ringmaster St. Clare broke this rule at such a terrifying moment only shows how deeply ran the confidence of the Bedlam Brothers.

Nothing happened under the big top for an uncomfortably long time. There was no music. There was no change in the lighting. Chick could feel the crowd squirm in unison. There was nothing to look at besides the amazing Lazarus Cole's mutilated, mangled body, its flesh torn open and exposed to the world, its blood run into pools, flooding into puddles around the lifeless remains. The scene was appalling, ghastly, traumatizing. Now, at last, as the shock transformed itself into the apprehension of truth, came the sounds of children wailing. And as if on cue, Fatos, the mule, fainted dead away. Nadja knelt to tend to him but her claws were shaking.

Finally, Renaldo St. Clare returned to his ring and stepped into the spotlight. He looked down on the body of Dr. Cole, looked up at his audience, looked back down at the body, removed his top hat and held it against his chest, over his heart. The ringmaster closed his eyes and lowered his head. The crowd did the same. With his eyes shut tight, the ringmaster cleared his throat and in a trembling voice, so low that the crowd leaned forward in unison, he said, "Might there be a doctor in the house?"

Heads turned from right to left as all eyes swept the bleachers. In the very last row, a man stood and began to make his way, slowly, deliberately, down the steep aisle toward the performance ring. He was small and wide, with a large dome of bare, sweat-drenched skull and a crown of longish white hair, and he wore a long and ill-fitting white coat.

The doctor approached St. Clare, shook his hand silently, then got down on one knee and put two fingers on the throat of Lazarus Cole. After a moment, the doctor leaned his trunk down and placed an ear against Cole's chest. Then he struggled to his feet with the help of the ringmaster, and addressed the crowd directly.

"I am Vernon Taber," he said, "assistant medical examiner, Hazor County. And I officially certify that this man," suddenly shouting and thrusting an arm out to point at Cole's corpse, "is dead as dead can be."

Taber let his pronouncement sink in, then he bowed at the waist toward the crowd, came upright, bowed his head toward the ringmaster, and waddled out of the spotlight.

Long moments passed and a lion's roar could be heard in the distance. When St. Clare opened his eyes, there were tears. When he spoke, there was a tremor in his voice.

"Ladies and gentlemen," he said, "you have witnessed this evening the beginnings of a miracle."

A handful of burly gazonies ran from the sidelines, shovels in hand, and began to spade over the bloody earth next to the dead magician. The ground had been prepared and the work proceeded quickly.

"I ask," said the ringmaster, "that you remember what you have seen here tonight at the start of our Jubilee."

When a grave of sufficient length and depth had been fashioned, four of the gravediggers dropped their spades, approached the body, and went down on one knee.

"For the Bedlam Brothers," said St. Clare, his voice increasing with volume and enthusiasm, "intend to astound you to your very core."

The diggers rose. Each took a hand or a foot. They lifted the heap that had been Dr. Cole and carried the corpse to its tomb.

"Each and every one of you is invited back to this festival a week from tonight, as guests of the Bedlam Brothers family."

The pallbearers dropped the body unceremoniously into the ground, retrieved their shovels, and began filling in the grave.

"For in seven short days," the ringmaster shouted, reclaiming his brightest bally, "you will see a man rise from the dead. The Amazing Dr. Lazarus Cole will live once again."

St. Clare raised his hat in the air and waved it around to show the earnestness of his declaration. The crowd responded, hesitantly at first, but then the band struck up the Bedlam anthem again, the house lights came up, and the full troupe parade came back for another pass, all of the performers as bouncy and gusto-filled as ever. Balloons were released into the air and the trained monkeys began to run up and down the grandstand aisles dispensing candy. The elephants blew trunks of water at the clowns. The jugglers lit torches and began throwing them skyward in tall, spinning arcs.

St. Clare began to sing along with the anthem and then, lifting his arms into the air, encouraged the crowd to join him. And join him they did. They sang loudly and with emotion. They clapped and swung heads from shoulder to shoulder, stamped their feet and hollered with the joys of the spectacle laid out before them.

"And now," shouted St. Clare above all the noise, "on with the show."

11

Sweeney knew next to nothing about the city. And he felt no great need to educate himself. It was another rust-belt mill town and he had no intention of finding a way into its gritty life. He'd make his home at the Clinic. Come into town when necessary, when he needed supplies or maybe to see a movie sometime.

He was about a mile from the Peck when he noticed the warning light on the gas gauge. The drive-away agency had guaranteed that the car would be delivered with a full tank. He drove a few blocks, trying to tamp down the anger, and then it was no good and he was yelling *son of a bitch* and pounding the dash.

He came to a red light and, thinking he heard the engine start to gasp, he took a sudden arcing swing at the windshield. His fist went numb for an instant as the center of the glass formed a web of thin cracks. He put his fist in his lap and the pain came alive across the knuckles. The light turned green. A car behind him honked. He looked across the intersection and saw an antique, two-pump gas station.

As an attendant filled his tank, he made his way to the men's room and ran cold water over his hand. It did nothing to alleviate the pain. He turned off the water, held both hands next to each other. One was already swelling but both were shaking. He tried controlled breathing for what seemed a ridiculous amount of time. Then he exited the toilet, paid for his gas, and asked where he could find the nearest shopping center.

The attendant seemed a little confused by the question and gave it all his concentration. He pointed down the road.

"The Mart might still be open," he said. "It's closing any day, but it might still be open."

A half mile east, Sweeney found a nearly deserted plaza, a relic from the pre-mall era. A dozen small stores — a pharmacy, a shoe repair, a barbershop — were anchored by a five-and-ten. The structure had a flat roof and sported a metal awning that ran the length of the sidewalk. All of the stores but the five-and-ten were empty and, from the looks, had been for some time. Some were shuttered, others had whitewashed front windows, but the barbershop was wide open, its door and window smashed in.

Sweeney parked and locked the car and decided he wouldn't linger. The Mart had automatic doors, but they weren't working and he had to struggle to open one manually. Inside, the lighting was dim and yellow, an effect he found at first unsettling and, somewhat later, almost charming. Most stores overdosed on the fluorescents.

He grabbed a red canvas handbasket and began to walk the aisles. There was no apparent order to anything. Nothing was grouped by department. He found spray paint next to beach pails. Cakes of soap next to goldfish bowls. It was like a trip back to his childhood and, had his hand not hurt so much, he might have managed to lose himself for a few minutes. There were a half-dozen items that he picked up and examined, not interested in purchasing any of them, but simply stunned that they were still manufactured.

He began to suspect that he was entirely alone in the store until he turned a corner and came upon the key-making booth. The old man inside, perched on a stool, dressed in full apron and a knobby cardigan, was smoking a cigarette. Sweeney tried to recall the last time he'd seen someone smoking inside a department store. The man looked bored and hot and Sweeney thought about handing over the car keys just to give the guy something to do.

Instead, he said, "I'm looking for boys' pajamas."

The old man blew out a lungful of smoke and said, "Try aisle seven."

Sweeney thanked him and moved on. None of the aisles were marked, so he continued to browse. As he looked at eggbeaters and cheese graters, clothesline rope and a full bin of rubber galoshes, he realized there wasn't much chance that he'd find what he was searching for. But then there they were, on a table that featured a red plastic flag that bore the last traces of the word *Special*, dozens of pairs of *Limbo* pajamas. Along with random piles of *Limbo* card games with their box flaps taped closed, a few issues of the comic books with the covers torn off, *Limbo* wall calendars from years past, and some tiny, green plastic freak figures that Sweeney had never seen before. About the size of toy soldiers. Some of them, he noticed, were missing their heads.

He picked through the pile, selected four summer-weight pajama sets in Danny's size. He held them up and out from his chest, sized them the way Kerry used to, and made sure there were no tears. He studied the design, tried to pick out as many characters as he could. Chick and Kitty and Bruno were easy, of course. But he could never remember the name of the lobster girl or the pinhead or the human torso. Though he could have told anyone that the human torso had lost his bottom half in a bear attack.

It was significant how someone became a freak. Danny had assured him of that. Some people, his son had explained, are just born that way. But some become freaks due to an accident.

He threw the pajamas in the basket and hunted down coffee, a percolator, a bottle of aspirin, plastic hangers for his lab coats, and three sets of twin sheets. Then he began tossing items that he didn't need into the basket. A box of magic markers. A jar of olives. A thermometer. A Big Chief writing tablet. A package of mothballs. As he stood paging through a 1972 atlas of the interstate highway system, he began to smell frying meat. It was still only midmorning but the aroma was wonderful and he tossed the atlas atop the mothballs and followed the scent to the rear of the store.

Where he found a lunch counter that had been preserved, unchanged since, perhaps, the summer of love. A dozen leather-topped stools were mounted before a marble ledge. The black and white menu on the wall above the grill was faded but legible and offered a handful of staples like chicken salad and lime rickeys. Sweeney stared at it, thinking the prices were impossible. That over the years, the menu had evolved into a piece of nostalgic art. Of the same era as the napkin dispensers and the cake plates with their glass domes, but no longer functional.

The old key maker was behind the counter but he'd removed his cardigan. He was bent over a spitting grill, moving a beef patty around with a spatula. A single customer was perched on the last stool at the end of the counter, a tall biker in full leather, including jacket, chaps, and boots.

The guy had his elbows resting on the counter and his hands folded in front of him, as if in prayer. And though he wore sunglasses, Sweeney had the sense that his eyes were closed. At least until the biker turned his head and said, "What are you looking at?"

The question contained just the right degree of threat. The key maker turned from the grill and gave Sweeney a look as if to say *Stop bothering the customer.*

"Nothing," Sweeney said. "I just didn't know they served food here."

The biker cocked his head until the old man slid a platter in front of him. The plate was bone white and heavy-looking and big enough to contain a rump roast but it held only a plump burger garnished with lettuce and tomato, a dill pickle, and a small pile of potato chips. Sweeney looked from the biker down to the platter and felt himself start to salivate.

"You going to order," asked the old man, "or can I shut down the grill?"

"Aren't you just opening?" Sweeney said, and the old man cleared his throat and let it suffice for an answer.

Sweeney put his basket down, slid onto the stool, and said, "I'll have what he's having," gesturing toward the other end of the counter.

The old man tilted his head and bulged his eyes a little, as if to confirm the order, but the biker paid no attention. He was taking fast, aggressive bites out of his burger, making snapping, doglike motions with his jaw, and wiping the resulting spray of grease off his chin with the back of his hand. By the time Sweeney's meal was ready, the biker had cleared his platter. He pulled a stack of napkins from the dispenser, wiped at his lips and then his fingers and deposited the saturated paper in the middle of his plate.

"Food of the gods, Myer," he said to the old man as he climbed off the stool. "I'll see you next Saturday."

The old man poured water onto the grill from a glass coffeepot and watched the liquid sizzle and spatter. He shook his head without turning around and began to scrape debris into a grease well. As the biker passed behind Sweeney on his way to the exit, Sweeney swiveled and said, "Excuse me."

The biker stopped walking and froze, overly dramatic. The old man, Myer, turned and put a hand to his forehead. Sweeney had taken a bite of pickle and began to talk with his mouth full.

"I wonder if you can help me," he said. "I'm new in town and I was wondering, you know, if you knew a good garage. I'm having some problems with my car."

The biker looked at Myer, then at Sweeney. He took a step forward and removed the sunglasses. He let his head sink down into his shoulders a little, then said, "I look like a fucking mechanic to you?"

Sweeney looked at Myer, hoping he'd step in or turn the moment into a joke. The old man looked infuriated.

"No," Sweeney said. "I'm sorry, I just — "

"You just what?" the voice getting even lower. "You just looking for a reason to talk to me?"

"No, I thought — "

"You some kind of faggot?" the biker said and looked at Myer. "You serving faggots in here now, Myer?"

The old man looked down to the floor and said, "Not that I know of, Mr. Cote."

"Look," said Sweeney, "I made a mistake. I'm sorry."

"You're goddamn right you're sorry. You trying to pick me up, you little cocksucker?"

"Jesus Christ," Sweeney said and put his hands up. "No, No You've got the wrong idea. I'm new. I'm new here."

The biker put a finger on Sweeney's chest and pressed in on the breastbone. "I'll bury your fucking ass, you want."

"For Christ sake," Sweeney said. "I didn't mean anything. I was looking for a garage."

The biker bit down on his bottom lip, seemed to think for a second. Then he removed his finger, reached past Sweeney, and took the uneaten burger off the platter.

"You're new to a town," he said and pointed with the bulky roll and Sweeney watched some grease drop onto the boots, "you watch your manners. You understand that?"

Sweeney shook his head. The biker bit into the meat, chewed and swallowed, then said, "Buzz Cote is no fucking mechanic, asshole." Then he put the burger back on the platter and left the lunch counter. Sweeney could hear his boots click on the tile floor all the way to the front of the store.

Myer took the platter and threw it in a rubber bus tub and said, "What the hell is the matter with you, mister?"

Sweeney looked up at him. "You heard me. I just asked the guy a simple question."

Myer threw a hand out, disgusted.

"Listen," Sweeney said, the weight of the encounter starting to settle on him, "I'm brand new in town. I've got some problems with my Honda. That's it. I swear to you."

"And why didn't you ask me?" Myer said, steadying himself with a hand on the counter. "I've lived here seventy years. Most of my life. I've been through more lousy cars than you can count. Why the hell didn't you ask me for a garage?"

"I just thought, you know, the guy must know bikes — "

"You just thought," wiping hands on a dishrag, disgust moving up a notch to contempt. "Did you find the pajamas?"

The shift in subject, if not tone, was so sudden that Sweeney was confused.

"The pajamas," Myer said, on the verge of yelling, "the pajamas. Me, you'll ask about boys' pajamas. You know I once lived next to a garage?"

"I didn't mean to cause any problems," Sweeney said. He got off the stool, bent down and lifted his basket, and took a step toward the checkout.

"Give me that," Myer said, extending his arms across the counter for the basket.

Sweeney handed it over, but said, "Don't you want to ring it up down front?"

"Something wrong with this register?" Myer said, indicating an antique brass machine located down by the soda taps. But he didn't go near the ringer. Instead, he rummaged in the basket, shifting items and muttering. "Gimme thirty bucks."

Sweeney was getting more confused by the second. "What are you talking about?" he said. "The percolator alone is twenty dollars. I've got three sets of sheets in there."

"You," Myer said, shaking his head, resigned to his annoyance, "are a disagreeable SOB."

"But you're cheating yourself."

Myer handed the basket back to him and said, "Gimme thirty bucks or get out of my store."

Sweeney went into his pocket, came out with a hundred. "I've only got big bills," he said. "Can you make change?"

Myer pushed air out between his teeth, his aggravation beyond words now. He snatched the bill, shuffled to the register, hammered the sale tab with the palm of his hand, planted the bill, grabbed change, and slammed the cash drawer with his hip. He moved back to Sweeney with a heavy head and handed him a fifty.

"This isn't correct," Sweeney said.

"Get the hell out," Myer said.

SWEENEY DROVE DIRECTLY back to the hospital. This morning, on his way down the hill, he'd thought about finding a comic book store and searching for some of the back issues of *Limbo* they were missing. Maybe he'd pick up some dumbbells at a sporting goods store and some rabbit ears, if they still made them, at a Radio Shack. But now he just wanted to get safely back to the Peck. He'd eat some lunch at the cafeteria and spend the afternoon with Danny.

He got lost twice because he couldn't stop replaying the incident at the lunch counter. His question about the garage was honest and innocent enough. Why had it provoked such an overreaction? Granted, it would have been smarter to ask the old man. And maybe most people would've avoided the biker out of a general sense of caution. But what bothered Sweeney more than his bad judgment was that this kind of thing had been happening for a year now.

Back in Cleveland, he'd find himself almost weekly in an instantaneous shouting match, often with customers and always, it seemed to him, with the most ridiculous instigation. In the last six months, he'd had arguments in parking lots, pizza houses, dry cleaners, and the public library. And more than a few of them had rushed right up to the brink of physical violence.

Because of the number of incidents, logic told Sweeney that, at least some of the time, he must have been the inciting party. But when he'd replay the scene after the fact, he'd find himself, invariably, the clueless victim. Slow on the uptake. Stumbling through an ineffectual defense.

He'd shared a few of the early incidents with the therapist in Shaker Heights. And it was the only time her manner had turned from professionally compassionate to suspicious. She'd interrogated him, asked insulting and provocative questions: *Are you sure that's what you said to the man? Are you sure that's how you said it?*

After each of those sessions, she had tried to sell him on a prescription. And he'd asked her, joking, kidding around to defuse the tension, if she'd taken a job with Pfizer.

Sweeney considered himself, if not a pacifist, then at least a man less comfortable with casual violence than the rest of his culture seemed to be. He found nothing appealing in the cheap brutality of boxing or hockey. The nightly spewing of blood and viscera on television appalled him — maybe even more than it did Kerry. In the pharmacy, he had occasion to see stressed and overtired parents give in to the urge and deliver the fast slap or pinch to fussy children. He called them on it every time and once had notified Social Services.

He'd been a quiet kid growing up, bordering, maybe, on withdrawn. Through high school, he'd had exactly one fistfight and it had been less than glorious, a short and awkward tussle with a next-door neighbor. In college, he'd gravitated to pot more than booze, spent long, slow hours in small, dim rooms with a handful of friends, passing pipes and eating pizza and listening to mournful songs.

His amiability had occasionally grated on Kerry. At dinner once, a few years ago, when he'd boasted to friends that he and his wife never argued, she put a hand on his shoulder and said, "I try, but he just won't fight."

But over the past twelve months, he'd been in more arguments than in the rest of his lifetime.

And then there were the outbursts of rage, so far directed only at inanimate objects. At the old house, he'd had to replace two closet doors and the mirror on the medicine cabinet before he could hire a Realtor to sell the place. At the pharmacy one night after closing, he'd knocked a shelf clean and thrown a can of Ensure across the room, gouging the wall. It was infantile stuff. Pure temper tantrum. And after the fact, it always scared him and sickened him.

What if his response to the biker's abuse had been to grab for his knife or fork? He'd have ended up in the hospital or, less likely, in lockup on assault charges. Either way, he'd be jeopardizing both his and Danny's stay at the Clinic.

Maybe he'd call Shaker Heights tonight and ask for a referral and a prescription. But probably he wouldn't.

12

The Honda made terrible noises all the way back to the Clinic. The girl from the drive-away agency had done something to the car. Sweeney parked in the back lot and killed the ignition and the engine went through a melodramatic death scene, bucking and coughing up clouds of gray smoke. After the last spasm, he noticed the cigarette burns in the dash and the cupcake wrappers peeking out from under the passenger seat. Sweeney reached under the driver's seat and pulled out two empty tequila nips and a half-empty can of Jolt. He put them in the handbasket — Myer hadn't offered to bag his purchases — and got out of the car.

He dropped everything but the pajamas in the apartment, went up to the cafeteria and was surprised to find it crowded. He got a coffee and was looking for an empty table when Nora Blake whistled to him from the back of the room.

He slid into the seat opposite her. Nora was finishing a turnover and a paperback novel that featured a blond pirate on its cover.

"I didn't know administrators worked Saturdays," Sweeney said, and Nora held up a finger and brought her head just a bit closer to the words on the page.

Sweeney waited, sipped his coffee, and watched the woman concentrate. The book was beaten up, the spine cracked and peeled and the cover sporting dozens of creases that did nothing to lessen the pirate's virility. Nora started to shake her head, a slow sway, side to side, and Sweeney couldn't tell whether she was enthralled or disappointed. Finally, she looked up at him and gave a sigh that was almost as dramatic as the Honda's.

"You like pirate books?" Sweeney asked. He noticed that Nora was wearing pearls.

She shoved the paperback into a purse that was slung on the back of her chair.

"I was a virtual widow for twenty years," she said. "And I'm in love with historical romance."

"How much is history," Sweeney asked, "and how much is romance?"

"This one," Nora said, pulling her Virginia Slims from a pocket, "was about seventy-five, twenty-five romance to history. And I think I'm being generous. So how was your first night in the Peck? And what've you got there in your lap?"

He answered the second question first.

"They're pajamas for Danny," he said. But he didn't bother to hold them up.

Nora grimaced. "They might not go for that," she said, "depending on the G-tube and all."

"Danny would want these," Sweeney said. "I'll talk to Alice."

"Oh," said Nora, still feeling the effects of the high seas, "it's Alice already?"

He ignored her and said, "As for my first night, you know anything about a card game called Limbo?"

She smiled, almost laughed, and sucked the life out of her cigarette, then pointed at him with it.

"Limbo is new," she said. "Ernie's game was Blue Migraine. We made close to two thousand dollars one season. I bought myself a portable Jacuzzi for Christmas."

"So you know about the game and it's all right with you?"

She put on a concerned grandmother face but Sweeney thought something mocking was in it as well.

"Does it bother you?" she said. "Because I was outraged at first. It's amazing I didn't go to Dr. Peck that night."

"Why didn't you?" Sweeney asked. "I'm thinking about telling Alice today."

"You think she doesn't know?"

Sweeney hadn't even considered the possibility.

"Does she?" he said, a little too loud.

Nora shrugged and said, "Drink your coffee. It's getting cold," and Sweeney did as told.

"Look, Sweeney, I didn't go to Dr. Peck because it isn't in my nature to be a fink. Even though I was mad as hell and for a while it made me think about pulling Ernie out of here."

"But you left him in."

"I wish you smoked," Nora said, stubbing out her cigarette even though half of it was left. "It was better when people smoked together." She shook her head and started again. "The more I thought about the game, the more I started to believe Griswold was right — "

"Who's Griswold?"

"He's the one who started the game. He's been gone a while now. But he insisted they were playing for the patients. And Griswold walked the walk, you know. He'd play as if he were just Ernie's hands. One time, they were playing Lost Weekend, and it was western rules, and so the pot was growing pretty quickly. And before the end of shift they ended up with six, seven hundred dollars on the table. And it's Griswold's turn to either call or fold. And I'll never forget this. The sun is coming up and everyone's overtired and getting nervous. You can hear stomachs groaning and all. And Griswold just takes his time and he gets up and climbs onto the bed with Ernie. And he holds the cards in front of my husband's face. And he starts whispering. This isn't some nut, okay? This guy was top of his class at Stanford Medical. So the whispering and conferring goes on for a while. And then Griswold gets up off the bed, shaking his head, saying, 'All right, Ernie, if that's what you want to do.' And he calls and it was one of those long moments, you know. Just like in a movie. Everyone waiting to see what happens. The tension just hanging there."

She paused, trying to recreate a little of the original suspense.

"And Griswold took the pot?" Sweeney said.

Nora gave up a big, self-satisfied smile. "No," she said, "Ernie took the pot. You're missing my whole point, aren't you? We gave Griswold seventy bucks and I bought Ernie and me the Jacuzzi down at the Mart."

Sweeney put his coffee down and he and Nora stared at each other for a second. Then he said, "Look, I don't want to upset you. But you don't find that story a little ..." he fumbled, then tried, "macabre?"

"Macabre?" she said.

"How about disrespectful?"

"Disrespectful to who?"

"To your husband and you," he said. "To the patient and his family."

She didn't get upset. She patted his hand.

"You know what I find disrespectful?" she said and didn't wait for an answer. "When they treated my husband like a vegetable in a warehouse. When they talked about him as if he wasn't there. When some prissy little doctor would study my husband's file as if Ernie was some math problem."

She took out another cigarette but didn't light it.

"Dr. Griswold said to me once, he said, 'They're still inside.' He was convinced of it and he convinced me of it. He said the best way we could help them was to show them some faith. To show them we accept their new consciousness — "

The word was a button that brought Sweeney to life.

"Oh for Christ sake," he said. "Their new consciousness? Jesus, Nora, this guy was a fucking nut."

He was aware of people around them turning their heads in his direction, and he lowered his voice.

"They *have* no consciousness. That's what this condition is. That's the goddamn definition. They've lost consciousness."

"If Danny has no consciousness," Nora said, calm and serene, "then why did his father buy him special pajamas?"

Sweeney opened his mouth and closed it just as quickly. The question was a slap and it had the effect of flipping his anger into fear.

"I guess," he said, "I bought them for myself."

Nora was good with a cigarette in the way lifelong smokers often are. She pointed it at Sweeney's chest and said, "There aren't that many ways to get through this. You know I speak from experience. I've lived through some nights that most people can't even imagine. Now you're telling yourself you're a stoic. And that's keeping you from following your wife's example. You've gotten rid of everything that existed before the accident. You've erased Cleveland. Everyone and everything you used to know. You've moved into this nightmare and you've started your vigil. Fine. But how long do you think it'll be before you either take a swing at something other than a wall? Or get so scared that you want to trade places with your son?"

Sweeney's throat was fully constricted. He said, "I'd give anything to trade places with Danny."

"That," Nora said, "we don't get to choose. But we do get to choose how to think about this. You really want to believe that your son is a turnip who can still suck air?"

He lifted his coffee cup to throw it but Nora didn't flinch.

"Or do you want to believe that Danny can't wait to get in those new pajamas? That he knows when you're next to him and that you still love him even though he's not what he used to be?"

"It's not a choice," he said.

"It's absolutely a choice," she said. "It's about the only option you've got left. Let me clue you in on something, honey. These doctors, they know a lot of impressive words and they've got enough attitude to choke a czar. But they have no idea what consciousness is. And don't you let them tell you they do."

All he could get out was her name and he said it like a request. He was exhausted and nauseated and he knew that no amount of breathing exercises would help.

Nora leaned over the table.

"If you don't want Danny to be part of the game, then don't let him. The game is nothing. But don't start accepting someone else's opinion about who your son is. They know their science. Maybe. But you know your boy. Right?"

He put down his cup and said, "I've got to go see him now."

Nora put her free hand to her throat and touched her pearls. "You worry me, Sweeney," she said.

He got up and left the cafeteria without another word.

HE RAN TO Danny's ward. People stepped out of his way. The floor out-side 103 was newly mopped and he slid on the way in and fell on his ass. Alice Peck, who was hunched over Danny's bed, turned and looked down at Sweeney.

"Are you all right?" she asked.

She started to offer a hand but he was already climbing to his feet.

"They should put up a sign," he said.

Alice had a penlight in her hand. She was dressed in fitted black pants and a silk blouse. There was no sign of her lab coat.

"I was just checking in with the little guy," she said. "But I can come back."

This was a first. Sweeney had never heard a doctor offer to adjust her rounds to accommodate him.

"No, please," he said, "I've got all day. I can come back later."

Alice shook her head. "There's no need. Unless it makes you uncomfortable to see him examined."

"Were you examining him?" He looked at the bed and the night table for files or stethoscope, latex gloves or a new tube kit. There was nothing but the penlight she held in her hand.

"Nothing major," she said. "Mostly I was just visiting."

She bent over and used her fingers to pull Danny's lids apart. She brought her head close to the boy's, almost touching. She thumbed her penlight on, shined it into Danny's right eye, and studied the eyeball for what seemed, to Sweeney, an unusually long time. She did the same thing with the left eye. Then, before raising her head, she did something that Sweeney had never seen any doctor do before. She kissed Danny on the forehead.

"Drives my father crazy," she said as she came upright and saw the surprise on Sweeney's face. "But it's part of the therapy." She smiled and added, "And I'm crazy for kids."

When Sweeney didn't respond, Alice said, "I'm sorry. Does it bother you?"

"Not at all," he said. "It's a nice change."

She looked back to Danny, reached down, and ran a hand over the side of his skull.

"His hair's like silk. I love it at this age."

"He's got his mother's hair," Sweeney said.

Alice nodded, took a last look at the boy, then motioned toward the hall with her head and said, "Be careful there. It still isn't dry."

Sweeney followed her outside. She looked up and down the corridor before she spoke.

"In the next week," she said, "we'll want to schedule a meeting with you."

"Is everything all right?"

"Everything's fine," Alice said. "This is standard procedure at the Clinic.

It'll be my entire assessment team, Dr. Gögüs and Dr. Tannenbaum, maybe a therapist or an attending nurse. And possibly my father."

"I've met Dr. Tannenbaum," Sweeney said.

Alice bobbed her head and said, "He's terrific, isn't he? We're thrilled to have him here."

"What happens at the meeting?"

"It's actually the first in a series of meetings. But in some ways it's the most crucial. We'll track through Danny's condition from every possible angle. We look at full medical history. We study prior diagnosis and prognosis. We look at and evaluate all previous therapies. And we revisit the incident itself."

"The accident," Sweeney said.

"I tell you this," Alice said, "to prepare you. For most families it's a pretty grueling session. It's tedious and it's technical and some highly emotional material is presented in a pretty clinical fashion."

"I might not like what I hear."

"You might not like what you hear," Alice said, "both in terms of the recounting and the final assessment."

"You took Danny," Sweeney said, "because you thought his case was promising. That's what Dr. Lawton told me."

"And that hasn't changed," Alice said. "But what we do here at the Peck is start from the beginning. And it can be painful going backwards. It's been a year since Danny's incident, right? You'd already found a routine at the St. Joseph. And you might find things changing here."

"And that would be a bad thing?"

Alice smiled at him and regrouped.

"This is what I'd like to do," she said. "At some point, before the meeting, I'd like to talk to you one-on-one. Outside a clinical setting."

Sweeney stared at her again and went mute.

"Away from the Peck," she said. "I want to sit down, in a relaxed atmosphere, and talk to you. About Danny. And about you and Danny."

"Anytime you want to talk about Danny," he said, "I'm available."

"I'll call you," Alice said and walked away before Sweeney could tell her that he didn't have a telephone yet. He watched her turn a corner and, in the same instant that she disappeared, the janitor, Romeo, turned onto the hall, pushing a wash bucket on casters with a long-handled mop. He swayed toward Sweeney with a relaxed, almost swaggering gait, water slopping over the lip of the bucket as he moved. He didn't stop to talk, but brushed by and said, "How we doin' today, friend?" The voice was low and it was still locked in street jive.

"You're making a mess," Sweeney said to his back and Romeo lifted a hand, waved it in the air, and kept moving.

Sweeney went back into 103, stood at the end of the first bed, and looked at his son. Then he walked across the room and looked at Irene Moore, Danny's roommate. She was still in the same position she'd occupied yesterday. He moved to the side of the bed, leaned down, and kissed her forehead. Then he immediately walked back to Danny.

He climbed in next to his son. He brought his head level with Danny's and got comfortable, rolled to his side and brought his lips to the boy's left ear.

"Dad's back, Danny," he whispered.

He took a few breaths. He reached down, took his son's wrist, and timed the pulse.

"Do you remember," he asked, "where we left off?"

He stared for too long at his son's face, waiting for anything that he could tell himself was a response. Then he opened the drawer of the nightstand, reached inside, and pulled out several issues of *Limbo*.

13

At some point, Sweeney dozed off and dreamed that Kerry and he were with Danny at Put-in-Bay. They were sailing a boat through a series of narrow canals. Danny's hair was long and summer blond. Kerry was wearing the teal bikini. He noticed a tattoo of the sun on her belly. And then it was a different boat, something larger with a tall mast and Sweeney was having trouble with the rudder. Kerry was down below getting lunch and he kept calling to her but she wouldn't answer. Danny had climbed up the mast and grabbed onto a line and was swinging out over the water. With each swing the boat tilted on its side. The waves were hitting Sweeney. His eyes were stinging. He was furious, screaming for Danny to climb down and Kerry to come up topside. Then a flock of birds blocked the sun and the lightning began.

He yelled out when the second-shift nurse woke him.

"You were having a nightmare," she said.

He swung his legs off the side of the bed, rubbed his eyes, and looked at his watch.

"What's that?" he asked as the nurse began to hang a new bag on the IV pole.

"Just his meds," she said without looking at him.

She checked the drip and moved on to attend Irene Moore. He wiped at his eyes again, pulled a peppermint from his pocket, and put it in his mouth. He leaned over the bed and kissed Danny, then went back down to the apartment.

HE EMPTIED HIS purchases from the Mart, hung his lab coats in the bedroom closet, and made up his bed with the new sheets. He changed into T-shirt and gym trunks, then assembled the percolator and made some coffee. No one used percolators anymore, he thought. And this was a shame because they made such a wonderful sound, gave off such a rich smell.

He started his routine of sit-ups but before he reached his quota the idea hit him. He sat up with the first notion, then went into the bedroom, got the Big Chief scratch pad and the felt markers, and brought them to the couch. But he found, immediately, that the ink bled through the paper, so he took the pencil from the logic puzzle book and began his notes on the second page of the scratch pad. When he'd filled a page, he felt confident enough to get up and pour himself the first of what would be many cups of coffee.

He wrote in outline form. One-line sentences. Nothing fancy. At this stage, he was unconcerned about language or style. He wanted only to get the facts down, the series of sequential events necessary to build a plausible bridge from point A to point B.

It would have been easier to make a new starting point, to lessen the desperateness of the freaks' situation. But that would have been a cheat. Danny knew the story by heart, so there was no choice but to play the cards that had been dealt.

SWEENEY WENT UP to the cafeteria and found it empty. He got a ham and Swiss sandwich from the vending machine but it smelled suspicious and he threw it in the trash. He bought several packs of peanut butter crackers and a can of cream soda and ate at a clean table at the far end of the room.

When he was done, he went to the pharmacy and found Ernesto Luga seething.

"What the fuck," Ernesto said. "I offer you my friendship and you rat me out?"

"I didn't rat you out," Sweeney said. "What's the problem here?"

He was still standing in the doorway of the vault. Ernesto threw a bag of Jevity at him and he caught it like a football.

"The problem?" Ernesto said, his accent getting thicker with the sarcasm. "The problem is that I come in tonight and Romeo's all over my ass 'cause he says I told you about the game. I didn't say shit about the game."

"And I didn't say you did."

Sweeney came into the vault and faced him down. Ernesto was only about five foot five and Sweeney towered over him.

"So where'd he get the idea?"

"How should I know? Maybe you've told other people about the game."

This brought Luga up short.

"I never told no one shit. It was Nora, wasn't it? That old bitch."

"Nobody told me about the game," Sweeney said. "The place was dead and I got bored. I took a walk and I found them — "

"Up to the third floor? You took a walk up to the third floor?"

"That's right," the anger starting to well now. "I was walking around up there and I heard them."

Ernesto said, "You're full of shit."

Sweeney slapped him in the face with the bag of Jevity. Ernesto was shocked more than hurt. He stepped back and blinked, then closed his right eye and said, "*Qué coño.*" There was, maybe, an instant when Sweeney could have walked out of the vault and given them both a few minutes to calm. Then it was gone and Ernesto was taking a wild swing, a hook that glanced off Sweeney's neck. Sweeney stepped in, kneed Ernesto in the balls, and as Lugo doubled up, Sweeney reached out both arms and grabbed him by the neck. Lifted him off the floor. Pivoted and ran and slammed Ernesto against the far wall. The scoops of Sweeney's thumbs and forefingers were pressing in and Ernesto started to choke. And the sound of the choking stoked Sweeney's rage. He lifted the pharmacist's body higher, pressed in tighter. A low, grinding gag came out of Ernesto's mouth, then stopped. Sweeney had his left leg out behind himself, bracing his weight. He leaned in harder, his arms thrusting up, his hands squeezing tighter. Ernesto's eyes began to swell. His legs and feet thrashed against the white wall, his heeled boots making scuff marks.

"Motherfucker," Sweeney said and let go.

Ernesto dropped like dead weight. Sweeney kneeled over him and said, "I told everyone it was you, you little fuck. Now get out."

He stood up, pulled Ernesto to his feet, and pushed him into the hallway. Ernesto went down again. Sweeney could hear him making little crying noises and trying to get his air back. After a second, he got on all fours, his head hanging almost to the floor. There was some more gagging and then he got up and ran for the stairwell.

In the distance, Sweeney heard a voice yell, "Ernesto, what's wrong?" but there was no reply.

He moved to a counter and leaned on his elbows. Then he began to open cabinets until he found what he was looking for — a bottle of bleach and some fresh cleaning rags. He soaked a rag, moved to the scuffed wall, squatted and started rubbing at the black smudges. But it was futile. They wouldn't come off.

When he got up, Nadia Rey was standing in the doorway. They looked at each other but neither one spoke. He capped the jug of bleach, moved back to the cabinet and stored it. The rag he tossed in the sink. He ran water and wrung it out.

"You have a script I can fill?" he said with his back to her.

She didn't answer but came into the vault and hoisted herself up onto the counter next to the sink. She was wearing a starched white skirt and white stockings. To Sweeney, it came off as campy and he sensed that was what she was going for.

"You know, pharmacists have this reputation for being easygoing people," she said. "But that's never been my experience."

Sweeney turned off the water and shook his hands over the sink.

"Is there something I can help you with?" he said.

"Why'd you hit Luga?" she said.

Sweeney shook his head and said, "I didn't hit him. He took a swing at me."

"Ernesto took a swing at you?" she said. "I don't think so."

He pulled some paper towels from the dispenser, finished drying his hands, and wiped around the edges of the sink.

"He thinks I told Romeo and the others that he was the one."

"The one what?"

"The one that told me about the card game."

She closed her eyes, let her head tilt back. "This is bad," she said.

He toed open the wastebasket and threw in the paper towel. He looked up to find her smiling, on the verge of a laugh.

"You think this is funny?" he said. "I'm two nights in a new job and I almost strangle my coworker."

She tried to suck in her cheeks. "Ernesto's fine," she said. "You just scared him."

"What if he doesn't come back?"

"He's leaving for Wonder Drug anyway."

"And what if he comes back with some friends?"

She slid off the counter and the skirt rode up. "Oh, please," she said. "He talks a lot but, trust me, he's a fruit drinker. He likes to play dice and chase after little girls. In an hour he'll be telling everyone at La Concha how he kicked your ass."

"I can't believe this happened," Sweeney said.

"It's over," Nadia said. "It was an incident and now it's over."

"This has been coming on," Sweeney said.

"It's understandable," Nadia said. "You're under a lot of stress and Ernesto pushed your button. He swung first, right?"

He didn't want to tell her about the Jevity bag so he just nodded.

"Try to forget about it. You had a little fight. It happens. You're in a new place and right away some idiot gets aggressive."

"It was a misunderstanding," Sweeney said. "I overreacted."

"You were defending yourself," Nadia said. "What were you supposed to do?"

Sweeney said, "I really overreacted."

She offered to bring him a coffee but he said coffee was the last thing he needed. She asked if he would like some food and he told her he'd just eaten.

"You've got a long night ahead of you," she said. "You've really got to get past this."

"This is my second night," he repeated. "They don't know me from Adam. I really need this job."

"Nothing's going to happen to your job," she said. She moved close, put a hand on his shoulder.

"What if Ernesto goes to Dr. Peck?"

"I know Ernesto," Nadia said. "I'll talk to Ernesto. Ernesto won't make trouble. Trust me, it's taken care of."

"You'll talk to Ernesto?" he said.

"Consider it done."

"I don't know what's the matter with me," Sweeney said.

"You're going through a lot of changes," Nadia said. "You've got to give yourself a break here."

"I just tried to strangle someone."

"You tried," she said, and couldn't help the smile, "to strangle Ernesto. Believe me, Sweeney, you're in good company."

He shook his head and put his hand on the counter. "I've got to get some help. This is out of control."

"Ernesto's fine," she said. "I saw him. You hurt his pride and that's about all."

"I had my thumbs in his throat."

"Ernesto's a big pussy," she said and the remark brought Sweeney up short.

"Excuse me," he said but Nadia didn't move. He pushed up the sleeves of his lab coat and turned on the cold water. He cupped his hands below the faucet, let the water pool, hunched over the sink and brought his hands to his face. He did this several times. Then he shut off the water and straightened up. Nadia was standing in the same position. Water rolled down Sweeney's face. He grabbed two paper towels and patted himself dry.

"I think I've made a big mistake," he said.

She folded her arms across her chest. She looked darker in the light of the vault. She looked, he thought, like a gypsy. And he was struck, for the first time, by the magnitude of her foreignness and her beauty.

"That's what I wanted to talk to you about," she said.

Sweeney waited for her to go on and when she didn't, he said, "I don't understand."

"My note," Nadia said. "Didn't you get my note?"

"The note," Sweeney repeated. "Of course, the note. I got it. Yes. You wanted to talk. About Danny."

"I thought for a minute you didn't get the note."

"Is Danny okay?" he asked. He had repeated this question so many times in the last year that at some point it began to feel like a prayer or a pledge.

"Not in here," Nadia said. "We can't talk here."

He looked around the vault and nodded.

"You want to go down to the cafeteria?"

Now she laughed.

"No," she said. "I mean I'm not comfortable talking here at work. In the Clinic."

She gave him a chance to suggest something and he failed.

"Listen," Nadia said, "I know a place near here. This little bar. It's open all night. Why don't I meet you around the back lot in fifteen minutes? Can we take your car? I got a ride in."

He looked at her, then up at the wall clock, and then back.

"What are you talking about? Shift just started."

"That's not a problem," she said. "Debbie will cover for me."

"I can't just leave here," he said.

He saw the indulgent smile and shook his head in response.

"You want me to just leave the drug room? On my second night of the job?"

"Oh, please," she said. "What? You're more essential than I am?"

"No, that's not what I'm saying. I just can't leave the room unmanned."

She walked to his in-box and lifted maybe three scripts.

"You waiting for the rush?"

"That's not the point."

"Sweeney, everyone knows where everything is. Just leave a note that you got called away. You had an emergency. They'll find whatever they need."

"Jesus Christ," he said. "You want me to just leave the vault open? Are you nuts?"

"Ernesto used to do it all the time."

"What the hell kind of place is this?" he said and she understood that he wasn't looking for an answer.

"This is not a big deal, Sweeney."

He lifted an arm, let it fall back and slap his thigh.

"Like almost choking someone to death isn't a big deal."

"God," she said, "you are tense."

"What is it you have to tell me about Danny?"

She just shook her head.

He sighed, exhausted. His stomach was churning.

"What's the name of this place?" he asked. "This bar?"

"It's called," she said, "Gehenna."

He stared at her. She widened her black eyes.

"You're kidding me," he said.

"Is there a problem?" she asked.

They stared at each other for a few seconds until he realized that she wasn't going to say anything else.

"Can we go after shift? I mean, it's open all night, right?"

She thought about it.

"I want to hear what you have to say," he said, "but I'm not going to walk out and leave the vault open."

She knew there was no use arguing.

"All right," she said. "I'll meet you in the lot at 7:15."

14

Motionless in his terrarium, silent but wide awake in the dimness of the study, the salamander waited. It was a blue-spotted newt, of the Ambystomatidae family, about five inches long, with splayed toes and a black belly. Its name was Rene and it had been last year's birthday gift from Alice Peck to her father.

An endangered species, the blue-spotted newt was typically found in the swamps and marshes of the American Northeast, where it fed on mealworms, beetles, millipedes, and aphids. Freedom, of course, has a price, and in its natural environment, a sallie's life expectancy was less than ten years. But here in the study, safe and well tended, Rene might live twice that long.

It was difficult at best, insane at worst, to ascribe emotion to a creature as inscrutable as a salamander. But, if forced, Alice might have said that she sensed from Rene a certain serenity, a contentedness, born of life in her father's study. Alice kept the terrarium tidy, filled it regularly with fresh moss scraped from the trees that lined the hill below the Clinic. Dutiful and vigilant, a good daughter, she misted the interior of the bowl each morning before her rounds and cleaned away any shed skin that Rene had failed to consume during the night.

For his part, Dr. Peck had come to consider Rene a necessary presence in the study, as essential to his work as the texts that rimmed the walls or the bottle of sherry in the bottom drawer of his desk. Over the course of the last year, Peck had discovered intriguing similarities between newt and neurologist. Both were naturally nocturnal. Both were deaf to conventional wisdom. Both were regenerators, magicians who could raise up that which had been lost or damaged or cut away. And both, Peck had become convinced of late, were the last mystics in this world — enigmatic shamans who could bend and shape consciousness itself. Which is to say, reality itself.

It might have appeared a contradiction, to label a man of science — a man whose life had been founded on and guided by logic, rationality, provability — a mystic and a shaman. But what Dr. Peck had come to understand, by way of hard, shaping experience, was that his work required terrifying leaps of faith into counterintuitive realms. What the doctor had learned about the human mind over the last decade had reconfigured everything he thought he knew about the way the world was put together. Now, like his blue-spotted confessor, he understood that the universe, the fabric of reality, was composed of nothing more than particles of longing, a kind of quantum desire for absolute connection. Dr. Peck understood that, from moment to moment, we are profoundly asleep and, so, profoundly alone. Like Rene, we are locked inside the glass terrariums of our lives. What the doctor needed to discover was how to wake us up. The path to that discovery began, he was certain, inside the craniums of his patients.

He knew that every arousal he achieved would bring him closer to answers that had more to do with the nature of consciousness than of coma. Every new patient was a fresh opportunity, one more chance to sound the alarm that would awaken the world itself. Which was why he had run from the surgical theater, down to the incinerator, and on to the study in the middle of the night. To share the latest good news with the newt. And to meditate, together, across the bounds of language and species, on what that news might mean.

Peck entered the study from the rear corridor that connected his residence to the Clinic proper. He was wearing his scrubs and carrying the black leather satchel. He moved to his desk, placed the satchel on his blotter, next to the terrarium, and stripped off his gown, cap, and mask. As he balled them together, he took note of the single drop of blood on the hem of the gown, then deposited the soiled laundry into the empty satchel for collection by Alice in the morning.

He left the latex gloves stretched over his hands, and when he felt the first tremor, he leaned forward and braced himself against the desk. Clad now only in his boxer shorts and slippers, he felt the chill more powerfully. He let himself tremble, let the small earthquake pass through his nervous system. It was happening more frequently of late, always after a session in surgery. He would not mention it to Alice — no need to worry the girl. It was, most likely, nothing more than a release of tension and stress, coupled with too many nights without any sleep.

As his body worked its way through the final few spasms, the doctor tried to recall the last time he had been to bed. But tonight, exhaustion had taken a toll on his short-term memory as well. So he waited for the episode to pass. And when it did, he began to collect the items he needed for his postoperative recovery. Rene, he knew, was waiting to hear the details. And the doctor was anxious to supply them.

From one desk drawer, he took the bottle of Manzanilla and the first edition of *Les passions de l'ame,* a volume that he had purchased to mark and celebrate his first arousal. From another drawer he removed the over-sized gray envelope that contained his newest patient's films — the latest scans, sent up by Dr. Tannenbaum yesterday afternoon — and a scuba diver's flashlight. He tucked book, bottle, flashlight, and envelope under his arms in order to free both of his hands. Then, gingerly, he lifted the terrarium, nestled it against his chest and climbed the spiral staircase that led to the cupola.

Halfway up, he stopped, as he often did, to study the painting of his long-dead wife. Practically life-size, she was captured in heavy oils and boxed inside a thick gilt frame. The darkness of the composition made her look willowy and ethereal, a spirit leisurely slipping free from the trap of the body. Only her eyes retained the piercing, hateful focus, which had never quite been tranquilized by the many medications. It still surprised Peck that he had chosen this woman for a mate.

"Look at her," the doctor said to Rene before moving on. "She wanted nothing more out of life than a prolonged nap."

Up in his perch, his nest at the top of the world, he carefully placed each item on the floor below the window seat, then lay down on the seat itself, stretched out on its red velvet cushion. He closed his eyes for a moment and pushed his nose against the cool glass of the window. Reaching down to the floor, he found the bottle of sherry, clutched it and brought it to his mouth. Eyes still closed, he guzzled until he needed air. Then he cradled the bottle and opened his eyes quickly, looking out on the pines. Lit up by a half-moon, the trees that sloped along the hill below the Clinic were swaying with the wind so that they looked like the waves of some alien ocean.

This time, it took almost thirty minutes for the doctor to find that scarce and precious moment when exhaustion and sherry allowed him to fade out of the Clinic and into the place where his mind could rage against the borders of rationality. The place where, he knew from experience, the most radical breakthroughs were conceived.

Unfortunately, the doctor rarely had enough time or solitude these days to roam out into the frontier of his imagination. He was a man of staggering responsibilities. Few could know the enormity of his obligations and fewer still could discharge them. And while some mundane satisfaction derived from executing one's duty, the cost was considerable — an ongoing sacrifice of the hours and the privacy needed to dream well and deeply.

But with his tools at hand and the right combination of sleeplessness and Manzanilla, Dr. Peck could dive down into a level of thought where language and history were increasingly irrelevant. These submersions tended to ravage him, like the pearl diver who plunges beyond all good sense in search of the ultimate gem. The pressure on the lungs and the temples becomes more severe with each additional foot of depth. The danger of dislocation more acute. The risk of remaining forever submerged, extraordinary. But Peck, like all visionaries, knew that there was no such thing as true exploration without true risk. In fact, that was where the thrill of discovery resided — in the heart of the peril. It was not work for cautious men, which is why it fell to the doctor. Whatever other traits his blood harbored, timidity was not among them.

Peck took a last long swallow of sherry and put the bottle down on the floor. He could feel himself arriving into that moment when discovery was possible. In the end, he knew, this was what he lived for: that instant of pure, galloping potential, that feeling of downrushing epiphany.

But calling forth fresh thought was, like summoning demons, a precarious process. And, for Dr. Peck, it required an instinctual blending of the right amounts of whimsy, research, fatigue, daydream, alcohol, and stress. It also required the right environment — the cupola was the only place that the notions would deign to be born. Finally, the summoning required a marriage of humility and patience that could allow the idea to reveal itself in its own manner and time. The idea, it must be understood, is always in charge.

From adolescence through the first years of his medical practice, Dr. Peck had believed that new knowledge was born of a specific process, reflection and experimentation coupling to yield results that were quantifiable, repeatable, and capable of being shared. But up here, in this womb at the top of the Clinic, in his boyhood sanctuary, he had learned otherwise. Genuine revelation, he determined, was nothing less than an explosion of new consciousness, a reconception of the mind itself. It did not accrete, building slowly and steadily upon existing information and tradition. It was, rather, a revolution and a rapture, a concussion that obliterated the past and re-created the world in the radiant light of newborn vision.

Seeking refuge from a spectral and unimpressed father and, later, a scornful and depressive wife and, later still, a daughter he loved too much, Peck had spent countless sleepless nights in the cupola, looking out over the ocean of pines and trying to dream his way into epiphany or, failing that, oblivion. Over time, the cupola had become a kind of petri dish or incubator, the glass uterus where the notions were conceived and matured. Peck had come to feel this was a place of holy asylum.

Once, years ago, Alice had found him on the window seat, calling out in his sleep, locked into one of those slow-motion nightmares in which the terror is inversely proportionate to the mundane image that triggers it. She was fourteen or so at the time, with hair trimmed short for the summer. Upon being woken, still tormented by his dreams, Peck had mistaken her for his son and struck her across the cheek. Shocked, she had dropped to her knees, eyes open and staring throughout the fall, her skin reddening with the prints of his fingers. When Peck realized his mistake, he pulled the girl into his arms and held her, too tightly, until sometime before dawn, both of them weeping with what the father wanted to believe was a shared understanding regarding the cost of genius.

On that night, Peck realized that the calling to medicine — at least the kind of visionary medicine to which he aspired — was more than a vocation; it was destiny. And as such, it called for a radical lifestyle. Doctors, like monks, were forever at risk of infiltration by the domestic world.

He concluded, much too late, that they should be solitary, if not entirely celibate, creatures. A people, as the saying goes, set apart. The modern clinic, he now understood, was the contemporary monastery, its labs the chapels where communion could be reinvented perpetually. In the case of the Peck Clinic, it would be a communion with the sleepers.

On impulse, Peck reached down into the terrarium for Rene, caught the sallie gently inside his fist, and lifted it out of the glass bowl. Bringing his mouth close to his cupped hand, Peck spoke into it.

"My apologies. Did I interrupt a dream?"

The doctor's query was nothing but a polite greeting, something to set the tone and begin the session. He knew that salamanders lived day for night. Through the latex, he could feel the newt move against his skin, a sensation he found comforting. The gloves were for the creature's protection, certain toxins in the human epidermis being poisonous to newts.

Peck reached down with his free hand, grabbed one of the filmy brain scans and laid it on his bare chest. He placed Rene on the scan and the newt remained there, frozen, staring up into the sky of the doctor's face.

"I won't keep you in suspense any longer," Peck said to Rene. "The harvest was a success. As you know, I had my doubts about the fetal source. But I feel certain now that we were within the nine-week limit."

While it is true that salamanders are deaf to airborne sounds, the doctor was confident that his confessor received and processed the vibrations of voice in some satisfactory manner.

"The oldest irony," Peck said. "We must go to the gutter in order to reach the stars."

When drunk, Dr. Peck had a tendency toward the theatrical. Rene, for his part, did not seem to mind. There was little cruelty in artifice and, in small amounts, the doctor's affectations could verge on the charming.

"Light out of darkness," Peck intoned, like some hammy Victorian actor, ready to reach for a skull or break into song. "Life out of death. Consciousness out of profound stupor. As Bishop Berkeley said to his sallie, *These are the miracles we work in the Clinic.*"

He belched, and then, taking in some air, laughed at his own performance. Rene quivered slightly on his chest.

"It's good to have a place," the doctor said, "where we can let down our guard. You and I are fortunate. For all that we sacrifice in our pursuit, we always know where we reside. We'll always have the cupola."

He brought his hand up slowly and stroked the newt along its back with his index finger.

"But the mind," he said, "the poor, lost mind, has no idea where it resides. The Greeks housed it in the stomach, you know. As good an address as any other. I once knew a physicist. Said he could move his mind into his shoulder or his big toe. A lunatic, I agree, though not without his appeal. But in the end, I seem to return to our favorite poet."

He stared down at the sallie and smiled.

"Would you like a taste?"

The newt remained impassive. Peck grabbed the volume from the floor, propped it on his belly, and opened it to a page bookmarked with a torn sheet of pulp — a garish piece of comic art. He lifted the bookmark. It was a scene of dark romance, featuring a sinister-looking man — a magician, perhaps, or an undertaker — dark-eyed and gaunt, dressed in a flowing black cape that gave just a hint of its brilliant red lining. The man wore black boots with long pointy toes. He sat cross-legged, halfway up an enormous cliff, in a notch between two boulders. A cobra's head cane rested across his lap. His elbows were planted on his knees, his chin cupped in his braced hands. And he appeared to be in the grip of some sort of trance, looking out over a raging sea, terrifying whitecaps breaking over the rocks below him.

Peck studied the image for a moment, frowned at it, unable to recall from where it had come. Then he dropped the bookmark to the floor and read, rendering the English from the old French:

> Languor is a tendency to relax and be motionless,
> and this is experienced in all the members;
> like tremors, it proceeds from the fact
> that sufficient animal spirits do not get into the nerves.
> A swoon, however, is not far removed from death,
> for death results when the fire
> which is in our heart
> is extinguished altogether,
> and we only fall into a faint
> when it is stifled in such a way

that there still remains some traces of heat,
which, afterward, may rekindle.

A pause to let the words have their effect.

"As you might imagine," Peck said, "and like everything else, it loses something in the translation."

The doctor took great pleasure in reading to Rene. It reminded him of those lost Sundays, years ago, when Alice would sit on his lap downstairs in the study rocker and he would perform her favorite story, shamelessly acting out the dialogue of the princess and the prince and the evil witch with her poisoned apple.

Now he dropped the book onto the floor and put his hands behind his head.

"But the point remains," he said. "Just like you, my friend. Theories come and theories go. But the salamander remains. Take Tannenbaum, for instance. Been here how long now? But still he believes — he insists — that consciousness is a collection of patterns residing in known space and time. Everything for him comes down to the firing of neurons. Transmission and reception."

A belch.

"Smug son of a bitch," looking down at the sallie. "There is a kind of doctor, you know. More common than you'd imagine. Never known a day of doubt. But, tell me, Rene, if you've never known doubt, how can you know true faith?"

Peck wanted to roll on his side but the newt looked so comfortable.

"I've had years composed of nothing but doubt. Two arousals, Rene," holding up fingers to illustrate, "two arousals in ten years. In all that time, the only thing I haven't doubted is the existence of my own mind. But make no mistake, self-awareness is both boon *and* curse."

He lifted his head to focus in on his confidant.

"Sometimes I think I amuse you with my confessions. But I can't help this sense that the mind has its *own* cupola. Its own refuge. And if I can locate the refuge of consciousness, I can break inside. If not through the front door, then through the back. If not through the back, then through a window. If I can find its lair, I can poke it. And if I can poke it, I can wake it up."

Suddenly invigorated by his own pep talk, he returned the newt to the glass bowl, then grabbed the flashlight from the floor. Sitting up, he peeled Daniel Sweeney's latest brain scan from his chest and fixed the film against the cupola window. He thumbed on the flashlight — it was a diver's lamp and its hundred-thousand-candlepower beam passed through the film and projected the image of the boy's sleeping brain out over the sea of pines. As the trees rippled in patterns with the wind, the brain itself, enlarged to ten times its true size, also appeared to ruffle and wave.

Peck studied the organ's topography as he spoke to Rene.

"Our problem, of course, is the father. Always the father."

He stopped himself and stared at the undulating map of the child's brain and in the long silence that followed, the newt began to lash his tail back and forth and excrete his toxins into the drying moss at the bottom of his bowl.

"But I promise you that we *will* deal with the pharmacist," Peck said. "And one way or another, I will step out onto that ocean and walk upon that water," face grimacing and fully theatrical now, as he used his finger to mark the places where he would cut open the child's skull and poke the brain with his monk's harpoon, spreading the new seed and birthing a new world.

But Rene was no longer listening. He had stopped at that moment when the makeshift bookmark had floated to the floor next to his bowl. And the caped sorcerer caught the salamander's eye and began to work his dark mesmerism across those vast expanses of myriad dimensions.

LIMBO COMICS

FROM ISSUE # 7: "A Bloody Ordeal"

. . . Needless to say, following the murder of Lazarus Cole, the freaks and their strongman moved through that first night of the Jubilee in a state of stunned disbelief. And yet, they seemed to be the only ones who experienced the aftershock of witnessing such a degenerate and orchestrated killing.

"But remember," Chick said to them just before the sideshow annex was opened for business, "the Jubilee comes through Mach'pella every year. And according to the bannerline, Lazarus Cole has been with them for seven seasons now."

"You're saying," said Milena as s/he applied talc in the dressing room, "that he's not really dead."

"He's a magician," said Aziz, doing his stretching exercises. "That's what he does. It's all a trick. It's the art of illusion."

"I've been on the circuit all my life," the lobster girl said, applying oil to her claws. "And I've dated my share of magic men. But I've never seen anything like this. It's obscene, is what it is."

Bruno had been sitting on a stool, trying to memorize a spiel that Milena had written for him.

"If it is an illusion," he said, "it's the best damned illusion I've ever seen. And I've shared bills and played cards with the best magicians in Bohemia."

"Even if it is an illusion," said Kitty, standing atop two orange crates, ironing an evening gown, "it feels like the trick is beside the point."

"Kitty's right," said Vasco, slicking back his hair.

"There's something wrong with this show," said Marcel, borrowing the comb and completing the thought.

"Well," said Milena, picking a feather boa from a steamer trunk, "right or wrong, we've got to get to work. It's showtime."

BRUNO DID HIS BEST. On this, all the freaks would agree. He made a valiant effort. And if good intentions could fill a sideshow, the annex would have been a straw house that night. He helped each member of the clan up onto his or her particular stage, helped them get positioned, and assisted with props. He rolled down each curtain—the Jubilee had reasonably appropriate banners for a hermaphrodite, a female dwarf, and Siamese twins. The rest got velvet drapes without any illustration. No one complained and everyone hit the boards as confident professionals.

Everyone, that is, except for Bruno. Put him in a ring, on a field, and he would shine. He could box or wrestle three men at a time. He could break chains, heave boulders, hoist the largest livestock on the farm. But what he could not do was bark.

Bruno Seboldt was no salesman. Not so long ago, he would never have imagined a time in his life when this fact would constitute a problem. But tonight, in the country of Gehenna, in the town of Mach'pella, in the company of the Roving Jubilee, it was nothing short of a crippling disability. And he found himself utterly tongue-tied and, for the first time, genuinely fearful.

He stood at the annex entrance, choking in a bow tie, sweating under the band of a straw boater, a bamboo cane looking like a child's toy in his hand. He tried to recite the patter that Milena had written for him but it was no use. The words he managed to remember came out stilted and ridiculous.

"Step right up," he began. "See the world's most astounding individuals. One small fee brings you face to face with eleven wonders of the universe."

And by the second sentence, his tongue had swollen and his mouth had gone dry. He was perspiring desperately.

"See the human mule and the lobster girl," he cried. "See the skeleton and the fat lady. See Vasco and Marcel, the Siamese twins."

But it came out as if he were reading from a laundry list. And the marks just gave him a suspicious or angry look and walked right by. Inside, the freaks waited, not so patiently, to hear the familiar noise of bodies filing into the sideshow annex, the voices of braggadocio and wonder, the nervous quips and laughter. Now, all they heard was Bruno's muffled and mangled attempts to bark up some business.

"The show starts in ten minutes," the strongman called. "One price buys you eleven freaks. See the human torso. See the pinhead. See the chicken boy."

But there were no takers. And this was a first. Bruno had traveled with circuses and carnivals all of his life. The freak show was the closest thing to a sure bet he'd ever encountered, through cities and villages, in good times and bad. The Goldfaden Freaks had drawn sell-out crowds all across Old Bohemia. Why weren't they drawing them in at the Jubilee?

The answer was provided with gleeful hostility by Chief Shawnee, the Jubilee's resident strongman. He approached Bruno minutes before showtime, peeked into the empty annex, and laughed, "Now that's a damn shame," though it was obvious that he relished the sight of the empty tent.

He held out a bottle to Bruno, who declined. The Chief shrugged and took his own swig, wiped his mouth with his forearm, and said, "You're the worst talker I've ever seen."

"It's not my specialty," Bruno agreed.

"Oh, that's right," said the Chief, "you're with the shovel brigade, aren't you?"

"I'm a strongman," Bruno said, "just like you."

"That right?" Micmac said, arching his brows and pulling down his jaw. "I heard you were a dung shoveler. I heard you were a lowlife, shit-slinging gazonie."

The sweat was pouring down Bruno's face and he could feel the muscles in his neck starting to pulse. He took a breath and said, "You heard wrong, Chief," throwing all the accent onto the last word and turning it into a mocking insult.

The Chief took a drink and gave a half laugh. "No need to be ashamed," he said. "Every circus needs its dung slingers. Hell," a pause to belch, "I'd even say it's a step up from trying to sell a bunch of sham freaks."

"They're not shams," Bruno snapped, too quickly. "They're the real things."

The Chief nodded condescendingly. "'Course they're shams. Everyone knows they're shams. Why do you think no one's buying a ticket? They all remember the last time the Jubilee offered up some freaks. They were all bogus. Every one of them. Frauds, fakers, and phonies."

Bruno stepped out from behind the ticket booth.

"My freaks," he said, "are genuine."

"Well, then," the Chief said, "you won't mind showing them to me." And he lifted the flap and strolled into the annex.

Bruno followed him inside, unsure of what to do. It was showtime, even if there was no audience. And if he refused to display the freaks, it would seem as if he were afraid of exposing their fraudulence.

"C'mon," the Chief said. "Bring up the curtains and let's have a look at your needle and thread monsters."

Conflicted and annoyed, Bruno stomped over to the riggings and took hold of all the tie-lines at once. Instead of bringing one curtain up at a time, the way the show was supposed to unfold, he yanked all of them up simultaneously. And the freaks were revealed together, in eleven dioramas: Chick behind pen fencing, Kitty among oversized furniture, Nadja laid out with conch shells and sea stones, Fatos next to a cardboard cactus, and so on.

The Chief was taken aback at first. He'd been hitting the bottle when the curtains went up and he spilled liquor down his chest at the sight of them. Bruno watched him bite his bottom lip and stare. Then he took a step closer and leaned his head forward and muttered something unintelligible. He moved over to the first stage, where Antoinette was posed on a wooden stool before a classroom backdrop. The Chief studied the pinhead for awhile, then began to walk from stage to stage.

He took his time, stroking his chin as he gaped, sometimes scratching at his head. The last stage belonged to Milena, who was posed on a loveseat, lounging in an elaborate costume that was half white silk nightgown and half black pajama shirt and pants.

The hecklers and the rowdies always saved their strength for the hermaphrodite. It had been the same back home. Milena had heard every comment and developed several standard responses. So when the Chief said, "You gonna' show them to me?" Milena didn't even think before s/he said, "Not till you show me yours first."

"I'm not the freak," said the Chief.

"We won't know that," said Milena, "until I get a good look."

Bruno was ready to launch himself if the Chief made a move toward the stage. But it wasn't necessary. Shawnee glared at Milena, threw a hand dismissively in the hermaphrodite's direction and uttered a single, disgusted syllable.

"Bwah," he said.

Then he turned to Bruno and smiled.

"There's only one thing," he said, "more humiliating than a strong-man playing wet nurse to a freak troupe."

Bruno waited for it silently. The Chief allowed himself a belt from the bottle before he continued.

"A fake strongman," he said at last, "playing wet nurse to a troupe of fake freaks."

Satisfied with himself, Micmac Shawnee began to exit the annex tent.

Bruno could have let it go at that. And, perhaps, on another night, in another town, he would have. But the feel of the bow tie at his neck and the boater, too tight, on his head, had abbreviated his capacity to suffer fools gladly. And as the Chief bent to push through the tent flap, Bruno lowered a hand onto his rival's shoulder and stopped Micmac's progress.

The Chief turned slowly.

"I'll say it again," Bruno said. "They're not fakes."

The Chief looked at Bruno and then beyond him to the freaks, who were still frozen on their stages, several of them wishing their curtains would fall.

"And I'll say it again," said the Chief. "They're the saddest bunch of frauds and imposters I've ever laid eyes on. It's so obvious, I can only think that the ringmaster took them on out of pity."

"Let me tell you what I pity," said Bruno. "I pity the paying customer who has to watch a drunken tub of lard like yourself dress up like a real man."

The Chief responded with a wild and off-balance roundhouse, telegraphed so far in advance of its arrival that none of the freaks even bothered to shout a warning. Bruno sidestepped the punch, pivoted and threw two shots to the Chief's kidneys. Shawnee went down on a knee, stunned, but only for a second. And when he bounced upright, he barreled into Bruno with an enraged tackle. Both men went to the ground this time, rolling in the dirt and weeds, each trying to squeeze the other into surrender.

The freaks dashed to the lips of their stages to watch the spectacle, except for Antoinette who ran, sobbing, back to the trailer. Chick wondered if he should fetch someone but decided against it, unsure of whom he could trust.

The rolling and groaning and grunting continued for several minutes, each of the giants trying to break the other's hold with a sudden twist or turn. But for a while, the two appeared well matched.

As it turned out, however, Bruno had youth and cunning on his side. He let the Chief tire himself, let the alcohol in the man's blood go to work. And as the Chief's strength began to ebb just slightly, the Bohemian Behemoth sensed his advantage and threw his opponent onto his back.

Bruno capitalized on the toss by rolling up into a sitting position on Shawnee's stomach, fastening a grip around the Chief's enormous neck. At once, Micmac began to struggle for air.

"Give," demanded Bruno.

The Chief only gasped and tried futilely to roll away.

"Give up," Bruno repeated with more ferocity in his voice. And Milena wondered just how the strongman would know if the Chief did, in fact, surrender.

"I'm telling you," shouted Bruno, leaning down close to the Chief's face, "give up and apologize. Or I'll break your miserable neck."

Chick and Kitty and Durga all flinched at this, but Bruno, drunk on adrenaline and testosterone and invested fully in the moment, didn't realize the significance of what he was saying.

The Chief's eyes began to flicker and the noise from his throat grew deeper and more raspy.

"Bruno, enough," Chick yelled, throwing over the fencing, jumping down from the stage and running at his patriarch.

Bruno saw the flash of feathers at his periphery and, in that instant, he looked up to see the chicken boy flying toward him. Then he looked back at Shawnee, suddenly conscious of what he was doing and horrified that he was doing it. He took his hands, at once, from the Chief's neck.

What happened next took only seconds: The Chief, panicked, gasping for breath, bucked. Bruno's weight shifted and he began to slide off the Chief's stomach. The Chief lifted his ass off the ground, reached around to the waist of his pants and pulled free his hatchet, then threw himself upward and brought the hatchet down with all his strength. The blade sank into Bruno's flesh where the arm was joined to the right shoulder, at the socket. It fell to the bone and then it passed beyond the bone, chopping through the hard calcium and into the marrow of the joint's core.

Blood spurted like a geyser. All of the freaks screamed in unison. Bruno tried to climb to his feet, staggered, swooned, and fell backward. The Chief ran to him, pulled free the hatchet and thought, for just a second, about burying it once again, this time in the skull of the foreign interloper. Instead, he climbed to his feet, waved the bloody blade, hex-style, at the freaks, and ran, wild-eyed, out of the annex.

Kitty jumped off the stage, as did Fatos and Milena. They ran to Bruno, who was in the arms of the chicken boy, whose feathers were turning black as oil, painted by the spray of the blood. Bruno was starting to slip out of consciousness. He tried to speak and managed only a weak grunt. Bubbles of saliva formed on his mouth. His wounded arm sagged next to his body, attached only by flaps of skin and ligament and sinew near the pit.

Kitty and Milena tore sleeves from their gowns and Chick tried to tie off the wound, but the gash was too deep and wide and the flow of blood too rapid. The rags were soaked in seconds and did nothing to stanch the hemorrhage.

"Fatos," Chick yelled, "run and get the canvasman."

The mule sprinted from the annex. Behind Chick, Jeta could be heard vomiting and Durga was trying frantically to find a way off her stage. Now, Nadja, Aziz, Vasco and Marcel came running to join the strongman.

The chicken boy looked at his compatriots and struggled for something reassuring to say. But he could feel his feathers and the skin beneath them becoming saturated with the strongman's blood and this made him lightheaded. He wondered for a second if he were about to fade into the Limbo. But the father voice remained silent. And then Fatos was back with Forrest DeWitt and Dr. Taber, the yokel who had certified Lazarus Cole's death. For a moment, Chick didn't understand what Taber was doing here until he realized that the man must truly be a doctor of some kind.

Taber took one look at the injury and said, "Oh, Christ, this isn't good."

DeWitt gave him a shove toward Bruno. Taber went down on his knees next to Chick, looked more closely at the wound, and said, "We've got to get him into the clinic."

Nodding gravely, DeWitt said to Chick, "We can take the ringmaster's truck. I've got it waiting outside."

Bruno passed out completely when DeWitt and the doctor tried to lift him. With the help of Fatos and Milena, they carried the strongman out of the tent and laid him in the open bed of a dilapidated pickup. Kitty and Milena started to climb in and DeWitt said, "I don't think that's a good idea."

"I'll go," said Chick, hopping up into the bed. "The rest of you wait here. I'll send word as soon as I can."

The others did as the chicken boy instructed, stepping back from the vehicle and huddling into one another.

Taber and DeWitt climbed into the cab and gunned the engine, producing several backfires and a cloud of black smoke. They eased the truck into gear and drove rapidly across the fairgrounds in the direction of the county road.

Chick lay beside the strongman, cushioning Bruno's head, whispering in the patriarch's ear.

"I'm sorry," Chick said, over the rush of the wind. "I wish it didn't have to be this way.

"I chose you out of the world," the chicken boy whispered to the unconscious behemoth. "And the world will not love those who are not its own."

16

Nadia was sitting on the hood of the Honda, looking like a different person. The nurse's whites were gone and she was wearing a short black skirt and red silk halter and a pair of high-heeled sandals. She had let all that thick black hair down and it changed the look of her face. Her cheekbones seemed higher, more pronounced, and Sweeney thought her eyes were more almond-shaped.

She smiled when she saw him.

"How'd you know it was my car?" he asked.

"You look," she said, "like an Accord kind of guy," and he thought there was no way to take it as a compliment.

He came to a stop at the bumper and she leaned forward onto her knees.

"Aren't you beat?" he asked.

She shook her head. "It always takes me a while to come down. It's like, being around all that sleep . . ." and she rolled her eyes and shook her head and the thick hair, wavy and bordering on wild, bounced around her face.

"So where is this place?" Sweeney asked.

Nadia put out her hand and said, "It's probably easier if I drive."

AS SHE PULLED out onto Route 16, Sweeney adjusted the rearview and looked at the Peck.

"Jesus, it's ugly," he said.

"Doesn't it kill you?" Nadia said. "More money than God and they build this monstrosity."

"Maybe in its day," Sweeney said as the Clinic slipped off the mirror.

"That place," Nadia said, "was a goddamn tomb from day one."

They rode in silence for a quarter mile. It was an odd feeling. Except in cabs to the airports, Sweeney hadn't been a passenger in over a year, and he'd rarely been one in his own car. But it wasn't unpleasant, and Nadia was a smooth and confident driver. She accelerated up a rise and he looked down at her leg and saw a gold chain tight around her ankle. He turned on the radio, rolled the tuner until he came to some Al Green.

"It's weird," he said. "This thing was giving me some problems this morning."

"I've got friends with a garage," she said. "Just let me know."

"You from around here?"

She laughed and it was low and throaty and Sweeney moved in his seat.

"God, no," she said. "Can you imagine being from here?"

"I haven't seen much of the actual city," he said.

She took a quick right and suddenly they were moving through a no-man's-land of forgotten industrial parks — brick and concrete bunkers surrounded by dead fields. Sweeney counted three cars that were burned down to the frames and abandoned on the side of the road.

"You've seen the Clinic," Nadia said, "then you've seen the city. A bunch of comatose patients lying in an ugly warehouse."

He flinched and she noticed and said, "I'm sorry. I forgot. It's just a big, grimy mill town. You're not missing anything."

"You wanted," he said, "to talk to me about Danny."

She nodded.

"I'd rather wait, you know, till we're at the place. Till we can relax a little."

He started to reply and she said, "Shit. I forgot my cigarettes." She looked over at him and said, "You don't smoke, do you? You look like a health nut."

This he took as a compliment.

"I ate a dozen peanut butter crackers for dinner last night," he said.

Nadia turned her head toward him, pushed out her big lips, then said, "Well, keep it up, it's working."

She watched him flush and fed the Honda some gas.

He said, "I was a pothead in college. But I never smoked cigarettes."

"You were not," she said.

"I swear to God. I was stoned day and night for years."

"You don't look the type," she said.

An ad came on the radio and Sweeney turned it off and said, "Things have changed."

She took another turn. He realized that though he'd been watching the landscape roll by — warehouses and foundries and obsolete chemical plants — he hadn't been paying much attention to the route and he probably couldn't find his way back to the Clinic.

"I thought this place was close by," he said.

"You've got someplace else to be?" Nadia asked and he was a little surprised and put off by the way it came out. Nothing soft about it. No smile in its wake.

"I just don't like to be too far from Danny," he said.

"Danny'll be fine," she said. "You're the one I'm worried about."

Now they were driving past tenements, crumbling brownstones and row houses, heading toward a downtown section full of neon and traffic.

"Worried about?" he repeated.

She sighed and reached to the dash and turned the radio back on. The Moments were singing "Love on a Two-Way Street." She looked at him for so long that he got nervous and said, "Drive the car."

"I really didn't want to do this," she said, "until we had a couple of drinks in front of us."

"Do what?"

"I've worked at the Peck for a year, okay?" she said. "And before that I worked at Rasicott Memorial in Cincinnati. And before that at the Ford-Masterson in Phoenix. All right? I've seen a lot of people like you, Sweeney."

"How like me?"

"Like they're so angry and so guilty and so sick with grief that they're staying alive just to punish themselves."

He kept silent for a long minute and then, unexpectedly, Nadia took a left down a wide, dark avenue and came to a stop in front of a gravel lot full of motorcycles.

She sat staring at him, waiting for the response. He reached over and killed the engine and said, "You don't know me at all."

They both took it as a threat. She let it hang there for a while, then said, "Why don't we argue about it over an eye-opener?"

Nadia got out of the car, slammed the door and started walking toward a red brick ark next to the lot. Sweeney let himself watch her ass. Even in the heels, she finessed the gravel. She moved as if she knew he was watching. He pulled the keys from the ignition and followed her. The air was cooler than he'd expected and a little wet. It felt good on his face and he didn't want to go inside a stuffy bar. But she'd already entered the building through a pair of towering steel doors. So he jogged up the front walk to join her.

Carved into the granite arch above the entrance, in huge block letters, were the words

HARMONY PROSTHETICS.

The doors below featured two heavy brass bars that required pushing down for entry. Sweeney leaned on one bar, then the other, but both refused to budge. He blew out some air and looked back at his car. Then he put the keys in his pocket and pounded on the doors with his fist.

There was no answer. He moved around the side of the building and came to the gravel lot full of bikes. They were all Harleys, parked as if on display in a showroom, perfectly aligned, the forks angled just so. But they were all a mess, mud spattered and grease-caked.

He walked down the line, inspecting them, came to the last bike and put his hand, lightly, on the throttle.

And he heard, "Don't you fucking touch it."

It wasn't yelled. The words came out slow and even. He turned around and saw the speaker, skinny and bearded, all denim and leather, ass perched on an iron rail that fenced a concrete loading apron, which hung off the back of the factory and wrapped around the side. The biker had his torso angled to see Sweeney and he clutched a chicken leg in one fist.

Sweeney took his hand off the throttle.

"I was just admiring the bike," he said. "That's all."

The guy on the loading dock brought the drumstick to his mouth, tore off some meat, and began to chew. Before he was finished he said, "How 'bout I admire your faggot ass?"

Then there were three more of them glaring from the dock and Sweeney bolted for his Honda. But the bikers vaulted the rail and were on top of him before he cleared the line of Harleys. The fat one threw a body check and Sweeney went down to the gravel, protected his head but felt his palms shred. They pulled him up into a crouch and the skinny one, still holding his chicken bone, planted a knee in Sweeney's groin. He collapsed and lost his air but they didn't let him hit the ground. He closed his eyes and waited for the next blow, but found himself, instead, being hauled across the lot, half carried, half dragged, up a few stairs, across the dock, and inside the mill.

They deposited him in a chair. It took a few minutes for his eyes to adjust to the dimness. Music was playing, some old Santo and Johnny, but it got shut off as soon as he recognized the tune.

There was a small platoon of them, fanned out in a semicircle, most of the arms folded over the chests and everything bulging. The place smelled like Colonel Sanders and skunk beer and wet towels. Sweeney put his hands over his balls.

"You think you can fuck with other people's property?"

He focused in on the voice and saw Buzz Cote, the guy from the lunch counter at the Mart.

Sweeney stayed silent and Buzz stepped out from the semicircle, put a boot on the lip of Sweeney's chair and tipped him back until his head met the wall. He stayed that way, on the edge of falling. Buzz leaned over his own leg, brought a hand down to his boot, and then there was a Buck knife out in the air and Sweeney pulled in a breath and said, "Please don't do this."

Buzz said, "I asked you a question, shithead," and Sweeney answered, "Please, I've got a kid."

From someplace deep in the room, Nadia Rey yelled, "C'mon, boys, play nice."

Behind Buzz, one of the bikers let a laugh fly. And then everything was happening quickly. The knife was back in the boot and the chair was upright and Buzz was pulling Sweeney to standing and bear-hugging him like a lost brother and clapping his back hard enough to clear his lungs. And then the circle was disbanding with war whoops and whistles and cans of beer were being tossed hand to hand and popped open. The music started up again and the room seemed to brighten and Buzz had turned and pulled Sweeney to his side, arm wrapped around Sweeney's shoulder, and was walking him through a maze of bodies and around an engine that was leaking onto a floral bedsheet spread out in the middle of the floor.

Nadia was seated at a long metal table at the far end of what appeared to be an antique cafeteria. The room was lit by dozens of votive candles melting over every gritty surface. Buzz eased Sweeney down next to Nadia on an aluminum bench. Sweeney stared at the woman but couldn't say anything. Buzz sat next to Sweeney, sandwiching him in.

Nadia put what looked like a pie tin in front of Sweeney and began reaching for the bowls that crowded the table. She heaped the tin full of fried chicken, chili, and scrambled eggs, then tore a heel from a fat rye loaf.

She said, "You can't live on peanut butter crackers."

Someone threw Buzz a can of Hunthurst and he popped the top and set it in front of Sweeney, clapped his back again and said, "Sorry about the shot to the jewels. I told the Elephant to take it easy, but the shithead's dumber than a sack of bones. Drink up, you'll feel better."

Sweeney lifted his hand, felt how his bloody palm had gone tacky on his crotch. He wrapped the hand around the iced can and left it there. Buzz grabbed a bottle of Jack Daniels from somewhere under the table and guzzled. Sweeney looked past him and surveyed the room. It was a drab, gray dining hall, with one wall lined with hulking coffee and soda machines that looked like museum pieces. On the opposite wall were framed industrial safety posters, one of which read

ALL THAT SEPARATES YOU FROM YOUR CUSTOMERS
IS YOUR CONCENTRATION.

Above the posters, up near the ceiling, in huge black letters, half-printed and half-cursive, someone had spray-painted

GEHENNA.

"Try the eggs," Nadia said. "It's my own recipe."

"The girl," Buzz said, offering the bottle to Sweeney, "can fuckin' cook."

It was clear that Buzz wanted to see some eating. Sweeney picked up a fork and shoveled up some chili and eggs and put it in his mouth. The food was steaming and he grabbed the Hunthurst and took a pull. The beer cooled his tongue enough for his taste buds to go to work and his mouth was at once awash with flavor. There was something sweet and acrid, sharp and buttery. He got some pepper and some sugar and something on the edge of sour. With his second forkful, he came to realize how hungry he was. And then he was eating like a glutton, like a prisoner, and he was breaking a sweat and his eyes were watering.

When the tin was cleared, Sweeney let himself take a breath and then drained his beer. Nadia began to scoop seconds onto the pie plate, ladling the chili right over the eggs this time and squeezing a chicken breast up against the mix. She was cheered on by Buzz, who raised up slightly off his ass to hover over the table and say, "That's right, let's not shortchange this boy. There's plenty for everyone."

Then he turned to the rest of the clan, which was milling out at the far end of the lunchroom, and he yelled, "All right, now, come and get it, you savages."

They raced like children, bumping up against one another, jostling for position, shaking the table as they climbed onto the benches. They started to grab for forks and spoons but Buzz lifted the bottle of bourbon in a toast and they froze as if someone had blown a whistle.

"I want to welcome a special guest to Gehenna," he said. "And I want to thank Nadia for bringing him here."

He smiled in a way that was not entirely benign and turned to look on the nurse. "She gets some insane fucking notions from time to time," he said. "But don't she come through in the end? Here's to our girl."

Buzz brought the bottle to his lips and gurgled it and his crew erupted, cheering and pounding the table with fists. Then the noise stopped as everyone followed suit and began swilling from cans and bottles. From there, it turned into a kind of farcical cartoon. They went into a seated dance, eating as they grabbed, mouths open, the sound of belches filling the air. These were inhuman sounds, the kind of gnawing and slurping cacophony heard only around the seediest zoos.

At one point Nadia got up and collected empty bowls and Sweeney watched her move through a swinging door into what must have been a kitchen because she returned with more food. This time it was some sort of jambalaya that featured shrimp and sausage but it looked unlikely that any of Buzz's boys cared about or maybe even noticed the new selection. They simply continued shoveling it in as fast as their lungs and their gullets would allow.

Later, long after Sweeney had dropped his fork into his pie tin and pushed it away, the meal turned into a test of wills, a kind of contest. A few of the men started to look sick in a hungover fashion, a bit green and breathless and disoriented. They did a little stumble away from the table and waddled out of the cafeteria. The ones who were left kept their eyes on Buzz, but furtively. As for Buzz, he was consistent, machinelike. Every few spoonfuls, he'd close his eyes and dip his head and savor, then he'd clear his palate with a pull of beer or bourbon and turn back to the job. He never spoke but he would nod to Nadia or bump shoulders with Sweeney.

Toward the end, Nadia retreated to the kitchen once again with an armful of empty bowls, but this time she returned with only two mugs of coffee. She held onto one and put the other in front of Sweeney while she kept her eye on Buzz. Sweeney took a sip. It was black and oversugared.

"Why don't you two settle out in back," Nadia said. "I'll be right out."

Buzz nodded and started to rise from the table. He seemed to be in a fine mood, suffering no ill effects from the meal. "Take your coffee," he said to Sweeney and led the way to the loading dock where two wooden rocking chairs had been set at the edge of the apron.

The lot behind the Harmony looked like the face of a meteor. It was a deep canyon of rocks and broken bricks and, here and there, random pieces of black metal and piles of obsolete machinery. In its day, this acreage had housed one of the region's first industrial parks. But every mill except the Harmony had been more or less knocked down.

"That," Buzz said, gesturing to the remains of what had once been an enormous, phallic stack, "is what's left of the county crematorium. I always get kind of a kick out of the fact that they were neighbors, you know? The Harmony trying to piece folks back together. And the incinerator next door trying to burn 'em down to nothing."

Sweeney stayed quiet and watched the bikers running wild over the ruins, working off their feast by playing some variant on King of the Hill. This version of the game allowed bricks and stones to be hurled like grenades at the enemy. Most of the players were stripped to the waist and were howling at each other like rabid coyotes as they tried to charge up onto the roof of what looked like an abandoned hearse.

"It's a '67 Miller-Meteor," Buzz explained. "A beautiful vehicle. If you have to go with four wheels."

He eased down into one of the rockers, tapped the arm of its companion and said, "Boys'll be boys, huh?"

Sweeney sat down with both hands around his coffee mug.

"Most boys anyway," Buzz said, then changed the tone of his voice. "Now listen, Sweeney, I don't want you being pissed off at Nadia. None of this is her fault. You want to be pissed at someone, you be pissed at Buzz. You understand?"

"I'm not angry with — "

"'Course you're angry," Buzz said. "You're fucking furious. Be something wrong with you if you weren't. Someone you barely know drives you out to who knows where, you get ambushed by a bunch of fucking animals? Shit, yes, you're angry. You start off scared, but underneath," and here he arced a spitwad off the dock, "you're goddamn enraged."

"I'm not enraged," Sweeney said.

Buzz nodded and held his cigarette so that the smoke clustered in front of his face.

"Two things, son," he said, though he was probably younger than Sweeney. "First off, you're either lying to me or yourself. And believe me, we should both be hoping it's yourself. And second, I'm sitting here telling you it's all right. You got a right to be angry. People fear the unknown more than anything else. And you, son, are in the middle of the fucking unknown."

There was a yell and one of the bikers had a hand over an eye. Buzz stopped speaking to watch for a second, took a long drag and muttered, "Goddamn idiots."

Nadia came out the door, moved to the railing and said, "Does the Ant need a bandage?"

"Not yet," Buzz said. "Honey, could you get me a coffee and put a little Jack in it?"

She was looking out at the ruins a bit distractedly, but turned and went back inside.

Buzz waited till Nadia had gone, then said, "Now this is the point I'm trying to make. You look at these two out there, throwing bricks like children. They're fucking morons's what they are. But they're family. And morons or not, you look out for family. I mean, you know that. Look at what you've done for your boy."

The words focused Sweeney. Buzz reached across the space between them, patted and then squeezed Sweeney's arm. "What I'm trying to say is, there's not much difference between you and me. We do what we have to do to take care of our people. You see my point?"

Sweeney nodded and Buzz released his grip.

"Now, I don't want you to think for a minute that we're going to leave you hanging out there in the unknown. You take one look around, you see what I've made here, you know I'm not like that. You're a smart guy. That's obvious. You understand cause and effect. And I'm hoping that, in addition to being smart, you're patient. I'm going to clear everything up for you. But right now, before she comes back, I want to get straight about Nadia."

"There's no problem with Nadia," said Sweeney.

"And there shouldn't be," Buzz said, "What she done, she done for you and your boy. That's the fucking truth, Sweeney. You're gonna know that in time. But right now you have to take it on faith."

Down in the ruins, the game had degenerated into a straight-out rock fight. Nadia returned to the dock with a coffee mug in one hand and a roll of gauze in the other. She crossed in front of Sweeney, her eyes on the canyon, handed the mug to Buzz and put the gauze down on the apron.

"Who started it?" she asked.

Buzz said, "Who do you think?"

"Don't you think you should stop it?"

"We'll let them vent a while," Buzz said. "Fluke and the Ant've been hissin' at each other all week." He turned to Sweeney and said, "You didn't know we had dinner theater, did you?"

Sweeney put his coffee mug down on the concrete. He stood up and looked at Nadia, then turned his eyes on Buzz and said, "You touch my son, in any way, and I'll kill you."

Then he walked off the dock, expecting to be tackled. Expecting Buzz to yell for his animals. But no one stopped him and no one said a word. He let himself into the Honda, kicked over the engine, and drove away.

Two miles up the road, he pulled to the shoulder, opened his door, and vomited. It took him over an hour to find his way back to the Clinic. The car spewed black smoke the whole trip.

17

Sweeney ran into room 103 to find the Pecks, father and daughter, on either side of Danny's bed. Eyes burning, shirt stained with puke and chili, he stopped short in the doorway and looked from his son to the two doctors and back again. Alice seemed confused by his appearance and her father was about one step from appalled, but it was Sweeney who asked, "Is everything all right?"

The father let the daughter answer.

"Danny has a slight fever," she said. "That's not unusual. We've put him on an antibiotic."

"Are *you* all right, Mr. Sweeney?" the father asked. He was wearing a banker's suit and a red tie. There were figures on the tie but Sweeney couldn't make them out. A nurse entered the room, glanced at the scene, and moved on to tend to Irene Moore.

Sweeney shook his head, put his hands on his hips. "Danny's okay then?" he said.

"His condition is stable," Peck said, then he shifted his eyes and asked, "What happened to your hands?"

Sweeney looked down to his palms. Alice stepped toward him, took a hand, and inspected it.

"It's nothing," Sweeney said. "I fell down in the parking lot."

"In the Clinic lot?" Peck said.

"It's just a scrape," Sweeney said. "It's nothing."

"Did you put anything on this?" Alice asked.

Sweeney took his hand away. "I'm fine," he said. "Can I ask what antibiotic you prescribed?"

In Sweeney's experience, physicians tended to bristle when questioned by a pharmacist. Peck wouldn't even acknowledge the question. But he forgot about the scraped palms and that was the point.

"Azithromycin," Alice said. "It's a low-grade fever. He's running a hundred one. I'm not overly concerned."

Sweeney stepped past her, leaned over the bed, and put his lips on Danny's forehead. The boy was warm but he'd spiked much worse in the past. Sweeney pinched the elastic neck of the pajama top and found it dry.

He straightened and said, "Well, thank you both for looking in on him."

"He'll be fine," Alice said.

Sweeney nodded. "I'm just going to grab a quick shower and change up. I should be back in twenty minutes."

Alice smiled but her father said, "Didn't you work last night?"

And here it was, the capper to the morning. Ernesto had reported him, had gone to Peck about the fight.

He made eye contact with the doctor and said, "I did."

"Then shouldn't you be getting some sleep?" Peck said.

"I sleep in the evening," Sweeney said. "So I'm fresh for my shift."

But he understood that Peck knew it was a lie.

DOWN IN THE CELLAR, he stripped, threw his clothes on the closet floor, and stood under a cold shower. His hands stung as he washed them and his balls were still tender from the knee he'd taken. He stayed in the shower until he shivered. Then he toweled dry and threw on a T-shirt and a pair of jeans.

He thought about brewing some coffee but settled for a glass of tap water. He thought about calling Dr. Lawton back at St. Joe's, seeing if Danny could get his old bed back. The CVS probably wouldn't rehire him but there were still a few mom and pops that could use a weekend druggist. He'd sell the Honda here. And if he couldn't, he'd leave it in the parking lot. Let the Clinic deal with it. He and Danny would fly back together this time. He could call Mrs. Heller, see if she'd do some private duty again. The house was gone but he could lease one of those condos down on Mercury Drive.

He rinsed the glass, turned it upside down on the counter to dry.

People made mistakes. People used bad judgment. And it wasn't like he'd dreamed up this whole move himself. Lawton and the rest had recommended the Peck, said it was top-notch. Just the place for Danny. Things happened in everybody's life. You tried to make the most of it. You coped to the best of your ability. You repaired what you could and you moved on.

Better that he found out now. It was a mistake coming to this city. It was a mistake moving Danny. There was no way to have known that until after the fact. The thing to do now was to get Danny set up back in the St. Joseph and start inquiring about a job and a place to live.

He wondered now why he had ever believed in this place, why he had ever allowed himself to imagine something better. Dr. Peck was an arrogant prick at best. And maybe nothing more than a sham. This city was a circus and the Clinic was starting to seem like a freak show. Cleveland may have been hopeless but at least it was a known despair.

Once he had a bed for Danny, he'd tell the Pecks it had all been a mistake. He'd given it a try but things weren't going to work out. Thanks for the chance and all, but we're going home now. It would take at least a week. He'd have to find a nurse to fly with them. He'd have to book the reservations and make all the special arrangements with the airline. Goddammit, why hadn't he turned on the phone yet?

They'd get back to Cleveland and he'd call the woman, the therapist in Shaker Heights, first thing. He'd agree to new sessions. He'd agree to a script. He'd do group again, if he had to. He'd get back to the way it had been, focus on Danny and the job. He'd work on acceptance. He'd stop telescoping, projecting. He'd stop searching for radical procedures and miracle treatments. He'd admit to his fear and his rage. He'd take responsibility for his actions, acknowledge what a grand disaster this move had been.

He'd tell everyone, *I'm the bad father but I'm trying now. I'm flawed but I'm doing my best.* He'd go to Shaker Heights and talk about his pain. He'd go to Shaker Heights and say, *Give me a script. I'm ready for the script.* Then he'd take the pills faithfully. He'd visit with Danny and he'd work the job and he'd take the pills.

The first thing to do was to make some phone calls. He'd drive back down into town. He'd call from a pay phone, use a credit card. He'd call Dr. Lawton and Mrs. Heller. He'd beg, if need be. He'd say, *We've made a mistake and we just want to come home.* Then he'd call the Realtor that had sold his house and ask her to find him a new place. An apartment. Someplace small and near the St. Joseph. He could erase the last week. The last month. He could get back into the routine. He could get his old job back or find a new one. He could get Danny his old bed at the St. Joseph.

His heart was racing and his palms were stinging again and he felt a sudden need to look in on his boy.

Sweeney ran upstairs, climbed onto the bed next to Danny, positioned his mouth near the boy's ear, and began to explain that Dad had made a mistake. That pretty soon they'd be going back home to Ohio, back to the St. Joe and Dr. Lawton and Mrs. Heller. Things would be better, Sweeney promised, once they got back to Cleveland. As soon as they made it back home, he swore, things would go back to normal. He fell asleep muttering promises and stroking the child's head.

A NURSE WOKE him just after six, an older woman with a tight, sparse perm. He blinked up at her and when she came into focus, he started.

"He's holding steady," she said, "at one-o-one."

He ran a hand over his face, a tongue around his mouth, and sat up in the bed on an elbow.

"I went out like a light," he said and fingered some sleep out of his eyes.

The nurse uncoiled a pressure cuff from its basket mount on the wall.

"I know," she said. "I've been in and out and you were snoring like a bear."

"Sorry about that," Sweeney said. "Feel free to wake me if it happens again."

"You weren't bothering anyone."

She wrapped Danny's arm and pumped the ball.

"I wish we could get his temp down," Sweeney said, putting a hand to Danny's forehead. "He usually responds pretty quickly to the meds."

The nurse studied the meter, then released the pressure, unwrapped the cuff, and placed Danny's arm back on the bed. "I'm sure he'll be fine by morning," she said.

"I'm his father, by the way," Sweeney said.

He expected her to introduce herself but she only smiled at him and asked, "Is Daniel your only one?"

Sweeney nodded. "Yeah," he said. "He's unique."

The word sounded ridiculous but the nurse didn't react.

"I've got five," she said, shaking her head as if still unable to believe the fact, "and they're all individuals. All characters. Every one of them."

"Do they live around here?"

She gave him a look that said he was joking and that it was a cruel joke.

"They get home for the holidays," she said. "And sometimes I go out there."

She straightened Danny's sheet, then wrote something on the chart that hung above the sphygmomanometer. When she was finished writing, she asked, "Is there anything I can get you?"

"No thank you," Sweeney said.

The nurse started to leave the room and he asked, "Aren't you going to check on Ms. Moore?" Irene was, as usual, curtained from his sight.

The nurse acted surprised. "I already did," she said, a little testy, and then exited the room.

Sweeney went to Danny's closet, found a facecloth, and soaked it with cold water. He wrung it close to dry, came back to the bed, and gently washed the boy's face and neck and arms. He threw the cloth in the hamper next to the closet, kissed his son, and went to the cafeteria.

Once again, the room was empty, but there was evidence of recent activity. A radio next to the utensil rack was playing "Don't Let the Green Grass Fool You," and the music in the empty room was just one more in a train of the day's unsettling sensations. Sweeney bought some machine coffee and a machine bagel, but gave up on the bagel halfway through. He picked up the local paper from an uncleared table and began to read about people and situations that were entirely unknown to him. The stories were close to unintelligible. He threw the paper in the trash with the bagel and, unsure of what else to do, started to clean up the cafeteria.

He was wiping down a table with a handful of napkins when he heard Alice Peck say, "Here you are."

He turned. She was dressed in a black skirt and a white blouse that shimmered a little under the fluorescents. Her hair was pulled back and up, and she wore dangling earrings. She had a black throw over her arm and was holding a glossy black clutch.

"Well," was what Sweeney managed, and then, "You look terrific."

Alice raised her eyebrows as if she'd been waiting for something else, but she said, "Thanks."

Sweeney threw the ball of napkins at the trash. It missed and dropped to the floor.

"Did you get called in unexpectedly?" he said, then flinched and added, "It's not Danny, right? I was just up there."

Alice shook her head.

"I guess we missed signals here. I thought we were going to dinner."

Sweeney took a step closer and said, "Excuse me?"

"Didn't you get my message? I left a message on your machine. I said I'd pick you up at seven."

"I don't have a machine," Sweeney said. "I don't have a phone."

"No," Alice said. "Human resources gave me the number."

"I'm not following this," Sweeney said. "I mean, I know we had talked about getting together outside at some point. But we didn't say tonight."

She began to shake her head and strands of hair came free and floated down by her ears.

"But we did," Alice said. "We specifically said tonight. Remember? Then I told you I'd call and confirm it? And I did. I called and left the message. I said I'd come by the apartment at seven."

"Jesus," Sweeney said. "I don't think so. I don't — "

She cut him off with a wave of the hand.

"You know what," she said, "it's not a problem. We'll do it another time. Or actually, we can just meet in my office."

"No, please. You're getting the wrong idea. I don't know what's the matter with me. I honestly don't remember specifying tonight. Jesus Christ. What the hell's the matter with me?"

She stepped in and touched his arm. She eased him into a chair, pulled up its mate, and sat down opposite him.

"It's all right," she said. "Stress can do some real damage to short-term memory. This isn't a big deal. You've had an overwhelming week."

"We decided on tonight?" he said. "Really, it was tonight?"

She nodded.

"I've got nothing," he said. "I have no recollection of that. I remember we said we'd talk, but that's it."

"You should really try to get some sleep," she said. "Sleep is the great healer."

They sat quietly for a while and he tried to think.

"I'm so sorry," he said. "This is pathetic. I feel awful."

He put a hand over his face and squeezed his eyes shut. He heard her say, "This is my fault. I was being presumptuous." Then he felt her pulling his wrist away from his face. He opened his eyes and saw her nails were painted a deep rose.

"Can you give me five minutes?" he said and she started to protest.

"Oh, no. That's not necessary."

"I think," he said, "maybe it is. I should get out of this place for a while and eat some real food and talk to someone who can talk back."

"Are you sure you're up to it?" she asked.

"Give me five minutes," he said and stood up. "I'll meet you out in front."

He held up his hand and splayed his fingers. "Five minutes," he repeated. "And I promise I won't forget."

She looked at the gashed palms and smiled and said, "I've got a better idea."

18

To get to the Peck residence from inside the Clinic one had to walk a long corridor off the third floor that bridged the main house to the east wing. There were no rooms off the corridor and no windows, just one narrow, tunnellike expanse piled with discarded rehab equipment. Everything was old and bulky-looking, wooden wheelchairs and tarnished brass walkers and even a few bell jars. Behind a mattress that was leaning against the wall, Sweeney spotted several prosthetic legs.

Alice had her key out before they got to the door.

"There's a separate entrance from outside," she said. "Normally, that's what I'd use. I like some division between work and home. But with the rain and all . . ."

She let the sentence trail off as she tried to work the lock.

"Can I help you with that?" Sweeney asked as she turned the bolt and opened the door onto a large, dome-ceilinged room. Sweeney crossed the threshold first. Alice snapped on the lights and locked up behind herself.

The room was a library, the walls book-lined and the floor covered with an enormous Indian rug over dark hardwood. The furniture was antique but masculine — English club chairs and a big Kipling desk devoid of photos or knickknacks, except for a glass terrarium in which a salamander sat so rigidly that for a second Sweeney thought it was made of porcelain.

"My father's study," Alice said.

"That would have been my guess," Sweeney said.

"He's out tonight. He still lectures at the med school."

He nodded and looked past her. Behind the desk, on the only wall not given over to shelving and books, was an oil painting, a formal portrait, dark and severe. The woman depicted was blond and a bit too fragile to be called beautiful. Sweeney looked from the painting to Alice and said, "Your mother?"

"My mother," Alice said. "She died when I was a child."

There was a credenza stationed beneath the portrait, and on top of it, a row of books, thick volumes, uniformly bound in red leather. Sweeney read the gilt titling on the spine and saw they were all copies of the same text — *Perchance to Wake: On the Causes and Treatments of Coma.* By W. Micah Peck.

"What's the W stand for?" Sweeney asked.

"William."

"What's he got against the name William?"

"Only his parents called him William," Alice said. "We should really go downstairs. My father doesn't like people in his study."

Sweeney followed her out of the room and down two flights of a semi-grand staircase to the first floor. In the foyer, they came upon a small, wide woman struggling into a yellow rain slicker. There were two bulging plastic bags resting near her feet.

"*Maneja con cuidado, Lucila,*" Alice said.

The woman pulled a hood up over her head and lifted her bags.

"*El cordero está en el horno,*" she said. "*Te veo el lunes.*"

Alice opened the front door for her and Sweeney could see the storm had picked up. The woman ran out to a battered Volvo in the driveway. Alice waited until Lucila was in the car before she closed the door.

"Our housekeeper," she said. "She's from Miravago."

She led him to the dining room, talking as she went.

"Her people disappeared years ago. Father and I are all the family she has left."

The dining room was small and, like what he'd seen of the rest of the house, dark and Victorian. A hearth on the interior wall had a fire blazing in it.

"But she doesn't live with you?" Sweeney said.

"She's got a place in the city," Alice said, and then put a hand out toward the table. "Sit. Get comfortable. I'll be right back." She started for the door, stopped, and turned back to him. "Do you eat lamb?"

"Lamb's great," Sweeney said. "Thank you. This is really nice of you."

"I eat alone much too often," she said and moved into the kitchen.

Sweeney walked to the hearth, thought about taking the poker and stoking the logs, but found himself, instead, studying the paintings that lined the walls. They were all portraits, all done in the same style as the one in the study, some of them, maybe, done by the same artist. The house, Sweeney realized, looking at all the pale and bony faces, was a museum to the Peck gene pool. There was probably a historical register up in Daddy's library that would trace a fairly straight bloodline of doctors and scientists. A few founders of cities and banks with maybe a hemophiliac or two dangling from the family tree.

He heard the clatter of china and then Alice backed her way into the room, pushing through the swinging door. She was carrying a serving tray that held plates, glasses of wine, and napkins full of silver. She placed the tray on the table, said, "Be right back," and vanished again into the kitchen.

Sweeney inspected the meal. A single, overlarge lamb chop was on each plate, and he knew they'd been cut from a full rack. Each chop was drizzled with a brown glaze and accompanied by a few tiny red potatoes, three stalks of asparagus, and a spoonful of mint jelly.

Alice returned with quilted placemats and a large box of stick matches. Sweeney hadn't seen matches like these in years. She set their places, transferred the plates and crystal from the tray to the mats, removed the tray to a sideboy, and lit two candles that rested in simple pewter holders at the center of the table.

"I hope the wine is okay," she said.

"I'm sure it's fine," Sweeney said.

Alice smiled, motioned for him to sit, and said, "No, I mean, I know you're working later."

"Actually," Sweeney said. "I'm off tonight. Unless you heard something different."

"No," she said. "I don't make out the staff schedules."

He couldn't tell if she was joking. They sat down and he raised his glass to her.

"Thanks again."

"You're welcome," she said. "Honestly, it's a pleasure to have some company. Half my meals, I read patient files."

He cut a piece of meat and put it in his mouth. It was tender but flavorless and he wondered what was the purpose of the glaze.

"This is delicious," he said.

Alice nodded, finished chewing, and said, "Lucila is a marvelous cook." She took a sip of wine and added, "There's more in the kitchen."

Sweeney speared a potato and glanced around the table for a salt or pepper shaker. There were none.

"You've lived here your whole life?"

"I was raised here," nodding and sipping. "I went away for college and medical school."

"You always knew you wanted to be a doctor?"

"It's in the blood," Alice said.

"I know what you mean," Sweeney said. "My father was a druggist. That's what he always called himself — a druggist. And my wife was one also. But the tradition comes to an end with me."

It was a stupid thing to say and he was embarrassed it had slipped out. They gave up a few seconds of silence and drank their wine. Sweeney clinked his crystal against his plate as he set the glass back on the table.

"Well," Alice said. "I'm in the same position."

He looked across the table at her and she smiled. And then it dawned on her what she'd said. She brought a hand to her mouth, then took it away.

"I'm so sorry," she said. "Of course, I'm not in the same position at all. I didn't mean —"

"It's okay," Sweeney said. "Relax."

"That was a foolish thing to say," she said. "What I meant was there's no one to . . ."

He started to let her struggle and realized he didn't want that.

"No heir," he said. "You meant that there's no heir. No one to carry on the Peck tradition."

She nodded, shook her head, tilted it back.

"You can see," she said, "why I dine alone."

"I can see," he said, and pointed with his fork to the portraits rimming the room, "why tradition could be a concern."

Alice smiled, and it seemed genuine and grateful. She brought her napkin up from her lap and dabbed at her lips and said, "Can we start over?"

"There's no need," Sweeney said. "We're doing fine."

Then she surprised him by saying, "So what really happened to your hands?"

He forked a stalk of asparagus and said, "Told you. I fell down in the parking lot. But in case you're worried, I'm not going to sue."

"You looked like you were having some difficulties this morning."

"I'm not a morning person," he said. "So why won't there be any Peck heirs?"

His question was a little harsh, maybe, but it sent the right message — we both have things we don't want to discuss. She finished the wine in her glass and said, "I should've brought the bottle in."

Sweeney rose and said, "Allow me," and Alice didn't object. He pushed through the swinging door and into the kitchen. It was large and old. Soapstone sinks and wainscoting and bad lighting. The Merlot was sitting next to a greasy roasting pan that held the rest of the chops. He grabbed the wine, moved back into the dining room, and filled Alice's glass to just below the brim.

He returned to his seat, topped off his glass and said, "You come up with an answer yet?"

"Nothing witty," she said. "Just the truth."

"And that is?"

"That the days when you could be married to medicine and raise a family on the side are gone."

"I knew a lot of doctors back in Ohio," Sweeney said. "And most of them were married and had kids."

Alice shrugged. "There's practicing medicine," she said. "And then there's the way the Pecks practice medicine."

Sweeney put on a mock grimace and said, "Excuse me." The wine made the words more sarcastic than he'd intended.

"I know what that sounds like," Alice said. "But like my father told me on my first day of med school, obsession is a requirement."

"And you still think Dad is right?"

"I know he's right," all kidding and flirting gone from her voice suddenly. "My father's always right."

Sweeney stayed silent, let the last words hang there, hoping she'd laugh at them. Instead, Alice continued.

"We're not bonesetters, Sweeney. We're out on the edge. Part of what my father and I do, maybe the most important part of what we do, is draw maps of the human mind. Our patients are helping us redefine beliefs about consciousness. Where it begins and where it ends and what it is."

"I'm glad," Sweeney said, "that Danny could assist you."

It was a snide comment but she'd been running toward pompous and he didn't like it. It made her resemble her father.

"I'm not trying to hurt you or offend you," she said. "And I'm certainly not trying to hurt your son. But you came to us because we're doing things that no one else in the field is doing."

"I came to you," Sweeney said, "because I was told you could help my son. I don't care what you do or don't discover in the process. And you don't have to talk to me like I'm on some grant committee."

"We don't take a dime," she said, rigid now, as if it were a point of honor, "from the federal government. Or from any private foundations. Or from the drug companies. We're funded exclusively by patients' fees, contributions, and the Peck Family Trust."

He'd touched some kind of nerve so he probed a little.

"And the reason for that would be?"

She looked at him as if the answer were obvious.

"We're not beholden to anyone," she said. "Outside of fulfilling our licensing and accreditation requirements, we can run the Clinic as we see fit."

"So independence is important to you," he said.

"In this area of research," preaching now, "it's crucial."

He worked his tongue to free a piece of gristle from between two teeth, then said, "Why?"

She repeated the word and he nodded and said, "I don't mean any disrespect, Alice. I really don't. But for almost a year now I've been hearing about this place. People talk in a kind of reverent way about the Peck" — she smiled at that — "like it's Lourdes, or something. Dr. Lawton said if I could get Danny into the Peck, I shouldn't hesitate. I had to go. So I read everything I could find on you people and I made application. And now here I am, and Danny's got a bed, and I'm having dinner with his neurologist. And I've still got no idea why this place is considered the Mecca."

"But you know about our results — " she began and he cut her off.

"You've had two arousals," he said.

She squinted at him, as if he'd wandered into a language she couldn't comprehend.

"That's right," she said. "And they were both persistent and semivegetative cases."

"And how do you know you were responsible for those wakings?"

"How do we know?" she said, stunned by the recklessness of the question. "For God's sake, we're scientists, Sweeney. We monitor our results scrupulously. We test and retest. We don't make claims we can't validate."

"Then why haven't the full case studies been published?"

"They will be published," she said. "Of course they'll be published. But there are procedures. These things take a lot of time. For precisely that reason, so results can be confirmed definitively. So we don't give false hope."

"I understand that," he said, more frustrated than he expected. "And I'm not suggesting the arousals were spontaneous. I'm sure they weren't. But you said yourself that your patients are helping you redefine your techniques — "

"Beliefs," she corrected. "I said beliefs."

He hurried so he wouldn't lose the thought.

"And my son is one of those patients now. And I have no idea what your beliefs, or your techniques for that matter, are. I'm his father. And I have no idea. What are you doing here that isn't being done elsewhere?"

She looked at him for a while as if trying to decide something, then took her napkin from her lap and put it on the table. She looked at her wristwatch and said, "You're not working tonight?"

He shook his head.

"Then let's do this," she said. "I'll clear the plates and you go into the living room and pour a couple of brandies and we'll talk some more."

She got up and started collecting the china before he could answer.

The living room was off the other side of the foyer. There were no ancestors here, but hung over the mantel was a gargantuan photo of the Clinic, matted and framed, pressed under heavy glass and dating, Sweeney guessed, from the turn of the last century. The building had been photographed at either dawn or dusk and the trees that today surrounded it had yet to be planted. As a result, the picture looked like a still from some early German horror film and he wondered what would possess anyone to make it the showpiece of the room.

On the opposite wall, hanging over an uncomfortable-looking couch that was too small for the room, was a family portrait, done in heavy oils. The portrait featured a young Dr. Peck, his wife, toddler Alice, and a scrawny preteen boy, who had to be an unmentioned son and brother. For such a young clan, and despite the artist's best efforts, the family looked so deeply unhappy that after a few minutes, Sweeney realized he preferred the photo of the Clinic above the mantel.

Logs were stacked on the grate of the fireplace but they hadn't been lit. He saw another box of kitchen matches on the mantel but decided to see if Alice wanted a fire. Next to the hearth was an antique grandfather clock and next to the clock, a small built-in closet with glass panel doors. He opened it and inspected the bottles inside, took down a cognac and filled the bottom of two snifters.

She came in and caught him with his nose above one of the glasses.

"Are you a connoisseur?"

"If you only knew," handing her a glass, "how funny that question would be to a lot of people back home."

She put her drink on the mantel and grabbed the matches, kneeled down before the grate and, in seconds, had a fire building.

"I would've done that," Sweeney said and helped her to her feet.

"It's fussy," she said. "Takes a special touch."

She held onto his hand and led him to the couch but they sat at opposite ends.

He took a sip of cognac and swallowed too quickly and in a second his eyes started to water. He blinked a few times and when he looked up she was staring at him.

"I know what you want," she said. "And it's impossible."

He let himself wipe at his eyes and said, "It is?"

"You want what they all want. All the loved ones. All the family members. Especially the parents. It's completely natural and completely unreasonable."

"I'm glad to know I'm not alone," he said.

She placed her glass atop a felt coaster on the coffee table and came

forward to lean on her knees. "All right," she said. "Let's get into it then."
She straightened her skirt over her knees and put her hands together as
if to pray. "You want me to take a lifetime's worth of highly specialized
research and give it to you in ten minutes. You want it jargon-free, trans-
lated into layman's terms. And you want the end result of that translation
to be an answer to your prayers."

He took another drink and made an effort this time to swallow correctly.

"You make it sound like a chore," he said.

"Am I wrong?" But it wasn't really a question. He looked across the
room to see that the fire had already died out.

"I doubt," he said, "that the Pecks are wrong very often."

When she ignored the comment and launched her spiel, he understood
that she agreed with him.

"Here's the problem. We're dealing with an extremely emotional issue.
And yet, in order to accomplish anything at all, I have to be blunt. From
your point of view, your son has been stolen from you."

"From my point of view," he repeated but she just went on.

"It's as if he's been kidnapped. And in a real sense, he has been. One instant, Danny was a normal, healthy six-year-old. And in the next instant,
he's something else altogether."

"He's still Danny," he said but there wasn't much conviction in it.

"Okay," Alice said, "this is where it gets tough. Is he really? Can we
honestly say he's still Danny?"

He bit down on the impulse to defend his son. He said, "I'm not sure
I'm following."

"We're talking about basic questions of identity, Sweeney. Who we are
is, in large part, determined by how we perceive our world."

He shook his head. "So if Danny doesn't perceive the world, what? He
doesn't exist?"

"You're going off track," she said. "You're trying to jump ahead of me.
I didn't say that."

"Jesus, Alice. You're making my son into a game for stoners."

"Try to stick with me," she said. "Listen to what I'm saying."

"If Danny falls in the woods," he said, "and I'm not there to hear him —"

"Calm down," Alice said. "You're not listening. One of the reasons that
coma is so frustrating — and fascinating — is that it forces us to deal with

some root beliefs. And *this*," coming down on the word, "is exactly where the Peck differs from every other facility I know of."

She let herself take a drink.

"The majority opinion would say that in most stages of coma, our sensory apparatus is shut down. Some sort of trauma causes the brain to turn off most of the higher functions. The patient exists in a state of profound unconsciousness."

He was listening but he was also thinking of Danny pre-accident. Flashing back to their last Saturday, the day of the accident. Thinking of his son, for some reason, propped up on a booster seat in the barber's chair, getting his hair cut. The barber was trying to ask him what he thought of the Indians this year, but Danny wouldn't answer. The boy just stared across the short distance between himself and Sweeney, his head looking so small above the tent of a blue nylon sheet that covered his body.

"What I'm saying is that the patient's brain is no longer receiving information along the sense pathways. So the patient is sent into a void. He's in a black hole. I know this is hard but it's necessary."

He mimicked Alice's actions, brought his drink to his lips and let a little brandy into his mouth. He heard her words and he understood them. He nodded to acknowledge this understanding. But he was thinking of Danny in a barber's chair.

"The average neurologist would tell you that soon after he arrives in that void, that black hole, the average coma patient becomes a vegetable. They lose any vestige of sentience."

There was nothing special about this trip to the barber's. There was nothing, no incident good or bad, that should have impressed such a vivid memory. But there it was, as clear, in this moment, as the woman lecturing before him. Danny, his mouth set in a manner that could turn, at any instant, into a smile or a frown, as flakes of his fine, soft hair floated down around him to rest on his nose and on the blue sheet.

"But there are two things wrong with this notion. The first is that there's no such thing as an *average* coma patient. And the second is that no neurologist that I know of has ever visited that black hole. So what they're telling us is conjecture."

Father and son never broke eye contact throughout the duration of the haircut. At points, Sweeney felt as if Danny were trying to tell him something. But mostly, in the midst of this mundane Saturday morning, this common and forgettable trip to the barbershop, he felt there was a moment of unexplained and binding love, radiating back and forth between the two of them.

Alice took another sip, looked across the room at the fireplace, then back at Sweeney.

"Everything that my father and I have discovered over the course of our careers tells us that those doctors have no right to their conjectures. The brain is a stunningly versatile organ. And the mind is an entity that we understand only in the most infantile ways."

And then the haircut was over and Barber Ray spun Danny in the chair, broke their eye contact. But only for an instant because Danny found Dad again in the mirror, watched his father rise and come forward to stand behind his son. He watched his father place a hand on the nylon sheet — Sweeney could feel it now, cool and silky against his skin — and barely squeeze the bony shoulder beneath. And Barber Ray was brushing off the cuttings, the small feathers of kid hair, as he asked Danny how he liked the haircut. And Danny said, "Good" — just the one word and not very loud. But he continued to stare at his father in the mirror. To look at the face, the eyes. As if to say, *I dreamed of you before I knew you.*

"What I believe, and what my father believes, is that if you shut down all sensory information to the brain, you do, in fact, separate the patient from our universe. From consensual reality, I'll call it. And maybe there is a period of passage through a void. A black hole. But I don't believe the patient's mind, their consciousness, dies. I don't believe they reside permanently in the void."

Her last words pulled him loose from the memory and he said, "Then where do they reside?"

"I think," she said, "they construct another reality. Another universe. One that doesn't need the prompts of touch and taste and smell and sight and sound."

"And what," he asked, "do they build that universe out of?"

"Who knows? I don't know. To say I do would be worse than arrogant. It would be a lie. But I can guess that, whatever the building materials, the comatose universe is entirely alien to our own."

Sweeney got up without being asked, moved to the fireplace, sat down on the floor and started to rearrange the logs.

"It's an interesting theory," he said. "But how does it help Danny? How do I get him back into my universe?"

"I want to answer your question," she said, "with another question. But it's a hard one for you to hear."

She got up from the couch and joined him, but left her shoes under the coffee table. She sat down on her heels and he watched her skirt ride up her thighs.

"I'm guessing," he said, "that I've withstood worse."

"How do you know," she said, "that he wants to come back?"

He lit a match, held it beneath a piece of kindling, and watched strands of wood start to glow. "He wants to come back," he said, "because he wants to be with me. Because his father loves him more than his own life."

"And he knows that?"

It seemed like a test, so even though he felt the anger coming on, he tried to keep ahead of it.

"He knows that, yes."

She didn't respond, just opened her eyes a little wider. It made her face lose a good deal of its beauty and he shook out the match just before it burned his finger. Then he lit another.

"He knows because before the accident I showed him every day. And since the accident, I've stayed next to him as much as I could and I've told him that I love him."

"There's a good chance," Alice said, "that he doesn't hear you."

He felt himself slip a bit, felt the defensiveness pushing its way into his voice. He said, "He hears me," and felt her shrug even though he didn't see her shoulders move.

"He's stage six," she said. "I'm not saying it isn't possible. But it isn't probable."

"Danny hears me when I talk to him."

"Do you think I'm being cruel?"

"You're being," Sweeney said, pausing, "a doctor."

"I'm preparing you," she said. "You're going to be invited to the first team assessment soon. It can be a difficult experience for the families."

"I'll cope."

She finished her drink and said, "I'm not so sure. You're functioning under some really debilitating stress. That takes its toll on everyone over time."

"I've spent a year being patronized by the best neurologists in Ohio," he said. "I'll handle the meeting."

In a week, he hoped, he'd be back in Cleveland, visiting Danny at the St. Joseph every day, working third shift at a Wonder Drug or an independent. Taking his medication and waiting for it to build up in his system. Waiting for the drug to accumulate enough power in his brain to numb down the rage and the fear.

"I'll help you out," Alice said, "as best I can. In spite of what I've said, I think Danny's a promising candidate for waking."

"Let's say the rest of the team agrees with you. What happens then?"

"Danny would be put in the RAT program."

He stared at her.

"Radical Arousal Therapies," she said. "We've gotten approval recently to start using a new battery of drugs and procedures. If Danny's recommended for the program, I'll go over all of them with you."

"And if he's not recommended?" he asked because he thought she'd expect it.

"Don't get ahead of yourself. Let's wait and see what happens at the assessment."

The second match managed to burn him. He dropped it and put his thumb in his mouth. She took his wrist, pulled the hand to her, and inspected the damage.

"Do you want me to get some ointment?"

He shook his head and she released his hand and he wiped the thumb on his pants leg and nodded toward the logs.

"I don't think it's going to catch," he said.

Alice hugged her knees. "There's something wrong with the flue. It's never worked right. I guess my mother was the only one who could make a fire in here."

"How old were you when she died?"

"I was about Danny's age," she said. "About six. I've got a few memories."

"Was it sudden?"

He watched her look down on her knees.

"It was to me," and she let out a small and awkward laugh. "She spent a year stockpiling Valium. And then she took them all in a single night."

"I'm sorry," he said, and thought of all the times he'd heard the same, feeble words.

"I guess she had a problem with it. I was a child. I didn't know anything. She went away once for treatment. But it didn't take."

"In my family," he said, "they called it the creature."

Her face lightened. "The creature," she said. "I like that."

Sweeney nodded. "It works," he said. "I had a couple of uncles. They were legendary."

"It's a genetic malady," Alice said. "People like you and me need to be careful."

He wondered if she'd smelled the beer off him this morning. "I don't know," he said. "It's never done much for me one way or the other."

She gave him a long look that he thought was going to evolve into another lecture. But then she smiled and turned her body and stretched out on her back on the floor next to him. It would have been a surprise move had there been a fire burning before them. Without the blaze, he found it just short of bizarre. She closed her eyes for a second, opened them, reached out, and put a hand on his knee.

That it made him feel like an adolescent was off-putting. But the sight of her, in the tight skirt and the silk blouse and the thin gold chain around the neck, was making him hard for the first time in a year.

And so, before he could think, before he could remind himself that he planned on running home in the next week, he leaned over and kissed her. Her eyes closed again and her hand found his head and the fingers plowed through the hair over his ears and he kissed harder, leaned lower, and brought a hand to the side of her waist. And then her tongue was easing into his mouth and they were like high school kids, panicked and thrilled by the rush of enzymes and hormones, sweat breaking, noises building in the throat. He swung a leg over her, straddled her, and came down chest to chest. He felt her wedge a hand between them and grab at his crotch through his pants.

He reared up in a kind of amazed fear, born of both the realization that he was still functional and the lack of control that he'd never before known. His hand pushed down her thigh, found the hem of her skirt, and started up again and the sensation of touching the warm, silken skin brought him, almost instantly, to the verge of coming. He began to clench and something changed and she began to push him off her body. Then he heard the car door slam in the drive outside and understood that her alarm had nothing to do with his hesitation and everything to do with the return of her father.

"You've got to go," she was saying, a panic in her voice that made her sound like a teenager. "It's Daddy."

She shoved him off and stood up, began straightening her clothing and hunting down her shoes. He looked around the room, helpless, infected by Alice's alarm. She was hopping on one foot, storklike, an arm behind her trying to jam toes into a shoe.

"Up to the study," she said, trying to yell through a whisper. "Leave the way we came in."

He ran for the stairs and on the second landing heard the front door open. Then he stopped running and walked, small steps, balls of his feet, to Dr. Peck's study. He let himself in and moved for the opposite door that led back to the Clinic. But before he stepped into the hallway, he took another look at the portrait of the doctor's wife, then helped himself to a copy of the doctor's book.

He closed the door to the study and looked out on the long, narrow corridor stretching in front of him. In that instant, the booze coupled with his exhaustion, and the hall began to tilt and expand. Sweeney placed a hand against the wall to steady himself. And as he did, the doctor's text fell open and the comic book pressed inside dropped to the floor.

Going down on one knee, he picked up the comic and stared at its cover, which featured the strongman, Bruno Seboldt, lying on a patch of straw and dirt, in a vast puddle of his own scarlet blood. The issue was in pristine condition, as if it had never been read. Used only, perhaps, as a place marker in the fat medical tome.

The surprise of finding the comic inside Dr. Peck's book gave way almost immediately to that reflexive fear, that compulsive desire to check in on Danny. As if the discovery of the comic were an omen. Sweeney stood up slowly and placed the issue back where he had found it, tucked the text under his arm and hurried down the corridor. And, in seconds, he was lost.

The route that Alice had taken from hospital to residence had been relatively short and direct, and Sweeney was certain that he had retraced it correctly. But at some point, he'd gotten himself turned around and ended up in a dim and narrow passage that dead-ended in an eaves that was crowded with dusty file boxes. He reversed direction and tried to work his way back to familiar ground. In minutes, he was completely disoriented and fighting a small panic.

And just when he was beginning to consider heading back to the Peck home, he found what he knew was the correct hallway and jogged to the door at its end. He pulled it open to find Romeo, the janitor, standing like a statue, his hands tight around a mop handle and a smile on his face as if he'd been expecting Sweeney.

"You out exploring again?" Romeo asked.

Sweeney stared at him for a second and then ran past him, sprinting all the way to Danny's room.

He found his son in his bed, clean and warm and safe. Sweeney sat down on the ward's empty middle bed and tried to breathe normally and stop his hands from shaking. After a time, as if it were the only way to calm himself, he pulled the issue of *Limbo* from Dr. Peck's book, lay back, and began to read.

LIMBO COMICS

FROM ISSUE # 8: "To Flee the Rising Moon"

The chicken boy waited in the corridor of the county clinic, a blanket wrapped around his blood-soaked feathers. Nothing, however, covered the protruding beak, and the few doctors and nurses and aides who passed by couldn't hide their shock and revulsion.

It was hours before the surgeon came. He was a tall, stout man who did not offer his name. He had the bearing of a sadistic policeman, though he was still dressed in yellow surgical garb that was stained about the midsection.

"You're the one who came in with him," the surgeon said.

Chick roused himself and let the blanket slip to the chair as he stood and nodded.

"You're both with the Jubilee, I take it?"

Another nod.

"I ask," said the surgeon, "because I've never seen you before."

"How is my friend?" Chick asked.

"He lost a considerable amount of blood," the surgeon said. "I'm afraid I had to amputate the arm."

Chick again nodded his understanding.

"He's stable," the surgeon continued. "You can go in and see him in a few minutes."

"Thank you," Chick said.

"Don't thank me," the surgeon said. "It only makes this more difficult."

"Makes what more difficult?" Chick asked.

"Normally," putting his hands on the small of his back and stretching, "a procedure like this, I'd like to keep the patient under my care and supervision for several days, perhaps a week."

"Normally," Chick repeated.

"But it's my understanding that this man is indigent."

Chick stared, unsure of what to say.

"Is that correct?" the surgeon asked. "He has no papers? No money? No insurance?"

"It looks that way," Chick said.

"Well, if that's the case—" the surgeon began but Chick interrupted immediately.

"I understand what you're saying. As soon as he's ready to travel, I'll take him with me."

IT WAS CLOSE to dawn when Bruno came awake. Chick was in the chair next to the strongman's bed, just coming out of a mild seizure. He wiped the bile from his beak and opened his eyes to see the patriarch staring at him, a slack anesthesia-cast to his huge face.

"You knew it would happen," Bruno said in a dry voice. "You knew they'd take my arm."

Chick shook his head, got up, and sat on the edge of the bed.

"You're going to be fine," he said. "You lost a lot of blood. But the doctor says you'll be okay."

"I'm going to be fine?" Bruno said.

Chick put a hand on the giant's chest.

"Let me ask you," Bruno said. "Have you ever known a strongman with only one arm?"

"I can't think of any," said Chick. "Which is why you'll be all the more unique."

Bruno bit down on his bottom lip and squinted. He drew a hitching breath, focused on the water-stained ceiling and said, "Don't patronize me, boy."

"Look at me," Chick said and waited.

After a few seconds, Bruno met his eyes.

"Would I patronize anyone?" Chick asked evenly.

"My life has been ruined," Bruno said, "since I took up with you and your tribe."

"I'm sorry," Chick said. "I'm honestly sorry for everything that's gone wrong. But understand something, Bruno. Every choice you've made has been your own. I know that's not what you want to hear right now. And trust me when I tell you that it's not what I want to say to you. But it's the truth. You chose to come warn us back in Odradek. You chose to deliver us from McGee. You chose to come to Gehenna with us and you chose to save us from drowning."

"So I'm a fool," Bruno said, his voice thick with drugs and exhaustion and despair. "And now, I'm a one-armed fool."

"Now," Chick said, "you're one of us."

Bruno tried to lift his head from his pillow.

"I don't want to be a freak," he said.

"You'll find," Chick said, "that it has its advantages."

"I'll try to remember that," Bruno said, "when I'm working as a gazonie for the bottom-feeders."

"There's nothing wrong with being a gazonie," Chick said. "But you're not made for a shovel and a broom. Not anymore, anyway. You're one of us now, Bruno. You're a freak. And one thing that every freak knows — better than the average person — is that life will throw catastrophe into your path. Not conflicts. Not challenges. Out and out catastrophes. And it's during those catastrophic moments, when we're at our most terrified and grief-stricken and enraged, that anyone can turn into a real monster. We all trip over catastrophe, Bruno. But some people turn into monsters and some don't. And maybe that has more to do with luck than anything else. But I doubt it. I think it has to do with the people around us. I think if anything keeps us from turning into monsters, it's the people we travel with. So you have to take real care when you choose your friends. And it seems to me, in this one area, you've chosen well. Most of us are good people."

Bruno was brought up short and a little confused.

"Most of us?"

Chick shrugged and said, "We still have a ways to go. There could be more catastrophes further down the road."

"Is this what your father told you?"

"My father said it's time for all of us to push on. He said we're due on the western coast. He said there's a town called Quaboag that sits at the edge of the ocean. He said he has a mansion on a cliff above the ocean. And that he'll be waiting for us. And he says that time is running out."

Bruno brought his hand up to his face and covered his eyes.

"I'm so tired," he said. "I only want to sleep right now."

"I understand," Chick said. "But they're going to throw us out of here very soon. And I'm not sure what will be waiting for us back at the Jubilee."

DR. TABER, the medical examiner, was waiting for them outside the clinic. This time he was driving a hearse. Bruno stretched out in the rear and Chick rode shotgun back to the fairgrounds. The freaks were waiting at their trailer, along with Renaldo St. Clare. No one said a word when Chick and the doctor helped Bruno through the door.

Milena and Fatos took charge of the strongman, pushing two cots together, helping him down to the mattresses and covering him with a quilt.

The ringmaster stood at the foot of the makeshift bed and bowed his head.

"I'm terribly sorry this happened," he said to Bruno. "Believe me when I tell you that the Chief feels just awful. He's never done anything like this before."

"You caught him?" Chick said, taking a cup of coffee from Kitty.

"Oh, he's in his trailer right this minute," said the ringmaster, "thinking long and hard about this whole matter. He says he's off the bottle for good this time and, truly, I believe him."

"He's in his trailer?" Chick repeated, approaching St. Clare. "What do you mean, he's in his trailer? Why isn't he in the town jail?"

St. Clare smiled at Chick and nodded, turned back to Bruno and bent down to pat the strongman's leg, saying, "If there's anything at all that you require, Mr. Seboldt, you need only ask and the Bedlam Brothers will be happy to oblige."

Then he turned to Chick, lowered his voice, and said, "Perhaps you and I should talk outside."

They exited the trailer and St. Clare immediately began to walk toward the midway. Chick hurried to keep up with him. The ringmaster looked at the rising sun as he began to speak.

"I think you'll agree that we've got a delicate situation here."

"I think," Chick said, "that it's pretty simple. Your strongman lopped off the arm of my strongman."

"Granted," said St. Clare. "But the brothers and I are not entirely sure that the best course of action would be to incarcerate the Chief."

"The Chief," Chick said, "is an alcoholic psychopath. One of these days he'll kill a mark."

"He felt threatened by Bruno," the ringmaster said. "He thought he was being replaced. This is really management's fault."

"Then management," Chick said, "should do the right thing and bring the Chief to the authorities."

St. Clare stopped walking next to the elephant track and decided it was time to level with the chicken boy.

"Look," he said, "we're out of here in a week. This town is a little goldmine for us. And we've got a full circuit booked on its heels. Chief Micmac is one of our headliners. All in all, it would be a financial disaster for us to deal with this situation in an official manner."

"Your Chief," Chick said, "attacked my friend and cut off his arm. He needs to pay."

"And pay," St. Clare said, seizing on the word, "is exactly what I've been instructed by the brothers to propose to you."

An elephant blew a trunk of water into the air. Chick said, "Go on."

"It's just that I spent the night talking to your colleagues," the ringmaster said, "and it's come to my attention that, like many people in our profession, you're all traveling without any documentation. You've got no passports. No citizenship papers. No inoculation cards. And worse than this, they tell me you've got no money. You're dead broke."

Chick sighed and waited for the pitch.

"I've been there," said St. Clare. "I know what that's like. Which is why I think there's a better way to deal with our situation. A better way for both of us."

"Bruno can't travel for a week," Chick said. "Doctor's orders."

"Okay, so you spend the week with us. Our guests. Food and lodging on the house. And no one need perform. You relax. You take it easy. You tend to your friend. And after the closing ceremonies, we part company without animosity."

"How much?" Chick asked.

"What did you have in mind?" St. Clare asked.

Chick stared at the man for a second, then knelt down and traced a number in the dirt with his finger. St. Clare looked at it, nodded, and toed it away.

"And some transportation," Chick said. "A truck or a bus that can hold us all."

St. Clare began to demur. "I'm not sure we have anything that—"

Chick cut him off, saying, "That's the deal. The money and the vehicle. And we let the Chief off the hook."

"I'll have to talk to the brothers," St. Clare said.

"You let me know what they decide," said Chick and, without another word, he walked back to his clan.

THEY TENDED BRUNO round the clock. Not that the strongman needed much nursing. Kitty and Durga changed his bandages when necessary. The others took turns bringing him food and water and a pipe of opium, twice a day, as prescribed by Dr. Taber. Mostly, the giant slept, troubled and mumbling in his dreams, saying prayers, on occasion, in some unknown tongue, and once begging his mother for forgiveness.

When he was awake, he rejected all attempts at conversation. Many of the freaks found this unnerving, but Chick understood the need for silence and repose. It takes time to make the change to a new consciousness, he advised his brothers and sisters. It takes time to get to know the new self.

The troupe stayed away from the Jubilee show. They huddled in the trailers like prisoners. At night they sat by the window and listened to the noise of the crowds and remembered, not without sadness and regret, the adulation they had known back in Bohemia, when the audience had embraced them each night. When the audience had paid homage to their differences.

On the last night of the Jubilee, just before the start of the closing
ceremonies, Bruno rose from his bed. Though a little unsteady on his
feet, he made his way, with the help of Chick, to the second trailer. The
freaks were listening to the sounds of a straw house, a capacity crowd
waiting to be amazed one last time. The giant and the chicken boy
came through the door like warriors home from a stalemate.

"I think," Bruno said to the clan, "we should go to the show."

Everyone looked to Chick, who said, "You heard Bruno. Get dressed.
He wants us all to see the show."

THEY GATHERED UNDERNEATH the main grandstand, watching
through a jungle of legs. Milena had been opposed to vacating the
trailer until they left for good. Chick found a compromise—they'd
view the finale but from a hidden vantage.

The closeout was a spectacle that handily demonstrated why the Jubilee was the biggest show on the central circuit. In terms of grandeur,
bravado, and pure showmanship, it exceeded the opening festivities
and raised itself into an event, the kind of performance a child will
carry to a distant grave. The wild beasts were more ferocious and nimble than any the troupe had ever known. The acrobats and wire walkers took risks that no sane man or woman would have considered. The
clowns were uproarious and innovative. The magicians, nothing short
of stupefying.

The freaks breathed a collective sigh of relief when it was announced that Chief Micmac Shawnee would not be performing due
to a continued illness. Ringmaster St. Clare apologized on behalf of
the Bedlam Brothers, and when he began to announce the final act of
the final night of the Jubilee, the crowd soon got over whatever disappointment it might have felt at missing the psychotic strongman.

"Ladies and gentlemen," the ringmaster said, his words echoing
around the big tent, "we now come to the moment you have all been
waiting, so patiently, to arrive."

The audience became silent in an instant and rose to their feet in
unison as the house lights came down and a single spotlight illuminated Renaldo St. Clare, standing in a cloud of swirling mist. The

freaks stared, as entranced as the rest, peeking through the fat calves of farm wives and around the boots of tractor salesmen.

In the middle of the center ring, St. Clare stood with his head bowed, looking down at what everyone knew to be the grave of Dr. Lazarus Cole. The ringmaster made a point of toeing the soft earth where the Resurrectionist had been interred. He stared down at the ground as if gazing on all of the failings of mankind. Then he lifted his head and spoke in a clean, strong showman's voice.

"One week ago," he said, "you all witnessed a terrible event here under our own joyous tents."

A pause to let the memories swim upstream.

"Here in this palace of marvels, you saw a dozen of your own citizens, your husbands, fathers, sons, brothers, step onto this midway and commit the greatest sin of all—the taking of another human life."

Additional spots were ignited and the eye of the crowd was drawn to a sad parade of twelve townsmen, now dressed in ill-fitting prison uniforms of black and white striped denim. The men shambled like condemned slaves, their feet shackled and each carrying a shovel over a sagging shoulder. They came to a stop before the ringmaster, who placed a hand on one head and watched as the lot of them fell to their knees facing the grandstand.

"You witnessed their fatal transgression," St. Clare said. "You saw them fall prey to their own murderous rage and do what only God may do. You watched as your own people became savage killers and dispatched a helpless man to a pitiful and agonizing demise."

Chick squinted and could see tears running down the cheeks of many of the killers. In the seats above him, he could hear weeping from the crowd.

"You saw that hideous spectacle one week ago," said the ringmaster. "And surely, you will never forget it. But we are called to forgive these murderers. Just as we, ourselves, are forgiven for our own failures and infractions. So let me ask you tonight, can you find it in your hearts to forgive these sinners who kneel before you?"

The murderers had hung their heads, cast their eyes to the ground.

One on the end was weaving and Milena wondered if he were drunk or simply overcome with the weight of his crime. Either way, it didn't seem to matter to the mob. They stood and cheered, clapped hands and stomped feet.

The ringmaster put his hand over his mouth for a second and then over his heart.

"You are," he said, "a compassionate people," and this goosed the cheering up into the realm of screaming.

St. Clare let it go on for a while and when it began to die on its own, he grabbed the collar of the murderer kneeling before him and yanked the man to his feet.

"Rise up," he said. "Every one of you. Rise up, now. Stand like men. You are blessed to live in a town of mercy."

When all of the killers were on their feet, the ringmaster came around and faced them.

"The people," he bellowed, "say we must forgive you. And forgive you we surely will. But first, before any forgiveness can be bestowed, it must be earned. Through a penance."

He turned sideways and threw an arm into the air as if presenting the killers to the audience for the first time.

"So let us see you work for your absolution."

As if coached, all of the murderers at once took their shovels in hand and attacked the grave of Dr. Lazarus Cole.

"That's it," bellowed St. Clare, "let us see you earn your acquittal. Let us see you sweat for this exoneration."

The murderers went to work with a fierce spirit, putting their backs into their labor, working up a lather of sweat. In no time they began to excavate the grave, descending into the soft earth under the breathless eye of the audience.

The ringmaster had the courage to forgo any narration and the crowd seemed to appreciate the credit he gave them. There was concentrated silence under the big top as the citizenry united in collective anticipation while the diggers sank deeper and deeper into the ground, opening a large pit around the perimeter of the grave proper.

Finally, one man stopped digging, hesitated a moment, threw his shovel aside, disappeared into the hole, came back into view and said, into Renaldo St. Clare's waiting microphone, "We found him."

St. Clare nodded but offered no instructions. The crowd inhaled in unison. Chick looked at Bruno, who had a hand placed lightly on his bandages and was sweating as profusely as the diggers.

Several of them now vanished down into the darkness of the hole. A series of grunts and groans became audible, as if they were struggling to move something heavy and bulky. Eight of the killers emerged from the pit and stood off to the side, leaning on their shovels, looking nervously from the ringmaster to the hole and back again.

It took a few minutes for the remaining four to climb into the spotlights. They rose slowly, moving as one. And when the crowd realized that they were carrying a corpse between them, a chorus of shrieks and howls filled the air.

The four bearers placed the body of Lazarus Cole at the feet of the ringmaster, then joined their colleagues on the other side of the pit. St. Clare looked down upon the crumpled and filthy pile of flesh and shook his head sadly. He cleared his throat and the noise of the clearing washed over the grandstand and silenced the audience.

"He was once the greatest magician on the circuit," St. Clare said solemnly. "And it was my honor and my privilege to know him as I did and to call him my friend."

Children could be heard crying despite their mothers' efforts to silence them.

"The lesson we can all draw from this tragedy," the ringmaster said, "is that sometimes the trick doesn't work."

Now the mothers were crying. The fathers were crying. Brothers and sisters and aunts and uncles and cousins were crying. Friends and neighbors were bawling. The entire audience was sobbing, heaving, awash in a sea of instant grief.

Which turned into shocked relief when the corpse at the ringmaster's feet suddenly jumped up, nonchalantly brushed down its tuxedo, rolled its head around its neck, stretched its arms out in the air, and loudly proclaimed, "And sometimes it works like a charm."

Then he gave a theatrical bow and the crowd exploded into an ovation that shook the grandstand and the big top and vibrated in the heart of every person gathered together for this macabre Jubilee.

Lazarus Cole was alive and well and no worse for the wear of a vicious beating and what appeared to be a week buried beneath the earth. He bowed twice more, once to the left and once to the right. Then in a gesture both grand and classy, he moved to greet his killers, embracing them one by one and planting a kiss on the cheek of each.

The action was too much for his murderers to bear and their shock and sorrow and joy blended and overflowed. The lot of them broke down, sobbing like infants at a harrowing birth. They embraced Dr. Cole and they embraced one another, until Dr. Taber appeared with a gazonie who led the absolved men out of the tent.

Taber received a smattering of applause but his shtick was fairly anticlimactic. He and Cole went through a pantomime of a physical exam, listening for a heartbeat, taking a pulse, checking ears, nose, and throat for normalcy.

When it was over, Taber faced the audience and proclaimed, "I find this man, Lazarus Cole, to be animate, healthy, and entirely alive."

This set off a new burst of applause and cheering and triggered the show's finale. The house lights came up, confetti descended, the band struck up the Bedlam Brothers anthem and the closing parade got under way, led this time by both Renaldo St. Clare and Lazarus Cole, joined arm in arm, high-stepping out of the big top, waving to an exultant crowd that had been remade into a vibrant and unified people by the ritual they had shared.

Milena was the first freak to speak. Over the ovation, she said, "Quite a trick, isn't it?"

It wasn't at all clear to whom s/he was speaking, but it was Nadja who answered. "I've never seen anything like it. He wasn't under there all week, was he?"

"Of course not," snapped the one-armed strongman. "It's an illusion. That's what magic is. It's nothing but another trick."

"But how—" began Vasco, before Bruno cut him off.

"I don't know how," he said. "How the hell would I? I'm not a magician."

"But we saw him pummeled," said Milena. "It sure looked to me like they beat him to death."

"There isn't a scratch on him," Marcel pointed out. "Not a single bruise."

"I'm sure there's a tunnel under the midway," said Aziz. "Isn't that right, Chick?"

There was no answer, and when they all looked to the chicken boy, he was on the ground, twitching and drooling.

Kitty went to him at once, but before she could manage to position his head in her lap, he was already coming out of the seizure.

"That was a short one," Milena observed.

"Bruno," Chick said, fighting off Kitty's attempts to calm him.

"What is it?" asked the strongman.

"The money and the truck," Chick croaked, choking on bile and fighting for air. "We have to leave now."

Bruno looked from Chick to Kitty, who raised her eyebrows to indicate her confusion.

"Now, Bruno," Chick tried to yell. "We have to go."

The strongman put a hand over the massive dressing taped from his shoulder to his ribs. Then he ran from beneath the grandstand.

THE BROTHERS, to their credit, did not attempt to cheat Bruno and his freaks. St. Clare had an envelope waiting, filled with cash and the keys to a semi that had been used to transport several of the elephants.

The ringmaster attempted to convince Bruno and the clan to stay for the wrap party, but seeing the strongman's urgency, he didn't try very hard.

Bruno found the truck, managed to get it going and pulled across the fairgrounds to the camptown where the freaks were waiting for him. He left the engine idling and ran around the back to unlatch the truck's gate.

The clan filed into the cargo box silently, most aware that something was wrong but afraid to ask anyone for details. Even Milena remained quiet despite the stench of elephant dung rising up from the floorboards.

Chick was the last to get on board, but before he could, Bruno secured the gate and put his last hand on the boy's shoulder.

"You're riding up front with me," Bruno said.

Chick didn't argue. He moved to the cab and climbed up to the passenger seat. Bruno joined him on the driver's side, slipped the vehicle into gear and steered for the county road.

After a few moments, the strongman handed the envelope across the seat to Chick, who took it and began to count the currency within.

When he was done, Bruno asked, "What was it? What did he tell you?"

Chick sighed and made a terrible sucking noise inside the beak.

"It's the Resurrectionist," he said.

"Cole?"

"He belongs to Fliess," Chick said. "He was waiting to grab us. As soon as the crowd was gone."

"How does he know?" Bruno asked and when Chick failed to answer, he turned his head to look at the boy. "How does Fliess know where we are?"

They had rolled onto the two-laner now and were picking up speed. Chick looked at Bruno, matched his stare for just a second, then looked back to the road and screamed. Bruno brought his eyes forward just in time to see Dr. Lazarus Cole standing in the middle of the road, pointing straight ahead at them. He was lit up by the truck's high beams and both driver and passenger could see the horrible, furious expression on his face.

And then they hit him. The body was sent sailing, bouncing off the hood and pinwheeling into the dark field to their left. The noise was loud and blunt. A starburst of blood covered part of the windshield.

Bruno hesitated only a second before turning on the wipers and simultaneously pressing down on the accelerator. And Chick didn't say a word.

20

At some point while reading, Sweeney fell into a heavy sleep. And sometime after that, he came awake, slowly and partially, into what he thought, for just an instant, was a dream. But when he opened his eyes, he saw a figure perched above him, sitting on top of him with its head thrown back so far that he couldn't see a face. He was still out of breath and he could feel his heart racing. He blinked and tried to sit up and the figure came forward and its arms pushed him down and he was too weak to fight. In that moment, sinking back into the bed, he realized he was fucking someone. That he'd been fucking someone for some time and that he was about to come. And the brain shut down and his buttocks and thighs tightened and he drove upward. And the person on top of him responded perfectly, speeded up the pace of her own rocking, began to gallop, short, hard slaps down onto his cock, her own noises increasing. In the midst of it, she drew one arm up to her throat and then used a hand to push her mane back behind an ear. And in the orange light, he saw that it was Nadia Rey.

She looked down at him, understood that he was fully awake and that he knew what was happening and who it was happening with. He put a hand on either side of her waist and adjusted their rhythm. They were grinding up against each other now. He could see the sweat on her forehead and cheeks. She was wearing her nurse's uniform, the skirt hiked up. She sat back for a second, rested her ass on his legs, and he heard her take a deep breath. And then she came forward again, put her hands on his shoulders, pinning him against the bed. She began to ride him faster and her mouth formed itself into an oval and she looked as if she could blow a smoke ring. Her nails went into his shoulders. He bore upward, felt her tighten, and saw her start to shake her head in little seizurelike motions.

He began to pump as fast as he could. Within seconds she came and reared up and back and then crumpled down on top of him. When he felt her full weight on his chest, felt her hair against his mouth, he let himself go and bit down on his bottom lip to keep from crying out.

The intensity ran to the edge of catastrophic. He felt as if his body would collapse through the mattress and the steel frame, fall through the whole of the bed to the floor below and fall through the floor into the basement, into the bed in his apartment and then through that bed as well and into the dirt and rock of this mistake of a city. And then he fell back into a dreamless sleep.

He was out for at least as long as it took for the drool around his mouth and the jism on his legs to dry. He was woken by a tap — and then a slap across his cheek. He reached up before his eyes opened, still stupid with sleep, and touched Nadia's face and felt the stubble of a new beard. This brought him to full consciousness at once and his head jerked off the pillow and his eyes opened. And he looked up at Buzz Cote, who was grinning and nodding and biting in on both of his lips. He pinched Sweeney's cheek until it bruised but his voice was low and excited when he said, "Well, we're brothers now, kimosabe."

That combination of friendly tone and rough physicality set the pattern for their exit from the Clinic. Buzz stood, grabbed Sweeney's shirt and pulled him into a seated position. And then he punched Sweeney, this quick jab that landed where the shoulder hinged under the breastbone. It connected perfectly and Sweeney felt as if the bone had chipped. But then it was another round of backslapping and arms locked as if to promenade.

"Nadia will meet up with us later," Buzz said. "You ready for your initiation ride?"

Sweeney didn't answer, but it didn't seem to matter. Buzz threw an arm across his back and gripped the bruised shoulder on the other side. Then he proceeded to waltz Sweeney out the front door of the Peck, past the delighted eyes of Romeo the janitor, who was dusting in the reception area.

In the predawn quiet, their steps crunched on the driveway gravel.

Buzz was moving quickly, spieling something about Nadia being one in a million, yes sir, and all the Abominations agreed about that and you haven't known a jones till you've had a piece of that honey there. The words mattered less than their speed, their charged tone and the way they jumped from Buzz's mouth. Sweeney had known a neighborhood speed freak in high school and had studied the symptomology in college. So he felt fairly certain that while he'd been dream-fucking Nadia, Buzz had spent the night injecting some high-test crystal meth.

They circled the west wing of the building and climbed the hill that led to the rear parking lot where Buzz's hog was waiting.

They came to a stop before the bike and Buzz said, "The boys are pleased, I can tell you that. The boys are very excited about this."

Sweeney didn't try to escape the embrace but he said, "Fuck you," in a clear, emotion-free voice.

"We'll see about that later," Buzz said without any smile or hesitation. "Right now, we got to get you initiated. And seeing how you don't have a bike, there's only one way that can happen."

"I'm not going anywhere with you," Sweeney said.

Buzz rubbed and picked a bit at a nostril with his free hand and said, "The thing is, Sweeney, you are. And you're not stupid. So you know you are. I can kick your ass from one end of this lot to the other and tie you to the back of this thing like a bitch. But neither one of us wants that. So just get on. You'll be glad you did. At some point, you're going to have to trust me."

Sweeney looked back to the Clinic.

"I can start screaming."

Buzz nodded. "You can. That's true. You could get a scream out. But two things, okay? First off, nobody in there likes you very much and they're not going to do shit to help you out. Okay? And second, I'd bust you in the throat as soon as you squealed and you'd end up puking and maybe passing out. I know you, Sweeney. You don't want Nadia to see that. She's watching you right now."

His eyes scanned the windows on the back of the building but he didn't see any shadows.

"So just get *on*," Buzz continued. "And let's run this fucker the way she's meant to be run."

Sweeney thought about bolting and then stepped up to the bike and mounted it. Buzz was delighted.

"You've made me happy," Buzz said. "It's gonna be much better this way."

Buzz mounted in front, kicked over the engine and throttled up a few times. Sweeney wrapped his arms around the driver's trunk and yelled, "What about helmets?"

Buzz thought this hysterical. He yelled, "You *are* the shit, man," put the bike in gear, and sprayed gravel to either side as they rode out of the lot and down to Route 16.

SWEENEY HAD NEVER owned a bike. But he'd ridden a few over the years, usually smaller rice burners loaned by friends and usually in empty parking lots or off road. And though he couldn't remember who gave it to him, he did recall one piece of motorcycle wisdom: sooner or later, everybody has to lay his bike down.

This occurred to him about ten minutes into his kidnapping, as Buzz negotiated a series of blind curves without reducing his speed in the least. Sweeney leaned into Buzz's back, turned his head sideways and watched the run of pines blur.

He kept waiting for the speed or the noise to decrease but they would not. When a new set of bends and curves appeared in the road, Buzz refused to slow down. And that was when Sweeney discovered a new breed of fear. Buzz was angling the bike to the road at suicide velocities, and Sweeney became convinced they were seconds from the kind of death that teenagers turn into legend. And with each instant that they did not die, Sweeney learned more about the fear. It was a living panic and in this way it sat in opposition to the dead panic he'd inhabited for the last year. There was a juice inside this terror, a surge, part electric and part chemical. The dead fear left him numb in its wake. But he knew that, should he survive this ride, he'd be anything but numb. He'd be overloaded and fused, twitching in the aftermath of maximal stimulation.

It went on this way for what seemed a long time, though the rush never faded. Sweeney's sense of time became degraded and then, irrelevant. Whatever Buzz was planning on doing to him at the end of this ride seemed, in those moments, unimportant. Because, for a while, it felt as if the ride would never end. He felt certain they'd passed out of the city, possibly out of the county, and maybe out of the state. Afterward, he realized that not once during the entire experience had he thought of Danny or Kerry or the accident.

Something changed when the scream of the engine's work became a chorus and Sweeney understood that they were being joined by the rest of the Abominations. The others came out of the wooded bluff on either side of the road. They appeared solo, falling in behind Buzz, one by one, a new addition every mile or two. When all twelve had surfaced and converged, they took over the route, riding on either side of the dividing line. The first car they encountered had to roll up the bluff to avoid them.

When the sun became fully visible over the trees to the left, their pace seemed to slacken a bit and Sweeney allowed himself a look behind for the first time. He expected to find Nadia Rey straddling the rear of a machine, but there was no sign of her. He swung forward just as Buzz kicked back into high, lurched ahead of the rest, and pulled the bike right, suddenly, off the highway, over the shoulder, and up a dirt trail that cut through the pines.

The trail threaded up a hill that might have qualified as a small mountain. Engine scream echoed farther and louder the higher they climbed and Sweeney could feel Buzz willing the hog skyward. They reached the far side of the rise and what had been hardpack turned into granite and though the trail became narrower, the climb got easier. Sweeney made the mistake of glancing to the right and saw the road's shoulder gave way to a plunge, maybe five hundred feet into a rocky chasm. After that, he kept his eyes on Buzz's back.

It took about a half hour to reach the plateau, a lip of rock that jutted out from the last wall of granite. The riders parked in that same formation that Sweeney had first seen outside the Harmony factory. They idled until Buzz cut his engine and dismounted. Then the rest of the pack followed suit. Buzz pulled Sweeney into a shoulder hug as soon as the passenger's feet touched granite. No one spoke. Buzz walked Sweeney to the edge of the plateau. Depending on one's feelings about height, the view was either spectacular or agonizing. The air held a hypnotic clarity. But looking down revealed a fatal plummet, the kind that, in movies, allows a human scream to echo into seeming infinity.

"You impressed?" Buzz said.

Sweeney nodded and Buzz slapped his back hard enough to make him pitch toward the brink, but held onto an arm to keep him in place.

"This where you do all your victims?" Sweeney said, staring at his own feet.

"Victims?" Buzz said and sounded genuinely surprised. "Ain't you got a complex? You fuck *our* woman and *you're* the victim?"

"I didn't," he started to explain and gave up immediately.

"You're no victim, Sweeney," Buzz said. "You gotta stop telling yourself that. That's one of your main problems. You are what you think you are. No one ever tell you that?"

"Why'd you bring me here?"

"For your own good, son," and there was that trace of down-home accent again. "You needed some air. And this is where you come when you need some air. You feel it?"

He let go of Sweeney and tilted his head back, took in a deep noseful, closed his eyes and shook his head.

"This is one of my favorite places. Thought I'd share it with you. You got to get out of the tombs from time to time, son. You'll become one of those people."

"My son's back there," Sweeney said, then regretted mentioning Danny.

"Yes, he is," Buzz said. "And it's one thing to want to be with him. And it's another to want to be like him."

He took Sweeney's chin and cheeks in his gloved hand and said, "You're one of us now, son. And you're starting to make some bad choices. For you and for the boy."

"I'm not one of you," Sweeney said.

Buzz squeezed in on the cheeks. "You fuck our woman," he said, "you're one of us." Then he started to pull Sweeney's face forward over the lip of the cliff. "Otherwise," he said, "what you did would be a problem."

He let the words hang, then he released the face and patted the bruised cheek, grabbed the front of Sweeney's shirt and pulled him back to where the others were standing next to their bikes, waiting.

"I think you know most of the family," Buzz said and he started pointing to each in turn. "Mouse, Turtle, Monkey, Rabbit, the Elephant — also known as Tubby — Crabs, Bear, Fluke, the Ant, Roach. And this here is

Piglet. You be good to Piglet and Piglet will be good to you. That right, Piglet?"

Piglet was small and a little sick-looking, with ashen skin and thin, straggly hair. His eyes were too small for his face, but it was probably the stubby, upturned nose that accounted for the name. In general, he looked greasier, more feral than any of the others by a factor of two or three.

Piglet didn't give an answer and Buzz smiled as if he really hadn't wanted one.

"Boys," Buzz said, "you all remember Sweeney."

Nobody moved except for the one called Monkey, who bobbed his head and showed some caramel teeth.

"Once we get to know you better," Buzz said, "you'll get your name."

Sweeney looked around the precipice. There was nowhere to run but back down the trail and they'd be on him in an instant. He had a sense that Piglet would love an excuse to toss him off the mountain.

"Now, listen," Buzz said, moving between Sweeney and the rest of the clan. "This is not gonna work out unless you trust us. What you got to do here, you got to make a leap. You got to ignore your own common sense and throw in with us, son. 'Cause whether you believe it right now or not, we're the best thing that's happened to you in a long goddamn time."

Buzz waited for an argument but Sweeney kept his mouth shut.

"And we're the best thing that's happened to your boy. We're sure as hell a shitload better than those fuckers down in the tombs. That shithead Peck and his little bitch of a daughter. They are poison. They're the last people can help you and Danny."

He was baiting but Sweeney wouldn't rise to it.

"Couple days, you're gonna look back and see that Buzz was right. And you're gonna thank me for doing what I had to do. You're just lucky we found you in time. You trust me, Sweeney, things are gonna get better. You're one of us now. Isn't that right?"

Buzz didn't bother to look, but Sweeney was sure that all the Abominations were nodding this time. Even Piglet.

"'Course you're one of us," Buzz said. "You helped yourself to a piece of Nadia and you had your first ride. Just one thing left for you to do."

Sweeney had been waiting and now here it was. Some kind of initiation. Something awful and lasting. They were going to take turns beating the life out of him or they were going to pin him down and cornhole him. They were going to cut him or brand him or maybe drag him down the mountain, tied to the back of Buzz's hog.

"It's nothing major," Buzz continued. "And it's nothing to be scared of. It's symbolic, s'what it is."

Sweeney picked out Fluke because he looked like the slowest and the dullest. Piglet was smaller but it was obvious he was pure psychotic. He tried to play it out in his head. He'd wait till they pulled out their knives or their ropes, then he'd charge the Fluke. He'd run head down and try to hit him midsection, drive the wind out. Then he'd go for the knife and, if there were any chance, mount the Fluke's bike and head for the trail.

But no one took out a knife or a rope and no one unhitched his jeans. Buzz came up to him and once again draped an arm over his shoulder. He began to walk Sweeney to the opposite side of the precipice, where some scrub brush was growing against the wall of shale that stretched another hundred yards into the sky.

"See, Sweeney," Buzz said, "we come up here every now and then. Get some fresh air and commune, you might say, with the natural world. Now last time we come up, we left something here."

He let go of Sweeney's shoulder and sank into a squat. He picked up a fallen branch and used it to push back some of the overgrown scrub. And in the mountain face behind, Sweeney saw a small hole cut into the granite, a little hollow that led into a cavity of some kind. It wasn't big enough to be called a cave. It was more like a burrow, a lair of some sort, fit for a fat possum or unusually small bear.

"We need you," Buzz said, "to scoot on in there and get it."

Sweeney stared at him.

"Don't worry," Buzz said. "You won't get stuck. It opens out once you get inside."

"What is it?" Sweeney asked.

"That," Buzz said, "would ruin the surprise. You gotta trust me."

Sweeney took a step forward, went down on one knee and tried to peer inside the hole.

"You want me to climb in there?"

Buzz nodded. "Like I said, it gets bigger once you're in."

"I bet it does."

"You go in. You get what we want. You come out."

"I come out."

"You come out. Right. What the hell you think?"

"I think," Sweeney said, "that once I'm in you'll block up the entrance and laugh your asses off while I suffocate."

Buzz looked back toward the tribe.

"You really got a low opinion of us," he said. He reached in his boot, pulled out a small box of kitchen matches, held them up for Sweeney to see, like he was about to do a magic trick. Then he tucked them in Sweeney's shirt pocket and said, "You're a real paranoid fucker. Nobody's going to block you in there."

"I'm not going in."

Buzz smiled and said, "Like you weren't coming with me in the first place. But here you are."

Sweeney just shook his head.

"Time you understood something, son," Buzz said. "I can be your savior. Or I can be the scariest fucking nightmare you ever had. I'll go either way. Whatever's required to take care of my family. So get in the fucking cave. 'Cause if I have to, I'll send Piglet in there with you."

21

He had to get down on his belly and crawl on his forearms to make it under the archway. His hips rubbed stone as he edged inward. The burrow was a bit longer than the length of his body. When he cleared it he got on his knees and reached his hands up in the darkness until he touched rock. There wasn't enough room to stand, but now he could get off his stomach and crawl on hands and knees. The air inside was cool and dank and smelled like charcoal. And the light from outside didn't make it in very far.

He began to crawl in an ever-widening circle, patting the earth and waving a hand to the side. He felt ridiculous, but he guessed that he was looking for some sort of contraband. A bag of dope or money or maybe even guns.

It took him a while to realize the initial chamber opened into a larger one, that the burrow was actually a series of caves, a honeycombed maze of linked vaults and passages. He struck a match and let it burn down to his finger and thumb. It didn't throw a lot of light but he'd never have seen the graffiti without it.

It was in the second chamber, at eye level if you were on your knees. And when he got closer he could see that it wasn't really graffiti. There were no obscene or obscure phrases, no insults or limericks or drawings of Kilroy or human anatomy. The writing was painted on the granite in Day-Glo lime but the numbers and letters were small and precise. The writer had etched them with a stick or a brush. This was not the work of some drunken teens with a spray can, but slow, close, methodical transcription.

Sweeney knelt in front of the first line, instinctively touched a random letter because the paint looked wet. It wasn't, at least not the lines he found in that second chamber. But he knew immediately what the lines meant. And he thought, incorrectly it turned out, that they'd been painted specifically for his discovery.

He found writing on the wall of every chamber he visited after that. But by the fourth room he could no longer translate it. The writing had gotten too small and the lines ran too long and became nonsensical with tangential notations above and below the main text. By then he'd burned through his last match. And lost his sense of where he'd entered the cave.

He didn't panic immediately.

The panic came when he called out for help and received an answer in the form of a laugh from somewhere close by. It was male and high-pitched and sloppy and it echoed. Sweeney couldn't pinpoint the laugh's origin but that didn't stop him from trying to run from it. He hit a wall almost at once, bounced off unhurt, but went down on his ass.

That was when the first beer can hit him. And when the laugh sounded again, it was in the same chamber. Sweeney scrambled backward, got his back against the stone, and said, "Who's there?"

More laughter, then the sound and the smell of someone urinating.

Someone belched, sniffled, said, "Buzz send you in for me?"

When Sweeney didn't answer, the voice said, "It's been a fuckin' week already?"

A flashlight beam snapped on, found Sweeney, and focused on his face. Sweeney put out a hand and shielded his eyes.

"You want a beer?" and a can landed in Sweeney's lap. "Warm as piss but what the hell."

Sweeney heard the cluck and hiss of a can being opened, then a moment of quiet and a second belch.

The beam of light came off Sweeney's face and swung up onto the wall next to his head. It ran down the line of letters and numbers painted there.

"You know what that means?"

"Some of it," Sweeney said.

"Buzz said you'd know. So you're Danny's old man, huh?"

The light moved again, jumped across the ceiling, and went into spasm. It darted back and forth over their heads until it blurred, then it vanished for a second, leaving an afterimage before Sweeney's eyes. When it snapped back on, it was positioned beneath the speaker's chin, lighting up the face Halloween style. The cheeks of the face were inflated, the eyes too large.

When he was done, he laughed for a while, his head lolled over one shoulder. An unseen hand turned on a Boy Scout lantern and illuminated most of the chamber. Sweeney looked out on a filthy Abomination. He wore the colors, but that was the only thing that marked him as part of the tribe.

He was small, scrawnier than Piglet, and wasted-looking, with spindly limbs and a tiny skull that sprouted stringy blond hair. Sweeney couldn't hang an age on him, but sensed he might be younger than the rest of the crew.

"I thought," he said, "I had a couple more days."

"Did they put you in here?" Sweeney asked.

"Put me? Is that what Buzz told you? Fuckin' Buzz."

"Do you know the way out of here?" Sweeney asked.

"'Course I know the way out of here. Why you in such a hurry? You don't like it in here?"

"I've got to get back to my boy," Sweeney said.

The man began to pat himself down and came up with a pack of cigarettes. He offered the pack across his knees toward Sweeney, who shook his head to decline.

"You mind if I smoke?" the man said. "It helps me think. Came in here with a fuckin' carton and this is all that's left." He searched himself again, found a Zippo this time, and lit up.

He took a long drag, pointed the butt toward Sweeney and said, "You don't need to be worrying about Danny. Danny's going to be okay."

"Everyone seems to know about my son," Sweeney said, "and his problems."

The man made a face, kind of pulled his head back on his neck and tucked his chin down toward his chest.

"That embarrass you?" he said.

Sweeney hesitated and then said, "Does what embarrass me?"

"Your son," the man said. He took another drag, expelled some smoke, and added, "And his problems."

"My son doesn't embarrass me," Sweeney said.

"That's good. That's good to hear. And I hope I wasn't out of line with the question. I apologize if I was. Takes me a while to get readjusted, you know? Get used to talkin' to people again."

Something occurred to him and he got up on his knees, a little unsteadily, and shuffled over to Sweeney. He put his hand out to shake and said, "I'm the Sheep, by the way."

Sweeney took the hand. It was crusted with dirt and dried paint.

"I'm Sweeney," he said.

"I know," the Sheep said and sat down next to Sweeney, shoulder to shoulder. "I know you are. Buzz said you'd be comin' for me. And Buzz doesn't lie. You say what you will about Buzz. He does not lie to anyone."

"You've been in here long?" Sweeney asked.

"Not sure," the Sheep said. "You lose the sense of time. I'd offer you a bite but I ran out last night. I hope to hell Nadia's got something going back at Gehenna."

"You know Nadia?"

That laugh again.

"Well shit yeah," the Sheep said. "And I'm guessing you do too by now. Buzz said you and Nadia'd be made for each other. Buzz knows people. He really does. That's the thing about being a great leader. You have to see into people. Not that many can do it. Buzz knows how to push people's buttons. He knows how to bring people together. Or push them apart."

"You have any idea," Sweeney asked, "why he sent me in here for you?"

"Believe me," the Sheep said, "he's got his reasons."

"What are you doing in here?" Sweeney asked, and tried to lean away from the man, who smelled more than a little like his name.

"This is where I come," said the Sheep, "when I need to block everything else out. I don't know how other people do it. When I need to focus, I need to focus, you know? I mean, I've got to just seal myself away. I gotta crawl under the rock. Any distractions and my whole train of thought just goes to shit."

Sweeney pointed to the writing on the wall opposite them.

"You're their chemist?"

"I'm kind of a freelancer," the Sheep said. "But I've been with these guys a while. They took me in. They really did. Most clients just treat you like the hired help, you know? But not Buzz. He gave me his colors. Set me up with Nadia. They're good people."

"You make crank for them?"

The Sheep blew out a long trail of smoke and laughed. He pointed at the wall with his cigarette.

"That look like any kind of crank you ever seen?"

Sweeney stared at the wall through the smoke for a while, then said, "So what is it?"

The Sheep got up on his knees, stubbed the butt into the ground, and crawled to the wall. He made a fist and knocked his knuckles across the line of symbols.

"It's my goddamned masterpiece is what it is," he said. "It's my life's work."

"Your notations," Sweeney said, "are a little unusual."

"Yeah, well, I use my own shorthand. You think I'm the only one livin' in these caves?"

The Sheep knee-walked to his little camp and started to tie up his bed-roll and stash his tins in his pack.

"What happens now?" Sweeney asked.

"What happens now is you follow me out of here and we go back to Gehenna."

"And what happens when we get to the factory?"

"Well, first, I'd like to freshen up a little," the Sheep said.

"I mean," said Sweeney, "what happens to me?"

The Sheep attached his roll to his pack and slipped it over his shoulders.

"That," he said, "is for Buzz to say. I can't speak for Buzz. I wouldn't even try. But I really hope we get a chance to work together."

He picked up the lantern, turned and started out of the chamber. It took a second for Sweeney to realize that the Sheep was heading deeper into the caves. He got up and followed.

"What do you mean," Sweeney said to his back, "work together?"

The Sheep began to move more quickly, passing into and out of chambers, holding the lantern at arm's length. Sweeney saw writing on every wall they passed. Some of the chambers came alive in Day-Glo as they entered, every inch of rock adorned with letters and numbers, some depicting basic chemical compounds and others simply nonsensical.

"I mean," the Sheep said finally, a little out of breath, "that I've been needing an assistant for a while now. I mean, don't get me wrong, Nadia tries. But she just doesn't have the training. But you, being a chemist and all . . ."

"I'm not a chemist," Sweeney said and the Sheep stopped and turned and held the lantern out to look at Sweeney's face.

"What do you mean," he said, "you're not a chemist?"

"I'm a pharmacist," he said. "Did Buzz tell you I was a chemist?"

The Sheep sniffed, let his head drop toward a shoulder. He stood thinking for a minute, then said, "You'll be okay," and began his march again.

And Sweeney followed, unable to think of anything else to do. They wound left and right, through the interlocking chambers, sometimes crouching, sometimes down fully on hands and knees. The Sheep kept an even pace. Sweeney thought he heard sounds, all of them distant and brief. Water running. A shouted name. A crack of thunder. The Sheep gave no indication that he heard anything.

He lost track of time in the cave. He began to think they were revisiting corridors and chambers they'd been through before. He began to think that the Sheep was crazy and that Buzz knew it. That they might walk through this granite maze until both of them dropped. That whatever exits once existed had been blocked and mortared closed by a pack of Abominations. He began to think that maybe this was what it was like for Danny: cold entombment. A maze that emptied, always, back into the same pathways. A web of dark and useless roads that circled into one another until time and space and meaning were all degraded into a blind, exhausting loop.

And then he was following the Sheep down an incline and around a bend. And the walls were widening considerably. And light began to emanate from someplace up ahead. The Sheep turned off his lantern and waited for Sweeney to come level.

"Admit it," the Sheep said. "You had your doubts."

Sweeney didn't know how to answer that. The Sheep took him by the arm and led him to a spacious mouth that emptied onto sand and rock and scrub. They stepped out into the air and Sweeney looked up at the sun and guessed that about an hour had gone by.

"Makes you appreciate the open," the Sheep said, "doesn't it?"

Sweeney nodded.

"What's that song?" the Sheep said. "You know that song? *Been through the desert of night . . .*"

Sweeney shrugged.

". . . *Now it's time for the wine and the friends.*"

"Never heard it," Sweeney said.

The Sheep smiled and handed off the lantern. "It's a good one. But what I'm saying is, everything gets better from here on in."

He walked about twenty yards and Sweeney thought he was looking for a place to take a piss. Instead, he pulled a bike from beneath a pile of bramble and walked it back to the mouth of the cave. The machine looked too big for its rider but the Sheep had no problem kicking it over.

He goosed the engine and motioned for Sweeney to climb on.

22

Sweeney hugged the lantern to his side and held onto the Sheep with his free arm as the Abomination opened up the hog. The speed might have alarmed Sweeney if the rush of cold air hadn't felt so good. As if it were washing away all the grit from the cave.

They came upon the Harmony from the rear, pulling into the ruins of the old crematorium where the Abominations had played King of the Hill atop the dilapidated hearse. The Sheep killed the engine and climbed off the bike. Sweeney followed him to the antique funeral car where the Sheep reached through the passenger window, popped the glove box open, and extracted a pack of cigarettes.

The Sheep moved back around to the front of the hearse, eased himself onto its hood, and lit up a smoke. Sweeney joined him and they sat silently and rested for a few minutes, staring out at the prosthetics mill as if mulling a night on the late shift.

After a few minutes of this, Sweeney said, "Why are we stopping? You're almost home."

"I got to prepare myself," the Sheep said, "before I can jump back into the crowd. It's not that easy a transition for me. To go from the solitude back to the noise of the tribe. I can't rush right back in."

Sweeney looked out at the monstrosity they called Gehenna. In the distance, he could see a couple of Abominations sitting on the loading dock and someone was working on his bike down in the gravel lot.

"We had some good times in this city," the Sheep said. "Personally, I'm gonna hate leavin' here."

Sweeney turned toward him.

"You're leaving?"

The Sheep nodded.

"If things work out," he said. "We'll be movin' on next week."

"Where to?" Sweeney asked.

The Sheep grimaced as if this were a painful subject.

"Not sure yet," he said. "Buzz has one idea. Nadia has another. But it'll get worked out. We'll know when we need to know. Buzz says we shouldn't try to think ahead so much. You kill all the spontaneity in life."

"Can I ask," Sweeney said, "how you met Buzz?"

"Sure you can ask," the Sheep said and then threw an elbow to show he was just kidding. "No, it's all right. It's a good story. They found me in Phoenix. And let me tell you, I was not in the best of shape, okay? I was not doing very well. I'd burned through all my money and I'd fallen in with some bad people. These were not good people. But, you know, it's just like that song — *When the sinner is ready, the savior comes along.*"

He saw the blank look on Sweeney's face and said, "You're not a big gospel fan, are you?"

Sweeney shook his head and the Sheep said, "Well I hope you don't mind, cuz I listen to gospel while I work."

"Speaking of work," Sweeney said, and before he could go on, the Sheep had both hands in the air, revival style.

"I know, I know," he said, "that's the million-dollar question. How did a chemistry Ph.D. from Stanford end up riding with the Abominations? I get the curiosity, I do. Sometimes I say to Nadia, my life'd be a hell of a movie. But I don't say it to Buzz. You don't even kid about stuff like that with Buzz."

"So how'd it happen?"

"How's anything happen?" the Sheep said, going all weary and mystical in an instant. "You make a couple of mistakes and, bang, you find out you're not who you thought you were. You find out the world isn't what you thought it was. You find out you don't want any of the shit everyone's been telling you to want since the day you were born.

"What happened with me," confidential now, "was I had a full-blown textbook breakdown. I mean I was fuckin' catatonic for months. Now I'm healed enough, at this point, to face the facts and take the responsibility. But the truth is — and I don't mean this as any kind of excuse — I had a real asshole for an old man. One of these you-just-can't-please-'em sons a bitches. And I tried to sort of follow in his footsteps and I couldn't do it.

And the pressure got so bad, my brain just shut the fuck down one day. And I ended up in the psych ward at Ford-Masterson out there. And I'll tell you somethin' right now. Wasn't for Buzz and the boys, I'd still be there. Eatin' poached eggs and starin' at *The Price Is Right* all day."

"How'd Buzz get you out?" Sweeney asked.

The Sheep gave him a look that said even Sweeney should know better.

"There's something Buzz wants, Buzz finds a way to get it."

"I guess what I'm asking," said Sweeney, "is how he found out about you. I mean, you're institutionalized at this point. How did he know about you? What was the connection?"

The Sheep squinted at him and Sweeney sensed some real disappointment.

"The connection," said the Sheep, in a slowed down voice, as if he were speaking to a child, "is your new girlfriend."

"Nadia?"

"Of course Nadia," the Sheep said. "It's always Nadia. I mean, c'mon, Sweeney, huh? She's a sweetheart. And she's got a body that'd make Jesus weep. But she's a born pimp."

"I'm sorry," Sweeney said. "I'm not sure I follow."

"Nadia," the Sheep said, "is a procurer. I mean Buzz might be Moses, but your girl Nadia, she's the burning bush. Hey, I like that. Burning bush. That works, doesn't it?"

He saw the confused look on Sweeney's face and took pity.

"Look, if you're asking me how it all started, I can't help you. I came in late. But at some point Buzz met Nadia. Or Nadia met Buzz. And that's where the thing really begins. You look at us now, okay, and you can say what you want. We don't much care, you know? We're nomads. We're a tribe in the desert. That's how we see ourselves. You want to say we're vampires, we're parasites, well, those're just words. We know the truth. We're as much family as those scumbags that run the Clinic. We're as much family as you and your boy. That's the truth. And the truth sets you free, every time. You'll find that out real soon, Sweeney."

Sweeney tried to pull him back.

"You called Nadia a pimp," he said.

The Sheep crushed out his cigarette on the fender of the hearse.

"It's a metaphor," he said. "Jesus Christ. You know what a metaphor is? I'm not insulting her. In fact—and I think the rest'd tell you the same thing if they had the balls — we're a matriarchy. That's what we really are. She lets Buzz think he's the big bad dad. But the truth is we follow where Nadia leads. All the way to the last clinic. She's got the plans. She's the one who's brought us to this point. And I'll tell you, she's gonna bring us across the border. Whether Buzz likes it or not."

He paused, looked down at his boots and said, "But don't tell him I said that."

Sweeney was suddenly thinking too hard to stop and reassure the Sheep.

"Nadia was your nurse," he said. "In Phoenix."

The Sheep looked up and smiled and said, "Who says you're slow?"

"And she knew the family needed a new chemist?"

"The guy before me, the Gerbil, he put his bike down in Oakland. Got run over by a Camaro."

"So you move from clinic to clinic."

"You got to go where the work is."

"And what?" Sweeney said, trying to talk over the anxiety that was rising in his throat. "You do something to the coma patients? What do you do to the patients?"

"We do *nothing* but help them," the Sheep said. "This is a total win-win situation here. And if you let us, we can help Danny too."

"I'm not going to let you near Danny."

The Sheep gave him a patronizing smile.

"What?" he said. "You're going to kill us all? You? The pharmacist? Don't be an idiot all your life, Sweeney. It isn't necessary. You could turn everything around here if you'd just let go of the fear and let in the truth. I know. Because I did it."

The stoner voice was slipping a little and Sweeney recognized something behind it.

"You don't have to be alone," the Sheep said. "You're not supposed to be alone. None of us are. Buzz and Nadia and all of us accept you for what you are. You need some family, Sweeney. And we want you. Nadia wants you, I can tell you that. You got to make the leap. That's all. You think it will kill you, but it's the only thing that'll save you at this stage. I don't think you know how far gone you are. But you can turn the whole thing around tonight."

"You're not going to touch my son," Sweeney said. But there was more panic than resolve in his voice.

"Someone," the Sheep said, "already touched your son. And it wasn't us. We didn't put the boy in the coma, did we? Somebody else did that to him. Somebody else took him away from you. And all those fuckin' doctors with their fuckin' promises, they can't do squat to bring him back."

Sweeney stared at him.

The Sheep ran a hand over his skull. His head fell back and he closed his eyes for a while before he continued.

"I can help you and I can help Danny. I know I can. I can arrange for a reunion. You want to be with your son again, Sweeney?"

Sweeney sucked on his lips for an answer.

"You got to make the leap," the Sheep said. "No one can do it for you. You got to be strong and you got to have some faith. I'm not sayin' it isn't hard. But you can't go weak in the middle. This is going to be difficult. I won't lie to you like those assholes back at the Clinic. It's going to be frightening. Maybe terrifying. This is dangerous shit. And, yeah, it's addictive as it gets. You've never known real *want* till you've come back from Limbo. But you keep the faith and you'll make it. Out and back. You trust in Nadia and she'll take you to the last clinic. That's the real deal. And you better believe it."

The Sheep did a little stretch, then he gave Sweeney a quick shoulder hug, stood up, and walked back to his bike.

"You're not going to be alone anymore," he said. "After tonight, you'll be part of the whole thing. Just trust me."

FROM THAT POINT ON, Sweeney was numb. Wordlessly, he climbed on the back of the Sheep's bike. They bounced over rocks and bricks as they rolled slowly toward the Harmony, but the passenger felt nothing. Holding on was only a reflex. And so he had no understanding that this was the state toward which he'd been striving for the last year. That place beyond fear and rage. Beyond desire. At last, detachment had found him.

When the Sheep parked, Sweeney sat loose and limp and not quite there. His sensory equipment was working — he saw the Abominations tinkering with a bike, heard their calls from the dock. He smelled oil and beer. Could still feel the shift in weight as the Sheep dismounted. These sensations were registering but without any significance. Their meaning, the ability of their input to shape his reality, had been lost in the moment of the Sheep's embrace.

Sweeney sat on the back of the bike and waited for nothing in particular, knowing that he could wait until his bones turned to ash.

And it was as if the Abominations sensed this, because after a moment of the usual celebratory uproar upon the Sheep's arrival, they fell quiet and uneasy. Sweeney heard saliva being gulped over the hump in someone's throat. He heard boots shuffle on gravel and slow flies circling someone's beard.

Then Buzz appeared out on the loading apron and looked down on the Sheep and on Sweeney.

"Knew you'd come," he said.

Sweeney shrugged and said, "Did I have a choice?"

Buzz shook his head.

When Sweeney didn't get off the bike, Buzz gestured to the Fluke and the Elephant, who lifted him by the arms and dragged him across the yard and up the stairs to the dock. They propped him up in front of Buzz, who looked disappointed.

"You gonna be a dick about this?" he asked.

"I'm not going to be anything at all," Sweeney said.

Buzz took a deep breath. Sweeney watched the chest fill.

"Shit, son," Buzz said, "don't make me bring the bad Buzz out again. Can't you just believe I'm here to help you?"

"I can't believe," Sweeney said, "anything at all."

The Sheep joined them. Buzz kept his eyes on Sweeney but spoke to the chemist.

"How about you?" he asked. "How'd things go in the cave?"

"I got what I needed," the Sheep said.

But the comment didn't seem to bring Buzz much pleasure. He nodded for a few seconds, then said, "So how long you figure this should take?"

The Sheep looked at the two men, then down to his boots.

"If Sweeney helps me — " he began and Buzz said, "Sweeney'll help."

"Then we'll be ready before you know it."

Another nod, then Buzz said, "You go ahead. I'll send him up in a minute."

The Sheep hesitated, but only for a second. He moved to go inside the factory, stopped, turned back to say something, then changed his mind again, and went through the loading bay.

"Nadia misses you," Buzz said.

Sweeney asked, "Is Danny inside?"

"Danny's back at the Clinic," Buzz said. "Safe and sound. Under warm blankets."

Buzz expected an expression of relief or at least confusion. But the druggist looked as if he'd been spiked with an assful of Thorazine. Maybe given a little electroshock for good measure. The face was slack. Bored-looking. The body was loose, as if a knee to the groin would bring nothing but a dull, slow slump. The guy looked as if he could be deposited on a free bed at the Peck and no one would notice for a week. What the fuck had the Sheep said to him?

"You hear me?" Buzz said, a little louder and faster than he'd intended. "I said your kid was okay."

"I heard you fine," Sweeney said.

Buzz leaned into him, dropped his voice. "What the fuck's the matter with you? You want some food or something?"

"I don't want anything," Sweeney said.

Buzz turned to the Fluke and said, "Get him a drink. Then take him up to the Sheep."

"I don't want a drink," Sweeney said, but Buzz had already turned away.

The Fluke took Sweeney by the arm and led him inside the mill. There were a couple of Abominations lounging in the lunchroom, drinking and reading back issues of *Limbo*. They looked over to see the Fluke throw a thumb over his shoulder, then they grabbed their bottles and left the building.

"You don't want a beer or nothin'?" the Fluke asked and Sweeney shook his head. They exited the cafeteria, found their way to a wide, steep stairwell and climbed to an upper floor. There was only emergency lighting at that level, and it reminded Sweeney of the basement of the Peck. The Fluke led the way down a corridor and came to a stop at a door that featured some fading words stenciled on its opaque glass window — RESEARCH & DEVELOPMENT.

Sweeney followed the biker inside and found what looked like a large high school laboratory from the middle of the last century. The room was lit by dozens of candles and a handful of lanterns, which created a competition of shadows. Everything seemed covered in layers of grainy brick dust. In the corner, a portion of the plaster ceiling hung down like a great gray tongue streaked with fat veins of brown water stain.

The center of the room was lined with long, slablike tables, some fitted with marble tops, others with an odd green laminate. The tables were covered with lab equipment — test tubes and vials, beakers and graduated cylinders, Bunsen burners and a centrifuge, and a coffee mug that held various syringes and thermometers. A lot of nontraditional equipment was also scattered around — a Waring blender, a car battery, and some jumper cables. Lots of coiled wire, a wooden toolbox overflowing with pliers and screwdrivers. Wire coat hangers, plastic milk cartons, smoked glass jugs that Sweeney recognized from the pharmacy. An acetylene torch and a hot plate and several barbecue tongs and a white plastic egg timer. Underneath the tables were dozens of empty beer cases and an orange crate or two. It looked like a yard sale for chem majors.

Sweeney heard a toilet flush and the Sheep came out of an adjacent room, wearing plastic goggles and buckling his belt as he walked. A rolled-up comic book protruded from the back pocket of his jeans. Sweeney looked away before he could read the title. The Fluke shook his head and said, "Have fun, ladies," laughing as he left the room.

The Sheep moved to the tables, squatted and rummaged through boxes until he found two vinyl bib aprons. He threw one to Sweeney and slipped the other over his head.

"You have any coffee recently?" he asked.

Sweeney shook his head.

"Well," said the Sheep, "we'll call down for some later. I can't give you any speed, sorry to say. But you'll be needin' some caffeine."

He pulled some latex gloves from beneath a spool of copper wire and began to work his hands into them.

"I think there's another pair down there," he said but Sweeney didn't move.

The Sheep didn't seem too upset by this.

"It's your skin," he said and began to clear some space on the table before him. "Could you at least find us some decent music?"

There was an old Grundig on the floor.

"I'd love some Ethel Waters, but put on whatever you want," the Sheep said. "No one's allowed inside the mill while I'm working. And Buzz backs me up on that."

Sweeney walked around the tables, got down on one knee, switched on the radio, and began to spin the tuner. He slid through static and talk and came to a stop at "Shame on the World."

"Now that," the Sheep said, "surprises me. I woulda figured you for an arena rock kind of guy. Real meat and potatoes, you know?"

Sweeney sat down on a metal stool and watched the Sheep prepare his workspace. There was a methodical ease to the guy, a comfort level among the equipment and the solutions that he'd never find with people. It was that lab rat sensibility, that chronic desire to live in the midst of a process. In the heart of something quantifiable and repeatable.

The Sheep felt himself being watched, but didn't seem to mind. He'd run a garden hose out of the bathroom tap and was filling a couple of beakers.

Sweeney surprised himself by saying, "That's some quality control."

The Sheep didn't flinch.

"Don't need any quality control," he said. "That's one of the things I learned in the cave."

He held a test tube out in the air and, without thinking, Sweeney got to his feet and took it from him. Now the Sheep was firing on all cylinders, using one hand to swirl the tap water in the beaker, another to hold a small brown envelope to his mouth that he tore open with his teeth. He spit the flap to the floor, brought the envelope to his nose, and sniffed. Then he held it out to Sweeney, who declined the scent.

"You got a steady hand?" the Sheep asked.

Sweeney took the question as rhetorical and held out the tube. The Sheep poured the crystalline contents of the envelope without spilling a grain. Then he threw the envelope to the floor and took the tube from Sweeney, who remained by his side.

"Some people," the Sheep said, "need to go into the desert for revelation. But I can't stand wide-open spaces. All that sky, it's terrible." He talked as he worked, pouring colored liquids from soup cans and beer bottles that looked as if they'd never been washed, let alone sterilized. "Maybe I'm agoraphobic. That's the word, isn't it? But if so, they never mentioned it. I heard *paranoid* and I heard *delusional* and a lot of other not-so-nice things. But to the best of my knowledge nobody ever said *agoraphobic.*"

He produced more envelopes and plastic baggies, making them appear out of seemingly nowhere. At points, he reminded Sweeney of a particularly intense teppanyaki chef that he and Kerry had liked at the Tokyo Gardens back in Cleveland.

"But my point is, for some people, they got to go out under that big sky, with no boundaries, in order to get the truth. Now I'm just the opposite. I need to go *inward,* you see. I need to burrow in. Caves are perfect for me. I'm like a mole, you know? The deeper and the darker, the better. If the answer's gonna come, it's gonna come in the caves."

The radio played "Take These Chains." Sweeney found himself assisting. The Sheep's instructions were never explicit, but Sweeney had no trouble determining what he wanted.

"And I gotta say, I think that's appropriate. Cuz I don't know how much Buzz might've told you, but we're headed *inside,* right? When all's said and done, *that's* where the real cosmos is, you know?"

Sweeney answered in grunts. The radio played "She's a Winner" and "Reap What You Sow." At some point, the Fluke came up to the loft carrying two mugs of coffee. The Sheep downed his in a single gulp. Sweeney washed out beakers, ran the centrifuge, boiled down liquids. On occasion, he caught himself identifying aromas, taking note of colors.

It was pleasant work, and the Sheep was good company. A little spacey, tripped-out for a lab rat, but warm and smart and funny. Eventually the focus of all their labor became a tin saucepan that simmered on low atop the hot plate. The Sheep stirred the contents with a wooden spoon, his face tilted down over the mouth of the pan and engulfed in its vapors. Sweeney joined him, looked down and saw a thin purple broth.

"Is it soup yet?" he asked.

"That's funny," the Sheep said. "That's what Buzz calls it. But personally, I like to think of it more like chili."

He tapped the spoon on the lip of the pan, then set it down in the dust of the worktable. "This," he said, "is just the beans. We're still waitin' on the meat, you might say. The meat's the most important part. I tried a dozen recipes, okay, and some were better'n others. But it wasn't till this last trip to the caves that I got everything worked out just right. The soup was always too thick or too thin. Like in Goldilocks, you know? Too little meat and everything's just pale and bland. And too much meat and you'll put the boys in their own fuckin' coma. That's the thing to remember. It's all about the meat."

"The meat," said Nadia, from the doorway, "has arrived."

She was dressed in her nurse's uniform, all cotton, white on white. Her hair was still pulled back, and Sweeney found it strange to see her Clinic persona playing here in Gehenna. She stared at the Sheep and ignored Sweeney.

Nadia reached into her pocket and withdrew a vial. It was small and plastic, capped with a green stopper and filled with a pink liquid. She handed it to the Sheep, who held it up to the light and closed one eye to look at it.

"You said it was okay if I got some blood with the fluid."

Nadia sounded brittle, a little defensive. But Sweeney could see that the Sheep was thrilled.

"A little blood," he said, "might be just the thing."

He moved to the hot plate, pulled the stopper with his teeth, and poured the pink liquid into the soup. Then he grabbed the wooden spoon and began to stir. Nadia looked from the Sheep to Sweeney and said, "The kid says hello."

Sweeney came around the tables toward her, and the Sheep, without taking his eye off the saucepan, said, "Don't fuckin' touch her."

Nadia couldn't stop the smile. She put a hand on her hip, gave an exaggerated roll of the eyes. "You chivalrous bastard," she said but Sweeney couldn't tell to whom she was talking.

"What was in the vial?" he said to Nadia.

"So much for the afterglow," she said but the Sheep answered the question.

"It's Danny's brain fluid," he said. "They check the pressure in his skull cavity and if they need to, they drain the fluid. You know that, Sweeney."

Sweeney couldn't stop staring at Nadia.

The Sheep went on.

"Don't make a big thing out of this. Normally, they'd throw the drainage in toxic waste and it'd be burned in the morning. We're taking something he doesn't need, Sweeney. Something that's poisonous to him."

"We're helping Danny out," Nadia said. "And if you can control yourself, we're going to help you out too."

He wanted to slap her. Knock her to the ground. Break an arm or a leg. But everything they were saying was true. They did have to drain Danny's shunt once or twice a week. They'd done it back at St. Joe's. It relieved the pressure on the brain. A simple procedure. And the fluid was nothing but waste product. He'd watched Mrs. Heller throw a hundred vials into the toxic box. He'd never given them another thought.

He turned to the Sheep and said, "You're going to *drink* this shit?"

Nadia laughed and the Sheep said, "Actually, we're gonna take it intravenously." He put down the wooden spoon again and turned to Nadia.

"Call the boys in," he said. "And tell Buzz soup's on."

23

The Abominations had built a little campfire inside a massive stew kettle. They'd placed the pan on the floor in the center of the lunchroom and were sitting around it in a semicircle. Buzz was prodding the makeshift kindling with a tire iron. Opposite him, Sweeney was staring at the faces, all of them warped by shadow. The bikers looked like kids on Christmas morning, made silent by a panicky desire for a specific gift and a concurrent terror that it might not be under the tree.

The Sheep was in the middle of the semicircle, on his knees, holding a tin beer tray that held a pile of syringes. While everyone watched, he began loading the spikes with the contents of the saucepan.

Buzz put down the tire iron and said, "Looks a little thin,"

The Sheep shook his head.

"Looks," he said, and snapped a finger against the last needle, "can be deceiving as a motherfucker."

Buzz smiled but he let his voice go low when he said, "Careful there, Alvin."

"How 'bout you take a taste, Buzz," the Sheep said, "and then tell me how thin it is?"

Sweeney had watched his son receive countless injections but this was something else. Something disconnected from the medical, and tied, entirely, to the ritualistic.

Buzz extended his arm. The fire lit a coating of sweat across the bulge of muscle and vein. It was cool in the room but Buzz was stripped to the waist. He made the Sheep come to him. There was no rubber tie-off, no alcohol swab or sterile gauze. The Sheep put two fingers in his mouth and wet them with his tongue. Then he popped them free and slapped them across the underside of Buzz's forearm. It was a sound that would stay with Sweeney.

The Sheep hugged the arm against his stomach, picked his line. He waited a second, concentrating, then looked up. He and Buzz stared at each other. Then he forced the tip of the needle under the skin and into the channel. He pushed until the hilt of the syringe came flush to the arm, then thumbed the plunger, forcing the soup into the bloodstream. Buzz didn't move. Didn't blink. But Sweeney thought he saw his lips tremble.

After a while, the Sheep pulled the needle free and threw the syringe into the fire. Buzz sat back on his heels. The Abominations studied him. He put his head in his hands, pulled in a long breath. He said something to himself. It might have been, "Oh, Jesus."

The Sheep gave a self-satisfied nod and handed the beer tray to the Ant, who took a syringe and passed the tray down the line. The rest of the crew fixed themselves, messy or neat, but all of them relatively silent. When the tray got to Sweeney, he handed it back to the Sheep.

"Your turn," said the Sheep, holding up a syringe. He smiled and thumbed the plunger just a bit to make the needle spurt.

"I don't think so," Sweeney said.

"I can't fix," the Sheep said, "until you fix. Buzz's orders."

"Buzz," Sweeney said, "is incapacitated."

"True enough," the Sheep said, glancing down at his leader, who was moving his mouth but failing to emit any sounds. "But he'll be better than new tomorrow. And he'll be disappointed if he finds out we didn't follow orders."

"Well," said Sweeney, "there's at least two ways around that."

The Sheep smiled but it was forced.

"Should I even hear them?" he asked.

"The simple way," Sweeney said, "would be for us to tell him what he wants to hear."

The Sheep shook his head, disappointed, patience exhausted.

"That won't work," he said. "For reasons you won't understand unless you take your medicine here."

"That leaves the second way, then."

And though the Sheep didn't want to ask, he said, "Which is?"

"Which is," Sweeney said, "I go outside and drain all the petrol out of your tanks. Then I come back inside and pour it all over these scumbags. And then I drop a match and run the fuck out of here."

The Sheep finally let the hand that held the syringe drop into his lap.

"I know we just met," he said, "but I don't think so. You're a fuckin' pharmacist from Cleveland."

Sweeney stood up, loomed over the Sheep, and said, "I'm tired of people who don't know shit about me thinking that they do."

The Sheep wouldn't back down.

"So you're saying," he said, "that you'd rather incinerate all of us than take a chance and find out what this is all about?"

"You're threatening my son. The only reason I wake up every day is to take care of my son."

"And you can't believe that we're here to help you both?"

Sweeney stared at him. The Sheep held up the syringe halfheartedly and said, "C'mon, take the leap."

"Take it yourself."

Which is what the Sheep did. He found a vein, low, on his left arm, inserted the spike and flooded himself with the soup.

"What is it with fathers," he said, eyes fluttering a little, voice slight and soft, "that they can't make the leap?"

Within a minute the Sheep went into a fetal crouch. The sight of it made Sweeney flinch. He looked at all of them, immobilized, lying on their backs or sides, faces waxy in the firelight. One of them — he thought it was the Ant — was drooling. Another, maybe the Rabbit, was twitching his hands in some logorrhea of signing.

Sweeney stepped over the Sheep, toed Buzz's body and got no response. He put his foot on Buzz's chest and started to apply pressure. Nothing. He kneeled down and put a hand to Buzz's face, pinched the nostrils closed and fixed a palm over the mouth. Buzz didn't struggle. Buzz didn't make a sound. Sweeney took his hand from the face and knew something was wrong.

The Abominations had gone to the trouble of kidnapping him, of sending him into the cave to find the Sheep, of making sure he was present for the creation of the soup. They'd told him about the origin of the fluid. They'd seated him around the fire and let him watch while they fixed, and then collapsed into something beyond stupor. And now here they were, unconscious, harmless, helpless. Entirely vulnerable. Temporarily comatose. He could do anything he wanted right now. He could baptize them in gasoline, as he'd threatened. Turn them to ash if he wanted.

And Buzz would've known that. Buzz would have taken precautions. He could have tied Sweeney down and shot him up. He could have waited until Sweeney was unconscious before he let his crew fix.

So what to do now? Calling the police would pull him into the middle of an ugly investigation. Which certainly would delay his departure from the city. And once he was tainted by the story, what clinic would accept Danny? And what pharmacy would offer a position?

But the alternative was to get rid of the Abominations on his own. To go through with his original idea — soak them in gas while they're incapacitated and incinerate them.

He was picturing the scene when Nadia entered the cafeteria. She was wearing a short robe, green and satin and clinging to her. Her hair was wet and pushed straight back over her head. Her feet were bare and she had a towel rolled around her neck.

She looked over her tribe and then at Sweeney and said indifferently, "Decided not to join them?"

"Yeah," Sweeney said. "Just like you."

She shook her head, used the end of the towel to dab some water from her nose.

"I never fix," she said. "I watch over them. In case they need me."

She started into the kitchen, calling over her shoulder, "You want a beer?"

He didn't respond. He waited until she returned and said, "Why didn't they make me do it? Why didn't they shoot me up?"

She brushed past him, went to a bench and sat down with her legs underneath her. The robe spread open on her thigh. She took a long drink from a bottle of Hunthurst and casually opened a copy of *Limbo* that was on the table.

"Buzz has this idea," and the way she accented the word conveyed a little contempt. "He can bring you to the water. But he can't make you save yourself. He's kind of earnest like that. It's one of his best virtues. Not a lot of imagination, but he's got the passion. For someone like Buzz, you know, the trip to Limbo is an end unto itself."

"And that's not your take?"

Nadia shook her head.

"This whole ritual," she said, "the traveling, the harvesting, the whole communion of the soup, I'm sorry, it's just bullshit to me. It's vampire theater. And it consumes too much time and money. At best, it's a means to an end. Honestly, I can't wait till we're done with it."

"Done with it?"

She put the comic book down, made her voice lower.

"There's a place," she said, "where you don't need the soup. A real place. A clinic in Old Bohemia. Very exclusive. Very hard to find. But I know I can get us there. And I know it's the last clinic we'll ever need."

"So go," he said. "Just go and leave me and my boy alone."

"It's not so simple. Buzz isn't up for the trip. He's hopeless. The eternal nomad. He wants to keep moving. I try to tell him — movement for the sake of movement is just another trap. It's reductive after a while. I want to take my boys to the next level. Where we won't even need the soup to move through the membrane."

"And what about Buzz?"

"I'm working," she said, "on saving Buzz. On saving everyone."

Sweeney took a few steps into the middle of the pile of Abominations. He rested a foot on the Elephant's hip and said, "Yeah, they look saved."

"Like the Sheep said, looks can be deceiving. Are you scared of it?"

"Am I scared? Of ingesting brain fluid and whatever other shit this idiot cuts it with?"

Nadia smiled and looked back to the comic book, shaking her head above her bottle.

"He's not an idiot, Sweeney. Trust me on that."

"Well, you should know. You're the one who found him in Phoenix."

"He told you?" she asked, unfazed, taking another sip of beer.

"He told me you're their pimp," Sweeney said. "You're the one who finds the fresh victims."

"Victims?" Nadia repeated. "Little dramatic there, don't you think? Who've we victimized?"

He stepped off the Elephant and moved to the table and looked down over her.

"Danny to start with," he said. "And me."

"You? Jesus, Sweeney, you live to be a victim. Did you feel like a victim last night? While you were fucking me?"

He put his hand around her throat and started to squeeze. She looked up at him, unafraid, giving away nothing.

"I'm leaving now," he said, but he kept the pressure constant. "I'm getting my son and I'm getting the fuck out of this city. And if you come after us, I'll kill every one of you."

Now she started to make the choking sounds. She dropped the beer bottle, reached up and put both hands around his wrist. He let go of the throat, but she held onto the hand. Pushed it down from her neck and inside the robe and across her right breast. He tried to pull away and she held firm.

And then he was untying the robe with his free hand and she was leaning back on the bench and pulling him down on top of her. The kinetics of it were fast and brutal. No grace, no tenderness. His mouth went down on her neck. She arched her back, pulled his hair. He pushed her legs open. She pulled off his shirt and threw it, pulled the T-shirt beneath out of the pants. They worked together to unbuckle and unzip, got his pants down past his knees and left them there.

Then he was in her and they were both bucking, working for the rhythm. He dropped his head. A nipple fell into and out of his mouth. She made a sound, grabbed at his shoulders. He got his hands up under her arms, felt her sweat, tried to lift her, reposition her. He felt her hands under his balls, on his ass, up his back. The speed and force of his thrusts increased. He looked at her face. The eyes were open but squinting. He looked down at the floor, saw the Abominations, immobile, staring at nothing. He looked at the fire, felt himself starting to come.

And then felt the stab of the spike.

He ejaculated but the orgasm broke off, went numb before climax. He yelled, tried to pull out and roll away but she had her legs wrapped around his waist and his own legs were strapped by his pants.

Then she released him and he fell to the floor, trying to turn around and look at his backside, hands flailing behind him. He was on his knees, turning from side to side. He heard her say, "I don't agree with Buzz," and looked up, saw her holding a syringe. Her legs were still splayed, her face shining, sweaty in the firelight. Her head was resting on the lunch table and she'd pulled the robe closed over her breasts.

She threw the syringe past him into the campfire. There was a bloody smudge across her fingers. She brought herself up to sitting, seemed to swoon a little before she steadied herself with her hands.

She looked at Sweeney and said, "I don't think you have to save yourself."

She pulled the comic book into her lap, leaned toward him over her knees. Her face started to fade and there were flashes of light behind her as if someone were taking pictures.

The last thing Sweeney heard was, "I'll see you on the other side."

LIMBO COMICS

FROM ISSUE # 9: "The Castle on the Cliff"

. . . The freaks rode in steerage out of the interior plains, packed in the darkness and stench of the elephant trailer. At night, they slept in open fields, under a moon that looked too big and clear to be real. And if they had heard the collision with the Resurrectionist, none of them spoke of it.

Though there was traveling money, they chose to scavenge their food from the wilds in order to avoid seeing others. They shared a need to be alone for a time, as family. To bind into one another in preparation for whatever lay ahead. And as they moved toward the western shores, they found even more untamed territories in which to hide. Much of Gehenna, it seemed, lay unconquered. The troupe spied the occasional sign of civilization, towns and villages that had sprouted around railstops. But from a distance, these settlements appeared more outposts than anything else, precarious—and maybe temporary—havens for the restless and the pursued.

Again they kept to the back roads and the wooded pathways. The chicken boy told Bruno when and where to turn, made all the fork-in-the-road decisions. His seizures were getting more severe if less frequent. And when he returned from Limbo, he rarely had much to say about what he had learned. He studied the sun and the stars, gave directions to the strongman, and withdrew more deeply into himself. Kitty was both hurt and worried. She watched as Chick scribbled ferociously in his diary. She tried to ignore his nighttime wanderings away from camp and into the dense forests where the troupe hid.

The chicken boy's confession finally came on the night that Aziz first smelled the salt of the ocean. They had pulled into a grove of enormous trees and were moving through the usual camp-making routines when the human torso tossed his head back, pulled in air through his nose, and announced, "I think we've reached the shores."

All of the other freaks froze in place and began to imitate Aziz. And after a moment they started to nod and then murmur their agreement. In the wake of the murmuring came the celebratory sounds of a homecoming—though, of course, none had ever been to the western shores before. Their joy and hope were born of a sense of destination achieved. The fact that this destination was an unknown landscape didn't matter very much at first.

Durga, Jeta, and Antoinette danced together in a small circle. Vasco and Marcel did their own little jig. Nadja and Milena embraced and hooted. Aziz hopped around on his knuckles like a frog. Only Chick maintained the gravity of the road, opening his beak in an effort to taste the salt that hung in the air. As if needing to confirm something.

Seeing the look on the chicken boy's face, Bruno tamped down the revelry and called the troupe to a meeting. When they were all settled on the ground, the strongman put his remaining hand on his hip and spoke.

"It seems," he said, "that we're very close now. The ocean is less than a day away. And, believe me, I'm as anxious as all of you to get off the road and rest for a while. But I think, right now, that the one who brought us here should say a few words."

He lowered himself to the ground with only marginally less grace than he'd once possessed.

Chick looked hesitant as he stood before the clan. He toed the earth as he thought about how best to begin. He scratched absentmindedly at his feathers and avoided eye contact.

Eventually, he said, "We've come a long way."

The words triggered a whoop of affirmation from Fatos. Chick ignored the mule and pressed on.

"I want to thank all of you for having faith in me. You took a great chance. A great leap. I've never claimed to understand what happens when I go into Limbo. I just know that I hear and see things. And that those things feel true and real to me. So I want to thank you for trusting in something that none of us understand. Your faith is what makes it so hard to tell you this last bit."

He paused and let the mood of the group change, felt the joy and excitement start to turn to anxiousness and suspicion.

"I know that we've all been looking for the same thing. We've been looking for a place where we can be our true selves, together. We've been looking for a haven. A place of refuge and sanctuary."

Jeta nodded her agreement. Milena began to scowl and lean forward.

"But the fact is, I can't promise you that place. It might be at the end of our road. And then again, it might not."

Kitty reached over, took Nadja's claw. Vasco and Marcel brought hands together nervously and cracked knuckles.

"All my life, I've been searching for my father. I think it's my father who led me through the Limbo. I think it's my dad who brought us to where we are tonight. And now, I think, he needs our help. And I think, if we help him, that he'll help us in return."

The chicken boy went quiet for a second and studied his comrades' faces. The freaks looked back at Chick, unsure of what to say or do. Except for Bruno, who decided to push the boy.

"Tell us," the strongman said, "exactly what you have to tell us."

Chick looked at Bruno and nodded.

"Tomorrow," Chick said, "we'll arrive at the western shore. And at the castle of Dr. Fliess."

At the mention of the name, Jeta burst into tears. At the sight of the tears, Antoinette became hysterical. Durga pulled both of them into her breast and looked to Milena for help. But the hermaphrodite only smiled at the fat lady and remained placid and unmoving.

"You've got to be kidding me," Bruno said, standing and walking up to Chick in order to tower over him. "We spend this entire time running *from* Fliess. And now you tell us we were actually running *to* him."

"I didn't know," Chick said, weakly. "Not until the last few days. Not for sure."

"You said *your father* would be waiting," Bruno said, confused.

Chick nodded. "Fliess has my father. And we have to free him."

"You want us to go to the castle?" Vasco asked, incredulous.

"And demand that Fliess hand over your poppa?" asked Marcel, out-raged.

"No," said Chick, backing up as more of them rose from the ground and came toward him. "Of course not. I have a way in. There are tunnels. A series of caves that lead into the castle. I know exactly where to find my father. And I know, if we can free him, he can help us."

That there was anger and outrage, disappointment and fear, did not surprise Chick. His own reaction to the knowledge of what lay in wait at the end of their road was profound sadness. The clan had relied on him to bring them to refuge. And instead, he had delivered them into their greatest terror and deposited them at the feet of their enemy. So he understood the bitterness that lay at the bottom of the troupe's surprise. And beyond this, he felt his own particular brand of grief surge back into every feather of his body, the anguish that had simmered, for years, from the beginning, just on the edge of his consciousness. And he realized that whether or not his freaks abandoned him in the end, he would go to Fliess's castle. And he would be saved or damned. But he would find whatever last truths were available to him. Because to live forever with a grief that deforms the heart is unacceptable—an abomination that must not be tolerated.

In the end, it was Milena who settled things and decided how the story would end.

"We're here," s/he shouted, drowning out the timorous carping of the others. "We've followed him this far. Now, we can call it a day and split up. Take our chances wandering around, looking for a show that will have us. Or we can trust in the chicken boy. We can play this out to the end. We can go to the castle and find his daddy and see what the man can do for us."

It was as simple as that. As if all that had been needed was for a hermaphrodite to state, succinctly, the facts of the matter, and the options those facts generated. Milena's tone was enough to indicate which option s/he had embraced. And once s/he declared her allegiance, the others began to fall in line. Their outrage and terror petered out rapidly and dissipated into little more than an undercurrent of grumbling. And suddenly, almost instantly, they were whole again.

Durga and Nadja got busy pulling together the night's supper. And though the clan ate in silence, even the pinhead understood that all of them would remain a family to the end. There would be no splintering of the freaks. Come salvation or oblivion, they would face the future together.

And so, over a dessert of fresh berries and nuts, Bruno consulted with Chick, and the decision was made to set out just before midnight. They broke camp, buried their fire, left the truck to rust in the woods and followed the chicken boy on a path that, though it did not deter the freaks, did nothing to calm or reassure them. Within minutes of setting out on their last trek, they were overcome with a stench that made the slaughterhouses of Maisel seem like cologne shops by comparison. The ground beneath their feet turned into a hard, cracked clay of some sort. They tramped with hands and claws covering mouths and noses, taking short, careful steps that left them prematurely tired and uneasy.

They moved into and out of a fetid, swampy patch, slogging through warm murky water or pulling their feet step by step from the sucking mud. They passed through an infestation of fat, buzzing insects whose bites left welts the size of kroners over any exposed areas of flesh or fur. The freaks cried and groaned and cursed and threatened to turn back. But finally they emerged just meters away from a cascade of enormous boulders that coalesced into a cliff wall, atop which sat what could only be the castle of Dr. Fliess.

It loomed, as if it had been waiting for them since the day of its unlikely construction, all black iron and terrible rivets, countless stories of dark metal and tiny bug-eye windows. At its top was a single turret of tall glass panes, like a lighthouse, revealing a single, dim light within. From the top of the turret, a black metal spire thrust up into the sky like a lightning rod. And from the spire flew an enormous red flag, visible in the moonlight, its undulations in the wind incapable of obscuring the Gothic black *F* imprinted on its face.

Antoinette brought a hand up to cover her eyes, as if the mere sight of the castle and its awful banner would turn them all to stone. Jeta began to edge backward into the marshland from which they'd just emerged and Milena had to hold the skeleton's hand to keep her from fleeing.

"That's where we have to go," Chick said, pointing to the turret. "That's where he's keeping my father."

He looked to Bruno, but the strongman only nodded his head, gesturing to the mountain of rocks before them. So Chick led the way to the bottom of the cliff, moving to a smooth purple boulder that sat flush against the granite wall. He inspected it quickly, put his palm against its cool surface, then turned to Bruno and said, "This is the one."

The others stepped back and made room for the strongman, who wasted no time putting his good shoulder to the shale and heaving all of his mass into the stone. It took time and effort to move the rock and at one point, Fatos attempted to offer assistance. But Chick warned him away with a look. They let Bruno grunt and heave, sweat breaking over his face, veins bulging across the dome of his skull. And gradually, the stone was rolled aside and an opening was revealed behind it, carved into the face of the cliff wall.

Chick smiled at the strongman, who was hunched down over his knees, blinking at his feet and breathing heavily. "It will be dark inside," the chicken boy said. "Let's stay close together." And with that he entered the black hole of the cave.

The others followed, single file, Durga just managing to squeeze through. The air inside was close and stale. The tunnel opened out almost at once, but as it did, the sound of their steps on the stone walkway beneath their feet echoed loudly. Bruno brought up the rear of their parade. The freaks had no torches, not even a kitchen match among them, so they proceeded by touch and sound. They could all feel the curve of the path they walked and its upward slant. They were spiraling, Bruno knew, up a slowly inclining ramp, toward the top of the castle.

Everyone lost his or her sense of time after a while. Random and unsettling noises came and went—growling of stomach, clearing of throat, and what might have been the skittering of vermin across the flagstones beneath their feet. At some point they heard a muted weeping or laughing, but when Milena attempted to shush Jeta, the skeleton denied the sound had come from her.

And before Milena could argue, Chick crashed, beak first, into something and the clan collided, one into the next, fronts into backs. The chicken boy brought up a hand and touched a smooth wood panel that angled down at him sharply from the ceiling of the cave. It was a hatch of some sort and it was freezing. He pulled his hand away at once and called for Bruno. The strongman had to get on his belly and crawl between Durga's legs, then squeeze past all the others until he arrived at the front of the line, where Chick indicated the door.

Bruno ran his hand over it, searching for a latch or a knob, but the chicken boy already knew the effort was futile.

"You'll have to break it down," Chick whispered, just as the realization dawned on his friend.

The strongman had an even harder time with the hatch than he'd had with the boulder at the base of the mountain. He had to work against gravity, to thrust his body upward into the impasse. With all his strength, he rammed his good shoulder into the hatch, as hard as he could, a dozen times before growing frustrated and angry. He pounded on the door with his fist. Slapped at it and punched it and then, in the instant when pique turned into fury, he bashed it with his head.

The bolt snapped and the trap flew upward and suddenly the freaks were illuminated by a dim yellow light that shone from above.

Bruno was bleeding from his brow but he ignored the gash, silently got down on his knees, and hunched his torso over. Chick understood that the strongman was offering himself as a stepstool and began to direct the troupe, one at a time, to climb up the patriarch's back and pull themselves into the turret. A single grunt issued from the Behemoth when Durga trod his spine. But Fatos and the twins pitched in to haul the fat lady to the top of the castle.

When Bruno used his remaining arm to pull himself up through the hatchway, he thought Chick was about to slide into Limbo. The boy was shivering and his eyes were locked in that unblinking daze. But, in fact, there was no seizure under way. Instead, the chicken boy was transfixed by the gaunt man, suspended from the dome ceiling of the turret by chains shackled to his wrists.

The man was dressed in simple black pants and a white peasant shirt. He was shoeless and his feet were dirty with dried blood. His skull drooped and rolled on his neck as if he were balanced on the edge of consciousness. His feet dangled just above Bruno's head. His arms looked as if, in the next second, they might tear away from the body at the shoulders.

But Milena was already removing the lantern from a small table that sat behind the hanging man, shoving the table forward and motioning for Bruno to climb on top of it. Bruno wasn't sure the table could support his weight, but he mounted it anyway, then proceeded to take hold of the chains that bound the prisoner.

The freaks stared while Bruno ripped the chains from the ceiling. The hanging man dropped to the ground at the chicken boy's feet. Chick went down on one knee, lifted the man's head in his hands. The man's eyes fluttered, then closed, as his mouth opened and the tongue inside batted around for a moment until he swallowed and found his voice and managed to say, "I knew you would come."

Without any difficulty, the man came up on his knees and embraced the chicken boy. Over Chick's shoulder, he surveyed the whole clan and, in a louder voice, said, "I knew you would all come."

And then things happened so quickly that Antoinette would not suspect the truth until hours later, when she heard the first shovels of sand being tossed atop her casket.

The hanging man transformed his embrace into something closer to a choke hold and called for his creatures, a horde of grotesque homunculi—half-naked gargoyles with red eyes and diminutive but overly muscular bodies—which emerged through the trapdoor and swarmed into the turret.

And in that instant, Chick knew that the Limbo had turned on him. And that the man they had just rescued could not be anyone but their dreaded enemy and pursuer, the demon at the heart of all of their nightmares, the mad Dr. Fliess.

Within seconds, Fliess's creatures had filled the turret, thronged over and captured all of the freaks. Bruno threw and kicked and stomped a dozen or more of the monstrosities before Fliess called the strongman's attention to the scalpel held at the chicken boy's neck.

Bruno and Fliess stared at each other until the doctor said, "Surely even a strongman knows when to surrender."

Antoinette was hysterical beneath a swarm of Fliess's monsters, who had her pinned on the floor. One of them bent back the cone of her head, as if making ready to snap the neck. Seeing this, Bruno gave up the fight and the creatures battened onto his legs and arm. The deformed angel on the pinhead's back moved its hands to cover her mouth and silence her.

"Very good," Fliess said, lifting himself and Chick to standing and walking to the far side of the room to get a better look at the entire troupe.

"You are more hideous," he said, "than even I could have imagined." He hugged Chick more tightly, brought his mouth to the chicken boy's ear and added, "And I have a vivid imagination."

Behind the doctor, out the turret's window, Milena could see a vast ocean that rolled beyond the far side of the castle. For only a moment, s/he wondered about her chances of crashing through the glass and diving to the water far below. But at the end of that moment, s/he knew the idea was simply life's last kick in the ass. A final instance of false hope.

"It's true," the doctor said to the freaks, "that I will never understand fear in the manner, or to the degree, that you understand fear. And yet, it breaks my heart and it angers me that you've allowed fear to damn you."

"I'm not afraid of you," Chick said, staring at the strongman.

The doctor shrugged awkwardly while maintaining his hold on the boy.

"Despite all appearances," he said, "you're human. And like all of us, you fear the unknown."

"You don't know anything about us," Bruno said, in a voice that should have held rage but, instead, contained only the sound of terminal failure.

"That's incorrect, Mr. Seboldt," Fliess said. "Try to remember that nothing is as it seems. That's the original good advice."

Then the freaks were marched out of the turret's proper exit and down a long series of stairs and dark landings that led, eventually, out of the front gate and down a steep and narrow stone stairwell cut into the cliff. They were brought out into a small circle of beach, a horse-shoe cove of hard, brown sand. There were no hysterics when they saw the graves that had been dug during the low tide or the simple pine boxes that rested next to their tombs.

Instead, Jeta and Antoinette wept and the others tried, with vary-ing degrees of success, to assume a stoic posture. Without any delay, the gargoyles brought the freaks, in groups of two or three, to their respective coffins. No one fought and no one tried to flee. As if they'd all come, at the same instant, to some unspoken understanding or ex-haustion. As if all of their spirits were like a circuit of circus lights and each one had gone out in the line.

The box for Durga was, of course, enormous. As was the one for Mar-cel and Vasco. Chick found himself wondering how the homunculi would manage to lower the crates into the ground. Then, ashamed at the thought, he found himself enraged. But when he spotted Kitty's tiny coffin, his emotions simply imploded. He collapsed against the mad Dr. Fliess in a convulsion of self-loathing and despair, crushed under the realization that he had delivered the people he loved most deeply, most truly, into oblivion. Into the hopeless and ceaseless Limbo.

With one hand, Fliess stroked the chicken boy's feathered cheek. With the other, the doctor adjusted the blade of his scalpel against Chick's neck and made the boy lift his head.

"I want you," the doctor said, "to witness this."

And so, Chick watched through tear-splintered eyes as Bruno, the strongest man in the world, climbed, of his own free will, into his cas-ket, and lay down, without a word of objection. One by one, the other freaks followed his lead.

The freaks had fought or run all the way across Gehenna. And now, here they were, models of acceptance and docility. More than anything else, in that moment, Chick wanted one final seizure, one last chance to fade out and quake and ask the reason for this gentle capitulation.

But the seizure would not come. There was no bile in his throat. No chill telegraphing up his spine. And so he tore his eyes off his clan as they lay down one by one. And turned his head upward to Dr. Fliess and asked, "Why?"

The doctor looked down at the chicken boy hesitantly, with a gaze that even a pinhead would call loving.

"Because," said the doctor, "I am a man of both science and compassion."

25

It was like cream at first. White on white and thick. And there was a richness, a hard sweetness. And cold moving toward freezing. That was where Sweeney first felt himself in the new moment. The sensation of his testicles rising with the cold, withdrawing — that's what made it real, that sense of his body, that awareness. That's what made it something more than a dream. Gave it a solidity that made it true.

He was still inside the factory. And Buzz and the Abominations were spread out around him, still in dream. That was his first sound, their collective respiration. He opened his eyes and blinked, surveyed the room and saw that Nadia was gone. He looked down to see that his pants had been pulled up and rebelted. There was a piercing sensation, like a bee sting, in the small of his back near the base of his spine. He rubbed it and only aggravated the pain.

He got to his knees and then, with some effort, to his feet. He made his way out of the cafeteria, through the kitchen, and out the loading bay onto the concrete apron. In the moonlight, he could make out the ruins behind the Harmony but everything was out of focus. He took his hand from his back, pinched the bridge of his nose and rubbed down into the circles beneath his eyes. When he looked again, his vision had cleared. In fact, everything now appeared hyperfocused, more real than real. And somewhere out among the debris of the back lot, he began to hear a noise.

At first it was difficult to locate the source. The sound echoed and distorted on its way across the yards of brick and stone. Without thinking, Sweeney jumped down off the loading dock and began to walk toward the abandoned hearse, where the Abominations had played King of the Hill.

Halfway to the hearse, he understood that the noise was a human voice, a child's cry of grief and fear. And then Sweeney was running.

When he got to the hearse, he ran from door to door, pulling at each handle. But they were all locked. He began to circle the vehicle, pounding on the smoked glass of the windows. And the more he pounded, the louder the crying grew. The sound was making him frantic. He drummed his fists against the windows but nothing happened. He jumped up onto the hood and began to kick away at the windshield with his heels, but he could not shatter the glass.

Sweeney began to sweat and his breathing became labored. But at last, near the point of exhaustion, he moved around the rear of the hearse, got on his knees, and reached down for a brick. Bringing it up above his head, he let gravity carry the red block down against the hearse's rear window, which cracked neatly down its center. Sweeney stood and dropped the brick, used his elbow to shatter the window, reached inside the hearse, and unlatched and swung open the gate.

Bending at the waist, he peered inside. And saw that the crying child was his son. And that his son's body was covered in feathers. In all other respects, the boy looked normal, healthy. He was simply shrouded in a layer of down.

At the sight of his father, Danny stopped crying and yelled, "Daddy."

Sweeney inserted his arms and extracted Danny from the hearse. Then the father fell back on his heels and cradled the child against his chest. And both of them breathed and shivered and held onto each other.

"I didn't know where you were," Danny said, starting to cry again. "I didn't know where you went."

"It's okay, Danny," Sweeney said, hugging his son more tightly, cupping the boy's head and easing it down to the shoulder. "I'm right here. Everything's okay."

"I couldn't find Mom," Danny said, his need to suck air fighting his need to speak.

"We'll find Mom. It's okay, Danny. It's all right."

"I got so cold, Daddy."

"I'll keep you warm," Sweeney said. "I'm here now."

"Can we go find Mom," Danny asked, "and then go home?"

"That's a good idea," Sweeney said, shifting the boy in his arms and struggling up to his feet. And when he looked around, he realized that the landscape had changed.

The ruins of the old factories now stretched as far as he could see. There were no bordering streets. No tenements or mills or city lights visible in the distance. Beneath his feet, what had been brick and rock and rubble was now something else — something like baked clay, hardpan, a gray and white expanse shot through with cracks. It was flat and it extended to the horizon. There was something intensely primordial about the landscape and it triggered sudden terror in Sweeney.

Sensing his father's panic, Danny said, "It'll be okay, Dad."

Sweeney wanted to ask *Where are we?* but was afraid of the answer. Instead, he said, "I don't know which way to go."

"Can I ride on your back?" Danny asked.

Sweeney hoisted him and, once secure, Danny extended his downy arm and pointed away from the Harmony factory. And they began to walk.

They covered what must have been miles, but Sweeney's feet and back carried his burden without complaint, though his eyes watered from the oppressiveness of the air. There was a chemical smell that got worse as they progressed, something like sulfur and cabbage. Danny either didn't notice it or didn't mind it.

They didn't talk much. Once Danny asked if Mom would be mad that they were late and Sweeney said, "How do you know we'll be late?"

"We're already late," Danny said.

After that they came to the first Joshua tree. It was growing up out of one of the larger cracks in the hardpan. Neither father nor son commented on it and soon they were spotting more of them and the new trees were bigger, fuller, their spearlike branches all pointing in the direction Sweeney was heading.

"Can you eat the flowers?" Danny asked and Sweeney said he didn't know. As they passed one of the branches, Danny reached out, pulled free a white blossom. Seconds later, a few petals floated down onto Sweeney's chest and leg.

And sometime after that they were in the thick of the trees. Their progress slowed considerably. The sky turned purple and the moon appeared low and to their right. Sweeney tried to hurry but the thicket of tree limbs made the going near impossible. There was no clear path. And the smell had grown putrid, a clogged leech field in high summer. He brought a hand up to shield his nose and mouth and from beneath the hand he said, "How can you stand it?"

"It's not so bad from up here," Danny said.

Sweeney felt his son's feathers against the back of his neck and head. He wanted to put Danny down for a while, but he knew it was crucial that they continued moving. And so he tried to ignore the fatigue and tramp on. But as the hardpan began to soften, go marshy, his legs began to ache and he had to ask Danny if he could walk for a while.

The boy agreed and his father lowered him to the ground. Soon after, the trees began to thin again and when they left the last one behind them, they were fully in the swamps. Now the smell was different. Just as strong and just as unpleasant, but more alive, derived less from decay and more from something fertile and ripe.

They held hands and took smaller steps. Their feet sank into inches of heavy, fetid water. Sweeney felt it seep through shoe and sock and touch his skin. His flesh prickled and he ground his teeth. But the swamp water didn't seem to have any effect on Danny. When it rose to the boy's knees, Sweeney hoisted him up on shoulders once again. And that's when the insects arrived. Fat, slow winter flies. They ignored his swatting hands, tried to land on him, their buzzing set to a ridiculous volume.

Sweeney breathed through his nose and shook his head. Within yards, the pests had swarmed into an infestation and he tried to run. But with each attempt to lift his leg and push out of the water, he planted a foot deeper into the bottom muck. Danny pressed his eyes into his father's head and wrapped his arms more tightly around Dad's neck. The flies began to mass on Sweeney's face. He shook his head wildly but they refused to dislodge. And that was when he tripped over the first body.

He went down on his knees, yet somehow Danny managed to stay on his back. The putrid water sprayed up, soaked his shirt and face, which loosed some of the flies. He wiped the rest away with the back of his arm and opened his eyes to look into the face of Ernie Blake. Though Sweeney had never met the man, he was certain this was Ernie, Nora's husband.

Blake was lying just beneath the skin of the water, floating in the murky pool. He was dressed in workman's coveralls that had gone filthy in the

swamp and sported a coating of slimy algae. Though he was fully submerged, his eyes were open and they tracked Sweeney's movement as he
tried to jump away from the body.

"It's okay," he heard Danny say behind him. "It's only Mr. Blake."

Sweeney didn't know what to do, if he should attempt to lift the man
out of the water. He felt his knees sinking into the mud and as he tried to
think, Ernie Blake opened his mouth and dozens of tiny black fish swam
out.

Danny began to laugh and Sweeney was horrified. He pushed himself
up to standing, tried once again to run and tripped, this time over the
floating body of Lawrence Belmonte, the footless hunter from Maine.
Belmonte's eyes were closed but his mouth was open and he was running
his tongue over his teeth. The tiny black fish were swimming into one of
the stumps at the bottom of the man's left leg and out of the stump at the
bottom of his right.

Sweeney tried to calm his breathing and failed. He stood up slowly
and, though the swamp was dim, lit only by a sliver moon, he could see
dozens of figures floating just beneath the water. And he knew they were
all patients from the Peck Clinic — Honey Lieb and Tara Russell and
Ginny Oliphant and all the others.

"Can they breathe under water?" Sweeney asked Danny.

But Danny just said, "I'm cold, Dad. Are we almost home yet?"

Sweeney's answer was to begin walking again. When they cleared the
swamp, they could finally see home. Only it wasn't the house in Cleveland
exactly. And it wasn't quite the Peck Clinic. And it wasn't entirely the
Limbo fortress of the evil Dr. Fliess. It was, instead, some horrible and
unlikely amalgam of all three structures. And it was looming above them
from the edge of a cliff, a haunted Gothic castle, with handicap ramps
and awnings, neon red crosses and enormous wooden shutters.

And looking up at it, Sweeney understood that it was the last place he
wanted to be. That he'd rather spend the rest of his life in the swamps
than in any room of this stone palace.

Danny sensed his father's hesitation.

"You have to, Daddy," he said. "You've got to bring me home."

Sweeney shook his head, felt the brush of the feathers.

"That's not your home, Danny," he said.

"It's my home now," Danny said. "I'm late, Dad. And Mom's worried."

"Mom doesn't have to be worried," Sweeney said. "You're with me."

"She's worried about you too, Dad. She's worried about both of us."

"But all those rocks," Sweeney said. "I don't know how to get up there."

"I know a way," Danny said. "I'll show you."

Sweeney stood for a minute looking up at the structure, then turned to look back toward the swamp. He started to say something about going back to the factory but was bitten on the hand by a green-headed fly. The sting and the after-burn were severe. He brought the hand to his mouth and sucked on it.

Danny said, "There'll be millions of them in a little while."

And so Sweeney started for the boulders without argument and began to climb. The stones were as big as cars, some of them larger, and they were slick with moss. Danny locked his arms around his father's neck and asked questions as Sweeney tried to find his footholds and pull them upward.

"Do you think someone could lift one of these?" he asked. "How much do they weigh? What's underneath the rocks?"

Sweeney replied in a monotone, "I don't know."

He slipped once, went down hard on his knee. The higher they rose, the steeper the rocks became. Had he been climbing alone, he would have had more options, but with Danny on his back he couldn't make use of the crevices between stones. At one point while he was trying to get a purchase somewhere on the sheer face of a wall that stretched to twice his height, Danny asked, "What's that say, Dad?"

"Danny," Sweeney yelled, "I'm trying to climb here."

His head was aching and his knee was throbbing and the boy was choking off some of his air. But when he heard the crying and felt the trembling against his back, he stopped attempting to pull them up and leaned his head back against Danny's face.

"I'm sorry, son," he said. "Dad's really sorry. But this is very hard."

"I just wanted," Danny said through hitching breath, each word standing on its own, "to know what it meant."

Sweeney looked up and backward now, to an outcropping of rock that formed a lip off the top of the cliff. Somehow, someone had spray-painted *Freaks Die* on the underside of the ledge.

"It doesn't mean anything," Sweeney said and instantly regretted it.

"It says something," Danny said.

"It's in another language," Sweeney said and turned back to the cliff wall and began to climb.

The rest of the way up they moved in silence. When they got to the top and Sweeney pulled them to level ground, they found freshly laid sod, a yard of meticulously clipped turf, too green to look natural. There was a brick walkway running through the center of the yard and it led to the oversized doors of the castle.

Sweeney sat on the grass, catching his breath and studying the doors. Danny sat next to him, imitating his father's pose and demeanor.

"They're not locked," Danny said.

Sweeney looked from the doors down to his son. The feathers seemed less strange now. But the mouth appeared even more beaklike, harder and more protruding.

"Have you been here before, Danny?"

The boy looked down in his lap and nodded.

"What am I going to find inside, son?"

Danny looked up and said, "Everything's going to be all right, Dad." But the voice and the tone and the body language gave it away as a lie.

"If I go inside," Sweeney asked, "will I wake up again?"

Now Danny looked genuinely confused.

"I don't get it," he said.

"I'm asking you," Sweeney said, "if the dream will end."

Danny shook his head and said, "This isn't a dream, Dad." Then he stood up suddenly, extended his hand to his father, and said, "I'll show you."

They walked up the path to the doors, which parted as they approached. Candles mounted in holders high on the walls lit the interior foyer. Father and son stepped inside and Sweeney took a moment to let his eyes adjust.

It was partly the Peck Clinic. It was partly the St. Joseph in Cleveland. And there were touches of the old house back home — an endtable that had been in their bedroom, the framed print that Kerry had bought on a trip to San Francisco. But mostly the castle was Dr. Fliess's Gothic laboratory, straight from the pages of *Limbo*.

In a corner of the foyer was an ornate, oversized grandfather clock, the same piece Sweeney had seen in the Peck residence. As soon as he looked at its face, the clock began to chime. And as soon as it chimed, as if it were a signal of some kind, Danny broke away from his father and sprinted up the center staircase to the second floor.

Sweeney yelled after the boy and started to run, but stopped when he heard his name called. He stood still, listened and heard it again, and followed the call into a parlor to the right of the stairs. The room was high Victorian, enormous but crowded with dark and heavy furnishings. Two wing chairs were positioned before a fireplace where a pile of logs was blazing. Someone was sitting in the nearest chair. He heard a crisp page being turned, smelled the cigarette smoke, and walked across the room to sit in the empty chair.

Nora Blake didn't look up but she held out the hand that braced her cigarette to indicate she'd be with him in a minute. He looked up at the painting hanging above the mantel — a depiction of the *Limbo* freaks done in the same somber style of the Peck ancestral portraits. Danny was the centerpiece of the work. The rest of the troupe was fanned behind him.

Nora closed the book, sighed, and heaved it into the fire. Embers flew and she shook her head, plugged the cigarette into her mouth, and sucked until her cheeks caved in.

Sweeney looked at the book as the flames consumed its title — *The Diary of a Young Chicken Boy.*

He said, "You didn't like it."

"I'm done with fiction," Nora said.

"Was it a pirate book?" Sweeney asked.

Nora shook her head, knocked some ashes onto the carpet.

"A love story," she said and he knew it was a lie. "Really frivolous. I just don't have the time or the patience anymore."

She blew out a stream of smoke, came forward, slapped his bad knee, and said, "So you finally made it. What the hell took you so long?"

"You were expecting me?"

"I was hoping," Nora said.

"To tell you the truth," Sweeney said. "I didn't have much say in the matter."

Nora gave him a sour look and made a dismissive sound, blew some air through pursed lips.

"Of course you did," she said. "Everyone has a choice. That's all you've got. Choices up the wazoo."

Sweeney didn't want to argue with her. "What is this place?" he asked.

"Didn't Danny tell you?" she said. "It's home."

"This isn't my home," he said. "I've never lived in a place like this."

"Sweeney, honey," Nora said, "your memory isn't what it used to be."

"I don't think I can stay here, Nora."

"You think too much, mister. I'd say that's your number one problem. You overthink everything. My Ernie had the same tendency, by the way."

"I've got bigger problems than that, Nora."

She closed her eyes, shook her head.

"I knew you'd say that, Sweeney. I really did. I'm sorry but you're as predictable as one of my romances." She leaned forward again and knocked her paperback deeper into the flames. In a lower voice, she added, "It drove Kerry nuts you know."

"You didn't know Kerry," he said and immediately regretted it. He realized that she was baiting him but couldn't stop himself from giving her what she wanted.

"Let me tell you something about Kerry," Nora said, angry now. "Kerry deserved better. Kerry deserved to be forgiven."

"I did forgive her," yelling now, "I swear to you I did."

Nora wouldn't look at him. She was staring at the fire. She said, "That's right, swear to me." And then she didn't say anything else.

He waited a few minutes, watched the last of the paperback turn black and crumple into ash. Then he stood and said, "I have to find Danny."

Nora rummaged in the chair cushion until she found her cigarettes. And Sweeney moved up to the second floor of the castle.

THE STAIRS WERE grand-hotel wide but much too steep. Sweeney had to concentrate to be sure of his footing. It was as if each ledge had been fashioned into different heights. There was no way to gain a rhythm and run to the landing.

When he reached the top, he stopped by the railing that formed a balcony over the foyer. He was dizzy and so winded that he wondered about the altitude. He looked down over the banister and was hit with a wave of vertigo. Turning around, he went down on his bad knee and let out a yell. It echoed a bit down the three corridors that stretched off the landing and ignited a distant burst of laughter.

The laughter seemed to come from the left, so he moved in that direction and suppressed the urge to call out for Danny. The corridor was tall but narrow, like the halls of the Clinic. The floor was marble, covered by a green runner. The walls were covered in wainscoting, but they were lined with mounted torches that threw shadows and left large pockets of darkness.

He found them in the billiard room. They were at the far end, beyond the tables, which were covered in animal skins — cow and leopard and zebra hides. He stood in the doorway for a while. Romeo, the janitor, saw him first but didn't acknowledge it, turned his eyes back to his cards and hunched down over his drink. It looked like a sullen crew, locked into one of those dead games that refuses to end. Ernesto Luga slouched down in his chair, eyes half-closed. Though they had their backs to him, Sweeney knew the other players were Tannenbaum and Gögüs, the Clinic's associate neurologists.

For the moment, he ignored them and moved to one of the billiard tables where Irene Moore was laid out like a corpse in its casket. Her skin had turned from white to a gray tinged with yellow. She was on her back, lit by a Tiffany lamp that hung from a chain of oversized metal links. Her skull was resting on two rubber bumpers. And she was naked.

"He's gonna climb on top of her," he heard Ernesto say. "I'll bet all my chips he's gonna slip her the chicken."

The words were dull and muted, as if spoken underwater. Sweeney ran the back of his hand over Irene Moore's cheek. The skin was icy but she opened her eyes at his touch and he jumped backward and collided with another table.

Then he felt a hand on his shoulder and turned to find Tannenbaum next to him. The doctor was looking down on Irene Moore, shaking his head theatrically.

"Why don't you sit in for me," Tannenbaum said. "I'm busted. And there's nothing you can do for this one."

Sweeney shook his head in agreement, then leaned down and brought his mouth to Irene's. Her lips were cold but smooth. He pulled some air in through his nose, pushed it out into the adjoining mouth. In response, he felt her tongue come to life and move against his own for a second, before continuing, pressing forward like a snake, until it touched the back of his throat and he began to choke. He jerked backward but she had her arms around his neck.

He swung his arm and broke her grip, fell to the floor, scrambled upright, and ran from the game room as the card players broke into hysterical laughter. He raced down corridors that merged into corridors. Took rights and lefts, vaulted more than one flight of stairs and didn't manage to control the panic until he was entirely lost.

Eventually, he found himself at the top of the castle. The ceilings were lower here and the corridors shorter. He walked them, throwing open each door and poking his head inside each room to find a series of identical cells, stark chambers fixed under the eaves, each outfitted with only a coffinlike bed, a porcelain washbasin, and a matching pitcher. The cells looked out, through a chapel window of blue glass, onto an expanse of roaring ocean on one side of the hall, and the marshlands and swamps on the other.

Entering the last room, he knelt down before the window and drank from the pitcher. The water inside was warm and stale but he couldn't get enough of it. He tipped the pitcher too quickly, spilling it down his chest. When he'd drained the last of the water, he dried his mouth with the hem of his shirt, unzipped his pants, and urinated into the basin.

On his way back out, he glanced at the bed and saw the book that was almost hidden beneath the pillow. He sat down and extracted it and found the final issue of *Limbo*. The issue that he and Danny had purchased on the day of the accident. The cover featured a jagged title balloon that screamed

"Freaks No More"
The End
of
Their Journey!

in scarlet lettering. The cover drawing depicted the troupe at the base of a towering cliff, looking up at the black iron castle of Dr. Fliess, the madman genius who had tracked them relentlessly.

Sweeney rolled the comic into a tube, tucked it in his back pocket and exited the cell. He moved to the last door at the end of the hall, put his hand on the knob and, in that instant, heard Danny's laugh from inside. He turned the knob and pushed, found the door bolted and began to pound. And as he hammered his fist against the freezing slate of the door, Danny's laughter turned to crying. And then to screaming.

Sweeney kicked at the door. Heaved his shoulder at the door. Began to yell for his son. His knuckles started to bleed. Something ruptured in his throat and his yell turned into a rasp. He got down on his back, stomped against the door with the bottoms of his feet. There was no give, no sense of progress.

He got to his knee and then stood, moved halfway down the corridor and ran at the door, threw his body into it, crashed and slumped, stunned. He sat up, blinked, brought a hand to his forehead and took it away bloody. He got back on his knees, put both hands on the doorknob and yelled, as loud as he could, for his boy.

Then he felt the knob turning in his hands and the door began to open and he was pulled into a dark room that he knew, at once, was cavernous. He felt the temperature change before his eyes could adjust. It was as warm as a sauna. He could hear waves crashing from an open window. He could hear the clink of metal against metal. But Danny's screams had stopped.

The lights began to come up as someone on either side lifted him off the floor. He smelled perfume and coffee and salt air. He felt himself being lowered and relaxed into something plush. Felt something soft and damp against his wounded forehead. And then his vision was restored, though the light was cobalt blue and railroad lantern red. In the dimness, he could see Danny about ten feet away. The boy was lying on an operating table, his head on a thin pillow, his body covered up to the chin by a sheet that reflected the comic book colors of the room. The boy looked tired but his eyes were open and he was smiling at Sweeney.

Danny's mouth opened and closed as if forming words, but no sound came from his lips. Sweeney tried to make out the words anyway.

"I knew you'd come," he repeated to himself and started to slump a bit.

A hand pressed against his chest and pushed him back in his seat. He looked to his left to see Nadia Rey, dressed in her nurse's whites, her hair pulled back and secured. He looked to his right and saw Alice Peck, in her three-quarter lab coat, with pearls around her throat and a stethoscope hanging from her neck.

Sweeney let his head loll back and touched glass. He sat up and surveyed the room and realized he was in the main turret at the top of the castle, a circular chamber, like the top of a lighthouse, with a peaked ceiling and narrow windows all around. He was on a section of the window seat that circled the room, which was, he now saw, a surgical theater. There were boxy metal carts everywhere, their tops covered in green sheets upon which rested all manner of bowls and basins, scalpels, scissors, chisels, retractors, bone saws, hypodermics, and roll after roll of cotton gauze.

A new kind of panic began to flood in and Sweeney attempted to get up, to go to Danny. But his legs couldn't seem to bring him to standing and each time he tried, Nadia and Alice restrained him. They did so in a gentle and easy manner, with soft shushing and patting of arms and legs. But they kept him held in place.

Danny, watching his father struggle, gave another smile and mouthed what Sweeney took as, *It's okay, Dad.*

And that was when Dr. Fliess appeared on the scene, as if out of no-where. Suddenly he was standing on the far side of the operating table, his hands on the guardrail, lowering it. He was stationed halfway down the table, near Danny's waist, wearing green surgical scrubs and latex gloves. To Sweeney, he looked as he'd been depicted in the various *Limbo* mediums — the comic books, trading cards, posters, TV cartoons, and films. He had the mad eyes that were somehow both bulging and beady. He had the terrible posture that made him seem humpbacked. He had the oversized ears that sprouted the wiry strands of white hair. But when he lowered the surgical mask, his face was that of Dr. Micah Peck.

He addressed Sweeney directly over his son.

"I'm honored to have an audience," he said, "on a day that will live in medical history."

Then he spoke to the two women in a sharp voice.

"Has the patient been prepped?" he snapped. "Where's my assistant?"

Nadia and Alice leaned out from either side of Sweeney and looked at each other. But before they could answer, the room filled with the sound of heels on tile. And out of the darkness came Kerry, the lost wife and mother. She was dressed in scrubs, but unlike Dr. Peck's, these were soiled. The front of her gown was saturated with blood. She ignored Danny and Peck and walked directly to Sweeney. She was carrying something in her arms.

When she reached her husband, she placed her burden in his lap. His legs and crotch began to burn and he made himself look down from Kerry's face and saw a fetus, swathed in blood and afterbirth, squirming and making heavy, breathless sounds. Sweeney brought the fetus to his chest, saw that it wasn't fully developed. Kerry took her husband's face in her hands, wiped blood and tissue down his cheeks, and moved back to the surgical table to join Dr. Peck.

Peck was nodding, impatient to begin the procedure. Still staring at Sweeney, he reached down to a table, grabbed a sleek, black-on-black bone saw, and slapped it into Kerry's hands in a theatrical gesture. As Kerry stepped to the head of the table, Sweeney tried to scream and run to her. But voice and legs both failed him, went numb and useless. And so he sat, embraced by Nadia and Alice, embracing the fetus, watching, unable even to close his eyes, as Kerry cut into Danny's skull, made a small, round hole, and removed a covering of bone as if it were the top to a cookie jar.

What saved Sweeney was the fact that Danny remained fully conscious during the sawing and that he did not cry out. His eyes blinked and glazed, but there were no screams, no convulsion.

Kerry ran her fingers along the edge of the new cavity, and then, in a calm and clinical voice, she said, "We're ready, Doctor," and Peck took a long breath and once again addressed Sweeney.

"I know," said Peck, his words clearly rehearsed, "that you question my methods. And that is appropriate. Many have doubted me before you. But I am here to lead, not to follow. And when the doubters have turned to ash in some forgotten boneyard, my work will live on."

Without looking, he reached down and lifted a cup into view. It was clear plastic and oversized and decorated with line drawings of the *Limbo* freaks. The kind of thing given away as a promotion at a fast-food joint. It had a purple, crazy straw protruding high above its rim, twisting and looping to its end. For a moment, Peck lifted the cup above his head, like a chalice or a trophy, then he passed it to Kerry. When he spoke again, there was no sense of a prepared speech.

"Do you know why you're here?" he asked Sweeney, staring.

"I'm here to help my son," Sweeney said.

"Do you think you're a good father?" Peck asked.

"I've tried my best," Sweeney said.

"But your best wasn't good enough," Peck said. "Was it?"

Sweeney shook his head.

"Where do you think you went wrong?"

Sweeney tried to wet his lips but found his tongue void of fluid.

"I didn't protect him," he said, and Peck yelled, "Speak up."

"I didn't protect him," Sweeney repeated. "I couldn't keep him from harm."

Peck nodded. Sweeney brought a hand up and covered his mouth.

"I had a son once," Peck said. "I understand your troubles."

Sweeney nodded, unaware that he had begun to weep.

"You want to be forgiven," Peck said. "You want the boy to forgive you."

Sweeney's head was bobbing faster now, his throat on fire and his lungs forgetting any sense of rhythm.

"But to be forgiven," Peck said, "you must forgive. That is an absolute."

"I forgive you," Sweeney yelled.

Peck bit down on his bottom lip, then said, "You have no reason to forgive me. I've done nothing to you or your boy."

"You have to forgive Kerry," Alice whispered.

"And Danny," Nadia said.

Peck wasn't pleased by their interruption.

"Do you know what grace is?" he asked, his voice too loud, and Sweeney nodded. "I'm giving you a gift today," Peck said. "You didn't ask for it and you'll never be able to repay me."

He looked to Kerry and gave a small nod. Kerry held the *Limbo* cup in her right hand and manipulated Danny's head with her left, tilting it back until a thin, slow stream of murky pink liquid began to pour from the hole in the skull and fill the plastic tumbler.

"Today you'll know what the child knows," Peck said. "And you'll feel

what the child feels. You'll know and feel these things without loss or dis-
tortion. Without the corruption of language. You'll know the truth. And
then you'll have to decide if you want the truth to set you free."

When the last of the fluid dripped from the boy's skull, the tumbler
was nearly full, and the liquid gave color to the skin of the freaks, whose
bodies were outlined on the plastic. Kerry positioned Danny's head back
onto the surgical slab, crossed the room to Sweeney and extended the
cup to him.

Sweeney stared up at her, unsure of what he should say or do. And in
the absence of any plan, he lifted a tacky hand to his wife and they traded
fetus for cup. Kerry smiled at him, brought the flesh in her hands to her
chest, up high, near her neck. Sweeney wrapped both of his trembling
hands around the cup, which was neither cool nor warm. He lifted it
slightly, noticed what seemed to be tiny bubbles popping just above the
rim. He brought his head down, fitting his mouth around the end of the
straw as he closed his eyes and began to suck. The fluid wound its way
through the looping track of the straw and flowed into the father's mouth,
over the tongue, down the throat and esophagus. It tasted like milk with
a hint of molasses, and Sweeney drank until the straw made the slurping
and sputtering that indicated the cup was empty.

He let the straw fall from his mouth, lowered the cup and opened his
eyes to the phosphorescent display of a thousand Roman candles arcing
across a deep blue sky. When the fireworks faded, he found himself staring at the back of his own head. And then the picture opened out, and his
head was boxed in the rear window of the Honda. He was backing out of
the driveway. He was headed down Oread Street on his way into work. He
honked twice, his standard goodbye to his wife and his son.

He knew this moment, but not from this perspective. This was Danny's
viewpoint. This was the last time that Danny had seen him. This was the
last glimpse of the father by the son. This, Sweeney knew, was what happened at home on the night of the accident.

While Sweeney was turning onto Williams, cranking up "Betcha by
Golly Wow" and hoping that it would lull him out of a sour mood, Danny
was watching the Honda disappear. Everything that Sweeney was about
to witness, he realized, would be through the boy's eyes. And what he
saw was a dash back into the house, from a shaky and low-to-the-ground

angle. Upon entering the kitchen, carpet changing into linoleum, the sprint transformed into a glide, as the *Limbo* slipper socks carried the boy almost across the length of the room, where Kerry was chopping produce for a salad.

Danny's eyes came to rest on his mother and Sweeney saw Kerry smile.

"Did you say goodbye to Daddy?" she asked.

Danny nodded and the picture tilted forward and back.

"Can I have some Oreos?" the boy asked.

Kerry glanced at the wall clock.

"Dinner's in a bit," she said, but Danny was already at the low cabinet where they kept the cookies. "Just a few, okay?"

A nod, a tilt, and the boy pushed his fists into the bag that held the cookies and retrieved three, four, and one in his mouth made five. Kerry let it go and Danny departed the kitchen, climbed the stairs to the second floor, singing around the Oreo, "I Don't Look Like a Hero," the theme to the last *Limbo* movie.

When he got to his room, he stacked the cookies on the night table next to the bed, opened the drawer beneath the stack, and lifted out, gingerly, the issue of the comic that he and his dad had purchased earlier in the day. He hoisted himself up onto the bed. Kneeled and balanced and turned on the lamp. The bulb illuminated its *Limbo* shade. Threw shadows onto the far wall, across the *Limbo* poster and the *Limbo* wallpaper that stretched beyond the poster.

Danny sat back and then lay down. Not quite comfortable, he put the comic on the bed and stacked a second pillow atop the first. He grabbed two cookies off the top of the stack, put one on his stomach and took a bite of the second. Crumbs rained down on his chin. Now that he was ready, he lifted the little magazine, its cover overloaded with colors, the gloss glaring a little in the light.

He opened the issue, rolled the cover around to the back without creasing it, and began to read the first page of the final *Limbo* story.

26

The first page was one full panel, a portrait of the troupe on the little beach, at the foot of the boulders that stretched up to Dr. Fliess's castle. The freaks fanned out behind the chicken boy like bowling pins, their heads tilted up in unison and the same look of caution *and* anticipation on each face. Above them, the black iron castle, the laboratory of the legendary renegade, Dr. Wilton Fliess, sat at the edge of the cliff, looking ominous and uninviting.

They have wandered so long

the narrative bar above their heads read

And suffered so much.
They have faced the good and the bad together
Bound by their deformities and their love
But today, they will learn what lies at the end
of their hard road
Deliverance or damnation.
Because today they have reached

and now came the title, floating down in the air above their heads like manna, in blood red ink

The End of Limbo!

Below their feet was a banner that read

Complete in this one issue, the last chapter of the Limbo epic
Written & illustrated
By Menlo

Danny made crunching sounds. Crumbs flew and settled. The noise of the page being turned was thunderous. A second cookie went into the mouth and then the hand came down and grabbed the *Limbo* blanket, a little throw that Kerry had picked up a few months before. Danny pulled it over his legs and began to read.

Dr. Fliess is hunched within the folds of his black cape, the red velvet interior just peeking into view. He is sitting cross-legged halfway up the cliff, in the notch where two boulders come together. His elbows are planted on his knees and his chin is cupped in his braced hands. It is clear he is locked in some sort of demonic trance.

He remains this way all night. His gargoylean homunculi burrow into crevices around him. All that can be seen of the servants are their red eyes, looking terrified. *What has happened to the Master?* they wonder.

But the Master is unaware of their terror. He is in the grip of his own destiny, waiting to see where a lifetime's obsession will bear him. He is inside the densest mysteries of nature now. And no one can touch him. He watches the tide come in with its careless fury, battering the beach, flooding over the newly covered graves. Seawater sinking down into the hard sand. The tide builds, rises. The tide reaches up to Fliess, engulfs his pointy-booted feet before it begins to recede. The wind does its part, howling, banshee mad.

But by morning, gulls are able to coast in the upsweep. And when the water has pushed back to its shallowest limit, Fliess emerges from the trance. He stands with the aid of his cobra's head cane. He flutters his cape and stretches in the rays of the rising sun. And then he gives the signal to his legion. A snap of the fingers is all it takes and they emerge from their crevices, half-naked and carrying their crude shovels.

They scurry down the rocks and scamper over the new graves, still marked despite the night's heavy tide. They get to work in groups of two and three, panning out the wet sand, heaps of grain flying through the dim air. They know what to do. Fliess need not shout commands. He controls them by thought alone at this point.

In no time at all, the graves are opened and the scoliotic little demons are pulling on braided ships ropes, ropes as thick as their own
necks. And as they pull, the coffins of the freaks begin to emerge from
the earth. The pine boxes come up in the order they were planted. The
last to reach the surface is, of course, the chicken boy.

Dr. Fliess comes down the cliff with the graceful movements of a
natural dancer, a dandy to the end. His creatures rock and moan, torn
between the urge to cower and the need to exult. Fliess paces around
the semicircle of coffins that sit in pools of wet sand and seaweed. He
is waiting, one might guess, for the rising sun to backlight his emi-
nence. He is lost in a meditation on his own long-sought fate. What
will happen this morning, in these next few minutes, will determine
who the doctor is, will clarify, once and for all, the nature of his character. The facts about his very identity.

The enormity of this moment in time is not lost on the doctor. He
understands all too well, better than anyone else could, the meaning
of the task he has attempted. He feels its immensity and density in
his marrow. It throbs there, pulsing like a vein in God's forehead. It
is what has driven him all these years. It is what has allowed him to
ignore the nasty legends and push on. His calling has isolated him
from any kind of fellowship. But that's the price the chosen must pay
for their gifts. The shaman integrates the tribe by remaining apart
from the tribe. The shaman integrates the world by standing, forever,
outside the world.

Gulls pool above the coffins, wretched birds that feed on the leav-
ings of others. Fliess looks to one of his creatures who jumps into the
semicircle and does a little war dance, thrusting its stubby, misshapen
arms and crying out in a high-pitched babble. The birds disperse for
the moment and the creature runs back to its station.

Fliess turns one last time and looks out at the water and the crown
of the sun as it breaks above the horizon.

"It is time," he whispers.

Like a magician suddenly bored with his own secrets, Fliess walks
to the first casket, Bruno's box, and flips open the lid without looking inside. He moves gracefully to Milena's box and opens it in the
same manner. And then the coffins of Fatos, Aziz, Nadja, Jeta, Antoi-

nette, Marcel and Vasco. He opens the piano-size coffin of Durga, the fat lady, and the miniature coffin of Kitty, the beloved dwarf. And he stops before the coffin of the chicken boy, puts a boot on the lid, closes his eyes, brings a hand to his mouth. Beneath the hand, he mumbles something, words of a different tongue, Latin perhaps. Then he bends from the waist and throws back the lid with more force than needed.

It is almost silent on the beach. Even the gulls cease their cawing. And if the waves continue to lap, the noise goes unnoticed.

Dr. Fliess brings his arms out to his sides. His cape spreads over his shoulder. Then he pulls his hands together to produce a clap that echoes off the rocks like gunfire. His face placid, he opens his mouth and says, "Good morning, my children. And welcome to your new life."

The first to rise is Bruno, the leader in all things. He has hair on his head. His Atlas tattoos are gone. His left arm has lost its grotesque bulge, reduced itself to more human proportions. And its mate has reappeared, grown fresh and new and entirely normal, from shoulder to the tips of the fingernails.

At last Fliess smiles, looks up to the sky, turns palms toward the fading stars and pantomimes a call to rise. From a sitting position, Bruno stretches his newly proportioned arms and stands slowly, looking around the beach as if he has found himself on a new planet or in the midst of an afterlife for which he has prayed since birth.

He climbs out of his coffin, eyes on his healer, the transforming agent of his new normalcy. Bruno moves to Milena's crate, reaches down and extends an arm that is taken by a small and well-manicured hand. And Milena rises, healed, void of penis and Adam's apple, fully female and entirely beautiful.

In turn, she moves to her neighbor and assists Fatos, who has lost his mule face and now looks like the prince of a Nordic tribe.

Fatos calls out Aziz, who has grown legs and feet.

Aziz springs Nadja whose lobster limbs have become perfectly delineated hands and feet, ten fingers and ten toes and each of them exquisite.

Nadja bids Jeta to wake and the human skeleton has grown a pink and healthy crop of flesh.

Jeta summons Antoinette, whose pinhead has bloomed and rounded into a skull that could carry the crown in any number of pageants.

Antoinette calls forth Marcel and Vasco who rise independently, Vasco stepping onto the sand with a look of shock on his face. Until he spies Marcel climbing out of the box to join him. They touch their hips simultaneously and then break into a little jig before waking Durga.

Who no longer needs three-quarters of her casket. She emerges onto the beach lithe and slim, unable to stop looking at her own arms and thighs, even as she invites Kitty to join her.

The beloved dwarf shows first one leg and then another and both of them long and perfectly shaped. She rises on these gams, tall and strong enough to captain a volleyball team.

But like the rest of her troupe, she is unable to revel in the joy of her new normalcy until the last one joins them and they are whole together. Kitty goes down on one knee, leans over the last coffin and reaches in to wake her man.

And then she draws back and crumples on the sand in a heap of silent tears. The others freeze in place, but Dr. Fliess runs to the coffin and falls beside it. Then he rears up and begins to scream, filling the cool morning air with obscene rage before collapsing, like Kitty, into a convulsion of bitter weeping.

Ever the patriarch, it is Bruno who moves to the casket and lifts the limp, soaked body up into the air. The boy is still covered in his feathers. His freak nature could not be rewritten. Fliess's magic could not touch him.

While Fliess continues his tantrum, his fists pounding the sand like a child denied a toy, the troupe gathers around the coffin. And Bruno, even without his brawn, has no trouble hoisting the body into his arms. He holds Chick for a time so that the others can draw around and stroke their brother and gaze on his beaked face. Bruno places this fallen bird into the arms of Kitty, who weeps like mother, sister, lover, her tears shed on feathers that, already, are going brittle and dull.

Bruno knows what must be done. He steps around the doctor, takes hold of Chick's coffin lid, and tears it free of the box. Kitty looks up at the sound. Bruno nods to her and, though her sobbing increases, she manages to nod back. This time, no one needs to explain a thing to Antoinette, the former pinhead. This time, Antoinette understands it all.

And Marcel and Vasco need not synchronize their steps as they lead the way down to the shore. And Durga has no need to stop to catch her breath as she follows. No, the tribe realizes this is, indeed, the last chapter. Realizes that there are no more Goldfaden Freaks. It is, suddenly, a story ready only to recede into a suspect history.

They break in two, their feet in the water up to their ankles and no more. Bruno walks between their columns, coffin lid under his arm like a surfboard. He places the lid on the surface of the water, puts a palm on it and makes sure it will float, and then he holds it in place as it bobs, trying to ride the gentle current pulling outward.

Kitty comes to the water now, her Chick in her arms. She wades in to her waist and the water laps up to her breasts. Bruno grips the lid with both hands and it fights him. Kitty places her love on his back, on the wood. She leans down, brings her mouth to the hard beak that she has known so well for so long. The kiss lingers and Bruno must take one hand from the board and place it on Kitty's shoulder. She straightens, as her whole body heaves. Behind her, someone, maybe Jeta, maybe Aziz, begins to keen with a kind of grief that the world has not known in ages.

Bruno takes this as a sign to let go. He shoves the coffin lid into the current and the body of the chicken boy begins to float off toward the horizon. The rising sun neither mocks nor comforts. The gulls begin to follow the tiny barge. The erstwhile freaks fall to their knees, one by one, the surf swirling in their laps. They make themselves study the progress of the barge through blurring vision.

The last picture of the last issue of *Limbo* is a close-up of the chicken boy's face, eyes open but lifeless, the rising sun looming in the upper right-hand corner of the frame. Inked below the face is the last message from the artist and author, from the creator of *Limbo*.

Not everyone

it reads

is meant to be normal.
Not every story

it reads

has a happy ending.

27

The final picture loses focus and stability, turns into a piece of carnival spin art, as Danny throws the comic book into the air. It hits the poster above his bed and knocks it to the floor.

What comes next is a moment that someone with medical knowledge might term *fugue*. Danny sits up as if prodded by electricity. But then he holds in place. Were he a cartoon boy, and were we able to remove the back of his skull like the lid of a cookie jar, we might see a literal overload of circuits, a convulsion of charges running too fast or too slow, but all in the wrong direction. This lost moment lasts under three seconds. And when it ends, the boy begins to scream.

At that moment, Kerry is in the kitchen, mixing up a homemade yogurt dressing for her salad. But Sweeney can't see this. He still can see only the squint-compressed vision of his son, his cartoon boy, in the midst of a nonsensical rage that has him shredding the *Limbo* pillow on his bed.

This is when Kerry enters the picture. She runs into the room to find the air filling rapidly with white and gray feathers. She tries to yell over Danny's screams.

"What's wrong?" she cries. "Danny, what's wrong?"

Sweeney knows the look of growing panic on her face. He hadn't seen it often but the few times it did appear made an impression. Danny throws what's left of the pillow at his mother. It hits her in the chest, falls to the floor. She moves to the bed, tries to grab the boy, her sweet, sunny child, who is pounding his bedroom wall hard enough to bloody his fist and to poke a hole in the plaster, using his stubby fingernails to tear off the *Limbo* wallpaper. Kerry climbs up onto the bed, grabs Danny around the waist, manages to turn him toward her. He is hysterical and enraged and incoherent. Kerry is on her knees, level with him, and Danny hauls off and hits her across the face.

Stunned, she releases the boy and he jumps, animallike, off the bed in one leap and flees the room, but not before he runs his arm down the length of his little bureau, sending *Limbo* lamp and *Limbo* coin bank and chicken boy action figure to the floor in a pile of glass and ceramic shards.

"Danny," the mother screams, now terrified.

She chases the boy into the hall, where he's catapulting himself from wall to wall, kicking and screeching and punching, trying to break and gouge everything he sees. He runs into his parents' bedroom, grabs a cast-iron doorstop from the floor, somehow hoists it and heaves it. The mirror above the dresser shatters as Kerry steps into the room. And on the heels of her disbelief comes her own outrage and anger.

"Danny," she screams at him, "what is wrong with you?"

He dashes past her but manages to kick her in the shin. It shocks more than hurts — he's not wearing his shoes. Kerry runs after him, catches up with her son on the second-floor landing, at the mouth of the stairway. She snatches an arm and goes down on one knee in the same motion. Danny flails, spitting, screaming, wailing. When he realizes he is caught, again he pulls back an arm and again he arcs it with all his might across his mother's face.

This one both shocks *and* hurts. This one dislodges her grip on rationality if only for a second or two. Which is all the time it takes for her to release the son's arm, cock back her own, adult arm, and bring it forward to crash across the boy's cheek.

Danny's head snaps with the blow. It carries his body out over the stairs. He sails into the air until gravity casts him halfway down the stairwell. He falls on a wrist and it breaks, shatters, in fact, small bones fracturing, splintering into rubble. But the body continues to fall. He bounces again on the second stair, makes a quarter turn, thus positioning the head to smash on the flagstone of the foyer.

An instant and an eternity, the fadeout is tipped sideways and involves Kerry's diminishing scream and the lake of blood that runs in a puddle until resolving into the last image — a red plain with a single bubble in its center.

And then sound and vision terminate.

SWEENEY SITS STILL for a moment and then, as if someone has whispered instructions, he stands and exits the surgical theater. When he pushes open the door he steps, not into the attic corridor, but outside into the cool salt air. At the end of the walkway, sitting on the edge of the cliff, legs dangling, he sees his chicken boy, waiting.

Sweeney joins his son on the lip of the cliff and they both stare out at the ocean for a time before Danny says, "I thought you should know what happened."

Sweeney nods. After a while, he says, "You didn't want the chicken boy to die."

Danny looks at him, somewhere between exasperated and confused.

"That's why you got so upset," Sweeney says. "Because the chicken boy died."

Danny remains calm, takes a breath, lets out a sigh, and shakes his head.

"I don't know what happened to me," he says. "But I got upset cuz the doctor changed the others. Cuz they weren't themselves anymore."

"But he made them *normal*," Sweeney says.

Danny shakes his head and says, "Right."

"And you didn't want them to be normal?"

"I wanted them," Danny says, "to stay themselves."

Sweeney tries to think about this.

"What is it you want now, son?"

Danny looks back to the ocean and says, "I want you to forgive me. And then I want you to forgive Mom. And then I want you to stop hating yourself."

"And can you tell me how to do that?"

"If you want it, you'll figure out a way."

Sweeney reaches over and takes Danny into his lap, cradles him as if the boy were still an infant. Danny burrows his head into his father's chest.

"I love you," Sweeney manages to say. "But I don't want to go back."

When it comes, Danny's voice is muffled.

"You have to go back, Dad. You're not done yet."

"I think I am," Sweeney says. "I think I'm done."

Danny shakes his head and, despite Sweeney's attempts to hold him in place, the boy wiggles out of his father's arms.

"You have to stop the doctors, Dad. They're trying to make me into someone else."

"They say they can bring you back to me."

"And you believe them?"

"I don't know what I believe," Sweeney says. "I'm so tired. I'm exhausted."

"You just need some sleep," Danny says.

Then the boy brings his feet to the lip of the cliff, his toes dangling over, and raises his arms above his head, hands pressed together. As he dives, Sweeney yells his name.

It's high tide and the ocean has pushed in and flooded the canyon of boulders below. Danny's arc is impressive but there's no way to tell if he'll clear the rocks. Rather than wait to find out, Sweeney stands and makes his own dive, screaming all the way down. There's nothing graceful about his fall. He flails as he plummets and he hits the water with a hard slap, stomach first.

It's freezing and it's murky. His eyes sting and his lungs begin to ache almost immediately. He searches for Danny. He pushes with his arms, kicks with his legs, but it's as if he is swimming through mud.

He thinks he sees movement below and angles his body downward. His progress is agonizing, each stroke and kick enervating him. But he does manage to descend. He feels the temperature of the water drop. Feels his skin contract and pimple. His genitals try to retreat inward. His body begins to quake but he continues to dive.

He sees something moving on the bottom of the ocean. Something waving to him. A pain ignites in his temples, a terrible pressure. He knows he's about out of air.

And then he sees them. Danny and Kerry. Mother and son. He floats in place above them and they stare up at him. Kerry tilts her head back, opens her mouth. Bubbles escape and rush toward the surface. She's naked and there is a blue tinge to her skin and Danny is in her scar-free arms. Danny is shrunken, an infant again, the size of a small hen. He is bald and featherless and blue like his mother. His mouth is clamped on Kerry's left breast and he feeds with a heavy, aggressive sucking.

Sweeney opens his own mouth to speak. To release the last, crucial words and give birth to an absolution that can change everything. The impulse begins in the brain, which sends the signals to activate this redemption. The lungs push his last breath upward through the trachea and against the vocal cords. The glottis bursts open and the cycles of contraction and expansion commence, causing the cords to vibrate the sound of an unmitigated forgiveness.

And in the instant that Sweeney speaks, an exchange is made. The words flow out to the mother and the child. And water rushes in over the father's tongue, past his teeth, and down his throat. It is the coldest water he has ever felt. Cold enough, he knows, to wake a dead man.

He is flooded with water, choking on water. His lungs and his stomach fill with cold water. He tries to push up to the surface but his arms and legs are entirely spent and he is paralyzed. And then everything begins to fade. Sound, vision, even the cold on his skin. And Sweeney slips, at last, into the dreamless vacuum.

28

Later, he thought he could remember being carried. He thought he could remember the sound of a doorbell, but muted, as if the chime were ringing underwater. And maybe he heard an engine throttling up as it receded into the distance. That was about it. The whole of the world was reduced to sound.

Vision didn't return for hours. The first thing he saw was Alice Peck's face. She was hovering over him, pulling something cool and damp across his forehead. Then he was out again for a while, until he heard pages being turned. He opened his eyes to see Alice sitting on the edge of his bed, reading the final issue of *Limbo*. He tried to speak but nothing came and the effort revoked his consciousness once more.

When he returned it was to the smell of chicken soup. He blinked and brought the bowl into focus. It was on the nightstand, steaming, and Alice Peck was stirring it with a spoon. She lowered herself to the mattress, brushed the backs of her fingers against his cheek.

"Do you think you can eat?" she said. "It'll help to eat."

He nodded, tried to sit up, and failed.

Alice lifted his head from the pillow with one hand, brought some broth to his mouth with the other. He slurped it, let it pool in his mouth and then slide down the throat. The effort was exhausting, even with Alice's support. She sensed this and eased him back onto the pillow.

"How long?" he asked. The words came out as a croak.

"I found you on my doorstep," she said, "about six hours ago."

"Danny," he said.

"Danny's fine," she said. "He's up in his room and he's fine."

And now he thought to look around. He was in his own bed, in his room in the basement, dressed in clean sweatpants and a T-shirt.

"Lucila gave me a hand getting you down here," Alice said. "No one else saw you. And I didn't get a look at whoever dropped you off. They were gone by the time I got to the door."

She reached out and pulled a bottom lid low and studied Sweeney's eye. She said, "More soup?"

He shook his head and said, "Danny."

Alice nodded. "I know. We'll get you upstairs to see him as soon as possible. But he's okay, I promise you."

He tried to sit up and she stopped him with a hand on his chest.

"I've called you in sick," she said. "Can you tell me what happened?"

He opened his mouth and managed only, "Danny."

She fed him another spoonful of soup, spilled most of it down the chin and mopped it up with a facecloth.

"Your blood pressure's back to normal," Alice said. "And so are your pulse and your pupils. You had me a little worried when you first arrived."

He said, "Danny," one more time and then he fell back to sleep.

ALICE WAS GONE when he woke up again. Nadia had taken her place. She was seated on the edge of the bed, reading *Limbo*. Without taking her eyes from the comic, she said, "I didn't think you'd ever come around."

When he didn't respond, she put the book down and studied him.

"First time can be overwhelming," she said, all tender concern, which was not her strong suit. "But you'll get used to it."

He forced an elaborate swallow and said, "Last I checked, my door had a lock."

She shrugged.

"I thought you'd be expecting me," she said. "Besides, locks are for the frightened. And you're not frightened anymore, are you, Sweeney?"

She looked a little haggard, he thought. Her eyes were dim and her hair was pulled back and limp. In a pair of jeans and a sweater, she looked more like a fatigued soccer mom than the matriarch of a biker tribe.

"Alice will be back soon," Sweeney said, his voice still a croak but getting stronger.

"No she won't," Nadia said. "Alice is upstairs telling Daddy that you're an addict and a menace to yourself and your boy and the Clinic. So let's get your ass in gear because we don't have a lot of time here."

He wondered for a second if this might be true. Then, more quickly than he intended, he said, "You can't have my son. I won't let that happen. You'll have to kill me first."

"For a pharmacist," Nadia said, "you're a dramatic little fucker. No one wants to kill you, Sweeney. You know that now, don't you? You've been there. You've talked to Danny. You know it's real."

He shook his head and felt his stomach seize up.

"I don't know what that word means anymore," he said and the weight of the fact made his whole body slump, as if it were about to cave in on itself.

"That's progress," Nadia said, nothing flippant or ironic in her voice. "But you still have to make a move here. You no longer have the luxury of being stuck, Sweeney. You need to make some choices. Right now."

"I throw in with you — " he said.

"Or you throw in with Peck," she finished.

"Either, or," he said, as if repeating the lyric of a well-known ballad.

"What would Danny want you to do?" Nadia asked. "What did he tell you?"

He struggled to sit up and they stared at each other.

"The Sheep told me," Sweeney said. "About the way things work. How you move from clinic to clinic. How you harvest from the patients till they're all used up."

She nodded. "I told him to tell you."

"But why?"

"So that when the time came," she said, "you'd be able to make the right decision. For yourself and for the boy."

One of her eyes twitched and Sweeney sensed that the depth of her exhaustion rivaled his own. And at the heart of the exhaustion was a desperate impatience that she was straining to contain.

"And you're telling me the time has come," he said, pushing her.

"There's a window," Nadia said, "when each coma patient is viable. That's not my fault. You can only draw for so long from any given source. We don't know why that is, though the Sheep has some interesting theories."

"And after that window closes?" Sweeney asked.

"The soup becomes progressively less potent. Until it expires completely. Until it just doesn't work anymore. That's why we have to move from clinic to clinic."

"And what happens to the patient at this point?"

Another shrug.

"And Danny?" Sweeney asked. "Is he about finished as a source?"

"It's hard to say. He could last another week or another year."

"And once he's finished — "

"He's finished," Nadia said. "Once you deplete the source, it's retired. There's no more contact. He can't wake into this world," indicating the bedroom with her hands, "and he can't bring you into his world. The patient can't commune."

Coming from her mouth, the last word sounded like a medical term somehow. As if it were a natural function of the body, a reflex, some thoughtless response of the nervous system.

"I just want him back," was all Sweeney could think to say.

"You can visit with your boy," Nadia said. "We've shown you that."

"But I want him back permanently," Sweeney said. "In my world. The way he was."

"That," Nadia said, "you can't have."

"I could still give him to Peck. Let Peck perform the procedure."

"You could," Nadia said, unfazed. "You could let the doctor put his needle in Danny's brain. Shoot the head full of stem cells and the rest of his shit. Might even work. But who would Danny be when he woke up?"

"He'd be my son," Sweeney said.

"No he *wouldn't*," Nadia snapped, her impatience breaking through. "Restoring consciousness doesn't restore Danny. It doesn't. Danny knows that. He *told* you that. Look, Sweeney, I don't know what else to do with you. We showed you the other side. You met with your son. What more do you need?"

"But Peck — "

"Peck can't help you, Sweeney. You leave the boy with Peck and you'll lose him. Period. You're out of time. Listen to your boy if you can't listen to me. They're upstairs now, sharpening the knives."

And he had no idea if she meant this literally.

"But I haven't signed the release," he said and realized, as the words came out, how foolish they sounded.

Nadia waited a few beats and then, in a low voice, she said, "C'mon, Sweeney, make the fucking leap already."

He took a breath and held it, ran his tongue around the dry well of his mouth. He thought about Danny. He thought about his son on the last day of his old life, enraged at a story that didn't turn out the way he wanted. He imagined his son, encased in feathers and waiting for a father who would not return.

He said, "Get me up. Then you can help me pack while you tell me what I have to do."

Nadia stood and smiled as she pulled back the covers. Sweeney looked past her and saw that his bags were already waiting by the door.

29

Peck had placed the terrarium on the metal cart next to him, among the rest of his tools. From this vantage, Rene, the salamander, had a fine view of the procedure as it began to unfold. To some degree, the newt's vision was affected by the curve of the glass bowl, which bent the light a bit and added just a touch of magnification.

The doctors were dressed in deep green gowns and caps. Their masks hung down at their necks, leaving their faces visible. The younger doctor seemed slightly manic, too jovial, bouncing on his feet, his gloved hands clasped tightly behind his back. The older doctor was serious if not severe. He stood at the head of the slab, a safety razor in one hand. The other hand held a swatch of gauze that he used to dab away the shaving cream.

"I've never trusted a surgeon," Peck said to Tannenbaum, "who doesn't personally shave his patient."

Tannenbaum mumbled his agreement, but his focus was on the structure framing and confining the child's skull.

"Everything today is about speed," Dr. Peck said. "About efficiency and economy."

The skull was held rigid within a gleaming metal halo that circled around the forehead, just above the delicate ears and the blond eyebrows.

"You'd think we were accountants," Peck said, a touch dreamily, but still in his lecture voice, "or train conductors."

The halo, in turn, connected to a series of metal rods, which formed an open cube and bolted to the surgical slab. The device was, Tannenbaum knew, the doctor's own invention and construction. Just as he knew that he would be acting as little more than instrument nurse throughout the procedure.

As if reading his thoughts, Peck handed his aide the straight razor and foamy gauze, then left his cutting hand extended, all the while continuing to stare at the boy's skull, as if it were a newly discovered planet. Tannenbaum took the refuse and placed it on the cart, grabbed a fat marking pen and slapped it into the doctor's waiting palm.

Peck uncapped the pen and brought its tip to the bare scalp, drew a crosshair in the appropriate location and darkened its intersection with a bull's-eye.

"Science has been degraded," Peck said to the room. "What was once a vocation has become a profession."

He recapped the pen, returned it to Tannenbaum. On the instrument cart, resting on a sheet of emerald cotton next to Danny's bulging medical file, was a collection of Peck family heirlooms — the straight razor with its scrimshaw handle, the steel cannula that had been brought back from a trip to Germany in the '30s, and the 150-year-old glass syringe, its bulging crystal bulb full of raw potentiality.

While he had hoped to use only Father's instruments for this procedure, in the end Peck had chosen a state-of-the-art Kopf stereotactic drill to bore through the skull. It was a beautiful piece of equipment — a hand unit, battery operated, with a flexible shaft and a speed range up to fourteen thousand revolutions per minute. The drill weighed only five ounces and accepted a wide variety of shanks and bits. For this case, the doctor had selected a diamond bit to make the opening.

Peck lifted the drill, switched it on and listened to the hum of the motor, eyes closing for just a second as if trying to place the title of an obscure sonata. The procedure itself was a relatively simple operation. The optimum site for reseeding — in the center of the disaster area, in the superior aspect of the basal ganglia — had been identified through CT scans. The doctor would cut through the dura with the craniotomy, then insert a stabilizing probe, plant Father's syringe, and slowly inject the contents of the crystal bulb — six million cells of potential consciousness. A personal wake-up call from Dr. Peck.

He shut the motor down and looked at his protégé.

"To be a doctor," he said, "is to accept a responsibility that most men can't comprehend."

Tannenbaum nodded, uneasy with the pronouncement, wanting to get on with the operation.

"We're not like other people," Peck continued. "A real doctor, a true physician, is a person set apart. We're a caste unto ourselves. We live outside the tribe. But we're responsible for its health."

"It's a great obligation," Tannenbaum said, because he felt a response was needed.

"I'm not speaking here," Peck said, "about viruses and infections. Fevers and broken bones."

"Of course not," Tannenbaum said.

"I'm speaking," Peck said, "about the essential well-being of the race itself. The protection and advancement of the species."

Tannenbaum nodded, his mask bouncing against his throat.

"I need you to understand what's at stake here," Peck said, "I need you to witness the magnitude and the meaning of what we're about to do."

"We're going to bring the boy back," Tannenbaum blurted and immediately regretted his words.

Peck stared at the younger doctor suspiciously for a second, then pulled the mask up to cover the lower half of his face. Without taking his eyes off his assistant, he thumbed on the drill once again and the noise of its motor filled the theater.

Tannenbaum reached down and lifted the antique syringe gingerly, cradling the glass bulb full of saline and fetal cells. Peck motioned for the young doctor to stand on the other side of the slab, where he'd have an unobscured view of the implantation.

Peck positioned himself directly behind the child's skull, the red bull's-eye looking scarlet under the yellow lights and against the milky white canvas of the boy's skin. Hunching, the doctor stepped in close and adjusted his weight across his hips, the way his father had advised so many years ago. He felt the control in his arms and hands; his muscles and nerves confident, assured, tremor-free. He could sense himself sliding into that place beyond thought, like a monk or an athlete, ready to fulfill his only reason for being. He brought the drill forward and made ready to bore into the boy's head.

And in that instant, the salamander began to react to the vibrations that were rolling forward down the hallway. Rene shifted his gaze from the doctor's hands to the theater's entrance, just as the doors were kicked open with enough force to snap both of the hinges.

At the sound of the tearing metal, Peck simultaneously pulled back from the skull and began to turn toward the doors, just in time to have the drill batted out of his hands. It fell to the floor, still purring. The surgical theater was suddenly full of bodies. Three men, huge and hairy, screaming obscenities, dressed in leather and fur and denim, rushed inside, followed by the patient's father and one of the clinic nurses.

The largest of the invaders, the Elephant, immediately grabbed the syringe from Tannenbaum and hurled it, shattering the bulb and showering the wall. Then the biker took Tannenbaum's throat in one hand and, seizing his crotch through his gown, lifted the young doctor horizontally into the air and heaved him against the wall, where he crashed into and dislodged the display of antique surgical instruments before falling to the ground. In full adrenaline rush, the Elephant ran toward the crumpled pile of doctor and began kicking and stomping along the prone body. The sound of bones snapping was audible until Sweeney yelled, "Don't kill him. Don't kill either one of them."

As Tannenbaum's bones broke, Peck was knocked to the floor by a euphoric Piglet, then lifted up and held in place by Nadia and the Fluke. Sweeney made himself wait while Piglet drove a knee into Peck's groin, then brought the cowering doctor upright again with two uppercuts to the head. Then Piglet noticed the drill still whirring away on the ground. He squatted quickly to snatch it, but stood slowly, as if savoring the many kinds of damage he could do with this tool. Positioning the drill before Peck's forehead, he said, "How 'bout I cut this asshole a third eye?"

At this, Sweeney stepped forward and touched Nadia on the shoulder.

Nadia looked from Sweeney to Piglet and then back to Sweeney, before she asked, "You sure?"

"I'm sure," Sweeney said.

Nadia nodded to her Abomination, who grudgingly shut off the drill and stuffed it in his back pocket. Sulking, he moved to the slab to start disassembling the brace and halo that held Danny's head.

Sweeney stepped in front of Peck and said, "I never gave you permission to touch my child."

Peck stayed silent but stared at the pharmacist.

Nadia slapped the doctor across the back of the skull and yelled, "Answer the man."

"You don't know what you've done," Peck said.

"Yes, I do," Sweeney said. "I'm leaving now. And I'm taking my son with me."

"He'll die," Peck said and Nadia felt a little admiration for the stones on this elderly fucker. "Without the proper care, the boy will die."

"I've made provisions," Sweeney said.

"He's all set," Piglet called, tossing the last of the halo's bolts over his shoulder.

"You report any of this," Sweeney said, "and we'll come back here. And the first person we'll visit is your daughter."

"Oh, fuck yeah," Piglet yelled, as if already in deep fantasy about the many ways he would defile Alice Peck.

Then the Fluke popped the old man in the kidneys, twice, and Nadia let go of Peck's bony arm and allowed him to slip to the floor.

The Elephant pulled a gurney in from the hallway and he and the Fluke gently moved Danny onto it. Sweeney reached into his pocket, pulled out his car keys and tossed them to Piglet.

"I'm parked at the rear exit, right next to the door," Sweeney said. "Give us about a half hour before you head back to the Harmony."

Piglet stared at the keys in his hand, squinted, looked from Sweeney to Nadia and said, "I ain't driving no fuckin' Honda."

Nadia smiled and said, "Move your ass."

Piglet heaved a sigh, started to turn, then, as if remembering something, pulled the surgical drill from his pocket and held it up defiantly, like a gun or a flag.

"I'm *takin'* this," he said to Nadia, who shrugged. Satisfied, Piglet led the way out of the theater and the Fluke and the Elephant followed, Danny on the gurney between them.

Nadia surveyed the room, motioned toward Tannenbaum with her head.

"That one will be out for a while," she said. "But this one," toeing Dr. Peck, "is still ambulatory."

Sweeney went down on one knee and watched the doctor curl up, fetal.

"My son for your daughter," Sweeney said, putting a hand on Peck's shoulder in time to feel the tremble.

Rising, Sweeney said to Nadia, "Go on. I'll be out in just a second."

Nadia gave him an uneasy look.

"There are some things that Danny will need," Sweeney said. "It'll just take me a second."

Nadia looked around the chaos of the room, nodded and departed.

Dr. Peck remained on the floor, knees bent up toward his belly, shoulders bent in toward the chest, both arms crossed and the eyes closed, as if in dream.

Sweeney moved to the surgical cart and lifted the shaving razor. Then he dropped it, gathered up Danny's medical file and stuffed the bulging folder inside his jacket. He turned to leave, hesitated, and turned back to the cart once more. This time, he picked up and pocketed the marking pen. Then he put his hand inside the terrarium and lifted Rene out of the bowl. He placed the salamander in his shirt pocket and walked out the broken doors.

30

Sweeney rode to the Harmony on the back of Nadia's bike, one hand around the nurse's waist, the other cupping his own shirt pocket, making sure the newt was secure. And as the wooded hills surrounding the Clinic gave way to the city, he felt Rene begin to move. Felt the tiny, damp feet raking down softly over the heart.

They rolled at an even speed past the foundries and the chemical plants, past acres of ghostly housing projects and antique tenements long gone dark. Eventually, they cut into the city proper and made for downtown, a Mardi Gras in perpetual decay, this crowded hive of clubs and bars, noodle dens and arcades, strip joints and chapels of the apocalypse, all of them announced in red and blue neon. To Sweeney it looked like the last nightmare. And it smelled like a third world circus — sweet and rancid and toxic.

They approached the Harmony from the rear, through the blocks of ruined brick and stone. Halfway across the lot, they could make out Buzz, sitting alone in the rocking chair on the loading dock, waiting like some sea captain's wife. Nadia parked the bike and killed the engine. They dismounted and climbed up onto the apron.

Buzz didn't say a word and Sweeney sat down on the rail, blocking his view of the ruins. Nadia went inside the factory without speaking and after a minute they could hear her running water in the cafeteria.

Buzz looked as if he were staring through Sweeney, still focusing on the broken bricks in the distance.

"I'm not a solitary person, usually," Buzz said and it sounded as if he were speaking to himself. "I like people around. I was alone a lot, growing up."

Sweeney didn't think the biker was looking for a comment, so he kept quiet.

"The thing is," Buzz continued, "sometimes, when you really need to think, there's no substitute for solitude."

Sweeney allowed himself a nod.

"The boys are off on a run," Buzz said. "And I don't mind telling you, I miss every one of those fuckers already."

"I'm sure you do," Sweeney said, not rushing anything. Letting Buzz Cote do this in his own way and time.

"They drive me bugfuck. They really do, sometimes. But I'm like any parent. I'd be lost without them. And I like to think they feel the same way about me."

"You're a family," Sweeney said and when Buzz's eyes focused in on him for the first time, he knew he'd chosen the perfect word.

"I've been sitting out here for hours," Buzz said. "I haven't moved a fucking muscle. I been sitting here trying to figure out what it was you were gonna do. And I was trying to decide what I was gonna do once you made your decision."

Sweeney took in air through his nose.

"I know sometimes I might seem erratic," Buzz said. "Maybe even weak. But I'm neither one. I'm focused. It's about being willing to become anything and everything to get what you need. To get what your family needs. To go hard or soft. Be sweet or sour. Eyes on the prize. Every fucking second."

"It's not easy," Sweeney said, "being a father."

"And I hope you understand how much I appreciate that."

"The thing is," Sweeney said, "I honestly do. I believe you get it."

Buzz leaned sideways just a little.

"It changes you," he said. "And not just in the ways you'd expect."

Sweeney's throat was dry. He wished Nadia would bring out a bottle.

"It's about sacrifice," Sweeney said. "To do the job right, you have to give up parts of yourself."

"Fuck, yes," Buzz said. "I swear to you, I'm not the man I used to be."

"You'd give an arm and a leg," Sweeney said, "to keep your child from getting lost. You'd give whatever was necessary."

"You'd walk through fire," Buzz said. "You'd kick God in the balls."

"You'd give up your own life," Sweeney said, "in a second. No hesitation."

"No thinking at all," Buzz said, "because that's who you become."

"But sometimes," Sweeney said, "the kid gets lost anyway. And there's not a thing you can do about it."

Buzz went quiet for several seconds. When he spoke again, his voice sounded edgier, on the verge of impatient and heading into angry.

"That," he said, "is where we disagree in a major fucking way."

Sweeney didn't say anything.

"You can always find him," Buzz said. "And you can always forgive him for getting lost in the first place. Always."

"The chicken boy tried to tell me the same thing."

"It was *Danny*," Buzz yelled, his voice suddenly loud enough to echo off the ruins.

He got up out of the rocking chair and joined Sweeney on the rail. The light on the dock was muddy and half of the biker's face was in shadow.

"Jesus Christ, Sweeney, I have tried to be patient. But you don't have an ounce of fucking faith. I gave you a goddamn chance to be with your boy for the first time in a year. And you come back the same zombie as when you left."

"I'm just not sure it was Danny — "

"Of course it was Danny," coming forward off the rail now and leaning down into Sweeney. "Who else you think it was?"

"I'm saying I'm not sure it was real."

"It was as real as it gets," Buzz yelled, raising an arm as if ready to backhand the pharmacist. But he caught himself and froze, took a breath, and made himself ease the arm to his side. He tipped his head back, rubbed his forehead, pushed out some air, lowered his voice, and said, "I'm sorry. I'm just running out of time here. I want to do this the easy way. The way that's right for everyone involved. I'm trying to do what's best for everyone — me and my people and you and your boy. But you're making it awfully fucking difficult for me, Sweeney."

"Think of it from my point of view — " Sweeney began and Buzz said, "I'm doing exactly that."

But Sweeney pushed on with his words.

"In a single night, I lost everything. I've been living in a nightmare for a year. Now you and Peck both come along. And both of you start tell-ing me I can wake up from the nightmare. Only Peck says he can bring Danny back into my world —"

"Peck is a lying sack of shit."

"— and you tell me you can bring me into Danny's world."

"And I proved it. We took you into Limbo. We let you talk to your boy. And he told you what to do, didn't he?"

"Someone," Sweeney said, "or something told me what to do. But he didn't tell me how to do it."

"You leap," Buzz said, on the verge of pleading now, the conversion so close he could feel it. "You take the fucking leap. You decide to be-lieve. And you become one of us. There's a family waiting for you here, Sweeney. Me and Nadia and all of the boys. We'll take care of you and we'll take care of Danny. And, in turn, you'll take care of us. That's the way family works. You don't have to be alone anymore, Sweeney. This is the way out of the nightmare, son. This is the way out of the grave."

"You can't imagine how much I want to believe you."

Buzz put a hand out into the dark air before him.

"Then do it," he said. "I'm standing right here waiting for you. Let go and fucking leap."

They stared at each other. No sound but the wind and their own breath-ing. White clouds of mist floated out from their mouths and nostrils.

Sweeney moved first. He reached a hand deep into his right pants pocket and slowly pulled out a glass vial filled to the top with a murky pink liquid. He held it up between their faces and then brought it down and placed it in Buzz's enormous hand.

Buzz's whole body gave up a single tremor. Sweeney saw the biker's chest heave and heard his respiration catch for a second. Then fingers closed over Sweeney's hand and the vial. And then the biker pulled the pharmacist into a long bear hug that ended only when Nadia came out onto the dock carrying a cocktail tray.

Sweeney and Buzz unclenched and turned to the woman. With one hand, Buzz lifted from the tray an uncapped bottle of bourbon and with the other he picked up two syringes. He leaned over and kissed Nadia on the brow, passed the bottle to Sweeney, and said, "Mother, the prodigal has returned."

Sweeney took the bottle, brought it to his lips, and guzzled. He handed the bottle back and said, "What would you have done if I'd walked away?"

Buzz smiled and raised the bottle and closed both eyes for a second while he took a long drink.

"I'm a father," he said, "I would've done whatever was necessary."

Nadia rested the tray on the dock rail, stepped into Sweeney, laid a hand on his shoulder, and kissed him on the cheek.

"You made the right choice," she said. "You'll see."

Buzz took another hit off the bottle and passed it back to Sweeney, then he slung an arm around Sweeney's and Nadia's necks, pulled both into him, released them just enough so that they could walk as a threesome back inside the factory.

Lit candles were on several of the lunch tables in the cafeteria and they gave the room a warm glow that hid much of its dinginess.

"The boys won't be back till morning," Buzz said, lowering himself into a Buddha posture in the center of the room and slapping the floor next to him, indicating that Sweeney should do the same. "I wanted the two of us to journey out together this time. We'll go give Danny the word. Together. I can't wait to see his face."

He handed the spikes back to Nadia and began to roll up a sleeve. "The Sheep cooked up this last batch for me before he left. But with the new meat you brought tonight, there'll be enough for everybody when they get home tomorrow."

Sweeney pushed up his sleeves and put a hand on Buzz's arm.

"You'll let me talk to Danny first?" he said. "There are some things I've got to say."

"When are you gonna realize," Buzz said, "that I understand."

"I know you do, Buzz," Sweeney said and then looked up to Nadia and nodded.

She got down on her knees between the two men. The candles lit up her face. She took Sweeney's arm in her hands, lifted it, and brought her mouth down to the inside crook and kissed the skin. Then she found the vein she wanted, plunged the needle in, and thumbed the soup home.

The puncture bled a little when she removed the spike. Sweeney looked from Nadia to Buzz and back. Then his head snapped back and he sucked in a fast lungful of air and keeled backward. He stared up at the ceiling, his mouth open a little, his jaw slack, his eyes unfocused, and one foot twitching at the end of his leg.

Buzz looked down on him approvingly.

"Let's go, darlin'," he said and held out an arm, "I told you everything would work out."

Nadia cradled his arm and poked it with a finger looking for a target. "Buzz," she said, "I never doubted you."

And then she jammed the needle into the side of his neck, an inch below his left ear. Buzz screamed but didn't manage to throw her to the floor until she'd flooded him with enough soup to overdose a trio of Abominations.

Nadia landed on her back at Sweeney's feet. She looked up at Buzz who was trying and failing to yank the syringe out of his neck, muscles already numbing up. Buzz tried to stand and fell onto his stomach. He tried to speak but his tongue was swelling, and all that came out was a soft and slobbery sound. He threw an arm forward and hit Nadia's leg but he was beyond a grasp by now.

Nadia sat up and kicked the hand away. She waited another second or two until she saw the eyes were dilated. Then she got onto her hands and knees, crawled to the incapacitated biker, pulled the needle from his neck and tossed it into a corner.

She put her hand over the seeping wound and said, "We'll take good care of you, Buzz. I promise that. And the boys will come to visit whenever they get a chance."

Taking a breath, she shifted position and said, "You okay?"

Sweeney sat up slowly and pulled down the sleeves of his shirt. He eyed Buzz cautiously and said, "You're sure it was enough?"

She took her hand off the neck, wiped her palm across Buzz's back, and said, "He's in Limbo. And he's never coming back."

It took about an hour to give the Harmony a mediocre wipe-down. They worked in silence and spent most of their time packing what Nadia said she needed from the factory. They crated a hodgepodge of equipment, left it on the dock, and sat down in the rocking chairs.

"Do I want to know what was in my spike?" Sweeney asked.

"Saline," Nadia said. "And some food coloring."

"And you're sure you won't have any problems with the others?"

"I can handle my boys," Nadia said. "Even the dumbest of the bunch knows he needs me more than Buzz."

Sweeney thought about this for a few seconds, then asked, "How long will it take us to get there?"

For a while, he didn't think she was going to answer. Then she said, "I'd like to make it to Tampico by Sunday. But you know, you can't really open up a hearse."

And as if on cue, they heard engines in the distance and looked out across the ruins to see the Abominations approaching. Near the end of the line of bikes he spotted his Accord. And bringing up the rear was the hulking, antique hearse. Both vehicles were spewing black smoke but managing to keep up with the convoy.

"I can't believe," Sweeney said, "they got the hearse up and running."

"That's been your problem from the start," Nadia said. "This is a talented family. We can fix almost anything."

"You're sure there's room," Sweeney asked, "for both of them?"

"There'll be plenty of room," Nadia said. "There's a lot of space when you take out the casket."

Then the engine scream got too loud to talk over and they sat in silence as the bikes and the hearse and the Honda fell into a semicircle before them, idling, rumbling. The bikers glanced expectantly from one to the other and then all eyes turned up toward Nadia and Sweeney. And the nurse and the pharmacist gazed down on this collection of freaks, overgrown children with the names of creatures, all of them looking as if they had been woken, too suddenly, from a sleep that was heavy with the odd logic of dreams.

Nadia leaned over the dock railing and let a small smile spread over her lips.

"Okay, kids," she said, "it's time to rise and shine."

LIMBO COMICS 2.0

"Rising and Shining"

. . . They came from the city of Quinsigamond, in the heart of the industrial rust belt, a land of bad dreams and rubble. They crossed the American continent in a southwestern arc, traveling in a convoy that fragmented and regrouped over a run of days and states. And they became a family in the way that only renegades can, by embracing their difference and taking the hard-line against consensus reality.

Make no mistake, however: traveling with the comatose is a complex undertaking. But Nadia had planned well and thoroughly and on those rare occasions when her plans failed to consider an eventuality, she was a genius at improvisation.

Fueled on amphetamine and fast food, the Abominations kept pace with their leader, gunning their bikes through the night, some of them blocking for the hearse, some of them covering its rear. Sleeping rough, out in the fields and forests, they huddled in their leathers. They torched the Honda and abandoned it in Newark. They lost the Fluke to a state cop somewhere in Delaware. They lost the Piglet to a county sheriff someplace in South Carolina. But Nadia had no worries. The boys would either catch up or disappear, she said, and there wasn't much anyone could do either way.

As for the hearse, it was left undisturbed, as if, in this land, death was always the final authority. The nurse and the pharmacist took turns driving, Danny and Buzz stretched out in the back. Nadia monitored her patients, tended their lines and sponged them down each night. She drew fluid from Buzz's makeshift shunt. Beneath the beer cans in a Styrofoam cooler at his feet, she stored the vials—the Sheep's new source of meat for the soup they'd consume while in transit. Danny's fluid she dumped out the window.

Behind the wheel, Sweeney was pleasantly surprised to find a radio in the dash. He fiddled with the dial until he found the Chi-Lites or the Stylistics, then he would let himself daydream. And when he rode shotgun, he transcribed the daydreams on the back of his son's medical reports, using Dr. Peck's surgical marker.

From his perch on the dashboard, Rene, the salamander, acted as compass, herald, and mascot. Once or twice, when passing through a rural stretch, Sweeney pulled over and collected some beetles and aphids for the newt. But Rene didn't seem interested in the grub and he began to eat less and less as the journey progressed. As if he were moving beyond food. As if he were preparing for a new kind of sustenance.

After a time, Sweeney started to follow Rene's lead, foregoing the greasy burgers and fries and reducing his intake to the speed and the beer. In this way, the trip became more and more like a story as they pushed southward and began to zero in on the border, made themselves ready to cross out of their homeland forever. And at some unnoticed point on a deserted road in the middle of nowhere, Sweeney succumbed to a profound repose. And he understood that this was what it felt like to believe.

Unlike Sweeney, Nadia remained insatiable. The hearse became littered with her refuse, crumpled and stained paper bags piling up amid crushed aluminum cans and Danny's issues of *Limbo*, which were now in a condition somewhat less than pristine.

Late in the night, as Nadia speeded along, one hand on the wheel, the other gripping a can or a bunful of meat, chattering about what they would find at the end of their journey, Sweeney would page through one of the comics, reading by the glove box light, searching out a needed name or nugget of history. Then he'd close the box and scribble in the dark on the back of a med sheet, sometimes right on an x-ray.

By Augusta, he came to feel, at last, that he understood the story of the freaks. By Tuscaloosa, he understood that the story was deficient. And by the time they crossed the border at Brownsville, he found that he was reading solely for reference.

To many, it might seem crazy to travel west in order to move east. But the only freighter bound for Old Bohemia that would consent to carry this troupe of misfits was the *Wyznanie*, an ancient Polish tramp with a crew of convicts and a captain who napped through much of the passage.

The ship departed from the Port of Tampico and steamed out of the gulf, headed for the old world. Nadia paid a fortune for transport, but they were able to drive the hearse right into the hold, where the Abominations set up camp.

The bikers stayed below deck throughout the journey, eating and sleeping among the freight—barrels full of colored inks and embalming fluid, crates full of barbiturates and the pulpiest of paper. They spent the nights curled together in blankets, rolling with the waves and dreaming of the castle on a hill outside of Maisel. Nadia had described it as the last clinic they would ever need. But Nadia never came down to the hold.

She remained, day and night, at the bow of the ship, Buzz in the deck chair behind her, wrapped in quilts, his eyes covered by sunglasses. Studying the Atlantic, Nadia searched for other ships that might be carrying other dreamers striving toward the same castle, that final clinic, the healing church of all sleeping freaks.

And like a mirror at the ship's stern, Sweeney watched everything recede. Behind him, Danny lounged and dreamed, wrapped in alpaca.

Near the end of the voyage, on a particularly foggy night, Sweeney took the complete *Limbo* story and began to throw it overboard, one issue at a time, like some kind of ritual. In the moonlight, he glanced at one garish cover after another and then let it drop into the ship's wake, watching it float for a moment or two before it sank into the blackness of the sea.

He spied Bruno swimming for the coast of Gehenna, Kitty on his back, the unconscious chicken boy cradled in one bulging arm as the strongman kicked the trio to safety. Sweeney focused in on the swimmer's face, looking, perhaps, for a sign of realization regarding the moment's meaning. And then he tossed the issue over the ship's rail.

Next he perused a tawdry death scene, showers of scarlet blood frozen midspurt as Lazarus Cole was pummeled to death by the enraged dozen. Sweeney saw the rocks and bricks, pipes and plates crashing down on the magician's body, tearing flesh, breaking bone, thrashing the skull until the brain began to turn itself off. This time, Sweeney closed his eyes for a moment as he sailed the comic into the dark and salty air.

When he opened them, he saw that the wind had selected a particular image in the last issue of *Limbo* and he looked down on a full page depiction of Chick, prone atop his own coffin lid, floating out into the watery expanse as the sun rose and his family folded itself, member by member, into unique shrouds of grief along the shore.

And as he studied this picture, Sweeney thought about all the places where the story's creator had gone wrong, fallen down on the job. It was as if the artist had come to hate his characters and his audience. And for Sweeney, this was a helpful exercise in learning how to craft his own tales.

Some stories, the *Limbo* author had written, do not have a happy ending.

And some stories, Sweeney would counter, have no ending at all. Were he to meet and confront this Menlo, the creator of *Limbo*, Sweeney would insist that some stories sail on and on, moving, perhaps, beyond their maker's vision, but floating, nonetheless, into worlds unknown. Carried by currents of need, whose source we may never discover.

If it is true that Danny was shattered by a story, then maybe it follows that he can be remade by a story. In this regard, Sweeney has ideas. Notions of wandering and adventure, of transgression and sorrow, penance and reconciliation. Beyond this, Sweeney has hundreds of sheets of medical reports and a surgical marker. And it is possible that this is all he needs for a communion of minds and shared memories. For a true dream in which human freaks engage an abominable world. And sometimes redeem it.

THE FATHER DROPS the last issue of *Limbo* into the sea and takes a seat next to his boy. Rene sits unmoving on Danny's shoulder, like some tiny, scaly parrot, studying the horizon. Sweeney pulls the cap off the marker, lifts the papers into his lap, turns his head and glances at his sleeping son.

Then he looks out at the black, unending ocean. And over time and miles, he begins to see the chicken boy, resting, unmoving on a slab of wood, on the splintered altar of a coffin door. Chick is bobbing on the ocean's waves, free from the flock of gulls that had circled and swooped for days, maybe weeks. Neither hungry nor thirsty anymore, he lives on story now, as he rides in perfect rhythm with the sea.

Dreaming that he is cruising on a tramp freighter to the old world, where his patriarch awaits. Dreaming of sanctuary and serenity. Of reunion and communion and the last and best redemption.

Dreaming of that moment on the horizon when he will open his bill, separate the maxilla from the mandible. When, by thought alone, he will release those keratin hinges that smell of cherry and coconut.

Dreaming of that instant when he will come fully awake, and open his beak and deliver the words that advance the story and make the future possible.

"I forgive you."

ACKNOWLEDGMENTS

I would like to thank:

Nat Sobel and Judith Weber for their faith, support, and tireless counsel.

Chuck Adams for his enthusiasm, graciousness, and keen insight.

And, especially, my family — N, C, & J —
for perpetually resurrecting this scribbling freak.